New York Times bestseller Jill Shalvis is the award-winning author of over four dozen romance novels, including her sexy, heart-warming contemporary 'Animal Magnetism' and 'Lucky Harbor' series. She won a RITA for *Simply Irresistible* and is a three-time National Readers Choice winner as well. Connect with Jill on her website www.jillshalvis.com for a complete book list and to read her daily blog, where she recounts her Misplaced City Girl adventures, or visit her at www.facebook.com/jillshalvis or @JillShalvis for other news.

Praise for Jill Shalvis:

'Packed with the trademark Shalvis humor and intense intimacy, it is definitely a must-read . . . If love, laughter and passion are the keys to any great romance, then this novel hits every note' *Romantic Times*

'Heartwarming and sexy . . . an abundance of chemistry, smoldering romance, and hilarious antics' *Publishers Weekly*

'[Shalvis] has quickly become one of my go-to authors of contemporary romance. Her writing is smart, fun, and sexy, and her books never fail to leave a smile on my face long after I've closed the last page . . . Jill Shalvis is an author not to be missed!' *The Romance Dish*

'Jill Shalvis is such a talented author that she brings to life characters who make you laugh, cry, and are a joy to read' *Romance Reviews Today*

'What I love about Jill Shalvis's books is that she writes sexy, adorable heroes . . . the sexual tension is out of this world. And of course, in true Shalvis fashion, she expertly mixes in humor that has you laughing out loud' *Heroes and Heartbreakers*

'I always enjoy reading a Jill Shalvis book. She's a consistently elegant, bold, clever writer . . . Very witty – I laughed out loud countless times and these scenes are sizzling' *All About Romance*

'If you have not read a Jill Shalvis novel yet, then you really have not read a real romance yet either!' *Book Cove Reviews*

'Engaging writing, characters that walk straight into your heart, touching, hilarious' *Library Journal*

'Witty, fun, and sexy – the perfect romance!' Lori Foster, *New York Times* bestselling author

'Riveting suspense laced with humor and heart is her hallmark, and Jill Shalvis always delivers' Donna Kauffman, *USA Today* bestselling author

'Humor, intrigu[e] . . . zanne Forster, *New York* . . .

By Jill Shalvis

Lucky Harbor Series
Simply Irresistible
The Sweetest Thing
Head Over Heels
Lucky In Love
At Last
Forever And A Day
It Had To Be You
Always On My Mind
Once In A Lifetime
It's In His Kiss
He's So Fine
One In A Million

Merry Christmas, Baby & Under The Mistletoe
(A Lucky Harbor omnibus)

Animal Magnetism Series
Animal Magnetism
Animal Attraction
Rescue My Heart
Rumour Has It
Then Came You
Still The One

Jill SHALVIS

lucky in love

headline
ETERNAL

Published by arrangement with Forever,
a division of Grand Central Publishing.

First published as an ebook in Great Britain in 2014
by HEADLINE ETERNAL
An imprint of HEADLINE PUBLISHING GROUP

First published in paperback in Great Britain in 2015
by HEADLINE ETERNAL
An imprint of HEADLINE PUBLISHING GROUP

2

Cataloguing in Publication Data is available from the British Library

ISBN 978 1 4722 2280 0

Offset in Times by Avon DataSet Ltd, Bidford-on-Avon, Warwickshire

Printed and bound by CPI Group (UK) Ltd, Croydon, CR0 4YY

Headline's policy is to use papers that are natural, renewable and recyclable
products and made from wood grown in well-managed forests and other
controlled sources. The logging and manufacturing processes are expected
to conform to the environmental regulations of the country of origin.

HEADLINE PUBLISHING GROUP
An Hachette UK Company
338 Euston Road
London NW1 3BH

www.headlineeternal.com
www.headline.co.uk
www.hachette.co.uk

To Laurie, Melinda, and Mary for finding all my mistakes. If there are more, it's all on me.

To Helenkay Dimon, Susan Anderson, Kristan Higgins, and Robyn Carr for the bestest limo ride I've ever had (okay, ONLY limo ride I've ever had) on the day after I'd turned in this book (and winning a Rita that night was the icing on the cake!).

To Jolie and Debbie for the help in putting Ty together.

To Robyn Carr, for just about everything else.

Love you all!!

lucky in love

Prologue

*All you need is love. But a little chocolate
now and then doesn't hurt.*

Lightning sent a jagged bolt across Ty Garrison's closed
lids. Thunder boomed and the earth shuddered, and he
jerked straight up in bed, gasping as if he'd just run a
marathon.

A dream, just the same goddamn four-year-old dream.

Sweating and trembling like a leaf, he scrubbed his
hands over his face. Why couldn't he dream about something good, like sex with triplets?

Shoving free of the covers, he limped naked to the
window and yanked it open. The cool mist of the spring
storm brushed his heated skin, and he fought the urge to
close his eyes. If he did, he'd be back there.

But the memories came anyway.

"Landing in ten," the pilot announced as the plane
skimmed just beneath the storm raging through the night.

In eight, the plane began to vibrate.

In six, lightning cracked.

And then an explosion, one so violent it nearly blew out his eardrums.

Ty dropped his head back, letting the rain slash at his body through the open window. He could hear the Pacific Ocean pounding the surf below the cliffs. Scented with fragrant pines, the air smelled like Christmas in April, and he forced himself to draw a deep, shaky breath.

He was no longer a SEAL medic dragging his sorry ass out of a burning plane, choking on the knowledge that he was the only one still breathing, that he hadn't been able to save a single soul. He was in Washington State, in the small beach town of Lucky Harbor. The ocean was in front of him, the Olympic Mountains at his back.

Safe.

But hell if at the next bolt of lightning, he didn't try to jump out of his own skin. Pissed at the weakness, Ty shut the window. He was never inhaling an entire pepperoni pizza before bed again.

Except he knew it wasn't something as simple as pizza that made him dream badly. It was the edginess that came from being idle. His work was still special ops, but he hadn't gone back to being a first responder trauma paramedic. Instead, he'd signed up as a private contractor to the government, which was a decent enough adrenaline rush. Plus it suited him—or it had until six months ago, when on an assignment he'd had to jump out a second story window to avoid being shot, and had reinjured his leg.

Stretching that leg now, he winced. He wanted to get back to his job. *Needed* to get back. But he also needed clearance from his doctor first. Pulling on a pair of jeans, he snagged a shirt off the back of a chair and left the room as the storm railed around outside. He made his way through the big and nearly empty house he'd rented for the duration, heading to the garage. A fast drive in the middle of the night would have to do, and maybe a quick stop at the all-night diner.

But this first.

Flipping on the lights, Ty sucked in a deep, calming breath of air heavy with the smells of motor oil, well-greased tools, and rubber tires. On the left sat a '72 GMC Jimmy, a rebuild job he'd picked up on the fly. He didn't need the money. As it turned out, special ops talents were well-compensated these days, but the repair work was a welcome diversion from his problems.

The '68 Shelby Mustang on the right wasn't a side job. She was his baby, and she was calling to him. He kicked the mechanic's creeper from against the wall toward the classic muscle car. Lowering himself onto the cart with a grimace of pain, Ty rolled beneath the car, shoving down his problems, denying them, avoiding them.

Seeking his own calm in the storm.

Chapter 1

Put the chocolate in the bag, and no one gets hurt.

The lightning flashed bright, momentarily blinding Mallory Quinn as she ran through the dark rainy night from her car to the front door of the diner.

One Mississippi.

Two Mississippi.

On three Mississippi, thunder boomed and shook the ground. A vicious wind nearly blew her off her feet. She'd forgotten her umbrella that morning, which was just as well or she'd have taken off like Mary Poppins.

A second, brighter bolt of lightning sent jagged light across the sky, and Mallory gasped as everything momentarily lit up like day: the pier behind the diner, the churning ocean, the menacing sky.

All went dark again, and she burst breathlessly into the Eat Me Café feeling like the hounds of hell were on her very tired heels. Except she wasn't wearing heels; she was in fake Uggs.

Lucky Harbor tended to roll up its sidewalks after ten o'clock, and tonight was no exception. The place was deserted except for a lone customer at the counter, and the waitress behind it. The waitress was a friend of Mallory's. Smartass, cynical Amy Michaels, whose tall, leggy body was reminiscent of Xena, the warrior princess. This was convenient, since Amy had a kick-ass 'tude to life in general. Her dark hair was a little tousled as always, her even darker eyes showed amusement at Mallory's wild entrance.

"Hey," Mallory said, fighting the wind to close the door behind her.

"Looking a little spooked," Amy said, wiping down the counter. "You reading Stephen King on the slow shifts again, Nurse Nightingale?"

Mallory drew a deep, shuddery breath and shook off the icy rain the best she could. Her day had started a million years ago at the crack of dawn when she'd left her house in her usual perpetual rush, without a jacket. One incredibly long ER shift and seventeen hours later, she was still in her scrubs with only a thin sweater over the top, everything now sticking to her like a second skin. She did not resemble a warrior princess. Maybe a drowned lady-in-waiting. "No Stephen," she said. "I had to give him up. Last month's reread of *The Shining* wrecked me."

Amy nodded. "Emergency Dispatch tired of taking your 'there's a shadow outside my window' calls?"

"Hey, that was *one* time." Giving up squeezing the water out of her hair, Mallory ignored Amy's knowing snicker. "And for your information, there really was a man outside my window."

"Yeah. Seventy-year-old Mr. Wykowski, who'd gotten turned around on his walk around the block."

This was unfortunately true. And while Mallory knew that Mr. Wykowski was a very nice man, he really did look a lot like Jack Nicholson had in *The Shining*. "That could have been a *very* bad situation."

Amy shook her head as she filled napkin dispensers. "You live on Senior Drive. Your biggest 'situation' is if Dial-A-Ride doesn't show up in time to pick everyone up to take them to Bingo Night."

Also true. Mallory's tiny ranch house was indeed surrounded by other tiny ranch houses filled with mostly seniors. But it wasn't that bad. They were a sweet bunch and always had a coffee cake to share. Or a story about a various ailment or two. Or two hundred.

Mallory had inherited her house from her grandma, complete with a mortgage that she'd nearly had to give up her firstborn for. If she'd had a first born. But for that she'd like to be married, and to be married, she'd have to have a Mr. Right.

Except she'd been dumped by her last two Mr. Rights.

Wind and something heavy lashed at the windows of the diner. Mallory couldn't believe it. *Snow.* "Wow, the temp must have just dropped. That came on fast."

"It's spring," Amy said in disgust. "Why's it frigging snowing in spring? I changed my winter tires already."

The lone customer at the counter turned and eyed the view. "Crap. I don't have winter tires either." She looked to be in her mid-twenties and spoke with the clipped vowels that said northeast. If Amy was Xena, and Mallory the lady-in-waiting, then she was Blonde Barbie's younger, prettier, far more natural sister. "I'm in a 1972 VW Bug," she said.

As Mallory's own tires were threadbare, she gnawed

on her lower lip and looked out the window. Maybe if she left immediately, she'd be okay.

"We should wait it out," Amy suggested. "It can't possibly last."

Mallory knew better, but it was her own fault. She'd been ignoring the forecast ever since last week, when the weather guy had promised ninety-degree temps and the day hadn't gotten above fifty, leaving her to spend a very long day frozen in the ER. Her nipples still hadn't forgiven her. "I don't have time to wait it out." She had a date with eight solid hours of sleep.

The VW driver was in a flimsy summer-weight skirt and two thin camisoles layered over each other. Mallory hadn't been the only one caught by surprise. Though the woman didn't look too concerned as she worked her way through a big, fat brownie that made Mallory's mouth water.

"Sorry," Amy said, reading her mind. "That was the last one."

"Just as well." Mallory wasn't here for herself anyway. Dead on her feet, she'd only stopped as a favor for her mother. "I just need to pick up Joe's cake."

Joe was her baby brother and turning twenty-four tomorrow. The last thing he wanted was a family party, but work was slow for him at the welding shop, and flying to Vegas with his friends hadn't panned out since he had no money.

So their mother had gotten involved and tasked Mallory with bringing a cake. Actually, Mallory had been tasked with *making* a cake, but she had a hard time not burning water so she was cheating. "Please tell me that no one from my crazy family has seen the cake so I can pretend I made it."

Amy *tsk*ed. "The good girl of Lucky Harbor, lying to her mother. Shame on you."

This was the ongoing town joke, "*good girl*" Mallory. Okay, fine, so in all fairness, she played the part. But she had her reasons—good ones—not that she wanted to go there now. Or ever. "Yeah, yeah. Hand it over. I have a date."

"You do not," Amy said. "I'd have heard about it if you did."

"It's a *secret* date."

Amy laughed because yeah, that *had* been a bit of a stretch. Lucky Harbor was a wonderful, small town where people cared about each other. You could leave a pot of gold in your backseat, and it wouldn't get stolen.

But there were no such things as secrets.

"I do have a date. With my own bed," Mallory admitted. "Happy?"

Amy wisely kept whatever smartass remark she had to herself and turned to the kitchen to go get the birthday cake. As she did, lightning flashed, followed immediately by a thundering boom. The wind howled, and the entire building shuddered, caught in the throes. It seemed to go on and on, and the three women scooted as close as they could to each other with Amy still on the other side of the counter.

"Suddenly I can't stop thinking about *The Shining*," the blonde murmured.

"No worries," Amy said. "The whole horror flick thing rarely happens here in Mayberry."

They all let out a weak laugh, which died when an ear-splitting crack sounded, followed immediately by shattering glass as both the front window and door blew in.

In the shocking silence, a fallen tree limb waved obscenely at them through the new opening.

Mallory grabbed the woman next to her and scurried behind the counter to join Amy. "Just in case more windows go," she managed. "We're safest right here, away from flying glass."

Amy swallowed audibly. "I'll never laugh at you about Mr. Wykowski again."

"I'd like that in writing." Mallory rose up on her knees, taking a peek over the counter at the tree now blocking the front door.

"I can't reach my brownie from here," Blondie said shakily. "I really need my brownie."

"What we need," Amy said, "is to blow this popsicle stand."

Mallory shook her head. "It's coming down too hard and fast now. It's not safe to leave. We should call someone about the downed tree though."

Blondie pulled out her cell phone and eyed her screen. "I forgot I'm in Podunk. No reception in half the town." She grimaced. "Sorry. I just got here today. I'm sure Lucky Harbor is a very nice Podunk."

"It's got its moments." Mallory slapped her pockets for her own cell before remembering. *Crap.* "My phone's in the car."

"Mine's dead," Amy said. "But we have a landline in the kitchen, as long as we still have electricity."

Just then the lights flickered and went out.

Mallory's stomach hit her toes. "You had to say it," she said to Amy.

Blondie rustled around for a moment, and then there came a blue glow. "It's a cigarette lighter app," she said, holding up her phone, and the faux flame flickered over the screen like a real Bic lighter. "Only problem, it drains my battery really fast so I'll keep it off until we have an emergency." She hit the home button and everything went really, really dark.

Another hard gust of wind sent more of the shattered window tinkling to the floor, and the Bic lighter immediately came back on.

"Emergency," Blondie said as the three of them huddled together.

"Stupid cake," Mallory said.

"Stupid storm," Amy said.

"Stupid life," Blondie said. Pale, she looked at them. "Now would be a great time for one of you to tell me that you have a big, strong guy who's going to come looking for you."

"Yeah, not likely," Amy said. "What's your name?"

"Grace Brooks."

"Well, Grace, you're new to Lucky Harbor so let me fill you in. There are lots of big, strong guys in town. But I do my own heavy lifting."

Grace and Mallory both took in Amy's short Army camo cargo skirt and her shit-kicking boots, topped with a snug tee that revealed tanned, toned arms. The entire sexy-tough ensemble was topped by an incongruous Eat Me pink apron. Amy had put her own spin on it by using red duct tape to fashion a circle around the Eat Me logo, complete with a line through it.

"I can believe that about you," Grace said to her.

"My name's Amy." Amy tossed her chin toward Mallory. "And that's Mallory, my polar opposite and the town's very own good girl."

"Stop," Mallory said, tired of hearing "good" and "girl" in the same sentence as it pertained to her.

But of course Amy didn't stop. "If there's an old lady to help across the street or a kid with a skinned knee needing a Band-Aid and a kiss," she said, "or a big, strong man looking for a sweet, warm damsel, it's Mallory to the rescue."

"So where is he then?" Grace asked. "Her big, strong man?"

Amy shrugged. "Ask her."

Mallory grimaced and admitted the truth. "As it turns out, I'm not so good at keeping any Mr. Rights."

"So date a Mr. Wrong," Amy said.

"Shh, you." Not wanting to discuss her love life—or lack thereof—Mallory rose up on her knees to take another peek over the counter and outside in the hopes the snow had lightened up.

It hadn't.

Gusts were blowing the heavy snow sideways, hitting the remaining windows and flying in through the ones that had broken. She craned her neck and looked behind her into the kitchen. If she went out the back door, she'd have to go around the whole building to get to her car and her phone.

In the dark.

But it was the best way. She got to her feet just as the two windows over the kitchen sink shattered with a suddenness that caused Mallory's heart to stop.

Grace's Bic lighter came back on. "Holy shit," she gasped, and holding onto each other, they all stared at the offending tree branch waving at them from the new opening.

"Jan's going to blow a gasket," Amy said.

Jan was the owner of the diner. She was fifty-something, grumpy on the best of days, and hated spending a single dime of her hard-earned money on anything other than her online poker habit.

The temperature in the kitchen dropped as cold wind and snow blew over them. "Did I hear someone say cake?" Grace asked in a wobbly voice.

They did Rock-Paper-Scissors. Amy lost, so she had to crawl to the refrigerator to retrieve the cake. "You okay with this?" she asked Mallory, handing out forks.

Mallory looked at the cake. About a month ago, her scrubs had seemed to be getting tight so she'd given up chocolate. But sometimes there had to be exceptions. "This is a cake emergency. Joe will live."

So instead of trying to get outside, and then on to the bad roads, they all dug into the cake. And there in the pitch black night, unnerved by the storm but bolstered by sugar and chocolate, they talked.

Grace told them that when the economy had taken a nosedive, her hot career as an investment banker had vanished, along with her condo, her credit cards, and her stock portfolio. There'd been a glimmer of a job possibility in Seattle so she'd traveled across the country for it. But when she'd gotten there, she found out the job involved sleeping with the sleazeball company president. She'd told him to stuff it, and now she was thinking about maybe hitting Los Angeles. Tired, she'd stopped in Lucky Harbor earlier today. She'd found a coupon for the local B&B and was going to stay for a few days and regroup. "Or until I run out of money and end up on the street," she said, clearly trying to sound chipper about her limited options.

Mallory reached out for her hand and squeezed it. "You'll find something. I know it."

"I hope you're right." Grace let out a long, shaky breath. "Sorry to dump on you. Guess I'd been holding on to that all by myself for too long, it just burst out of me."

"Don't be sorry." Amy licked frosting off her finger. "That's what dark, stormy nights are for. Confessions."

"Well, I'd feel better if you guys had one as well."

Mallory wasn't big on confessions and glanced at Amy.

"Don't look at me," Amy said. "Mine isn't anything special."

Grace leaned in expectantly. "I'd love to hear it anyway."

Amy shrugged, looking as reluctant as Mallory felt. "It's just your average, run-of-the-mill riches-to-rags story."

"What?" Mallory asked, surprised, her fork going still. Amy had been in town for months now, and although she wasn't shy, she was extremely private. She'd never talked about her past.

"Well rags to riches *to rags* would be a better way of putting it," Amy corrected.

"Tell us," Grace said, reaching for another piece of cake.

"Okay, but it's one big bad cliché. Trailer trash girl's mother marries rich guy, trailer trash girl pisses new stepdaddy off, gets rudely ousted out of her house at age sixteen, and disinherited from any trust fund. Broke, with no skills whatsoever, she hitches her way across the country, hooking up with the wrong people and then more wrong people, until it comes down to two choices. Straighten up or die. She decides straightening up is the better option and ends up in Lucky Harbor, because her grandma spent one summer here a million years ago and it changed her life."

Heart squeezing, Mallory reached for Amy's hand, too. "Oh, Amy."

"See?" Amy said to Grace. "The town sweetheart. She can't help herself."

"I can so," Mallory said. But that was a lie. She did like to help people—which made Amy right; she really couldn't help herself.

"And don't think we didn't notice that you avoided sharing any of *your* vulnerability with the class," Amy said.

"Maybe later," Mallory said, licking her fork. Or never. She shared just about every part of herself all the time. It was her work, and also her nature. So she held back because she had to have something that was hers alone. "I'm having another piece."

"Denial is her BFF," Amy told Grace as Mallory cut off a second hunk of cake. "I'd guess that it has something to do with her notoriously wild and crazy siblings and being the only sane one in the family. She doesn't think that she deserves to be happy, because that chocolate seems to be the substitute for something."

"Thanks, Dr. Phil." But it was uncomfortably close to the truth. Her family was wild and crazy, and she worked hard at keeping them together. And she did have a hard time with letting herself be totally happy and had ever since her sister Karen's death. She shivered. "Is there a lost-and-found box around somewhere with extra jackets or something?"

"Nope. Jan sells everything on eBay." Amy set her fork down and leaned back. "Look at us, sitting here stuffing ourselves with birthday cake because we have no better options on a Friday night."

"Hey, I have options," Grace said. "There's just a big, fat, mean storm blocking our exit strategies."

Amy gave her a droll look and Grace sagged. "Okay, I don't have shit."

They both looked at Mallory, and she sighed. "Fine. I'm stalled too. I'm more than stalled, okay? I've got the equivalent of a dead battery, punctured tires, no gas, and no roadside assistance service. How's _that_ for a confession?"

Grace and Amy laughed softly, their exhales little clouds of condensation. They were huddled close, trying to share body heat.

"You know," Amy said. "If we live through this, I'm going to—"

"Hey." Mallory straightened up in concern. "Of course we're going to live. Soon as the snow lets up, we'll push some branches out of the way and head out to my car and call for help, and—"

"Jeez," Amy said, annoyed. "Way to ruin my dramatic moment."

"Sorry. Do continue."

"Thank you. If we live," Amy repeated with mock gravity, "I'm going to keep a cake just like this in the freezer just for us. And also..." She shifted and when she spoke this time, her voice was softer. "I'd like to make improvements to my life, like living it instead of letting it live me. Growing roots and making real friends. I suck at that."

Mallory squeezed her hand tight in hers. "I'm a real friend," she whispered. "*Especially* if you mean it about the cake."

Amy's mouth curved in a small smile.

"If we live," Grace said. "I'm going to find more than a job. I want to stop chasing my own tail and go after some happy for a change, instead of waiting for it to find me. I've waited long enough."

Once again, both Amy and Grace looked expectantly at Mallory, who blew out a sigh. She knew what she wanted for herself, but it was complicated. She wanted to let loose, do whatever she wanted, and stop worrying about being the glue at work, in her family, for everyone. Unable to say that, she wracked her brain and came up with something else. "There's this big charity event I'm organizing for the hospital next weekend, a formal dinner and auction. I'm the only nurse on my floor without a date. If we live, a date would be really great."

"Well, if you're wishing, wish big," Amy said. "Wish for a little nookie too."

Grace nodded her approval. "Nookie," she murmured fondly. "Oh how I miss nookie."

"Nookie," Mallory repeated.

"Hot sex," Grace translated.

Amy nodded. "And since you've already said Mr. Right never works out for you, you should get a Mr. Wrong."

"Sure," Mallory said, secure in the knowledge that one, there were no Mr. Wrongs anywhere close by, and two, even if there had been, he wouldn't be interested in her.

Amy pulled her order pad from her apron pocket. "You know what? I'm making you a list of some possible candidates. Since this is the only type of guy I know, it's right up my alley. Off the top of my head, I can think of two. Dr. Josh Scott from the hospital, and Anderson, the guy who runs the hardware store. I'm sure there's plenty of others. Promise me that if a Mr. Wrong crosses your path, you're going for him. As long as he isn't a felon," she added responsibly.

Good to know there were some boundaries. Amy thrust out her pinkie for what Mallory assumed was to be a solemn pinkie swear. With a sigh Mallory wrapped her littlest finger around Amy's. "I promise—" She broke off when a thump sounded on one of the walls out front. Each of them went stock still, staring at each other.

"That wasn't a branch," Mallory whispered. "That sounded like a fist."

"Could have been a rock," Grace, the eternal optimist, said.

They all nodded but not a one of them believed it was a rock. A bad feeling had come over Mallory. It was the same one she got sometimes in the ER right before they got an incoming. "May I?" she asked Grace, gesturing to the smart phone.

Grace handed it over and Mallory rose to her knees and used the lighter app to look over the edge of the counter.

It wasn't good.

The opened doorway had become blocked by a snow drift. It really was incredible for this late in the year, but big, fat, round snowflakes the size of dinner plates were falling from the sky, piling up quickly.

The thump came again, and through the vicious wind, she thought she also heard a moan. A pained moan. She stood. "Maybe someone's trying to get inside," she said. "Maybe they're hurt."

"Mallory," Amy said. "Don't."

Grace grabbed Mallory's hand. "It's too dangerous out there right now."

"Well, I can't just ignore it." Tugging free, Mallory wrapped her arms around herself and moved toward the opening. Someone was in trouble, and she was a sucker for that. It was the eternal middle child syndrome and the nurse's curse. Glass crunched beneath her feet, and she shivered as snow blasted her in the face. Amazingly, the aluminum frame of the front door had withstood the impact when the glass had shattered. Shoving aside the thick branch, Mallory once again held the phone out in front of her, using it to peer out into the dark.

Nothing but snow.

"Hello?" she called, taking a step outside, onto the concrete stoop. "Is anyone—"

A hand wrapped around her ankle, and Mallory broke off with a startled scream, falling into the night.

Chapter 2

*If it's a toss up between men and chocolate,
bring on the chocolate!*

Mallory scrambled backward, or tried to anyway, but a big hand on her ankle held firm. The hand appeared to be attached to an even bigger body. Fear and panic bubbled in her throat, and she simply reacted, chucking Grace's phone at her captor's hooded head.

It bounced off his cheek without much of a reaction other than a grunt. The guy was sprawled flat on his back, half covered in snow. Still holding her ankle in a vice-like grip, he shifted slightly and groaned. The sound didn't take her out of panic mode but it did push another emotion to the surface. Concern. Since he hadn't tried to hurt her, she leaned over him, brushing the snow away to get a better look—not easy with the wind pummeling her, bringing more icy snow that slapped at her bare face. "Are you hurt?" she asked.

He was non-responsive. His down parka was open, and

he was wet and shivering. Pushing his dark brown hair from his forehead, she saw the first problem. He had a nasty gash over an eyebrow, which was bleeding profusely in a trickle down his temple and over his swollen eye. Not from where she'd hit him with the phone, thankfully, but from something much bigger and heavier, probably part of the fallen tree.

His eyes suddenly flew open, his gaze landing intense and unwavering on her.

"It's okay," she said, trying to sound like she believed it. "It looks like you were hit by a large branch. You're going to need stitches, but for now I can—"

Before she could finish the thought, she found herself rolled beneath what had to be two hundred pounds of solid muscle, the entire length of her pressed ruthlessly hard into the snow, her hands yanked high over her head and pinned by his. He wasn't crushing her, nor was he hurting her, but his hold was shockingly effective. In less than one second, he'd immobilized her, shrink-wrapping her between the ground and his body.

"Who the hell are you?" he asked, voice low and rough. It would have brought goose bumps to her flesh if she hadn't already been covered in them.

"Mallory Quinn," she said, struggling to free herself. She'd have had better luck trying to move a slab of cement.

Breathing hard, eyes dilated, clearly out of his mind, he leaned over her, the snow blowing around his head like some twisted paragon of a halo.

"You have a head injury," she told him, using the brisk, no-nonsense, I'm-In-Charge tone she saved for both the ER and her crazy siblings. "You're hypothermic." And he was getting a nice red spot on his cheek, which she suspected was courtesy of the phone she'd hurled at him. Best not to bother him with the reminder of that. "I can help you if you let me."

He just stared down at her, not so much as blinking while the storm railed and rallied in strength around them. He wasn't fully conscious, that much was clear.

Still, testosterone and dark edginess poured off him, emphasized by his brutal grip on her. Mallory was cataloguing her options when the next gust hit hard enough to knock his hood back, and with a jolt, she recognized him.

Mysterious Cute Guy.

At least that's how he was known around Lucky Harbor. He'd slipped into town six months ago without making a single effort to blend in.

As a whole, Lucky Harbor wasn't used to that. Residents tended to consider it a God-given right to gossip and nose into people's business, and no one was exempt. All that was known about the man was that he was staying in a big rental house up on the bluffs.

There'd been sightings of him at the Love Shack—the town's bar and grill—and also at the local gym, and filling up some classic muscle car at the gas station. But Mallory had only seen him once in the grocery store parking lot, with a bag in hand. Tall and broad shouldered, he'd been facing his car, the muscles of his back straining his shirt as he reached into his pocket to retrieve his keys. He'd slid his long legs into his car and accelerated out of the lot, as she caught a flash of dark Oakleys, a firm jaw, and grim mouth.

A little frisson of female awareness had skittered up her spine that day, and even wet and cold and uncomfortable beneath him, she got another now. He felt much colder than she, making her realize she had no idea how long he'd been out here. He was probably concussed, but the head injury would be the least of his problems if she didn't get him warmed up and call for help. "Let's get you inside," she said, ceasing to struggle beneath him, hoping that might calm him down.

No response, not even a twitch of a single muscle.

"You have to let me up," she said. "I can help you if you let me up."

At that, he seemed to come around a little bit. Slowly he drew back, pulling off her until he was on his knees, but he didn't let go of her, still manacling both of her wrists in one hand. His eyes were shadowed, and it was dark enough that she couldn't see their color. She couldn't see much of anything but she didn't need a light to catch the tension coming off of him in waves.

His brow furrowed. "Are you hurt?"

"It's you who's hurt."

"No, I'm not."

Such a typical guy response. He was bleeding and nearly unconscious, but he wasn't hurt. Good to know. "You're bleeding, and we need to get you warmed up, so—"

He interrupted this with an unintelligible denial, followed by another groan just before his eyes rolled up. In almost slow-motion, he began to topple over. She barely managed to grab onto his coat, breaking his fall with her own torso so he didn't hit his head again. But he was so heavy that they both fell.

"Oh my God," came Grace's quavering voice. "That's a lot of blood."

Mallory squeezed out from beneath him and looked up to see both Grace and Amy peeking out from between the fallen tree branches and the door frame.

"Holy shit," Amy said. "Is he okay?"

"He will be." Mallory scooped Grace's phone from the snow and tossed it to her. "I need help. I told him I'd get him inside but my car's better, I think. My phone's there, and I have reception. We can call for help. And I can turn on the engine and use the heater to warm him up."

Amy leaned over him, peering into his face. "Wait." She looked at Mallory. "You know who this is, right? It's Mysterious Cute Guy. He comes into the diner."

"You never told me," Mallory said.

Amy shrugged. "He never says a word. Tips good though."

"Who's Mysterious Cute Guy?" Grace wanted to know.

"When you get reception on your phone, pull up Lucky Harbor's Facebook," Amy told her. "There's a list of Mysterious Cute Guy sightings on the wall there, along with the Bingo Night schedule and how many women managed to get pulled over by Sheriff Hotstuff last weekend. Sawyer's engaged now so it's not as much fun to get pulled over by him anymore, but at least we have Mysterious Cute Guy so it doesn't matter as much."

Grace fell silent, probably trying to soak in the fact that she'd landed in Mayberry, U.S.A.

Or the Twilight Zone.

Mallory wrapped her arms around Mysterious Cute Guy from behind, lifting his head and shoulders out of the snow and into her lap. He didn't move. Not good. "Grace, get his feet," she said. "Amy, take his middle. Come on."

"It's karma, you know that, right?" Amy said, huffing and puffing as they barely managed to lift the man. Actually *dragged* was more like it. "Because you promised you'd go for the first Mr. All Wrong who landed at your feet. And here he is. Literally."

"Yes, well, I meant a conscious one."

"He's going on the list," Amy said.

"Careful!" Mallory admonished Grace, who'd dropped his feet. Too late. With the momentum, they all fell to their butts in the snow, Mysterious Cute Guy sprawled out over the top of them.

"Sorry," Grace gasped. "He weighs a ton."

"Solid muscle though," Amy noted, being in a good position to know since she had two handfuls of his hindquarters.

Somehow, squinting through the snow and pressing into the wind, they made it to Mallory's car. She hadn't locked it, had in fact left her keys in the ignition, which Grace shook her head about.

"It's Lucky Harbor," Mallory said in her defense.

"I don't care if it's Never Never Land," Grace told her. "You need to lock up your car."

They got Mysterious Cute Guy in the backseat, which wasn't big enough for him by any stretch. They bent his legs to accommodate his torso, then Mallory climbed in and again put his head in her lap. "Start the car," she told Amy. "And crank the heat. Get my phone from the passenger seat," she said to Grace. "Call 9-1-1. Tell them we've got a male, approximately thirty years of age, unconscious with a head injury and possible hypothermia. Give them our location so they can send an ambulance."

They both did her bidding, with Amy muttering "domineering little thing" beneath her breath. But she started the car and switched the heater to high before turning toward the back again. Her dark hair was dusted with snow, making her look like a pixie. "He still breathing?"

"Yes."

"Are you sure? Because maybe he needs mouth to mouth."

"Amy!"

"Just a suggestion, sheesh."

Grace ended her call to dispatch. "They said fifteen minutes. They said to try to get him warm and dry. Which means one of us needs to strip down with him to keep him warm, right? That's how it's done in the movies."

"Oh my God, you two," Mallory said.

Amy turned to Grace. "We're going to have to give her lessons on how to be a Bad Girl, you know that, right?"

Mallory ignored them and looked down at her patient. His brow was still furrowed tight, his mouth grim. Wherever he was in dreamland, it wasn't a happy place. Then suddenly the muscles in his shoulders and neck tensed, and he went rigid. She cupped both sides of his face to hold him still. "You're okay," she told him.

Shaking his head, he let out a low, rough sound of grief. "They're gone. They're all...gone."

The three women stared at each other for a beat, then Mallory bent lower over him. "Hey," she said gently, knowing better than to wake him up abruptly. "We've got you. You're in Lucky Harbor, and—"

He shoved her hand off of him and sat straight up so fast that he nearly hit his head on her chin, and then the roof of the car.

"We've called an ambulance," she said.

Twisting around, he stared at her, his eyes dark and filled with shadows.

"You okay?" she asked.

"Fine."

"Really? Because the last time you said that, you passed out."

He swiped at his temple and stared at the blood that came away on his forearm. "Goddammit."

"Yeah. See, you're not quite fine—"

He made a sound that managed to perfectly convey what he thought of her assessment, which turned into a groan of pain as he clutched his head.

Mallory forced him to lie back down. "Be still."

"Bossy," he muttered. "But hot."

Hot? Did he really just say that? Mallory looked down at herself. Wrinkled nurse's scrubs, fake Uggs, and she had no doubt her hair was a disaster of biblical proportions. She was just about the furthest she could get from *hot*, which meant that he was full of shit.

"Mr. Wrong," Amy whispered to her.

Uh huh, more like Mr. *All* Wrong. But unable to help herself, Mallory took in his very handsome, bloody face, and had to admit it was true. She couldn't have found a more Mr. All Wrong for herself if she'd tried.

Ty drifted half awake when a female voice penetrated his shaken-but-not-stirred brain.

"I'm keeping a list of Mr. Wrongs going for you. This one might not make it to the weekend's auction."

"Stop," said another woman.

"I'm just kidding."

"I still vote we strip him down." This was a third woman.

Wait. Three women? Had he died and gone to orgy heaven? Awake now, Ty took stock. He wasn't dead. And he had no idea who the fuck Mr. Wrong was, but he was very much "going to make it." He was stuffed in the back of a car, a *small* car, his bad leg cramping like a son-of-a-bitch. His head was pillowed on...he shifted to try to figure it out, and pain lanced straight through his eyeballs. He licked his dry lips and tried to focus. "I'm okay."

"Good," one of them repeated with humor. "He's fine, he's okay. He's also bleeding like a stuck pig. Men are ridiculous."

"Just stay still," someone close said to him, the same someone who'd earlier told him that he'd been hit by a branch. It felt more like a Mack Truck. Given where her voice was coming from, directly above him, it must be her very nice rack that he was pillowed against. Risking tossing his cookies, he tilted his head back to see her. This was tricky because one, it was dark, and two, he was seeing in duplicate. Her hair was piled into a ponytail on top of her head. Half of it had tumbled free, giving her—both of her—a mussed-up, just out-of-bed look. Looking a little bit rumpled, she wore what appeared to be standard issue hospital scrubs, hiding what he could feel was a very nice, soft, female form. She was pretty in an understated way, her features delicate but set with purpose.

A doctor, maybe. Except she didn't have the cockiness that most doctors held. A nurse, maybe.

"I know it looks like you've lost a bit of blood," she said, "but head injuries always bleed more, often making them appear more serious than they are."

Yeah. A nurse. He could have told her he'd seen more head injuries than she could possibly imagine. One time he'd even seen a head blown clear off a body, but she wouldn't want to hear that.

Her blessedly warm hand touched the side of his face. He turned into it and tried to think. Earlier when he'd woken up to the nightmare, he'd gone to work on the Shelby before taking it for a drive. He'd needed speed and the open road. Of course that had been before the snow hit, because even he wasn't that reckless. He remembered winding his way along the highway, the cliffs on his right, and far below on his left, the Pacific Ocean. The sea had been pitching and rolling as the storm moved in long, silvery fingers over the water. He remembered making it into town, remembered wanting pie and seeing the lights in the diner, so he'd parked.

That's when it'd started to snow like a mother.

He'd gotten nearly to the door when his memory abruptly ended. Damn. He hated that. He tried to sit up but six hands pushed him back down. Christ. That'd teach him to wish for a dream about triplets.

Someone's phone lit up, giving them some light, and Ty ordered himself to focus through the hammering in his skull. It wasn't easy, but he found that if he squinted he could see past the cobweb vision. Sort of.

Leaning over the back of the driver's seat was the waitress from the diner, though she was looking a little bit like a drowned rat at the moment. The woman riding shotgun next to her was a willowy blonde and unfamiliar to him.

As was the woman whose breasts were his pillow. "Thanks," he said to her. "For saving my ass."

"So…would you say you *owe* her?" the waitress asked.

"Amy," his nurse said in a warning tone. Then she shot Ty a weak smile. "You've had quite a night."

And so had she. She didn't say so—she didn't have to—it was all there in her doe-like brown eyes.

"The ambulance will be here soon," she said.

"Don't need one."

She didn't bother to point out that he was flat on his back and obviously pretty damn helpless. She kept her hands on him, her gaze now made of steel, signaling that in spite of those soft eyes, she was no pushover. "We'll get you patched up," she said. "And some meds for your pain."

"No." Fuck, no.

"Look, it's obvious you're hurting, so—"

"*No narcotics*," he growled, then had to grip his head to keep it on his shoulders, grinding his teeth as he rode out the latest wave of pain. Stars danced around in front of his eyes, shrinking to pinpoints as the darkness took him again.

"They passed us up," Grace said worriedly, twisting to follow the flashing blue and red ambulance lights moving slowly through the lot and back out again.

"Did you tell them that we were inside my car, and to look for us here?" Mallory asked.

"No. Dammit." Grace grabbed Mallory's phone again. "Sorry. I'll call them back right now."

Mallory looked down at her patient. Dark, silky hair. Square scruffy jaw. An old scar along his temple, a new one forming right this very minute on his eyebrow. His eyes were still closed, his face white and clammy, but she could tell he was awake again. "Easy," she said, figuring she'd be lucky if he held off getting sick until they got him out of here.

"What happened?" he said, jaw tight, eyes still closed, his big body a solid weight against her.

It was not uncommon after a head trauma to keep forgetting what had happened, so she gave him the recap. "Tree on the head."

"And then Nurse Nightingale here came to your rescue," Amy told him. "And you said you owed her."

"Amy," Mallory said.

"She needs a date this weekend," Amy told him.

"Ignore her." Over his head, Mallory gave Amy the universal finger-slicing-at-the-throat signal for *Shut It.*

Amy ignored her. "If you go with her to the charity auction on Saturday night at the Vets' Hall, you'd save her from merciless ridicule. She can't get her own date, you see."

Mallory sighed. "Thanks, Amy. Appreciate that. But I can so get my own—"

Unbelievably, her patient interrupted her with what sounded like a murmured ascent.

But Amy grinned and bumped fists with Grace. "Five bucks says Mr. Wrong will rock her world."

Grace looked down at the prone man in Mallory's lap with clear doubt. "You're on," she whispered back.

Mallory gave up trying to control Amy and eyed her patient. Even flat on his back, he was lethally gorgeous. She could only imagine what he'd be like dressed to the nines and on his feet.

"She'll meet you at the event, of course," Amy said to

him. "Because even though this is Lucky Harbor, we're not giving you her address. You might be a serial killer. Or worse, just be a completely Mr. Right."

Another sound of ascent from Mysterious Cute Guy. Which, actually, might have been more of a moan of disbelief that he'd agreed to this craziness.

Right there with you, Mr. Wrong. Right there with you.

Chapter 3

*By age thirty-five, women have only a few taste buds
left: one for alcohol, one for cheese,
and one for chocolate.*

One week later, Mallory was walking around in a cloud of anticipation in spite of herself. The auction was tonight, and although she knew damn well Mysterious Cute Guy wasn't going to show up, she could admit a tiny part of her wanted to be proven wrong.

Not that she'd actually *choose* to date a man like him, with the guarded eyes and edgy 'tude. She didn't even know his name. Not to mention she'd chucked a phone at his face.

Mr. Wrong, aka Mysterious Cute Guy...

Truthfully, that whole stormy night at the diner was still pretty much a blur to her. The ambulance had eventually found them and loaded up her patient. The snow had stopped, and Mallory had been able to drive home, after a solemn pinky-swear vow with both Amy and Grace to meet weekly, at least for as long as Grace stayed in town.

Chocoholics—CA for short—was their name, chocolate cake was their game.

Mallory had then spent the rest of the week alternating between long shifts in the ER and working on the auction. A portion of the evening's take would go to her own pet project, the Health Services Clinic she planned to open in conjunction with the County Hospital Foundation. HSC would be a place for anyone in the county to get community recovery resources, teen services, crisis counseling, and a whole host of other programs she'd been trying to get going for several years. She still needed hospital board approval, and hopefully the money from the auction would ensure that. It's what should have been foremost in her mind.

Instead that honor went to one Mysterious Cute Guy. For the first time that day, Mallory walked by the nurses' station and eyed the computer. Thanks to HIPPA, a very strict privacy act, she couldn't access a patient's records unless she'd actually worked on the patient that day. This meant that if she wanted to know his name, she'd have to ask the nurse who'd seen him in the ER that night. Unfortunately, her own mother had been his nurse, so she decided against that option.

Luckily, she had six patients to keep her occupied. The problem was that her counterpart, Alyssa, was very busy flirting with the new resident, doing none of her duties. This made for a long morning, made even longer by the fact that one of Mallory's patients was Mrs. Louisa Burland. Mrs. Burland was suffering from arrhythmia complicated by vasovagal syncope, a condition that was a common cause of dizziness, light-headedness, and fainting in the elderly. She was also suffering from a condition called Meanness. "I brought you the juice you asked for," Mallory said, entering Mrs. B's room.

"I asked for that three hours ago. What's wrong with you? You're slower than molasses."

Mallory ignored this complaint because it'd been five minutes, not three hours. And because Mrs. B was so bitter that even the volunteer hospital visitors skipped her room. Before retiring, the woman had been a first grade teacher who had at one time or another terrorized most of town with a single bony finger that she liked to waggle in people's faces. She was so difficult that even her daughter, who lived up the road in Seattle, refused to call or visit.

"I remember you, you know," Mrs. Burland said. "You peed yourself in front of your entire class."

Mallory was surprised to find that she could still burn with shame at the memory. "Because you wouldn't let me go to the bathroom."

"Recess was only five minutes away."

"Well, obviously, I couldn't wait."

"And now you make me wait. You're a terrible nurse, letting your treatment of me be clouded by our past interactions."

Mallory ignored this too. She set the juice, complete with straw, on Mrs. Burland's bedside tray.

"I wanted *apple* juice," Mrs. B said.

"You asked for cranberry."

Mrs. Burland's hand lashed out and the juice went flying, spilling across the bedding, the floor, the IV pole, and Mallory as well. Juice dripping off her nose, Mallory sighed. Perfect. It took twenty minutes to clean up the mess. Ten more to get Mrs. Burland back into her now fresh bed, which had Mallory huffing a little with the effort.

Mrs. B *tsk*ed. "Out of shape, or just gaining some weight?"

Mallory sucked in her belly and tried not to feel guilty about the cinnamon roll she'd inhaled on a quick break two hours ago. She reminded herself that she helped save lives, not take them, and walked out of the room, purposely not glancing at herself in the small mirror over the sink as she went.

Paramedics were just bringing in a new patient, a two-year-old with a laceration requiring stitches. Mallory got him all cleaned up and prepped the area for the doctor. She drew the lidocaine, got a suture kit, 4x4s and some suture material, and then assisted in the closing of the wound.

And so it went.

At her first break, she made her way to the nurses' break room and grabbed her soft-sided lunch box out of the fridge. Her older sister Tammy was there and Mallory sidled up to her. Once upon a time, Tammy had been wild. For that matter, so had Mallory's younger brother Joe. And Tammy's twin, Karen. All three of them, as out of control as they came.

Not Mallory. She'd always been the good one, attempting to distract her parents from the stress of raising wild, out-of-control kids.

Then Karen had died.

Tammy and Joe had carried on for Karen in the same vein, but for Mallory, everything had pretty much skidded to a halt. Blaming herself, she'd fallen into a pit of desperate grief. She'd always walked the straight and narrow path, but she'd taken it to a new extreme, terrified to do anything wrong, to screw a single thing up and make things worse for her parents. Once during that terrible time, she'd accidentally forgotten to pay for a lip balm and had turned herself in as a thief. The clerk of the store had refused to press charges, instead calling Mallory's mother to come get her.

Mallory had felt as if she'd needed to be punished in some way for not paying enough attention to Karen, for being a bad sister, for something, *anything*. She'd put all of her energy into healing her family, but had not been even remotely successful. Her parents divorced and her father had left to go surf in Australia. He'd never come back, and Tammy and Joe . . . well, they'd gone even further off the deep end.

Joe was doing better these days, spending far less time at cop central and more time on the job. Tammy had improved, too. Sure, last year she'd headed to Vegas for a weekend and had come home with a husband. But to everyone's shock, the wedding hadn't been because of an unplanned pregnancy. It hadn't even been alcohol-related.

Well, it might have been a little bit alcohol-related, but unbelievably, Tammy and her hotel security guard-turned-shotgun husband were still married. She'd applied for and landed a housekeeping job at the hospital and—gasp—had actually held onto the job, the same as her marriage. And since their mother was a supervisory nurse, that meant there were *three* Quinns at the hospital working together. Or, more accurately, Tammy and Ella working as opposing magnets, with Mallory doing her best to hold onto them both.

Tammy had been on shift the night of the freak storm, and because she liked to know everything, in all likelihood she knew Mysterious Cute Guy's name.

Mallory knew that asking her would be better than asking her mom—or looking in the computer and losing her job, not to mention completely invading the guy's privacy—but not by much. Her best hope was for his name to come up in a conversation, all casual-like, maybe even "accidentally." The trick was to not let Tammy know what Mallory wanted, or it'd be Game Over.

The break room was crowded, as it usually was at this time of the day. Mostly it was filled with other nurses and aides. Today Lucille was sitting on the couch as well, sipping a cup of coffee in her volunteer's uniform.

No one knew exactly how old Lucille was, but she'd been running the art gallery in town since the dawn of time. She was also the hub of all things gossip in Lucky Harbor, and she gave one-hundred percent in life. This included her volunteering efforts, and since she knew *everyone*, she'd been hugely influential in helping Mallory gain interest in the Health Services Clinic. Fond of her, Mallory waved, then sat next to Tammy at the large round table in the center of the room.

Tammy smiled and put down her phone. "Heard about tonight."

Mallory stopped in the act of pulling out her sandwich. This might be easier than she thought. "What about tonight?"

"Rumor is that you have a hot blind date for the auction."

"No, I—" She went still. "Wait a minute. How did you hear that?"

"I'm psychic," Tammy said and stole Mallory's chips from her lunch bag.

Dammit, she *needed* those chips. Then she remembered what Mrs. Burland had said about gaining weight and sighed. "Just because you paid for an online course to learn to manage your Wiccan powers does not mean you actually *have* powers. How did you hear about the date?"

"Amy told me when I grabbed lunch at the diner yesterday."

Okay, she'd kill Amy later at their chocoholics meeting. For now, it was just the opening Mallory needed. "First of all, the date thing is just a silly rumor." Even if she was secretly hoping otherwise. "And second...did Amy happen to tell you *who* this silly rumor date might be with?"

"Yep." Tammy was munching her way through the chips and moaning with pleasure, damn her. Mallory hoped she gained five pounds.

"I can't believe you actually landed Mysterious Cute Guy," Tammy said, licking salt off her fingers.

"*Shh!*" Mallory took a quick, sweeping glance around them, extremely aware of Lucille only a few feet away, ears aquiver with the attempt to eavesdrop. "*Keep it down.*"

Unimpressed with the need for stealth, Tammy went on. "It's pretty damn impressive, really. Didn't know you had it in you. I mean, your last boyfriend was that stuffy accountant from Seattle, remember? The only mysterious thing about him was what you saw in him."

"You were here last weekend when he came in," Mallory said.

"The accountant?"

"My *date*."

Tammy smiled. She knew she was stepping on Mallory's last nerve. It was what she did. And this wasn't going well.

"So is it a silly rumor?" Tammy asked. "Or a real date?"

"Never mind!" Mallory paused. "But... did you hear anything about him?"

"Like...?"

Lucille was nearly falling off the couch now, trying to catch the conversation. Mallory turned her chair slightly, more fully facing her sister. "Like his name," she whispered.

This got Tammy's attention in a big way. "Wait a minute. You don't know his name?"

Shit.

"Wow, how absolutely naughty, Mal. You haven't done naughty since you were sixteen and turned yourself in for shoplifting. Now you may or may not have a date with a guy whose name you don't know. A fascinating cry for attention." Tammy turned her head. "You catching all of this, Lucille?"

"Oh, you know I am." Lucille pulled out a Smartphone and began tapping keys with her thumbs. Probably writing on the Facebook wall. "This is good; keep talking."

Mallory dropped her head to the table and thunked it but unfortunately she didn't lose consciousness and she still had to finish her shift.

After work, she drove home and watered her next door neighbor's flowers because Mrs. Tyler was wheelchair-bound and couldn't do it for herself. Then she watered her grandma's beloved flowers. She fed the ancient old black cat that had come with the house, the one who answered only to "Sweet Pea" and only when food was involved. And before she showered to get ready for the night's dinner and auction, she clicked through her e-mail.

Then wished she hadn't.

She'd been tagged on Facebook.

Make sure to buy tickets for tonight's elegant formal dinner and auction, folks! Supported by the hospital, organized by the nurses and spearheaded by Mallory Quinn, all proceeds will go into the Hospital Foundation's coffers toward the Health Services Clinic that Mallory's been working on shoving down our throats. (Just kidding, Mallory!).

And speaking of Ms. Quinn, rumor is that she'll 'maybe' have a date for the event after all, with Mysterious Cute Guy!

Go Mallory!

p.s. Anyone at the event with their cell phone, pictures are greatly appreciated!

Chapter 4

Chocolate will never fail you.

Ty's routine hadn't changed much in the six months he'd been in Lucky Harbor. He got up in the mornings and either swam in the ocean or went to the gym, usually with Matt Bowers, a local supervisory forest ranger and the guy who owned the '72 GMC Jimmy that Ty was fixing up.

Matt was ex-Chicago SWAT, but before that he'd been in the Navy. He and Ty had gone through basic together.

When Ty had injured his leg again, Matt had coaxed him out West to rehabilitate. They'd spent time hitting the gun range, but mostly they enjoyed beating the shit out of each other on the mats.

They had a routine. They'd lie panting side by side on their backs in the gym. "Another round?" Matt would ask.

"Absolutely," Ty would say.

Neither of them would move.

"You doing okay?" Matt would then ask.

"Don't want to talk about it," Ty would say.

Matt would let it go.

Ty would hit the beach, swimming until the exhaustion nearly pulled him under. Afterward, he'd force himself along the choppy, rough rocky beach just to prove he could stay upright. He'd started out slow—hell, he'd practically crawled—but he could walk it now. It was quite the feat. Or so his doctor kept telling him. He supposed this was true given that four years ago, he'd nearly lost his left leg in the plane crash thanks to a post-surgical infection.

Which was a hell of a lot less than Brad, Tommy, Kelly, and Trevor had lost.

At the thought of that time and the loss of his team, the familiar clutching seized his gut. He hadn't been able to save a single one of them. He'd been trained as a trauma paramedic, but their injuries, and his own, had proven too much. Later he'd been honorably discharged and he'd walked away from being a medic.

He hadn't given anyone so much as a Band-Aid since.

Working in the private sector had proven to be a good fit for him. In actuality, it wasn't all that different from being enlisted, except the pay was better and he got a say in his assignments. But six months out of work was making him think too much. He wasn't used to this down time. He wasn't used to being in one spot for so long. His entire life had been one base after another, one mission after another. He was ready to get back to that world.

He *needed* to get back to that world, because it was the only way he had of making sure that his team's death meant something.

But Dr. Josh Scott, the man in charge of his medical

care until he was cleared, took a weekly look at Ty's scans and shook his head each time.

So here Ty was, holed up and recuperating in the big, empty house that Matt had leased for him, the one that was as far from his world as he could get. Far away from where he'd grown up, from anyone he'd known. Just as well, since they were all gone now anyway. His dad had been killed in Desert Storm. His mom had passed two years ago. With his closest friends resting beneath their marble tombstones in Arlington, there was no one else: no wife, no lover, no kids.

It made for a short contact list on his cell phone.

Instead of thinking about that, he spent his time fixing cars instead of people—Matt's 1972 Jimmy, his own Shelby—because cars didn't die on those they cared about.

On the day of the big hospital auction, after replacing the transmission on Matt's Jimmy, Ty degreased and showered, as always. Unlike always, he passed over his usual jeans for a suit, then stared at himself in the mirror, hardly recognizing the man looking back at him. He still had stitches over one eye and a bruise on his cheek from the storm incident. His hair was on the wrong side of a haircut, and he'd skipped shaving. He'd lost some weight over the past six months, making the angles of his face more stark. His eyes seemed...hollow. They matched how he felt inside. His body might be slowly getting back into lean, mean fighting shape, but he had some work yet to do on his soul. He shoved his hand in his pocket and pulled out the ever-present Vicodin bottle, rolling it between his fingers.

The bottle had been empty for two months now, and

he'd still give his left nut for a refill. He had two refills available to him; it said so right on the bottle. But since Ty had started to need to be numb—with a terrifying desperation—he'd quit cold turkey.

This didn't help his leg. Rubbing it absently, he turned away from the mirror, having no idea why he was going to the auction.

Except he did. He was going because the entire town would be there, and in spite of himself, he was curious.

He wanted to see her again, his bossy, warm, sexy nurse.

Which was ridiculous. It'd been so dark the night of the storm that he honestly wasn't sure he even knew what she looked like. But he knew he'd recognize her voice— that soft, warm voice. It was pretty much all he remembered of the entire evening, the way it'd soothed and calmed him.

Shaking his head, he strode through the bedroom, slipping keys and cash into his pockets, skipping the gun for the night although he'd miss the comforting weight of it. His cell phone was up to fifty-five missed calls now, which was a record. Giving in, he called voice mail and waited for the inevitable.

"Ty," said a sexy female voice. "Call me."

Frances St. Claire was the hottest redhead he'd ever seen and also the most ruthless. The messages went back a month or so.

Delete.

"Ty," she said on one of them. "Seriously. Call me."

Delete.

"Ty, I'm not fucking around. I need to hear from you."

Delete.

"Ty, Goddammit! Call me, you bastard!"
Delete.

As the rest of the calls were all variations on the same theme, with slurs on Ty's heritage and questionable moral compass, he hit *delete, delete, delete...*

There was no need to call her back. He knew exactly what she wanted. Him, back at work.

Which made two of them.

Mallory paced the lobby of Vets' Hall in her little black dress and designer heels knock-offs, nodding to the occasional late straggler as they came in. From the large front gathering room, she could smell the delicious dinner that was being served and knew she should be in there. Eating. Smiling. Schmoozing. Getting people fired up for the auction and ready to spend their money.

But she was missing one thing. A date.

Her Mr. All Wrong hadn't showed, not a big surprise. She hadn't really expected him to come, but...hell. Amy had gotten her hopes up. And speaking of Amy, Mallory blinked in shock as the tall, poised, *gorgeous* woman stopped in front of her.

"Wow." She'd never seen Amy with makeup, or in a dress for that matter, but tonight she was in both, in a killer slinky dress and some serious kick-ass gladiator style heels, both of which emphasized endless legs.

Amy shrugged. "The hospital thrift store."

"*Wow*," Mallory repeated. "You look like you belong in a super hero movie."

"Yeah, yeah. Listen, I came out here to ask you if we need to review your mission tonight with Mr. Wrong."

"Nope. Mission cancelled."

"What? Where's your date?"

"We both know that I didn't really have a date." Mallory shook her head. "You look so *amazing*. I hardly even recognize you."

"Can't judge a book by its cover," Amy said casually. "Have you seen Grace? She didn't know any guys in town, and there's no one I'm interested in, so she's my date tonight."

In the time since Amy had shown up in Lucky Harbor, Mallory had never known her to go out on a date. Whenever Mallory asked about it, Amy shrugged and said the pickings were too slim. "Maybe I should be making you two a list of Mr. Rights," Mallory said.

Amy snorted. "Been there, done that."

Matt Bowers walked by and stopped to say hi to Mallory. She was used to seeing him in his ranger uniform, armed and in work mode. But tonight he was in an expensive dark suit, appearing just as comfortable in his own skin as always, and looking pretty damn fine while he was at it. He was six feet tall, built rangy and leanly muscled like the boxer he was on his off days. He had sun-kissed brown hair from long days on the mountain, light brown eyes, and an easy smile that he flashed at Mallory. "Hey," he said.

She smiled. "Hey, back."

Matt turned his attention politely to Amy, and then his eyes registered sudden surprise. "*Amy?*"

"Yeah, I know. I clean up okay." Her voice was emotionless, her smile gone as she turned to Mallory. "See you in there."

Matt's gaze tracked Amy as she strode across the lobby and vanished inside. Yeah, he looked very fine tonight—and also just the slightest bit bewildered.

Mallory knew him to be a laid-back, easygoing guy. Sharp, quick-witted, and tough as hell. He had to be, given that he was an ex-cop and now worked as a district forest ranger supervisor. Nothing much ever seemed to get beneath his skin.

But Amy had. Interesting. This was definitely going on the list of topics to be discussed during their next little chocoholics meeting. "You forget to tip her at the diner or something?" she asked him.

"Or something," Matt said. With a shake of his head, he walked off.

Mallory shrugged and took one more look around. At first, she'd been so busy setting up, and then greeting people, that she'd been far too nervous to think about what would happen if Mr. Wrong didn't show up.

But she was thinking about it now, and it wasn't going to be pleasant. She paced the length of the lobby again, stopping to look once more out the large windows into the parking lot. Argh. She strode back to the dining area and peeked in.

Also filled.

This was both good and bad news. Good, because there was lots of potential money in all those pockets.

Bad, because there was also a lot of potential humiliation in having to go in there alone after it'd been announced that she had a date.

Well, she'd survived worse, she assured herself. Far worse. Still, she managed to waste another five minutes going through the displays of the auction items for the umpteenth time, and as she had every single one of those times, she dawdled in front of one display in particular.

It was a small item, a silver charm bracelet. Each of its charms were unique to Lucky Harbor in some way: a tiny Victorian B&B, a miniature pier, and a gold pan from the gold rush days. So pretty.

Normally, the only jewelry Mallory wore was a small, delicate gold chain with an infinity charm that had been Karen's. It had been all she ever needed, but this bracelet kept drawing her in, urging her to spend money she didn't have.

"Not exactly practical for an ER nurse."

Mallory turned and found Mrs. Burland standing behind her, leaning heavily on a cane, her features twisted into a smile, only named so because her teeth were bared. "Mrs. Burland. You're feeling better?"

"Hell, no. My ankles are swollen, my fingers are numb, and I'm plugged up beyond any roto-rooter help."

Mallory was well used to people telling her things that would never come up in normal conversations. "You need to stay hydrated. You taking your meds?"

"There was a mix-up at the pharmacy."

"You need those meds," Mallory said.

"I tried calling my doctor. He's an idiot. And he's twelve."

Mrs. B's doctor was Dr. Josh Scott. Josh was thirty-two, and one of the best MDs on the West Coast.

"Trades on his cute looks," Mrs. Burland sniffed.

Mallory wouldn't have described Josh as cute. Handsome, yes. Definitely striking as well, and … serious, even when he smiled. So serious that he always looked like he'd been to hell and back. And had learned plenty along the way.

None of which had anything to do with his ability to

do his job. Josh worked his ass off. "You're being very
unfair to a man who's given you your life back. I'll check
into the med issue for you first thing in the morning."

"Yes, well, see that you do. Where's your date?"

Mallory took a deep breath. "Well—"

"You've been stood up? A shame, since you're dressed
to put out." Then the woman walked away.

Mallory went back to staring down at the bracelet.
Mrs. B was right about one thing: it *was* totally impractical for anyone who had to be as practical as she did on
a daily basis. The charms would snag on everything from
patients' leads to the bed rails.

"Sweetheart, what are you doing out here?"

Perfect. Her mother. Ella was in her Sunday best, a
pale blue dress that set off the tan she'd gotten on the
hospital's upper deck during her breaks, where she sat
reading romance novels and plotting her single daughter's
happily-ever-after. "Pretty," Ella said of the bracelet,
"but—"

"Impractical," Mallory said. "I know."

"Actually, I was going to say it's the type of thing a
boyfriend would buy you. You need a boyfriend, Mallory."

Yeah, she'd just pick one up at the boyfriend store
later.

"Where's your date?"

Oh good, her favorite question.

"Oh, honey. Did you get stood up?"

Mallory made a show of looking very busy straightening out the description plaque with the bracelet display.
"Maybe he's just running a little late is all."

"Well, that doesn't bode well for the relationship."

Yeah, and neither did the fact that they didn't *have* a relationship. "You should have a date too, Mom."

"Me?" Ella asked in obvious surprise. "Oh, no. I'm not ready for another man, you know that."

Mallory did know that. Ella had been saying so for the past decade, ever since The Divorce, which Mallory—however twisted—still one-hundred-percent blamed herself for.

"You look a little peaked, sweetheart. Maybe you're catching that nasty flu that's going around."

No, she was catching Stood-Up-Itis. "I'm good, Mom. No worries."

"Okay, then I'm going back inside. Dessert's up next." Ella kissed her on the cheek and left.

Mallory walked around the rest of the auction items. She checked the parking lot again for Mysterious No-Longer-So-Cute Guy. By then, dessert was just about over. When the lights dimmed and the PowerPoint slide show started—the one she'd put together to showcase the auction items—she sneaked in. Tip-toeing to one of the back tables, she grabbed the first empty seat she could find and let out a breath.

So far so good.

She took a surreptitious peek at the people at her table but it was too dark to see across from her. To her right was an empty chair. To her left was a man, sitting still in the shadows, his face turned to the slide show. She was squinting, trying to figure out why he seemed so vaguely familiar when someone came up behind her and put a hand on her shoulder. "Mallory, there you are."

Her boss. *Crap*. She craned her neck and smiled. "Hello, Jane."

"I've been looking everywhere for you. You're late." Jane Miller was the director of nurses, and probably in her previous life she'd been queen of her very own planet. She had a way of moving and speaking that demanded attention and subtly promised a beheading if she was disappointed in the slightest.

"Oh, I'm not just getting here," Mallory assured her. "I've been behind the scenes all night."

"Hmm," Jane said. "And...?"

"And everything's running smoothly," Mallory quickly assured her. "We have a full house. We're doing good."

"Okay, then." Rare approval entered Jane's voice. "That's terrific." She eyed the chair to the right of Mallory. The empty spot. "Your date didn't show up?"

And here's where Mallory made her mistake. She honestly had no idea what came over her: simple exhaustion from a very long week, or it might have been that her heels were already pinching her feet. But most likely it was sheer, stubborn pride—which her grandmother had always told her would be the death of her. "My date is right here," she whispered. As discreetly as she could, she gestured with her chin to the man to her left, praying that his date didn't take that moment to come back from the restroom.

"Lovely." Jane smiled politely at the back of his head. "Aren't you going to introduce us?"

Oh for God's sake. Mallory glanced over at the man, grateful he was paying them no attention whatsoever. "He's very busy watching the slide show."

Jane's smile didn't falter. She also didn't budge. It was her patent alpha dog stance, the one that hospital administrators, politicians, and God himself bent over backward for.

Mallory gritted her teeth and again glanced at her "date," expecting him to still be watching the slide show.

He wasn't.

He was looking right at her, and naturally the slide show ended at that very moment and the lights went up.

He had a bandage above his eye, which she knew covered stitches, and there was a small bruise on his cheek, where she'd nailed him with Grace's cell phone.

Mysterious Cute Guy.

Chapter 5

Do Not Disturb: Chocolate fantasy in progress.

Mallory's first thought at the sight of Mysterious Cute Guy: *Holy smokes.* The night of the storm she hadn't gotten a good look at him, but she was getting one now. Edgy expression, dangerous eyes, long, hard physique clothed in the elegant, sophisticated packaging of a dark suit. He'd managed to pack a wallop while prone and bleeding but that had been nothing compared to what happened to her now when he was upright and conscious. Before she could speak, a spotlight hit the stage, revealing a microphone.

"That's you," Jane said, pulling Mallory out of the chair. "You're introducing the auction, yes?"

Saved by the bell. Or by the end of the slide show. "Yes, that's me."

"Well?" Jane said to Cute Guy. "You're her date, aren't you? Escort her up there."

The expression on his face never changed from that

cool, assessing calm. And even though Mallory had no idea what he did for a living, or even his name, she'd bet the last three dollars in her wallet that few people, if anyone, *ever* barked an order at him. "Oh," she said in a rush to Jane. "It's okay, he doesn't have to—"

But he was already on his feet, setting his hand at the small of her back, gesturing for her to go ahead of him.

Craning her neck, she stared up at him.

He stared back, brow arched, mouth only very slightly curved.

Hot, he'd called her. Sure, he'd also called her "bossy," and he hadn't been in full possession of his faculties at the time, but even now, the memory gave her a tingle in some places that had no business tingling.

"Mallory," Jane said in that Displeased Queen voice again. "Get on with it."

"Yes, *Mallory*," her "date" said, his voice low and grainy, with just a touch of irony. "Let's get on with it."

She nearly let out a short, half-hysterical laugh but she slapped her hand over her mouth. Later. She'd die of embarrassment later. She forced a smile for anyone looking at them, and *everyone* was looking at them. Speaking out of the corner of her mouth for his ears alone, she whispered, "You don't have to do this, pretend to be on the date you didn't want in the first place."

For the briefest flash, something flickered in his eyes before he smoothed it out and went back to his impassive blank face. Confusion? She wasn't sure, and it no longer mattered. Sure, an apology for standing her up would be nice, but beggars couldn't be choosers. For whatever reason, he was willing to play along, and at the moment, with Jane staring holes in her back, Mallory was grateful.

She threaded her way through the tables to the stage, managing a smile at everyone who caught her eye. But she couldn't have come up with a single name to go with those faces. Not when she was so completely aware of that big, warm hand at the small of her back to go along with the big, strong, gorgeous guy escorting her. He was close enough for her to catch his scent.

Which, by the way, was still fantastic, damn him.

As they got to the stage stairs, she caught the fact that he was limping. She glanced down at his leg. What had happened? He hadn't injured his leg in the storm that she knew of. "Are you okay?"

"Later," he said, and nudged her up the stairs to the stage.

With five hundred sets of eyes on her, she let it go and took the mic. "Good evening, Lucky Harbor," she said.

The crowd hooted and hollered.

In spite of herself, she felt a genuine smile escape at their enthusiastic greeting. She'd grown up in this town, had found her life's passion working as a nurse in this town, and knew that even if she somehow ended up on the other side of the world some day for whatever reason, she'd always smile at the thought of Lucky Harbor. "Let's make some money for health care tonight, okay?"

More wild applause. Then someone yelled out, "Who's the hottie with you?"

This was from Tammy, of course, sitting at one of the front tables, her hands curled around her mouth so that her voice would carry to the stage.

Mallory ignored her sister's heckling as best she could and turned to the big screen behind her. "Okay, everyone, get your bidding paddles ready because we have some great stuff for you tonight. Our favorite auctioneer, Charles Tennessee, is going to come up here, and I expect to see lots of action. I want cat fights, people. Hair-pulling if necessary. Whatever it takes to keep the bidding going. So let the fun begin—"

"We want to meet your date!"

Mallory let out a breath and looked down at Lucille, sitting at another front table.

Lucille gave her a finger wave, which Mallory also ignored, but it was hard to ignore the *"Do it, do it, do it"* chanting now coming from Tammy's table. Her brother was there too, looking every bit the part of the mountain biking bum that he was, with the perpetual goggle tan, the streaked, long brown hair. Tall and lanky lean, Joe sat with an arm slung around the blonde he was dating this week. Mallory caught movement at her right and glanced over as her so-called date strode up the stairs to the stage. Oh God, this wasn't going to help anything, and she shook her head vehemently at him to stop, to go back.

Instead he joined her.

She shook her head again, and she'd have sworn he was laughing at her without his mouth so much as twitching. His eyes were sharp with intelligence, wit, and absolutely no hint of remorse or shame at standing her up. She should probably get over that—and quickly—because the entire audience was now fixated on both of them, the anticipation palpable. With no choice but to be as gracious as possible, Mallory shook her head at the crowd. "Bloodthirsty lot, all of you."

Everyone laughed.

"One of these days," she said. "You're all going to get a life."

Everyone laughed again, but she knew no one was going to move on to the auction until she did this, until she introduced Mysterious Cute Guy. "Fine," she said. "But don't try to tell me you don't know the man standing next to me. I've seen his FB stats."

More laughter, and what might have been slight bafflement from the man himself. "Everyone," she said. "Meet..." She trailed off with one thought. *Crap*. Hard to believe that she could possibly have yet another embarrassing moment in her tonight, but she shouldn't have underestimated herself. Drawing a deep breath, she had no choice. She turned to him and she knew damn well that he knew what she needed.

His name.

Again, the very hint of a smile touched the corner of his lips as he looked at her, brow quirked. He was going to make her *ask*, the big, sexy jerk. Well, that's what she got for wanting Mr. All Wrong. Mr. Bad Boy. Mr. Smoking Hot. He was going to burn her, for sure, and she would lay the blame at the chocoholics' feet. But she'd yell at Amy and Grace later. For now, she had to deal with this. The question was how? She hadn't a clue. *Uncle*, she finally mouthed to him.

Leaning in close so that his broad chest bumped her shoulder, he wrapped his fingers around hers on the mic. They were tanner than hers, and work-roughened. And the touch of them made her shiver.

"Mallory's just being shy," he said to the audience, then slid her a look that she couldn't begin to decipher. The man was most excellent at hiding his thoughts. "I'm Ty Garrison. The...date."

Shy her ass. And she knew damn well he hadn't known

her name either, not until Jane had said it. And now he was giving her that bad boy smirk, and she wanted to smack him, but at least she finally knew his name.

Ty Garrison.

It suited him. She'd known a Ty once in first grade. He'd pulled her hair, torn up her homework, and told Mrs. Burland that she'd stolen his. It fueled her temper a little bit just thinking about it. "So there you have it," she said, commandeering the microphone. "Now let's get to the auction, and have a good time." She quickly introduced the auctioneer and gratefully stepped down off the stage, happy to be out of the spotlight.

She walked quickly through the crowd, even happier to note that no one was paying her any attention now; they were all glued to the auctioneer.

Except Lucille.

Lucille, in a silver ball gown that looked like a disco ball, snapped a photo of Mallory with her phone and then winked.

Mallory sighed and was bee-lining for her seat when she was waylaid by her mom, who pulled her down for a hug. Mallory had no idea where her supposed date had gone. Apparently he'd vanished when she'd left the stage, which worked for her. She did not want to subject him to her mother.

The auction had begun with her bracelet, and Mallory quickly grabbed an auction paddle from Ella's table, unable to help herself. No one else was bidding, so she told herself it was a sacrifice for the cause, and raised her paddle.

"Mallory," her mother admonished. "You can't afford that bracelet."

This was true. Annoying but true. "I'm thirty, mom. I

get to make my own dumb decisions now, remember?"

"Like going out with a man whose name you didn't even know?" She sounded scandalized. "That's as bad as finding a man on..." She lowered her voice to a horrified whisper, as if she was imparting a state secret. "—the *Internet!*"

"I'm not looking for a man on the Internet. And it's just a one-night thing with Ty."

Someone behind them won the bracelet, and the auctioneer went on to the next item.

"Listen to me, honey," Ella said. "Ty Garrison is not the kind of man who's going to marry you and give me grandchildren."

Well, her mom was absolutely right on that one. "I'm not looking for that, either." At least not right this moment.

"What *are* you looking for?"

Good question. "I don't know exactly." She looked around at the social crowd, who were all far more into the party atmosphere than bidding. "I guess I'm...bored."

Her mother looked as if she'd just admitted to smoking a crack pipe.

"And I'm restless too," Mallory said. "And...sad, if you want to know the whole ugly truth." She hadn't even realized that was true until it popped out of her mouth without permission, but she couldn't take it back now.

"Oh, honey." Ella squeezed her hand, her eyes suspiciously damp. "Out of all you kids, you've always been my easy one." The crowd got louder and so Ella did too. "The good one, and sometimes I forget to check in and make sure you're okay. Especially after Karen—"

"I *am* okay." And if she wasn't, well then she could

handle it. But dammit, she was tired. Tired of doing what was expected, tired of feeling like she was missing something.

"Mallory," Ella said softly, concerned. "You've also always been the smart one. I depend on that from you, honey." She paused. "You're not going to do anything stupid tonight that you'll regret later, right?"

Well, that depended on her mother's definition of *stupid*. As for regrets, she tried hard to live without them. "I hope so."

Her mother looked at something over Mallory's shoulder and made a funny little noise in her throat. Mallory froze, closing her eyes for a beat before turning to find— *of course*—Ty.

Looking bigger than life, he stood there holding two glasses of wine. He handed one over to her while she did her best to stay cool. Downing half the glass went a long way toward assuring that. *Please let him not have heard any of that....*

"Ty Garrison," Ella said as if testing out the name. "Is my daughter safe with you?"

"*Mom*," Mallory said quickly. "Jesus."

"Don't swear, honey." But Ella held up a hand in concession. "And fine. I'll reword." She looked at Ty. "Are you going to hurt my daughter?"

Ty looked at Mallory as he answered. "She's too smart to let that happen."

Okay, so he *had* heard every word. Terrific. God, she was so far out of her league she could no longer even *see* her league. Her mom had asked if she was going to do anything stupid. And Mallory was pretty sure that the answer was a resounding yes.

As if he could read her thoughts, Ty gave her a sardonic little half toast with his glass, then surprised her by moving away.

Which meant *he* was smart too. "Well," Mallory said. "This has been lots of fun."

"I'm going to assume that was sarcasm," her mom said.

"Always knew I got my smarts from somewhere." Mallory leaned in and kissed Ella's cheek, then went back to her own table where she'd left her purse. That's when she realized that her problems were bigger than her own stupidity issues. Although the room was filled with the sounds of happy, well-fed people, they really were doing far more socializing than bidding. When a "Boating at the Marina" package came up and no one lifted their paddle, Jane locked her unhappy gaze on Mallory's.

Mallory smiled reassuringly while quivering inside. *Someone bid, someone please bid*, she thought with desperation, trying to make it happen by sheer will.

Finally, someone did, but it didn't bring in the money she'd expected.

The next item was a big ticket one, an expensive night on the town in Seattle, which included a limo, a fancy dinner, and an orchestra concert. The bidding began at another low, modest rate, and Mallory's heart landed in her throat.

They were going to have to do better than this. Much better. Again her gaze locked in on Jane, and her unease grew. Someone sank into the chair next to her and since her nipples got hard, she knew it was Ty. "Go away," she said, not taking her gaze off the stage.

Ty said nothing, and she glanced over just as he rose

his paddle, bidding two hundred dollars higher than she could have even *thought* about offering.

She stared at him. "What are you doing?"

He didn't even look at her, just eyed the crowd with interest and a smile she hadn't seen from him before. It was a killer smile, she admitted to herself, and when someone joined him in the bidding across the room, he flashed it again and raised his paddle to up the bid.

And then the oddest thing happened.

More people joined in. Unbelievably, the bidding for the "Night on the Town" continued for five more minutes, until the money offered was nothing short of dazzling.

Ty won.

Apparently satisfied, he set down his paddle and leaned back, long legs stretched out in front of him, perfectly at ease as he watched the proceedings. Mallory should have been watching too, but couldn't take her eyes off him, while around them the night kicked into full gear with a new excitement. Everyone in the whole place was now bidding on all the items, playfully trying to outdo each other, or in some cases, not so playfully. It was...wonderful. But she couldn't get her mind off the fact that Ty had spent hundreds of dollars to get it going. "What are you going to do with that package you just won?"

"Have a night on the town, apparently."

There was no way he was an orchestra kind of guy. "But—"

"Trouble at three o'clock," he said casually.

She turned to look and found Lucille and another biddy from her blue-haired posse bidding fiercely for the next auction item—a date with Anderson Moore, the cute owner of the hardware store in town.

"This Anderson guy," Ty said to Mallory, still watching the old ladies upping the bid with alarming acerbity, "he's ninety, right?"

The auctioneer jokingly suggested the two older women share the date, and the bidding ended peacefully.

Ty winced in clear sympathy for Anderson, who now had to date not one, but two old ladies.

"Don't feel sorry for him," Mallory said. "He's got it coming to him. He goes after anything with breasts."

Ty slid her a look. "You have a little bit of a mean streak."

She laughed. It was true, even if not a single soul in Lucky Harbor would believe it. She had no idea what it said about her that Ty, a perfect stranger, saw more of her than anyone who actually knew her.

At her smile, Ty leaned close, his gaze dropping from her eyes to her mouth. "I like a woman with a mean streak."

She stared into his eyes, nearly falling into him before letting out another low laugh, this time at herself. God, he was good. Really good. "Save the charm. I'm immune." And look at her displaying another shockingly bad girl characteristic—lying through her teeth.

"Explain something to me," he said.

"What?"

"Why does everyone think I was your date tonight?"

She stared at him. "Last weekend, when I pulled you out of that storm, Amy told you about the auction and how I needed a date, remember?"

"No, actually."

She gaped at him. "Seriously?"

"I remember the storm," he said slowly, as if wracking

his brain. "I remember getting hit by the tree. I remember you."

She was wondering if that was good or bad when he added, "Sort of."

Sort of? He "sort of" remembered her? What did *that* mean? She reached for her wine, wishing it was something harder.

"I remember there being a list," he said. "A list of...Mr. Wrongs."

She choked on her wine.

"And I definitely remember waking up in the ambulance with a mother of a headache."

She was silent for a shocked beat while she digested this astonishing fact. He had absolutely no memory of the fact that he was supposed to be her date tonight. Well, that certainly explained a lot of things. Like being stood up. Damn, it was going to be hard to hold that against him, though she was willing to give it a try. "So I guess that the next time I make a date with a concussed guy, I should pin a note to his collar so he doesn't forget."

"Good plan." His hand was next to hers on the table. He let his thumb glide over her fingers, a small, almost casual touch that sent a shudder through her. "I'm sorry I forgot our date," he said. He was so close she could see every single hue of green in his eyes, and there were many. She could feel the warmth of his exhale at her temple. In the crowded Vets' Hall, their nearness was no different from any other couple in the room, discussing their next bid, or laughing over a joke. But Mallory wasn't bidding or laughing. Her heart was suddenly pounding in her throat and there were butterflies going crazy low in her belly.

"Am I on that list, Mallory?" he asked, low and husky. "Am I a Mr. Wrong?"

Oh God, she was in trouble now, because she liked the sound of her name on his lips. Too much. "Don't get too cocky. There are others on the list." She lifted her hand to touch the bruise on his cheek.

He caught her hand in his. "Not what I asked."

"Yes," she admitted. "You're on the list. You're at the top of the list."

Chapter 6

What came first, woman—or the chocolate bar?

Ty had no idea what the hell he thought he was doing, flirting with Mallory.

Scratch that.

He knew exactly what he was doing. He was feeling alive for the first time in six months. Possibly in four years.

She was looking at him, her sweet brown eyes lit, cheeks flushed. She was feeling alive too, he was guessing. But she probably wasn't wondering if he still had a condom in his wallet, trying to calculate how old it might be.

But if she had a list, so did he. A short list of one, and she was it. "Why does a woman like you need a list at all?"

"Like me?"

"Pretty. Smart. Funny."

She laughed, then shook her head. "I don't know. I guess I don't have a lot of time to date."

He could understand that. Hell, it'd been a long time

since he'd dated. It'd been a long dry spell without a woman at all, and she was all woman. Her dress was a deceptively modest black number that had little straps criss-crossing across her back and fell to mid-thigh, molding her curves and whetting his appetite for more. Her heels were high and strappy, emphasizing world-class legs that had been hidden beneath her scrubs. She had her hair up in some loose twist with a few tendrils falling across one temple and at the nape of her neck. Her only jewelry was a little gold necklace—no earrings, nothing to stop his mouth from nipping her throat along his way to her ear where, if he was so inclined, he'd stop to whisper promises.

He shouldn't be inclined. Mallory Quinn was sweet, warm, and caring. She was a white picket fence and two-point-four kids. She was a diamond ring.

She was someone's keeper.

Not his. Never his. He didn't do keepers.

And yet in that beat, with her mouth close to his, a smile in her eyes, he... ached. He ached and yearned for something. Someone. He wanted to wrap his arms around a woman, *this* woman, and lose himself in her.

A woman tapped Mallory on the shoulder, the same woman from before; tall, thin, and coldly beautiful, with a tight pinch to her mouth that said she was greatly displeased about something. Or possibly constipated. She wore authority and bitchiness as easily as she wore the strand of diamonds around her neck.

Mallory glanced up and straightened, her expression going carefully blank. "Jane," she said, in a tone that told Ty that the woman was either her boss or her executioner.

"I need a moment," Jane said.

Boss, Ty thought.

"Absolutely." Mallory followed Jane out of the hall and into the foyer.

The auction was moving ahead at full steam now, and people were into it, jumping up and waving as they bid. Telling himself he had to stretch his aching leg, that he wasn't at all curious about what had come so briefly over Mallory's face, Ty left the hall.

In the entranceway, Mallory had her back to him, facing Cruella Deville. "Absolutely," she was saying. "I'll go upstairs and get it right now. Thank you for your addition, Jane."

And then Jane went one way and Mallory the other, her sweet little ass sashaying as fast as she could move in those sexy heels.

Let it go, man. Let her go, he told himself. He'd heard enough from her mother to know she was a good girl just looking for a walk on the wild side. Probably she'd grown up in Lucky Harbor, which was pretty much the same thing as being in bubble wrap all her life. She was not for him.

Except.

Except here she was, clearly doing her damnedest to meet some pretty tough expectations from family and work and whatever, all while looking to spread her wings. She had guts, and he admired that. She was sexy and adorable, but no matter what she did to spread her wings, she wasn't going to match him in life's experiences.

Not even close.

She was clean and untainted and *not* jaded. She was his opposite. She was too good for him. Far too good, even when she was out there risking it all. She deserved *way* more than he had to offer, and he needed to just walk away. After all, he was out of here, maybe as soon as one more week. Gone, baby, gone.

He told himself all this, repeated it, and then followed her down the hallway anyway.

Mallory walked up the stairs, cursing the heels that were pinching her toes. Jane had sent her up here on a wild goose chase for an antique vase that had been accidentally left off the auction chopping block.

Mallory knew Jane's family had built the Vets' Hall in the early 1940s. Apparently the missing vase had sat in the entry for years, until last spring when the building had been renovated. The vase had never been put back on display and now Jane wanted it gone.

All Mallory had to do was find it.

The second story ran the length of the building. On one side was a series of rooms used by the rec center and other various groups like the local Booster Club. The other side was one big closed-off storage room. Mallory let herself in and flipped on the lights. Far above her was an open-beam ceiling and a loft area where more crap had been haphazardly shoved away. Mallory hoped like hell she wouldn't have to climb up there in her dress and annoying heels to find the vase.

The place was warm, stuffy, and smelled like neglect. She took a good look around and felt a lick of panic at the idea of finding her way out of here, much less locating the missing vase. She moved past a huge shelving unit that was stuffed to the gills with long-lost play props and background sets, and various other miscellaneous items for which there was little use.

Not a single vase.

She walked past more shelves and around two huge, fake, potted Christmas trees before coming to a large stack of boxes leaning against the wall. Assuming the vase wouldn't be stuffed away, she walked farther, gaze searching. Near the center of the room, she came to another long set of shelves. Here were some more valuable items, such as office equipment and furnishings, and miraculously, sitting all by itself on a shelf, a tall vase, looking exactly like the one Jane had described. Mallory couldn't believe it. She picked it up and turned to go, and ran directly into a brick wall.

A brick wall that was a man's chest.

Ty.

He'd appeared out of thin air, scaring her half to death. The vase flew out of her hands and would have smashed to the floor except he caught it.

His sexy suit might have given him an air of sophistication, but it did nothing to hide his bad-boy air. His hair was a little mussed, like he'd run his fingers through it repeatedly. In another man, this would have softened his look but not Ty. She wasn't fooled. There was nothing soft about him. He was sheer trouble, and she knew it. "What are you doing?" she gasped, hand to her pounding heart.

"What are *you* doing?"

She snatched the vase from his hands. "Working."

"Well, I'm helping my date work then."

"You're not my real date. You didn't even know you had a date."

He looked amused. "So you're one of those women who holds a grudge?"

"No! I'm—"

From somewhere far behind them, the storage room door opened. "Hello? Mallory, dear?"

"*Shit*," Mallory whispered, horrified. "It's Lucille."

"Your mother told you not to swear."

She narrowed her eyes at him.

"Mallory?" Lucille called out.

Mallory slapped her hand over her own mouth.

"Yoo-hoo...I saw your hot date follow you in here. I just want to get a picture of you two for Facebook."

Oh no. No, no, no...Mallory turned in a quick circle in the warm, dusty, overstuffed storage room, desperate for a place to hide.

Ty must have seen her panic because he briefly held a finger to her lips to indicate he needed her silence, then took the vase in one hand and her wrist in his other and tugged her along, farther into the shadows.

She followed, walking on her tiptoes to avoid the clicking of her heels, when suddenly Ty pressed her against the wall. "Shh," he breathed in her ear.

Stealth. She got it. She was depending on it. She also got something else, an unexpected zing from the feel of his mouth on her ear and his body pressing into hers.

"*Mallory*?" Lucille called out.

Ty had gone into 007 mode. His eyes were searching their surroundings, his body ready and alert. He opened a panel she hadn't even noticed, then pulled something from his pocket and used it inside the panel. In the next second, the lights went out.

Startled, she nearly gasped but he slid a hand over her mouth. That, combined with the way he was holding her against the wall, caused a tsunami of inappropriate feelings to rush through her.

"Don't move." He remained still until she nodded, and then he was gone.

Only not completely gone.

She jumped when she felt his hands on her ankles. He was crouched before her, removing first one heel and then the other. Her hands went out for balance and smacked him in the head. She heard his soft laugh, then he had her hand again and they were on the move. She couldn't see a thing, but Ty didn't appear to have that problem. He was navigating them both with apparent ease, leading her through the maze of the vast storage unit as if he could see in the dark. They turned corners and squeezed into spots, his hands sliding to her hips, guiding her exactly where he wanted her to go, taking care that she didn't bump into anything. She had no idea how he could see, or even know where they were going, but she followed him.

Blindly.

It was better than the alternative.

Each time they stopped, she was pulled up against his big, warm body, until she began to anticipate it.

Crave it.

"Mallory?" Now, accompanying Lucille's voice came a small beam of light.

Good Lord. The woman was using the same Bic app that Grace had. "Oh for the love of—"

Warm lips covered hers. "*Shh*."

Right. Shh. Her knees were still melting. Her one hand was in his, trapped between their bodies, but her other hand slid up his chest, around the back of his neck and into his hair. Because she needed a hand grip, she told herself.

"How bad do you want to keep out of her sight?" Ty

wanted to know, each syllable rumbling from his chest and through hers. He'd set the vase down, freeing up both his hands. She felt herself rock into him and tighten her grip on his hair, and it took a long moment to process his words because her brain was no longer firing on all cylinders.

"Mallory."

God, she liked the sound of her name on his lips. And she liked the feeling that had come over her too, the languid yet throbbing beat of anticipation. She certainly wasn't bored or sad now. "Hmm?"

"How bad?"

How bad did she want him? *Bad.*

With a little huff against her jaw that might have been another low laugh, he tightened his grip on her and spun her away from him, setting her hands on something that felt like cold steel.

"Hold on tight," he whispered and nudged his big body up behind hers, his biceps on either side of her arms, his chest against her back.

Her mind went utterly blank, but her body didn't. Her body went damp at the wicked thought of doing it right here, like this. From behind.

"Up," he said, and the fantasy receded. No, he didn't want sex. He had her in front of a ladder and wanted her to climb it.

Good thing it was dark because it hid the heat of the blush she could feel on her face. She pulled herself up, *extremely* aware that her butt was in his face, and then she was directly above him.

He was still apparently able to see in the dark. Which meant that he could see right up her dress. She was wearing a brand new silky black thong, her very best, but still, it couldn't be a very good angle for her.

At the top of the ladder was the loft. Moonlight slanted in from the sole round window, revealing more stored items, a couch and a large table with chairs. The table was stacked with more stuff. There were also rows of framed pictures and empty planters, and a whole horde of other crap. Everywhere.

Mallory moved aside for Ty to join her but the standing space was so small she lost her balance and fell onto the couch.

Ty followed her down.

On the night of the storm, Mallory had been beneath him too, but it felt different this time. Sexy different, and she let out a small, half hysterical laugh.

Ty covered her mouth with his hand, shifting a little to get the bulk of his weight off of her. In the execution, one of his thighs pushed between hers and *oh sweet baby Jesus*. She promptly stopped laughing and moaned instead. A total involuntary, accidental moan that sounded needy and wanton. And horrifyingly loud.

Ty's hands tightened on her and they both stilled, craning their necks, looking down into the dark storage area, following the little beam of light as Lucille weaved through the aisles below.

Ty pulled his hand from Mallory's mouth. "Unless she can climb a ladder, we're good here until she gives up and leaves."

Yes. Yes, they were good here. Or very bad, depending on how one looked at it.

Above her, Ty was still as stone, a solid heated package of testosterone and sinew holding her down on the couch.

She wasn't sure what it said about her that she felt just a little bit powerless and helpless, and that she liked it.

A lot.

Another thing she liked? The fact that every time he breathed, his leg shifted up against her core, putting her body on an entirely different page than her brain.

On the *get-more-of-him* page.

"She won't give up," she whispered, more than a little breathless.

"Watch." Ty shifted again—oh God *his thigh!*—and pulled something from his pocket, which he threw.

Mallory heard the ping of the coin as it landed with deadly precision all the way across the huge room near the storage room entrance.

Holy shit he could throw.

"Oh!" they heard Lucille exclaim, whipping around toward the sound. "You're escaping, you smart girl. Darn it all!"

They watched as the little beam of light wobbled back through the room to the entrance, and then in the next moment, vanished completely.

Silence reigned.

Well, except for Mallory's thundering heartbeat. She was in an attic loft, flat beneath her Mr. Wrong. Her common sense was screaming *flee!* But her secret inner bad girl was screaming *oh please, can't we have him? Just once?*

"You okay?" Ty asked.

Loaded question. "You have some impressive skills," she said. "I feel like a Bond girl."

"You weren't so bad yourself," he said. "The way you shimmied up that ladder is going to fuel my fantasies for some time."

So he *could* see in the dark. And now that they were up here with moonlight coming in the window, she could see too. She bit her lower lip because she could feel, too. She could feel him, *all* of him. Her breasts were mashed up against his chest, plumping out of her dress suggestively. She wasn't sure he'd noticed, but then he very purposely dropped his head, his lips just barely brushing her exposed skin. She sucked in a breath and felt him stir against her.

Yeah. He'd noticed. "I have lots of ladder practice," she said inanely.

"Yeah?" he asked, sounding intrigued. "You climb a lot of ladders in the ER?"

"Uh, no." Nerves had her laughing. And babbling. "But I had to clear the gutters on my house last fall before the rains hit. I nearly fell when I found a fist-sized spider waiting for me but managed not to accidentally kill myself."

A low laugh escaped him.

"So why did you do it?" she asked.

"The ladder? Nowhere else to go but up."

"No, I mean why did you help me hide? And thanks, by the way. You pretty much saved my butt." *Again.*

He slid a hand down her arm, squeezing her hip before shocking the hell out of her when he slid that hand further, cupping said butt. "My pleasure."

At the words, at the touch, her body liquefied. Or maybe that was his fingers, tightening on her hindquarters, making her want to squirm and rock into him.

The brand new bad girl in her took over and did exactly that.

Ty went still. She wasn't sure what that meant exactly,

but she was feeling things she hadn't in far too long, and she intended to go with those feelings. So she squirmed again.

"Mallory." There was a warning in that low, sexy tone of his, a very serious warning.

She'd wanted a kiss, but hearing him say her name like that was almost as good. And now she wanted more. She wanted things she didn't even have names for. So she wriggled some more, hoping like hell she was getting her message across because she wasn't all that practiced in the bad girl department. Amy had been right; she needed lessons. She made a mental note to address this as well at the next chocoholics meeting. For now, she'd wing it. "Yeah?"

"Are you coming onto me?"

"Well, technically, you're on top of me," she pointed out. "So I think that means that *you're* coming onto *me*."

With a groan, he pressed his forehead to hers and swore beneath his breath, and not the good kind of swear either. And though she should have seen this coming, she hadn't.

He didn't want her.

It was perfect, really. Perfect for the way the rest of the night had gone. Horrified, humiliated, she pushed at him. "Sorry. I got caught up in the moment. I'm not very good at this, obviously." He didn't budge so she shoved him again. "Excuse me."

He merely tightened his grip. "Not good at what, exactly?" he asked.

"Really? You need me to say it?"

When he just waited, she sighed. "Attracting men. I'm not good at attracting men. Now if you could please *get off.*"

He lifted his head and cupped the back of hers in one big hand, his eyes glinting with heat. "You first," he said rough and gravelly, leaving no mistake to his meaning.

She gasped, and he took advantage of that to kiss her, his lips moving against hers until she gasped again, in sheer pleasure this time.

Things went a little crazy then. Ty's mouth was firm and hungry, his tongue sliding against hers, and God, she'd almost forgotten what it was like to be kissed like this, like there was nothing on earth more important than her. That long-forgotten thrill of feeling soft and feminine rushed over her.

Then Ty lifted his head, and she realized she was touching his face, the stubble on his jaw scraping against the pads of her fingers.

"To be clear," he said, "I'm *very* attracted to you." And she believed him because the proof of that statement was hard against her hip.

"I think it's your eyes," he said.

She was a little startled by the unexpected romance of that. And then she was drowning in *his* eyes, which were smoldering. But then they were kissing again, and she couldn't think because he happened to be the world's most amazing kisser. Ever. She lost herself in it for long moments, loving the fact that he didn't seem to be in a hurry at all, or using the kiss as a means to an end. Kissing her was an act all unto itself, and she was panting for air when he finally broke from it. He shifted to pull away and she reflexively clutched at him. "Wait—We're stopping?"

Dropping his head, he rubbed his jaw to hers. "Yeah."

"But…why?"

He let out a low, innately male groan. "Because you're not the fuck-a-stranger-in-a-storage-room-with-her-boss-waiting type of woman."

Well, when he put it like that...Damn. Her inner bad girl retreated a little. More than a little.

You don't think you deserve to be happy.

Amy's words floated in her head. No, she'd never been the type to let a stranger into her heart, much less her body.

But this wasn't about her heart.

And Ty was no longer a complete stranger. He was the man who'd good-naturedly stepped in tonight when she'd needed him. Multiple times. He was the man who'd just given her the most amazing kiss of her life.

She wanted him to also be the man to vanquish her restlessness and loneliness. "I am for tonight," she said, and wrapped herself around him.

"Mallory." He stared down at her, the moonlight casting his features in bold relief. "I'm not a long-term bet. Hell, I'm not even a short-term bet."

"I just want this," she said. "Here. Now. With you."

This won her another long look, interrupted by a very rough, very male groan when she undulated against him, trying to sway the game in her favor.

"Christ, your eyes," he said on a long breath. "Come here then." Before she could, he pressed her down farther into the couch, his mouth trailblazing a path over her throat and collar bone.

Apparently, he wasn't one to over-think or second-guess a decision. Good to know. And when he came up against the material of her dress, he wasn't deterred by that either. A quick tug of his fingers and her straps slid down her shoulders to her elbows, trapping her hands at her sides and baring her breasts all in one economical movement.

Apparently, Ty didn't waste energy unnecessarily. Also good to know.

"Mmm," he said, a growl of approval low in his throat. He made his way to her breasts, paying such careful homage to her nipples that she was writhing beneath him by the time he moved down her stomach.

"So soft," he murmured against her, his breath gently caressing her skin. But there was nothing gentle about him as his work-roughened fingers pushed the hem of the dress up to her waist. He looked down at her black thong, gave another low growl of approval, then slid the tiny swatch of black silk to one side. This bared all her secrets both to the night air and his hot gaze. Lowering his head, he put his mouth on her, using his lips and his tongue, making her arch up into him. She was crying out within minutes, her hands fisted in his hair as stars exploded behind her eyes.

Before she'd even stopped shuddering, he'd shoved off his jacket, then unbuckled, unzipped, and was rolling on a condom. The sight made her moan, and then he was pushing inside of her and she lost her breath. He gave her a moment to adjust to his size, then his mouth found hers again and she could taste herself on his tongue. It was wildly sensuous, and so far out of her realm of experience she could only dig her fingernails into his back and hold on.

He swallowed her cries as he thrust into her, running a hand beneath her knee, lifting her leg up to wrap around him so he could get even deeper.

Deeper worked. Oh, how it worked. He took her right out of herself, and she thrilled to it. He was powerful and primal, and if he hadn't taken such care to make sure she was right there with him, she might have doubted herself. Instead, she rose to meet him halfway, unable to do anything but feel as he pushed her over the edge again, his hard length pounding into her, his tongue mimicking his body's movement as he claimed her. And it was a claiming, a thorough one. She was deep in the throes when he joined her, shuddering in her arms, his hands digging hard into her hips as he lost himself in his pleasure.

In her.

The knowledge nearly sent her over again, as did the low, hoarse, very male sound he made when he came. Tearing his mouth from hers, he dropped his head into the crook of her neck, his broad shoulders rising and falling beneath her hands as he caught his breath.

He was still buried deep inside of her when he lifted his head to see her face.

"What?" she whispered.

"Wanted to make sure you're okay. You're smiling."

"Am not." But she was. God, she so was. It would probably take days to get rid of it. But apparently she'd taken the Chocoholics modus operandi to heart. She'd just had her Mr. Wrong.

In a storage room.

Which just proved exactly how wrong Mr. All Wrong was for her, because she'd never had sex without a commitment in her entire life. She braced herself for the guilt.

None came.

In fact, Mallory felt unexpectedly fantastic. "No regrets," she whispered.

He gave her a curious look, then that almost-smile. "I like the way you think."

She ran a finger over the Band-Aid on his forehead, and then along the bruise on his cheek. "I'm sorry about this," she said. "About throwing the phone at your head when I thought you were a bad guy."

He shook his head, but his almost-smile became a full smile. "I don't remember that part."

"Oops. Then never mind." She heard a thunderous applause from below them and remembered. The auction! "Oh my God, we've got to go. You first. Hurry." She gave him a nudge but he didn't move.

"I'm not going to just leave you up here," he said.

"Yes, you are! We can't be seen leaving here together." Just the thought brought more panic, and she pushed him again. "Go. Hurry!"

Not hurrying at all, he looked at her for another long moment. Leaning forward, he pressed his lips to her damp temple and finally pulled away. He helped her straighten out her clothing before taking care of himself.

She was still lying there with no bones in her body when he disappeared over the edge of the loft, vanishing into the night, giving her exactly what she'd asked for. Just this, here, now.

And now was over.

Chapter 7

There is no kiss sweeter than a chocolate kiss.

Ty slept hard that night, and apparently lulled by post-orgasmic glow, he didn't dream. Sex was the cure for nightmares. Good to know. His morning went pretty much status quo. Matt met him on the beach, and they'd gone several miles when Matt got a cramp and went down.

Ty was too far away, and his heart nearly stopped before he got to Matt and dragged his ass out of the water.

Matt rolled around in agony on the sand while Ty dug his fingers into Matt's calf and rubbed the cramp out. When he had, he collapsed to the sand next to Matt. "No more."

Matt was gasping for breath. "You're right. You're a fucking animal in the water. No one should be able to swim that long and hard."

"No, I mean because you nearly drowned yourself."

"Well," Matt managed, sitting up with a smile. "Only half drowned, thanks to you."

"Fuck it, Matt, I'm not kidding. You're not swimming with me anymore."

Matt's smile faded as he studied Ty for a long moment. "You do realize that not everyone's going to die on you, right?"

"Shut up."

"What crawled up your ass today?" Matt asked. "You had a good time last night. I saw you actually crack a smile at Mallory."

Mallory. God, Mallory. Ty pushed upright and despite his trembling limbs, he started walking.

"Good talk," Matt called out after him.

Ty kept going, heading back to the house. He wanted to run but his leg didn't have the same want. Brooding about that, he pushed hard, forcing himself to stay at the tide line where the sand was the softest and choppiest because that made the going extra teeth-grindingly difficult.

Difficult worked. He wanted to feel the pain, to remind himself why the hell he was here. Which was *not* to dally with the sweet, warm, giving, sexy-as-hell Mallory Quinn.

Though God, she'd been all those things and more, and she'd revved his engine but good. Every time he thought about how hot she'd looked lying all spread out for him on that couch, he got hard.

Stupid. What he'd done last night had been *beyond* stupid and he knew it. It was also selfish, and he had no excuse other than she'd blindsided him with her open, honest sweetness. He should have ignored the attraction, had fully intended to, but that hadn't worked out so well for him.

And now he could add being an asshole to his list of infractions. Because taking advantage of Mallory last night had been a real dick move. But she was...well, everything he wasn't.

Still, she didn't deserve the likes of him, or what he'd done. Probably she already hated him for it. He told himself this was for the best and took a long, hot shower. He pulled on clothes while eyeballing the empty Vicodin bottle on the dresser. This was a ritual, the stare down. In the end, he shoved the bottle into his pocket as he always did, wanting the reminder close at hand. The reminder to keep his head on straight, keep his mind on the goal—getting back in the game.

With that in his head, he left for his doctor's appointment.

"Looking better," Josh said an hour later, eyeing the latest screen of Ty's leg.

"I feel all better," Ty said, lying through his teeth. After this morning's exercise, he hurt like hell.

Not fooled, Josh gave him a long look.

"I'm good for light duty."

"Uh huh." Josh leaned back in his chair and studied him. "Lighter duty than what, rappelling out of helicopters, rescuing dignitaries, etcetera?"

This was the problem with having your boss put you on leave until you were medically cleared. Thanks to Frances, Josh knew far too much about him. Ty blew out a breath. It wasn't Josh's fault. He was a good guy, and under different circumstances, would even be considered a friend.

If Ty had friends. He didn't. He'd let his friends die on a mountaintop four years ago.

So what was Matt, a pesky little voice asked. *Or Mallory*? Accidents, he decided.

"Look," Josh said, leaning forward, "you want out of here. I get that. You're getting closer. But let's give it another week, okay?"

Another fucking week. But reacting badly wasn't going to help him. He'd use the week to finish Matt's Jimmy. And the Shelby. He couldn't leave without the Shelby. "Fine. But *you* tell her."

"Frances?" Josh smiled grimly. "Gladly."

When Ty got back to the house, his phone was blinking missed calls. He deleted them without a glance, then went to work on Matt's Jimmy. Later he switched to his real love, the Shelby, stopping to look up some parts on the Internet. There he got distracted by an e-mail from Matt with a link.

He'd been tagged on Facebook. In fact, on the Lucky Harbor page there was an entire note on him, listing sightings and news. They called him *Mysterious Cute Guy*.

It was enough to give a guy nightmares.

Except he was already having nightmares...

He waited until hunger stopped him and drove into town. Lucky Harbor was nestled in a rocky cove, its architecture a quirky, eclectic mix of the old and new. The main drag was lined with Victorian buildings painted in bright colors, housing the requisite grocery store, post office, gas station, and hardware store. Then there was a turnoff to the beach itself, where a long pier jutted out into the water, lined with more shops, the arcade and Ferris wheel, and the diner.

Eat Me was like something from an out-of-time Mayberry, except in Mayberry he'd probably not have gotten laid at Vets' Hall, in a storage attic above the entire town.

Noticing the brand new front door, he entered the diner and took a seat at the counter. Amy silently poured him a mug of coffee. This was routine; they'd been doing the same dance for months, rarely speaking. He really appreciated that in a waitress, and he liked her infinitely more than the eternally grumpy diner owner. Jan scared him, just a little bit.

Then Amy dropped the local paper in front of him and cocked a hip tableside.

Ty slowly pushed his sunglasses to the top of his head and gave her a level look. Her return look had bad attitude all over it. She wore a black tee with some Chinese symbol on the front and the requisite frilly pink apron that looked incongruous with her short denim skirt, boots, and general kick-ass attitude. She gestured with a short jerk of her chin to the paper, and he took a look.

The headline read: COUNTY HOSPITAL'S AUCTION—A HUGE SUCCESS.

So far so good, he thought, then read the first paragraph, which credited the success of the auction to the nurses, specifically Mallory Quinn, who along with her new boyfriend had gotten the entire Vets' Hall on its feet by starting off the bidding with a bang.

Ty reread the article. New boyfriend? *Mysterious Cute Guy*? He graced Amy with his no-nonsense, don't-fuck-with-me look. It had cowed many.

But Amy didn't appear impressed or even particularly intimidated.

He set down the paper and pushed it away.

She pushed it back with a single finger.

"Do you have a point?" he asked.

"Several, actually. First, Mallory's my friend. And I recently encouraged her to make a change in her life. You were that change. Don't make me sorry."

Ty wasn't much used to threats, however sweetly uttered. Never had been. He'd been raised by two military parents who'd taken turns parenting him when one or the other had been on tour overseas. He'd been loved, but weaknesses had not been tolerated. Even his current job added up to a life lived by rules, discipline, sheer wits, and honor.

The honor part was troubling him now.

Somehow in spite of himself and his reclusiveness, he'd managed to find celebrity status in this crazy-ass, one-horse town, and even worse, there was Mallory, wanting him to take her for a walk on the wild side.

Bad idea.

The *baddest*.

He'd done it anyway, fallen captive to those melted chocolate eyes, even knowing he planned on being out of Lucky Harbor any minute now. "She's a big girl," he finally said.

Amy stared at him for a long moment, then shook her head and walked away, muttering something beneath her breath about the entire male race being genetically flawed.

Ty was inclined to agree with her. He paid for his coffee and received another long, careful look from Amy.

Message received.

As to whether he was going to heed the warning, the jury was still out. He went straight back to his big, empty house. Cranking the music to ear-splitting levels, he worked on the Shelby. He'd seen the car in the newspaper on his first day in Lucky Harbor had hadn't been able to resist her.

He'd never been able to resist a sweetheart of a car.

Or, apparently, a sweetheart of a woman...

Mallory sat in a hospital board meeting surrounded by a bunch of administrators that included her boss and her mother, in what should have been the meeting of her life. Instead, her mind was a million miles away. Or more accurately, in a certain storage room.

Memories of that storage room, and what Ty had done to her in it, were making her warm. *Very* warm.

She still couldn't believe how fast she'd gotten naked with him.

Well, not quite naked, she reminded herself. She'd been in such a hurry that she hadn't even lost her panties, not completely.

Ty had simply slipped them aside with his fingers.

Just remembering made her damp all over again. God. She'd never gone up in flames so hard and fast in her entire life.

Heaven.

He'd taken her to heaven in seven minutes. A record for her. And she'd do it again, in a heartbeat.

That is, if the man who'd taken her to heaven hadn't vanished from the auction without a word. That should teach her to have completely inappropriate sex with a man whose name she'd learned only twenty minutes earlier.

But all it'd really taught her was that she'd been missing out. Man, had she been missing out. Worse, she knew the magnitude of her attraction for him now, and she was afraid that the next time she saw him, she was going to shove him into the nearest closet for round two.

And round three.

Mallory took a moment to fantasize about that, about what she'd be wearing the next time. Maybe her little black dress again; he'd seemed to really like it. And maybe next time she'd leave the panties at home—

"Mallory?"

She blinked away the vision of Ty and her panties and came face to face with a *not amused* Jane.

"The amount?" Jane asked in a tone that said she'd repeated herself several times already.

"Eighteen thousand." Mallory looked down at the check in her hands, a check she was incredibly proud of—the total of the proceeds from the auction. "You said the board would donate twenty-five percent of it to the Health Services Clinic."

"There isn't an HSC," Jane said. "Not yet."

Mallory bit back her retort, knowing better than to show weakness. "There will be. We've proven need."

"Have we?" Jane asked.

"Yes." Mallory forced herself to look the other board members in the eyes as she spoke, no matter how resistant they were. Dr. Scott was there, rumpled and gorgeous as usual. His eyes warmed when he met her gaze. No one else made eye contact. She took a big gulp of air. "The need is obvious. There's nowhere else in the entire county providing drug programs, teen pregnancy counseling, women's services, or an abuse hotline. We all know that. The ER is losing money because we're taking on patients who'd be better served by a Health Clinic."

"You mean people who can't, or won't, pay." This

from Bill Lawson, head of the board of directors. He was tall, lean, and fit, looking forty instead of his fifty-five. He had sharp eyes, a sharper mind, and was all about the bottom line. Always. He *was* listening though, and Mallory appreciated that. This was important to her, had been since Karen had died because she'd had no place to go and get the services she'd so desperately needed.

People rarely talked about Karen and what had happened to her. But Mallory hadn't forgotten a thing, and she intended to make sure that no other scared eighteen-year-old girl ever felt the helplessness and terror that Karen had.

"We've run the numbers," she said, talking directly to Bill now. The hospital, just outside of Lucky Harbor, serviced the entire county but was private, run by a board of directors who all tended to bow to Bill's wishes. She needed his support. "A Health Services Clinic is eligible for programs and funding that the ER isn't. I've written the grant requests. If you go with my proposed plan and allow use of the old west wing, then one hundred percent of the HSC revenue will go right back into the hospital's pockets."

"It would also mean that the full financial responsibility for the Health Services Clinic would be the hospital's," Bill pointed out.

He already knew this. He just didn't like it. "Yes," she agreed. "But with the grants and donations, HSC will run in the black, and in the long run, it'll save your ER losses. We've got most of the first year's funds already."

"You're short ten big ones."

"True, but I won't stop until we have the rest," she promised. "This makes sense for our community, Bill, and it's the right thing to do." She paused, then admitted the rest. "I'm going to be a pain in your ass over this."

"Going to be?" Bill shook his head wryly. "Listen, Mallory, I believe in what you're trying to do, and I want to be on your side. But let's face the truth here—your proposed programs will bring a certain...demographic to Lucky Harbor, a demographic we typically try to divert away to other parts of the county. The town isn't really behind this."

"The town can be persuaded. People are in need, and HSC can meet that need."

Bill was quiet a moment, and Mallory did her best not to fidget. She was only moderately successful.

"I'll make you a deal," Bill finally said. "At this week's town meeting, I'll give everyone a formal spiel, then ask for thoughts."

People went to town meetings like they went to the grocery store or got gas. It was simply what everyone did. If Bill asked for opinions, he'd get them, in droves.

"If we get a positive response, I'll consider a one-month trial run for HSC. One month, Mallory," he said when she smiled. "Then we'll reevaluate on the condition of the actual costs and the bottom line at that time. If you've got the budget for the rest of the year after that month, and if there've been no problems, you're on. If not, you drop this." He gave her a long look. "Is that acceptable to you?"

There was only one answer here. "Yes, sir," she said with carefully tempered excitement.

"Oh, and that budget of yours better not include paying you to go to the pharmacy and pick up meds for our patients and then delivering them."

He was referring to how she'd picked up Mrs. Burland's meds for her just that morning and brought them to the woman's home. How he'd found out wasn't too much of a mystery. Lucky Harbor had one pharmacy. It was located in the grocery store, and everyone in town was in and out of that store often. Anyone from the pharmacist, to the clerk, to any of the customers could have seen her, and she hadn't made a secret of what she was doing.

Nor had Mrs. Burland made a mystery out of how she'd felt about Mallory delivering her meds.

"Do you expect a tip?" she'd asked. *"Because here it is. Put on some makeup and do something with your hair or you'll never catch a man."*

At the memory, Mallory felt an eye twitch coming on but she didn't let it dampen her relief. She was closer to opening the HSC than she'd ever been. "I did that on my own time."

Bill nodded. "And if by some miracle, the town meeting goes well, how long would you need to get up and running?"

She'd had volunteer professionals from all over the county on standby all year. "I would open immediately with limited services, adding more as quickly as I can get supplies and staff scheduled."

"See that 'immediately' is actually immediately," Bill said. "And I'll expect to see numbers weekly."

"Yes, sir."

An hour later, Mallory was on the ER floor, still doing the happy dance. Finally she had something other than sexy Ty to think about, because hoping for town approval and actually getting it were two very different things.

Not that she had time to think about that either, thanks to a crazy shift. She had a stroke victim, a diabetic in the midst of losing his toes, a gangbanger who'd been shot up in Seattle and made it all the way to Lucky Harbor before deciding he was dying, two drunks, a stomach-ache, and a partridge in a pear tree.

In between patients, she worked the phones like mad, preparing for a *very* tentative Health Clinic opening the following week.

The west wing in the hospital had once been the emergency department before the new wing had been built three years ago. It was perfectly set up for the clinic, easily accessible with its own parking lot. It needed to be cleaned and stocked. And she needed staff on standby. The list of what she needed and what she had to do went on and on.

When she yawned for the tenth time, Mallory went in search of coffee. As she stood there mainlining it, waiting for it to kick in—her mind danced off to revisit a certain storage room . . . *big, warm hands, both rough and gentle at the same time, stroking her—*

"Mallory, my goodness. Where are you at in that pretty little head, Disneyland?"

Mallory blinked and the daydream faded, replaced by the sight of her mother, who stood in front of her smiling with bafflement. "I called your name three times. And the same thing happened in the board meeting. Honey, what in the world are you thinking about today?"

She'd been thinking about the sound Ty had made when he'd come, a low, inherently male sound that gave her a tingle even now. "Dessert," she said faintly. "I'm thinking about dessert."

"Hmmm." Ella looked doubtful but didn't call her on it. "You've seen the paper."

"You mean the local gossip rag masquerading as legit news?" They'd labeled Ty her *boyfriend*. Who'd run the fact check for *that* tidbit? "Yeah, I saw it." Every person she'd come across had made sure of it.

"Honey, I just don't think it's a good idea to risk so much on a man you know nothing about."

"It's not about taking risks, mom." And it wasn't. Mallory had risked nothing, not really. Well, maybe she'd risked getting caught having wild sex in a public place, but she'd felt safe enough or she'd never have done it. No, for her it'd been about being selfish for the first time in recent memory, taking what she wanted. And yeah, maybe that was going to wreak some havoc on her personal life. But since when was worrying about what people thought a life requirement?

Since a long time ago. Since she'd got it in her head that she had to be good to be loved.

"Mallory, honestly," Ella murmured, her tone full of worry. "This is so unlike you, seeing a man you don't even know."

Yes, Mallory, the shock. The horror. The good girl actually wanting something for herself. How dare she? "We're not seeing each other," she said. At least not how Ella meant.

"But the newspaper said—"

"We're not," Mallory repeated. Ty hadn't said so in words, not a single one in fact, but he couldn't have been more clear as he'd vanished.

"So you're telling me that I'm worrying about nothing?" Ella asked.

"Unless you enjoy having to wash that gray out of your hair every three weeks, yes. You're worrying about nothing."

Her mother patted her brunette bob self-consciously. "Four weeks and counting. Do I need a touch-up?"

Just then, Camilla came running through, looking breathless. Camilla was a fellow nurse, twenty-two years old and so fresh out of nursing school she still squeaked when she walked. She was a trainee, and as such, got all the crap jobs. Such as signing in new patients. "He's here," she whispered dramatically, practically quivering with the news. "In the waiting room."

"He?" Mallory asked.

Camilla nodded vigorously. "*He.*"

"Does 'he' have a name?" Ella asked dryly.

"Mysterious Cute Guy!"

Her mother slid Mallory a look. But Mallory was too busy having a coronary to respond. *Why was he here?* "Is he hurt or sick?"

"He asked for Dr. Scott," Camilla said in a rush. "But Dr. Scott's been called away."

Mallory moved around Camilla. "I'll take him."

"Are you sure?" Camilla asked. "Because I'd be happy to—"

"I'm sure." Heart pounding, Mallory headed down the hallway toward the ER waiting room, taking quick mental stock. She had nothing gross or unidentifiable on her scrubs, always a bonus. But she couldn't remember if she was wearing mascara. And she really wished she'd redone her hair at break.

Ty was indeed in the waiting room. There was no noticeable injury. He was seated, head back, eyes closed, one leg stretched out in front of him. He wore faded Levi's and a black T-shirt, and looked like the poster boy for Tall, Dark, and Dangerous. Pretty much anyone looking at him would assume he was relaxed, maybe even asleep, but Mallory sensed he was about as relaxed as a coiled rattler.

He opened his eyes and looked at her.

Inexplicably nervous, she glanced at the TV mounted high in a corner, which was tuned to a soap opera. On the screen was a beautiful, dark-haired woman getting it on with a guy half her age in a hot tub. She was panting and screaming out, "Oh, Brad. Oh, please, Brad!"

Oh, good. Because this wasn't awkward enough. She hastily looked around for the remote but it was MIA. Naturally.

Ty's brows went up but he said nothing; he didn't need to. The last time she'd seen him, he'd been pouring on the charm and getting into her panties with shocking ease.

Okay, maybe not so much on the charm. Nope, he'd drawn her in with something far more devastatingly effective—that piercing, fierce gaze, which had turned her on like she'd never been turned on before.

Apparently nothing much had changed in that regard. She'd just handled three emergencies in a row without an elevation in her heart rate, but her heart was pumping now, thudding in her chest and bouncing off her rib cage at stroke levels.

He'd walked away from her, she reminded herself, clearly not intending to further their relationship—if that's what one called a quickie these days.

The woman on the TV was still screaming like she was auditioning for a porno. "Oh God, oh Brad, *yes!*"

The air conditioning was on, which in no way explained why she was in the throes of a sudden hot flash. Whirling around, she continued to search in desperation for the remote, finally locating it sitting innocuously on a corner chair. It still took her a horrifyingly long time to find the mute button, but when she hit it, the ensuing silence seemed more deafening than the "Oh Brad, please!" had been.

She could feel Ty looking at her, and she bit her lower lip because all she could think about was that he'd made her cry out like that too.

But at least she hadn't begged.

"I'd offer a penny for your thoughts," he said. "But I have the feeling they're worth far more."

"I'm not thinking anything," she said far too quickly, then felt the heat of her blush rise up her face.

"Liar." He rose from the chair and shifted closer, and she stopped breathing. Just stopped breathing. Which wasn't good because she *really* needed some air.

And a grip.

Ty leaned into her a little bit, his lips brushing her ear. "You weren't quite as loud as she was."

She closed her eyes as the blush renewed itself. "A nice guy wouldn't even bring that up."

He shrugged, plainly saying he wasn't a nice guy. And in fact, he'd never claimed to be one.

Of course there was no one else the waiting room, but just across the hall at the sign-in desk were Camilla and her mother, neither of them bothering to pretend to be doing anything other than staring in open, rapt curiosity.

Mallory turned her back on them. "I wasn't loud," she whispered.

Oh good Lord. That hadn't been what she'd meant to say at all, but it made him smile. A genuine smile that crinkled the corners of his eyes and softened his face, making him even more heart-stoppingly handsome, if that was possible. "Yeah," he said. "You were."

Okay, maybe she had been. But she couldn't have helped it. "It'd been a while," she admitted grudgingly. And he'd *really* known what he was doing.

As Tammy had reminded her, Mallory's last boyfriend had been Allen, the Seattle accountant, who'd decided Mallory wasn't worth the commute. That had been last year. A very long, dry year...

Ty's eyes softened, and she realized that they weren't clear green, not even close. Lurking just beneath the surface were layers of other shades, which in turn softened *her*. He'd held her like no other, whispered sweet, hot nothings in her ear as she'd indeed panted and cried out, and begged him just like the soap opera actress. Damn, but she could still get aroused at just the memory of the strength of his arms as he'd held her through it, that intoxicating mix of absolute security and wild abandon.

"It'd been a long time for me too," he said, surprising her. How did a guy who looked as good as he did and exuded pheromones and testosterone like they were going out of style *not* have sex for a "long time"?

On the screen behind him, the woman was still going at it, and watching her without the sound made it seem even more X-rated. "I did *not* go on like that," she murmured, and though Ty wisely held his tongue, his expression said it all. "What, you think I *did*?" she asked in disbelief.

His gaze flicked to the screen, then back to her face. "If it helps, you looked way hotter and sounded much better while doing it."

Oh, God. She turned away from him and was at the

door before his low, husky voice sounded again. "Where are you going?" he asked.

"Walking away. You should recognize it."

"I'm actually here as a patient."

At the only words in the English language that could have made her turn around, she did just that. "You are? Are you sick?"

He pointed to his head. "Josh told me to come back in ten days to get the stitches out."

Josh? He was on a first-name basis with Dr. Scott? "Dr. Scott got called to Seattle." She let out a long breath. "But if he left the order, I can remove the stitches for you."

Her mother and Camilla were still watching, of course, now joined by additional staff who apparently had nothing better to do than attempt to eavesdrop on Mallory and Mysterious Cute Guy. Mallory would lay odds that *this* Cute Guy sighting would go wide and be public by the end of her shift.

Nothing she could do about that. "Let's get this over with."

"Is it going to hurt?"

She looked at Ty, at his big, tough body, at the way he limped ever so slightly on his left leg, and then into his eyes. Which were amused.

He was teasing her.

Well, fine. She could give as good as she got. "Something tells me you can handle it."

Chapter 8

Eve left the Garden of Eden for chocolate.

Ty followed Mallory through the double doors to the ER and to a bed, where she then pulled a curtain around them for privacy.

In the military, Ty had learned defense tactics and ways to conceal information. He'd excelled at both. As a result, concealing emotion came all too easily to him. Not to mention, there wasn't much room for emotion in the underbelly of the Third World countries he'd worked in. So he'd long ago perfected the blank expression, honed it as a valuable tool. It was second nature now, or had been.

Until Mallory.

Because he was having a hell of a hard time pulling it off with her. Like now, for instance, when he was relieved to see her and yet struggling to hide that very fact. Clearly not so relieved to see him, she said "I'll be right back" and vanished.

Fair enough. As she'd pointed out, he'd vanished on

her, and a part of him had figured he'd never see her again.

But another part had hoped he would.

He'd known that she worked here and imagined she was a great nurse. On the night of the storm, she'd been good in an emergency, extremely level-headed and composed.

Unlike at the auction, in his arms. Then she'd been hungry, and the very opposite of level-headed and composed. He'd loved that about her. Now she was back to the calm persona. She looked cute in her pale pink scrubs with the tiny red heart embroidered over the pocket on her left breast. He especially liked the air of authority she wore.

Hell.

He liked everything he knew about her so far, including how she'd tasted. Yeah, he'd really liked how she'd tasted. Which was the only explanation he had for being here, because he sure as hell could remove his own damn stitches.

From nearby, someone was moaning softly in both fear and pain. He stood, instinctively reacting to the sound as he hadn't in four years. Four years of ignoring the call to help or heal.

The moan came again, and Ty closed his eyes. Christ, how he suddenly wished he hadn't come. Unable to help himself, he stuck his head out the curtain of his cubicle. In the next bed over, a guy was hooked up to a monitor, fluids, and oxygen. He was in his early forties, smelled like a brewery, and either hadn't showered this month or he'd rolled in garbage. His hair was gray and standing straight up, missing in clumps. A transient, probably, looking small and weak and terrified.

"You okay?" Ty asked, staying where he was. "You need the nurse?"

The man shook his head but kept moaning, eyes wide, his free hand flailing. His eyes were dilated, and there was a look to him that said he was high on something.

Cursing himself, Ty moved to the side of his bed. He glanced at the IV. They were hydrating him, which was good. Catching the man's hand in his, Ty squeezed lightly. "What's going on?"

"Stomach. It hurts."

The guy's clothes were filthy and torn enough to reveal a Trident Tattoo on his arm, and Ty let out a slow breath. "Military," he said, feeling raw. Too raw.

"Army," the man said, slurring, clearly still heavily intoxicated, at the least.

Ty nodded and might have turned away but the guy was clinging to his hand like it was a lifeline, so Ty continued to hold onto him right back as he slowly sank onto the stool. "I was Navy," he heard himself say. He left out the Special Ops part; he always did. It had nothing to do with not being proud of his service and everything to do with not wanting to answer any questions. And there were *always* questions. "I'm out now."

Technically.

"You never get out," the man said.

Well, that was true enough.

"They should pay us for the long nights of bad dreams." The guy took a moment to gather his thoughts. This seemed to be a big effort. Ty wanted to tell him not to work too hard but before he could, the man spoke again. "They should give us extra combat pay for all the ways our lives are fucked up."

Ty could get behind that. They sat there in silence a moment, the man looking like he was half asleep now and Ty feeling a little bit sick. Sick in the gut. Sick to the depths of his soul. Yeah, definitely the hospital had been a stupid idea. This was absolutely the *last* time he let his dick think for him.

"I still think about them," the man said softly into the silence.

Ah, hell. Ty didn't have to ask who. He knew. All the dead. Ty swallowed hard and nodded.

The man stared at him, glassy-eyed but coherent. "How many for you?"

Ty closed his eyes. "Four." But there'd been others, too. *Way* too many others.

The man let out a shuddery sigh of sympathy. "Here." He lifted a shaky hand and slid it into his shirt, coming out with a flask. "This helps."

Mallory chose that very moment to pull back the curtain. "*There* you are," she said to Ty, then smiled kindly at the man in the bed. "Better yet, Ryan?"

Ryan, caught red-handed with the flask, didn't meet her gaze as he gave a jerky nod.

"Why don't I hold that for you, okay?" Gently, she pried the flask from Ryan's fingers, confiscating it without another word.

Ty didn't know what he'd expected from her. Maybe annoyance, or some sign that she resented the duty of caring for a guy who was in here for reasons that had clearly been self-inflicted. But she ran a hand down Ryan's arm in a comforting gesture, not shying away from touching him.

More than duty, Ty thought. Much more. This was the

real deal, *she* was the real deal, and she cared, deeply.

"I've called your daughter," she told Ryan. "She'll be here in ten minutes. We're just going to let the bag do its thing, refilling you up with minerals, potassium, sodium, and other good stuff. You'll feel better soon." She patted his forearm as she checked his leads, making physical contact before she looked at Ty, gesturing with her head for him to follow her.

"Is he going to be okay?" Ty asked quietly on the other side of the curtain.

"Soon as he sobers up."

"He's on something besides alcohol."

"Yes."

"Does he have a place to stay?"

She gave him a long once-over. "Look at you with all the questions."

"Does he?"

She sighed. "I'm sorry, but you know I can't discuss his case with you. I can tell you that he's being taken care of. Does that help?"

Yeah. No. Ty had no idea what the fucking lump the size of a regulation football was doing stuck in his throat or why his heart was pounding. Or why he couldn't let this go. "He's a vet," he said. "He's having nightmares. He—"

"I know," she said softly, and reached out to touch him, soothing him as she had Ryan. "And like I said, he's being taken care of." She paused, studying him for a disturbingly long beat. "Not everyone would have done that, you know. Gone in there and held a vagrant's hand and comforted him."

"I'm not everyone."

"No kidding." The phone at her hip vibrated. She looked at the screen and let out a breath. "Wait for me," she said, pointing to his cubicle. "I'll be right there." And then she moved off in the direction of the front desk.

In front of Ty was yet another bed. This curtain was shut but it was suddenly whipped open by a nurse who was talking to the patient sitting on the bed. "Change into the robe," she was saying. "And I'll go page your doctor."

The patient had clearly walked in under his own steam, but he wasn't looking good. He was a big guy, mid-thirties, dressed in coveralls that had the Public Utilities Department logo on a pec. He was filthy from head to toe, clearly just off the job. As Ty watched, he went from looking bad to worse, and then he gasped, clutching at his chest.

Oh, Christ, Ty thought. Why the hell was he here? He should have left. Instead, he was hurtled back in time, back to the mountain, squinting against the brilliant fireball that had been a plane. He'd sat on the cliff holding Trevor in his arms, Trevor clutching at his crushed chest.

A million miles and four years later, the guy on the hospital bed groaned, dropping the gown he'd been holding. He slithered to the floor, his eyes rolling up in the back of his head.

Ty took a step back and came up against a rolling cart of supplies even as his instincts screamed at him to rush over there and help.

But the cart moved out from behind him, and he staggered on legs that felt like overcooked noodles.

Then suddenly people came out of the woodwork, including Mallory.

"He's coding," someone yelled.

And the dance to save the man's life began. Someone pulled Ty out of the way and back to his cubicle, where he waited for what might have been five minutes, or an hour.

Or a lifetime.

Mallory finally came in. When she found him still standing, she gave him a sharp look. "Sorry about that. You okay?"

"The guy. Is he . . . ?"

"He's going to make it." She gestured to the bed. "Sit. You look like you could use it."

Like hell he did.

"Sit," she said again, soft steel.

Fine. He sat. On the stool, not the bed. The bed was for patients, and he wasn't a patient. He was a fucking idiot, but he wasn't a patient.

"Not a big hospital fan, huh?" she asked wryly.

"No."

She washed her hands thoroughly. "Personal experience?"

He didn't answer, wasn't ready to answer. Apparently okay with that, she pulled on a pair of latex gloves, then opened a couple of drawers. "Are you squeamish?"

He didn't answer that either. Mostly because only yesterday he'd have given her an emphatic *no*. Except what had just happened to him in the hallway said otherwise.

He'd changed.

Once upon a time, nothing had gotten to him, but that was no longer true. Case in point was Mallory herself. She got to him, big time.

She lifted a big, fat needle, and he blinked.

She smiled and put the needle down, and he realized

she'd been fucking with him to lighten the mood. He heard the surprised laugh rumble out of him, rusty sounding. Muscles long gone unused stretched as he smiled and shook his head. "Guess you owed me that."

"Guess I did." After she'd loaded up a tray with what she wanted, she came at him. She set the tray on the bed and perched a hip there as well, letting out an exhale that spelled exhaustion. "If you don't want to sit here, I sure as hell do."

He found himself letting out another smile. "Tired?"

"I passed tired about three hours ago." She soaked a gauze in rubbing alcohol.

"So you're an RN."

"Yes," she said. "I bought my license online yesterday." She dabbed at the wound over his eyebrow and then opened a suture kit, which he was intimately familiar with. As a medic in the field, he'd gone through a lot of them patching guys up.

"Don't worry," she said, picking up a set of tweezers. "I've seen a guy do this once."

He wrapped his fingers around her wrist, stopping her movement.

"I'm kidding," she said.

"Oh I know. I just don't want you to be cracking yourself up when you put those things near my eye."

"Actually, I'm not all that amused right now," she said.

"What are you, then?"

She hesitated. "Embarrassed," she finally admitted.

This stopped him cold. That was the *last* thing he wanted her to be. "Don't be embarrassed," he said. "Pick something else, *anything* else."

"Like?"

"Mad. Mad would be better."

"You want me to be mad at you?" she asked, looking confused. "Why? I'm the one who said the 'here' and 'now,' remember?"

Yeah, he remembered. He'd loved it.

"And *I'm* the one who wanted a one-time thing," she said. "No strings attached."

"So why be embarrassed then?"

She sighed.

"Tell me."

"Because I'd never done that before." She lowered her voice to a soft whisper. "Sex without an emotional attachment," she clarified. "And now..." Her eyes slowly met his. "I'm thinking I should have requested a two-time thing."

This left him speechless.

She winced, shook her head, then laughed a little at herself. "Never mind." She leaned in close to look at the stitching. "Nice work. Dr. Scott's the best," she said. "But you'll probably still have a decent scar. Shouldn't be too much of a problem for you, women like that sort of thing. Apparently they'll fall all over themselves to sleep with you."

Still holding her wrist, he ran his thumb over her pulse. "You didn't fall all over yourself," he said quietly.

"Didn't I?"

"If you did, there were two of us doing the falling."

Again, her eyes met his, and he watched her struggle to accept that. "Well," she finally said, pulling her hand free, "as long as there were two of us." Some of the good humor was now restored in her voice. Which meant she was compassionate, funny, *and* resilient. His favorite qualities in a woman.

But he wasn't looking for a woman. He wasn't looking for anything except to get back to his world where he functioned best.

She leaned in close and used the tweezers to pull up a stitch, which she then snipped with scissors. "A little sting now," she warned, and pulled out the suture. "So what was it that you said you do?"

Oh, she was good, he thought. Very good. "I didn't say."

She pulled out another stitch and then gazed steadily at him.

She had the most amazing eyes. Mostly chocolate brown, but there were specks of gold in there as well. And a sharp wit that stirred him even more than her hot, curvy little bod.

A woman poked her head around the curtain, the same one who'd been at the front desk. Young. Eager. "Need help?" she asked Mallory, her eyes on Ty.

"Nope," Mallory said. "I've got this."

Her face fell, but she left without further comment.

Two seconds later another nurse appeared, and this one Ty recognized as Mallory's mother from the night of the auction.

"New arrival," she said to Mallory, eyeing Ty.

"It's your turn," Mallory told her.

Her mom frowned. "*Mal.*"

"*Mother.*"

The curtain yanked shut, and they were alone. "She hates when I call her 'mother.'"

"You work with your mom."

Mallory took a page from his book and went silent. It made him smile. *She* made him smile.

"She looked pissed," he said, fishing. Which was new for him. He never fished. He hated fishing.

"Oh, she is," Mallory said. She pulled another stitch, and he barely felt it. She had good hands, as he had reason to know.

"Because of me?" he asked.

"Now why would you think that?" she asked. "Because I left my own fundraiser to have sex in a storage room with a man whose name I barely knew?"

"Really great sex," he corrected. When she slid him a long look, he added, "Imagine what we could do with a bed."

She let out a short laugh, and he stared at her face, truly fascinated by her in a way that surprised him. She was supposed to be just a woman, a cute nurse in a small town that soon he'd forget the name of.

Except...he wasn't buying it.

"Hey, Mal." Yet another woman peeked into the cubicle, this one mid-thirties and wearing a housekeeping outfit. "Need anything?"

"*No!*"

"Jeez," she said, insulted. "Fine, you don't have to take my head off."

When she vanished, Mallory sighed. "My sister." She dumped the instruments she'd used into the sink, and still facing away from him, spoke. "What about your leg?"

"What about it?"

"Does it need to be looked at, too?" she asked.

"No."

She turned to look at him with an expectant air, saying nothing. It made him smile. "You can't use that silence thing against me. I invented it."

"What silence thing?" she asked innocently.

"You know what silence thing, where you go all quiet and I'm supposed to feel compelled to fill it in with all my secrets."

She smiled. "So you admit to having secrets."

"Many," he said flatly.

Her smile faded. "You're engaged. Or worse, you're married. You have ten kids. Oh my God, tell me you don't have kids."

"No. And I'm not engaged or married. I'm not...anything."

She just looked at him for a long moment. "Some secrets are toxic if you try to keep them inside. You know that, right? Some secrets are meant to be told, before they eat you up."

Maybe, but not his. In no time, he'd be long gone, back to a very fast-paced, dangerous life that would eventually, probably kill him. But not her. She'd find someone to share her life with, grow old with. "You watch too much *Oprah*."

She didn't take umbrage at this. She pulled off her gloves and tossed them into the trash.

"Does your whole family work here?" he asked, running a finger over the healing cut, now sans stitches. She'd done a good job.

"Just my mom, my sister, and me," she said. "And I also work at the Health Services Clinic."

"I didn't know there was one here."

"Well, there's not. Not yet. But if we get approval at the town meeting tomorrow night, it's a go for a tentative opening this weekend."

"Is there a need in a town this small?"

"This hospital services the entire county," she said. "Not just Lucky Harbor. And there's a huge need. We have a high teenage pregnancy rate, and drug abuse is on the rise as well. So is abuse and homelessness. We need counseling services and advocacy and educational programs. And there's going to be a weekly health clinic on Saturday for those who can't afford medical care."

God, she was so fierce she made his heart ache. They could use her at his work, he thought, but was doubly glad that she pretty much embodied Lucky Harbor. Hopefully she'd never live through some of the horrors out there, or lose her genuine compassion to jaded cynicism. "So what makes a woman like you take on such a thing?" he asked.

"What do you mean?"

"Usually this sort of thing is driven by a cause. What's yours?"

She turned away, busying herself with washing her hands again.

"Ah," he said. "So I'm not the only one with secrets."

She turned back to him at that, eyes narrowed. "Tell you what. I'll answer one question for every question you answer for me."

He knew better than to go there. He might have treated her like a one-night stand but he knew damn well she was different. By all appearances, she was pretty and sweet and innocent, but beneath that guileless smile, she held all the power, and he knew it. She'd have him confessing his sins with one warm touch.

She isn't for you...

"Yeah," she said dryly, hands on hips. "I figured that'd be too much for you."

It was. Far too much. He was leaving...and yet he

opened his mouth anyway. "What time do you get off?"

This shocked her, he could tell. Fair enough. He'd shocked himself too.

"Seven," she said.

"I'll pick you up."

"No," she said. "You know the pier?"

"Sure."

"I'll meet you there. In front of the Ferris wheel."

She didn't trust him. Smart woman. "Okay," he said. "In front of the Ferris wheel."

"How do I know you're going to remember to show up for *this* date?"

A date. Christ, it was utter insanity. But he looked into her beautiful eyes and nearly drowned. "Because this time I'm in charge of all my faculties," he said.

Except, clearly, he wasn't.

Chapter 9

Stress wouldn't be so hard to take if it were chocolate covered.

As Mallory got into her car after her shift, her phone rang from an unfamiliar number.

"He came to the hospital to see you?" Amy asked.

Mallory didn't bother to ask how Amy knew Ty had been at the hospital earlier. It was probably put out as an all points bulletin. "Whose cell phone is this?"

"I just found it at the diner. Don't tell Jan; she likes to keep all the leftover phones for herself."

"Amy! You can't just use someone's phone."

"And that," Amy said dryly, "is why you need Bad Girl lessons. Okay, impromptu meeting of the Choco-holics commencing right here, right now, because you're in crisis."

"I am not."

"Lesson number one," Amy went on without listening. *"Always* use a situation to your benefit."

"*That's* lesson number one?" Mallory said. "What's lesson number two?"

"Lesson number two is *not* to get your exploits recounted on Facebook. Rookie mistake, Mal."

Mallory sighed. "Do you have any wisdom that might actually be helpful?"

"Yeah." There was some muffled talking, and she came back on. "Grace is here. She needed a big, warm brownie after pounding the sidewalk today looking for a job. She says lesson number three is to understand that guys are about the visuals, and she's right. Always wear Bad Girl shoes and Bad Girl panties. They create the mood."

The panties were self-explanatory. "Bad Girl shoes? *You* wear steel-toed boots."

More muffled talking as Grace and Amy conferred on this subject.

"Okay," Amy came back to say. "Grace thinks it's a frame of mind. I'm a shit-kicker, so the boots work. You're...softer. You need high heels. Strappy. Sexy."

The thought of high heels after being on her feet all day made Mallory want to cry. Then she remembered how it had felt when Ty had put his hands on her ankles and removed her heels for her. She'd liked that, a lot. "My only heels hurt my feet."

"Get another pair. Lesson number four," Amy said. "Get a hold of his phone and scan through the contacts."

"I'm not going to run through his contacts!" Mallory paused and considered. "And what would I be looking for, anyway?"

"Anyone listed as *My Drug Dealer*. That's when you'd run not walk."

Mallory blinked. "The guy who left his phone at the diner has a contact that says *My Drug Dealer*?"

"And also *Bitch Ex-Wife*. Oh, and *Mommy*." Amy sighed. "*Not* a keeper."

Grace got on the phone then, her mouth sounding quite full. "You're going to have to make the next meeting in person, Mallory. This brownie is orgasmic."

She could use an orgasmic brownie. "One of you take a turn now."

"Well, Grace here has been turned down for all the jobs she applied for from the Canadian border to San Diego," Amy said. "So I'm considering pouring her a shot of something to go with the brownie. In the meantime, I called Tara at the B&B, and they had no problem giving her the local discount to keep staying there for cheap, since she's a local now. As for me," Amy said, "I'm status quo. Waiting for warmer weather to make my move."

"Your move on what?" Mallory asked.

"Life. In the meantime, we'll concentrate on you," she said. "You're the most screwed up so it makes the most sense. Get some bad girl shoes."

Mallory hung up and drove to the pier. When she got out, she took a moment to inhale the salty ocean air as the sound of the waves hitting the shore soothed her antsy nerves. At the pier's entrance, flyers were posted, one for an upcoming high school play, another for a musical festival the following week. But it was the flyer for the town's monthly Interested Citizens Meeting that caught her interest.

This was where Bill Lawson would pitch her Health Services Clinic and get the town's collective reaction.

In the meantime, she had another meeting, one that,

according to her heart rate, was imminent. She'd changed into a summer dress she'd borrowed from Tammy's work locker. Tammy had superior clothes. This was what happened when one was married to a mall cop. By way of her husband, Tammy got a hell of a discount.

Walking to the Ferris wheel, Mallory took quick stock of her appearance. Not too bad, she thought, although her walking sandals were definitely not up to Bad Girl code.

Next time.

The night was warm and moist, and the waves rocked gently against the pylons far below the pier. The power beneath her feet made the pier shudder faintly with the push and pull of the tide, which matched the push and pull of anticipation drumming through her.

You are not going to sleep with him again, she told herself firmly. *That was just a one-time thing. You're only here now because you're curious about him.*

And also because he'd looked hot today at the hospital. Damn, she had a problem. A big, attracted-to-him-like-a-moth-to-a-flame-type problem. How that was possible, she had no idea. Their good-bye on the night of the auction had been... abrupt. Although *nothing* about what had occurred before that had felt abrupt. Nope, everything had been... *amazing*.

She stopped at the entrance to the line for the Ferris wheel. When her inner drumming turned into a prickle at the base of her neck, she turned in a slow circle.

And found Ty watching her.

He was leaning back against the pier railing, legs casually crossed at the ankles, looking for all the world like a guy who made it a habit to be carefree enough to walk a beach pier.

They both knew that wasn't true.

And good God, just looking at him did something to her. His hair was tousled, like he'd been shoving his fingers through it. Stubble darkened his jaw, and his firm, sensuous mouth was unsmiling. The scar above his brow was new and shiny, and the mirrored sunglasses only added to the whole ruffian look he had going on.

It suited him, in a big way.

He was dressed in cargoes and a dark T-shirt snug across his broad chest and loose over his abs. He looked big, bad, built, and dangerous as hell.

And he was hers for the evening.

Hers.

Not one of her smartest moves. But stretching her wings wasn't about keeping her head. It was about...being. Living.

Feeling.

And the man definitely made her feel, a lot. Already in their short acquaintance, he'd made her feel curious, annoyed, frustrated, and the topper...

Aroused.

She was feeling that right now in fact, in spades. She wanted to shove up his shirt and lick him from Adam's Apple to belly button.

And beyond.

Slowly he pushed the sunglasses to the top of his head and his stark green eyes locked unwaveringly on hers. She knew he couldn't really read her mind, but she jumped and flushed a little guiltily anyway for where her thoughts had gone.

He pushed away from the railing and came toward her, all those muscles moving fluidly and utterly without thought. She had no idea what she'd expected, but it wasn't for him to take her hand in his and pull her around to the side of the Ferris wheel, out of view, between a storage shed and the pier railing.

"W-what are you doing?"

He didn't answer. He merely put his big hands on her, lifted her up to her tiptoes, and covered her mouth with his.

Her purse fell in a thud at her feet. Her fingers slid into his hair. And when his tongue slid over hers, all her bones melted away.

Then before she knew it, the kiss was over and she was weaving unsteadily on her feet, blinking him into focus. "What was *that*?"

He scooped up her purse and handed it to her. "I lost my head. You're distracting."

"And you're not?"

His eyes heated. "We could fix that."

"Oh no," she said. "You said you weren't a long-term bet. You said you weren't even a short one."

"But I'm on your list. Your list of Mr. Wrongs."

"Yeah, about that. I've rearranged the order of the list." This was a bold-faced lie. She'd not rearranged the list. He *was* the list.

He raised a brow. "Did what's-his-name from the hardware store get ahead of me? The one who sleeps with anyone with boobs?"

"Maybe."

"I was at the hardware store today," he said. "Anderson was there, flirting with some cute young thing." Leaning in, his mouth found its way to her ear. "You can take Anderson off your list."

Oh no he didn't. He didn't just tell her what to do. "I—"

He pressed her into the railing and kissed her again. Apparently he didn't want to hear it. That was okay, because she forgot her own name, much less who was on her list. She had her tongue in his mouth, her hands in his silky hair, and her breasts mashed up to his hard, warm chest. She'd have climbed inside him if she could.

You came here to ask him questions.

In an attempt to go back to that, she squeezed her thighs, thinking *keep them together*, but his knee nudged hers, and then he slid a muscled thigh between hers. Good. Lord. He felt so... *good.* Drawing on some reserve of strength she didn't know she had, she pushed on his chest. For a beat he didn't budge, then he stepped slowly back, his eyes heavy-lidded and sexy.

"Okay," she said shakily. "Let's try something that's *not* going to lead to round two of sex in a public place." His expression was giving nothing away. Not exactly open, but she was a woman of her word, and she wanted to know he was a man of his. "What do you do for a living? Are you... military?" she asked, letting loose of the one thing she couldn't seem to get out of her head. It was the way he carried himself: calm, steady, looking ready for anything, and that bone-deep stoicism. Not to mention how he'd looked while at Ryan's bedside—like he knew to the depths of his soul what Ryan was feeling.

A low, wry laugh rumbled out of him. "So we're going to ease into this then."

"Yeah." She was glad to see the smile. "You don't know this about me, but I tend to jump in with both feet."

"I noticed." He looked at her, his eyes reminding her that he knew other things about her as well, things that made her blush. "At the moment I'm rebuilding a few cars."

This didn't exactly answer her question, and in fact, only brought on *more* questions. "So you're a mechanic?" she asked.

"While I'm here in lucky Harbor."

"But—"

"My turn. The other night. Why me?"

She squirmed a little at this, although it was a fair enough question. He already knew that what they'd done that night at the auction had been a first for her, but what he didn't know, *couldn't* know, was that she'd only been able to do it at all because she'd felt something for him. Which was crazy; they'd been perfect strangers. "Like I said, it'd been a long time."

"So I was handy?"

"Well, Anderson already had a date, so..."

He growled, and she laughed. "I don't know exactly," she admitted. "Except..." *Just say it.* "I felt a connection to you."

He was looking very serious now, and he slowly shook his head. "You don't want to feel connected to me, Mallory."

"No, I don't want to. But I do. And there's more."

"The whole bored and restless thing?" he asked.

So he'd *also* overheard her entire conversation with her mother. The man had some serious listening skills.

"You used me to chase away your restlessness," he said quietly.

"Yes." She winced. "I'm sorry about that."

"Mallory, you can use me any time."

"But you said one-time only," she reminded him.

"Actually, *you* said that. And plans change. Apparently

I left you needing more, which is the same thing as un-satisfied in my book." His gaze went hot and dark. "We'll have to fix that."

She felt her body respond as if he'd already touched her. He hadn't left her unsatisfied at all. In fact, she'd never been more satisfied in her life. "Ice cream," she whispered, her throat suddenly very dry. "I think I need ice cream."

He smiled knowingly but didn't challenge her. They walked to the ice cream stand. The server was small for a guy in his early twenties and painfully thin, but the warm smile he flashed at Mallory distracted from his ill appear-ance. "Hey, Mal," he said. "Looking good today."

Lance gave her this same line every time that he landed in the ER. He could be flat on his back, at death's door—which with his Cystic Fibrosis happened more than any-one liked—and he'd *still* flash Mallory those baby blues and flirt.

He was one of her very favorite patients. "Where's your pretty girlfriend?" she teased, knowing he'd been dating another nurse, Nancy, for months now.

An attractive brunette poked her head out from behind Lance and smiled. "She's right here. Hey, Mallory" Nancy's eyes locked onto Ty and turned speculative. "Seems like Lance isn't the only one with a pretty date."

Mallory laughed at the look on Ty's face. He actually didn't react outwardly, but it was all in his eyes as he slid her a glance. She decided to take mercy on him and wrap things up. "I'll need a double scooped vanilla."

"So the usual," Lance said. "You ever going to branch out? Add a twist of cookie dough, or go for a walk on the wild side and add sprinkles?"

Mallory very carefully didn't look at Ty. "Not this time." She'd already taken her walk on the wild side, and wild walk on the dark side was standing right next to her.

Lance served Mallory, then looked at Ty, who shook his head. No ice cream for him.

Which was probably how he kept his body in such incredible shape, Mallory thought as she reached into her pocket for cash. Ty beat her to it, paying for her ice cream.

"Watching your girlie figure?" Mallory asked him, licking at the ice cream as they walked.

His eyes never left her tongue. "Girlie figure?"

There was nothing girlie about him, not one thing. "Maybe you're dieting," she said. Another lick. "Fighting the bulge."

Ty Garrison didn't have an ounce of fat on him, and they both knew it. But he did have a very dark, hot look as he watched her continue to lick at her cone. Like maybe he was a hungry predator and she was his prey. The thought caused another of those secret tingles.

"You think I'm fighting the bulge?" he asked softly.

She reached out and patted his abs. Her hand practically bounced off the tight muscles there. "I wouldn't worry about it. It happens to all of us," she said lightly, taking another slow lick of her ice cream. "Does your break from work have anything to do with your leg?"

"Yes." His eyes never left her mouth. She was playing with fire, and she knew it.

"You know this whole man of mystery thing isn't as cute as you might think," she said. "Right?"

"I'm not cute."

"No kidding!"

A very small smile curved his mouth as he studied her for a moment, as if coming to a decision. "You asked if I'm military. I was."

Her gaze searched his. "And now?"

"Like I said, I'm working on cars."

"And when you're not working on cars?" she asked with mock patience. "What do you do then?"

Again he just looked at her for a long beat. "It's in the same vein as mechanics. I locate a problem and...rectify it."

"But...not on cars."

"No," he agreed. "Not on cars."

Huh. He was certainly *not* saying more than he was saying. Which wasn't working for her. "And the leg?" she asked.

"I was in a crash."

He hadn't hesitated to say it but she sensed a big inner hesitation to discuss it further. "I'm sorry," she said, not wanting to push. She knew exactly what it felt like to *not* want to discuss something painful, but she was definitely wishing he'd say more. And then he did.

"I'm in Lucky Harbor until I'm cleared," he said. "Matt and I go way back. He set me up in a house to recoup."

"Are you...recouping okay?" she asked softly.

"Working on it."

She nodded and fought the ridiculous urge to hug him. He wouldn't want her sympathy, she knew that much. "The leg is giving you pain. Are you taking anything for it?"

"No," he said, and with a hand on the small of her back, led her into the arcade. Conversation over, apparently. He handed some money over to the guy behind the first booth.

Shooting Duck Gallery.

"What are you doing?" she asked.

"I'm going to shoot some ducks. And so are you."

"I'm not good at shooting ducks," she said, watching him pick up the gun like he knew what he was doing. He sighted and shot.

And hit every duck, destroying the entire row.

"Show off," she said, and picked up her gun. She didn't know what she was doing. And she didn't hit a single duck. She set the gun down and sighed.

"That's pathetic." Ty handed over some more cash and stood behind her. "Pick up the gun again." He corrected her stance by nudging his foot between hers, kicking her legs farther apart. Then he steadied her arms with his.

This meant he was practically wrapped around her, surrounding her. If she turned her head, she could press her mouth to his bicep. His very rock-solid bicep. It was shocking how much she wanted to do just that. She'd bet he'd taste better than her ice cream.

He went still, then let out a low breath, his jaw brushing hers. "You're thinking so loud I'm already hard."

She choked out a laugh, and he pressed himself against her bottom, proving he wasn't kidding. "How do you know what I'm thinking?" she asked, embarrassingly breathless. "Maybe I'm thinking that I want another ice cream."

"That's not what you're thinking. Shoot the ducks, Mallory."

With him guiding her, she actually hit one, and her competitive nature kicked in. "Again," she demanded.

With a rare grin, Ty slapped some more money onto the counter. "Show me what you've got," he said to her, and to her disappointment, this time he remained back a few steps, leaving her to do it alone.

She hit one more out of the entire row, which was *hugely* annoying to her. "How do you make it look so easy?"

"Practice," he said in a voice that assured her he'd had lots. "Your concentration needs some work."

Actually, there was nothing wrong with her concentration. She was concentrating just fine. She was concentrating on how she felt in his arms, with his hard body at her back.

She liked it. Far too much. "Maybe I don't care about being able to shoot a duck."

"No problem." He tossed down another few bucks and obliterated another row of ducks himself.

"Dude," the guy behind the counter said, sounding impressed as he presented Ty with a huge teddy bear as a prize.

Ty handed it to Mallory. "My hero," she murmured with a laugh, and he grimaced, making her laugh again as she hugged the bear close, the silly gesture giving her a warm fuzzy. Which was ironic because nothing about the big, tough Ty Garrison should have given her a warm fuzzy.

She knew he didn't want to be her hero.

He dragged her to the squirt gun booth next, where he proceeded to soundly beat her three times in a row. Apparently he wasn't worried about her ego. He won a stuffed dog at that booth, and then laughed out loud at her as she attempted to carry both huge stuffed animals and navigate the aisles without bumping into anyone.

Ridiculously, the whole thing gave her another warm fuzzy, immediately followed by an inner head smack. Because no way was she going to be the woman who fell for a guy just because he gave her a silly stuffed animal that she didn't need. *You're not supposed to fall for him at all*, she reminded herself. "This is very teenager-y of us," she said.

"If we were teenagers," he said, "we'd be behind the arcade, and you'd be showing me your gratitude for the stuffed animals by letting me cop a feel."

"In your dreams," she quipped, but her nipples went hard.

They competed in a driving game next, the two of them side by side in the booth, fighting for first place. Ty was handling his steering wheel with easy concentration, paying her no mind whatsoever. Mallory couldn't find her easy concentration, she was too busy watching him out of the corner of her eye. When she fell back a few cars as a result, Ty grinned.

Ah, so he *was* paying attention to her. Just to make sure, she nudged up against him.

His grin widened, but he didn't take his eyes off the screen. "That's not going to work, Mallory. You're going down."

Not going to work, her ass. She nudged his body with hers again, lingering this time, letting her breast brush his arm.

"Playing dirty," he warned, voice low, both husky and amused.

But she absolutely had his attention. She did the breast-against-his-arm thing again, her eyes on the screen, so she missed when he turned his head. But she didn't miss when he sank his teeth lightly into her earlobe and tugged. When she hissed in a breath, he soothed the ache with his tongue, and her knees wobbled. Her foot slipped off the gas.

And her car crashed into the wall.

Ty's car sped across the finish line.

"That's cheating!" she complained. "You can't—"

He grabbed her, lifting her up so that her feet dangled, and then kissed her until she couldn't remember what she'd meant to say. When he set her back down, she would have fallen over if he hadn't kept his hands on her. "You started it," he said. He gave her one more smacking kiss and then bought them both hot dogs for dinner. They sat on the pier, she and Ty and the two huge stuffed animals, and ate.

"So what are you doing to recover from the crash?" she asked.

"Swimming. Beating the shit out of Matt." He took the last bite of his hot dog. "Who's Karen?"

If her life had been a DVD, in that moment it would have skipped and come to a sudden halt, complete with the sound effect.

"I heard your mother say her name," he said, watching her face carefully. "And you got an odd expression, just like now."

"Karen's my sister." She paused, because it never got easier to say. "She died when I was younger."

Concern flashed in his eyes, stirring feelings she didn't want to revisit. Thankfully he didn't offer empty platitudes, for which she was grateful. But he did take her hand in his. "How?"

"Overdose."

His hand was big and warm and callused. He had several healing cuts over his knuckles, like he'd had a fight with a car part or tool. "How old were you?" he asked.

"Sixteen."

He squeezed her hand, and she blew out a breath. "You ever lose anyone?" she asked.

He didn't answer right away. She turned her head and looked at him, and found him studying the little flickers of reflection on the water as the sun lowered in the sky. "I lost my four closest friends all at the same time," he finally said and met her gaze. "Four years now, and it still sucks."

Throat tight, she nodded. "In the Army?"

"Navy. We were a crazy bunch, but it shouldn't have happened."

"All three of my siblings are a crazy bunch," she said. "Not military, of course, just . . . crazy."

He smiled. "Not you though."

"I have my moments." She blew out a breath. "Well, moment."

"Us."

She nodded.

"So I really am your walk on the wild side." He paused, then shook his head. "I'm still not clear on why you chose me."

"I'm not clear on a lot of things about myself." She met his gaze. "But in hindsight, I think it's because you're safe."

He stared at her, then laughed and scrubbed a hand over his face. "Mallory, I'm about as unsafe as you can possibly get."

Yeah. But for some reason, she'd somehow trusted him

that night. She still did. "If you're swimming," she said, "you must be healing up pretty good. When do you get cleared to go back to work?"

He looked into her eyes, his own unapologetic. "Soon."

"And it won't be in Lucky Harbor," she said quietly. She knew it wouldn't, but she needed to hear it, to remind herself that this wasn't anything but an . . . interlude.

"No," he agreed. "It won't be in Lucky Harbor."

The disappointment was undeniable, and shockingly painful. She'd really thought she could do this with him, have it be just about the sex, but it was turning out not to be the case at all. With a sigh, she stood. He did as well, gathering their garbage and taking it to a trash bin before coming back to stand next to where she was looking out at the water.

"I can't do this," she whispered.

He nodded. "I know."

"I want to but I—"

"It's okay." He brushed a kiss over her jaw and then was gone, proving for the second time now that he was, after all, her perfect Mr. All Wrong.

Chapter 10

*Chocolate is cheaper than therapy, and you
don't need an appointment.*

Two days later, Mallory entered the Vets' Hall for the town meeting and felt the déjà vu hit her. Pointedly ignoring the stairs to the second floor storage room, she strode forward to the big central meeting room. It was full, as all the town meetings tended to be.

Heaven forbid anyone in Lucky Harbor miss anything.

With sweaty palms and an accelerated heart rate, she found a seat in the back. Two seconds later, her sister plopped down into the chair next to her.

"Whew," Tammy said. "My dogs are tired." She leaned back and wriggled her toes. "You medical professionals are slobs, you know that? Took me an hour to clean up the staff kitchen, and I was ten minutes late getting off shift. And I was scheduled to have a quickie with Zach on his twenty-minute break too. We had to really amp it up to get done in time."

"That's great. I really needed to know that, thank you." Mallory glanced over at the glowing Tammy. There was no denying that she seemed... well, not settled exactly, and certainly not tamed, but *content.*

"Why are you looking at me like that?" Tammy asked. "Do I look like I just had a screaming orgasm? Cuz I totally did."

Mallory grimaced. "Again, thanks. And I'm looking at you because you look happy. Really happy."

"I should hope so. Because Zach just—"

Mallory slapped her hands over her ears, and Tammy grinned. "Wow, Mal, you almost over-reacted there for a second. One would almost think you hadn't had sex in forever, which isn't true at all."

"How in the world did you know that?"

Tammy grinned. "Well, I didn't know for sure until now. Mysterious Cute Guy, right? When? The night of the auction when you vanished for an hour and then reappeared with that cat-in-cream smile? *I knew it.*"

Mallory choked. "I—"

"Don't try to deny it. Oh, and give me your phone for a sec."

Still embarrassed, Mallory handed over her phone, then watched as Tammy programmed something in. "What are you doing?"

"Making sure you can't forget your new boyfriend's name," Tammy said. "Here ya go."

Mallory stared down at the newest entry in her contact list. "Mysterious Cute Guy, aka Ty Garrison." She stared at Tammy. "Where did you get his number?"

"He left a message for Dr. Scott at the nurse's desk, including his cell phone number. I accidentally-on-purpose memorized it."

"You can't do that—"

"Oh relax, Miss Goodie Two-Shoes. No one saw me."

"Tammy—"

"Shh, it's starting." Tammy turned to face forward with a mock excited expression as the meeting was called to order.

Mallory bit her fingernails through the discussion of a new measure to put sports and arts back in the schools, getting parking meters along the sidewalks downtown, and whether or not the mayor, Jax Cullen, was going to run for another term.

Finally, the Health Services Clinic came up. Bill Lawson stood up and reiterated the bare bones plan and the facts, and then asked for opinions. Two attendees immediately stood up in the center aisle in front of the microphone set up there. The first was Mrs. Burland.

"I'm against this health clinic and always have been," she said, gripping her cane in one hand and pointing at the audience with a bony finger of her other. "It'll cost us— the hardworking taxpayers—money."

"Actually," Bill interrupted to say. "We've been given a large grant, plus the money raised at auction. There's also future fundraising events planned, including next week's car wash." He smiled. "Mallory Quinn talked everyone on the board into working the car wash, so I'm expecting each and every one of you to come out."

There was a collective gasp of glee. The hospital board was a virtual Who's Who of Lucky Harbor, including some very hot guys such as the mayor, Dr. Scott, and Matt Bowers, amongst others.

"Even you, Bill?" someone called out.

"Even me," Bill answered. "I can wash cars with the best of them."

Everyone *woo-hoo*'d at that, and Mallory relaxed marginally. Bill had just guaranteed them a huge showing at the car wash. People would come out in droves to see the town's best and finest out of their positions of honor and washing cars. They'd pay through the nose for it as they took pictures and laughed and pointed.

Lucky Harbor was sweet that way.

Still in the aisle, Mrs. Burland tapped on the microphone, her face pinched. "Hello! I'm still talking here! HSC will bring *undesirables* to our town. And we already have plenty of them." Her gaze sorted through the crowd with the speed and agility of an eagle after its prey, narrowing in on Mallory way in the back.

"Bitch," Tammy muttered.

Mallory just sank deeper into her seat.

"You all need to think about that," Mrs. Burland said and moved back to her seat.

Sandy, the town clerk and manager, stood up next. "I'm also against it," she said with what appeared to be genuine regret. "I just don't think we need to deplete our resources with a Health Services Clinic. Not when our library has no funds, our schools are short-staffed due to enforced layoffs, and our budget isn't close to being in balance. We could be allocating donations in better ways. I'm sorry, Mal, very sorry."

The audience murmured agreement, and two more people stood up to say they were also against the Health Services Clinic.

Then it was Lucille's turn. She stood up there in her

bright pink tracksuit and brighter white tennis shoes, a matching pink headband holding back her steel grey/blue hair. She took a moment to glare at Mrs. Burland in the front row. The rumor was that they'd gone to high school together about two centuries back, and Mrs. Burland had stolen Lucille's beau. Lucille had retaliated by eloping with Mrs. B's brother, who'd died in the Korean War— not on the front lines but in a brothel from a heart attack.

Lucille was so short that the microphone was about a foot above her head. This didn't stop her. "A Health Services Clinic would be nice," she said, head tipped up toward the microphone, her blue bun all aquiver. "Because then, if I thought I had the clap, I'd have a place to go."

The audience erupted in laughter.

"What?" she said. "You think I'm not getting any?" She turned and winked at Mr. Murdock in the third row.

Mr. Murdock grinned at her, his freshly washed dentures so unnaturally bright white they appeared to be glowing.

Lucille winked back, then returned to the business at hand. "Also, we couldn't have an HSC in better hands than those of our very own Mallory Quinn. She's a wonderful nurse and has her degree in business as well. She's one smart cookie."

Tammy turned to Mallory. "Did you actually graduate with both of those degrees?" she asked, clearly impressed.

Mallory slid her a look. "You were at my graduation."

Tammy searched her brain and then shook her head. "I've got nothing. In my defense, I spent those years pretty toasted."

Lucille was still talking. "I know some of you might

say that Mallory's too sweet to handle such a big responsibility as the HSC, and that her programs involving drug
rehab and teenage pregnancies will be overrun by dealers
and pimps. But we're not giving our girl enough credit.
If she can't handle the riffraff that her clinic brings into
town, well then her new boyfriend certainly can."

"Oh my God." Mallory covered her eyes. "I can't
look."

Tammy snorted. "At least she didn't call him your
lover. And that's not even your biggest problem. That
honor goes to the fact that your only supporter so far is a
crazy old bat."

"You know, *you* could get up there and support me,"
Mallory said.

"Not me," Tammy said. "I'm shy in front of a crowd."

Yeah, right.

Lucille took her seat. Four more people had their say,
not a single one of them in favor of the HSC. Tammy had
to practically sit on Mallory to keep her in her chair.

"Beating them up isn't going to help," Tammy said.

Mallory's phone was buzzing with incoming texts, like
the one from her mother that said:

He's your boyfriend?

Finally, a tall, broad-shouldered guy in faded jeans and
mirrored sunglasses stood at the microphone, which came
up to his chest.

Ty Garrison.

By this time, Mallory was so low in her chair that she
could hardly see him, but to make sure she couldn't, she
once again covered her face with her hands.

"Gee, Mallory, that works like a charm," Tammy whispered. "I can't see you there at all."

Mallory smacked her.

Ty spoke, his voice unrushed and clear. "The Health Clinic will improve the quality of life for people who'd otherwise go without help."

The audience murmured amongst themselves for a beat. Then came from one of the naysayers, "There's other places in other towns for people to get that kind of help."

"Yeah," someone else called out. "People here don't need the HSC."

"You're wrong," Ty said bluntly. "There are people in Lucky Harbor who *do* need the sort of services that HSC will provide. Veterans, for instance."

No one said a word now, though it was unclear whether they were scared of Ty's quiet intensity or simply acknowledging the truth of what he said.

"You can keep sticking your heads in the sand," he went on. "But there are people who need help managing their addictions, people who don't have a way to find a place to go that's safe from violence, teens who can't get STD education or birth control. These problems are real and growing, and a Health Services Clinic would be an invaluable resource for the entire county." He paused. Could have heard a pin drop. "And Lucille's right," he said into the silence. "You couldn't have a better person running such a place than your own Mallory Quinn. Each of you should be trying to help. I'll start by donating enough money for a program for veterans, where they can get assistance in rehabilitation or job opportunities, or simply to re-acclimate to society."

Mallory's mouth fell open.

The entire place went stock still. A real feat when it came to the people of Lucky Harbor. No one even blinked.

"He is so hot," Tammy whispered to Mallory. "You really ought to keep him."

"Can't," Mallory said, staring at Ty in shock through the fingers she still had across her eyes. "We've agreed it was a one-time thing."

"Well, that was stupid. You can put your hands down now. It's safe. No one's going to dare cross him. He's pretty badass."

He *was* pretty badass standing up there, steady as a rock, speaking his mind. *Offering his help...*

"Hey, didn't he also save your ass at the auction too by getting the bidding going?" Tammy asked.

Yeah, he had, and here he was at it again. Saving her ass.

As if sensing her scrutiny, he met her gaze for one long charged beat across the entire audience before walking back up the aisle to leave.

He'd stood up in front of the entire town and defended her. Her, a one-night stand. *What did that mean?* It meant he cared, she decided. The knowledge washed over her, and she sat up a little straighter, craning her neck to watch him go.

"My boyfriend's ever so dreamy," Tammy whispered mockingly.

Mallory smacked her again.

In spite of Ty's rather commanding appearance, the next three people who stood up opposed the clinic. Then Ella Quinn had her turn. Still in her scrubs, she grabbed the microphone. "This is poppycock," she said. "Anyone against this clinic is selfish, ungiving, and should be ashamed of themselves. As for my daughter Mallory, you all know damn well that she can be trusted to handle the HSC and any problems that might arise. After all, she's handled her crazy family all her life without batting so much as an eyelash." She searched the audience, found Joe in the fourth row, and gave him a long look. "And call your mamas. No one's calling their mamas often enough. That is all."

Joe slunk in his seat, his shoulders up around his ears. The little blonde sitting next to him gave him a hit upside the back of his head.

The meeting ended shortly after that, and Mallory was rushed with people wanting their questions answered. Would she really be supplying drug dealers? Doling out abortions? It was an hour before she was free, and even knowing she wouldn't find him, she looked around for Ty.

But he was long gone.

That afternoon, a spring storm broke wild and violent over Lucky Harbor. Ty worked on the Shelby, and when he was done, he drove through the worst of the rain, flying through the steep, vivid green mountain canyons, his mind cleared of anything but the road. For once he wasn't thinking of the past, or work.

He was thinking of a certain warm, sexy nurse.

He'd shelved his emotions years ago at SEALs training camp, long before he'd ever met one Mallory Quinn. But no amount of training could have prepared him for her.

She was a one-woman wrecking crew when it came to

the walls he'd built up inside, laying waste to all his defenses. Only a few weeks ago, there wasn't a person on earth who could have convinced him that she would have the power to bring him to his knees with a single look.

And yet she could. She had.

A few hours later, the storm was raging as he came back through Lucky Harbor. At a stop sign, he came up behind a stalled VW. Through the driving rain, he could see a woman fiddling beneath the opened hood, her clothes plastered to her. Well, hell. He pulled over, and as he walked toward her, she went still, then reached into the purse hanging off her shoulder.

Ty recognized the defensive movement and knew she had her hand on some sort of weapon. He stopped with a healthy distance between them and lifted his hands, hopefully signaling that he was harmless. "Need some help?"

"No." She paused. "Thank you, though. I'm fine."

He nodded and took in her sodden clothes and the wet hair dripping into her eyes. Then he looked into the opened engine compartment of the stalled car. "Wet distributor cap?"

Her eyes revealed surprise. "How did you know?"

"It's a '73 VW. Get the cap wet, and it won't run."

She nodded and relaxed her stance, taking her hand out of her purse. "I was going to dry the cap on my skirt but it's too wet." She shoved her hair back from her face and blinked at him. "Hey, I know you. You're Mysterious Cute Guy."

Christ how he hated that moniker. "Ty Garrison."

"I'm Grace Brooks. One of your three guardian angels in that freak snowstorm last week." She flashed a grin. "I'm the one who called 9-1-1."

"Then the least I can do is this." He came closer and took the distributor cap from her, wiping it on the hem of his shirt, which hadn't yet gotten drenched through. When he had the inside of the cap as dry as it was going to get, he replaced it and got her off and running.

Back in his own car, he ended up at the diner. Amy and Jan were there, Jan's gaze glued to the TV in the far corner. *American Idol* was on, and she was very busy yelling at the screen. "Okay, come on! That *sucked*. God, I miss Simon. He always told it like it was."

Amy rolled her eyes and met Ty at a table with a coffee pot. Guardian Angel Number Two, in a pair of low-slung cargoes and a snug, lacy tee. Normally she was alert as hell and on-guard but tonight her face was pale, her smile weak. "Pie?" she asked.

"Sure."

She came back two minutes later with a huge serving of strawberry pie. "You're in luck," she said. "It's Kick Ass Strawberry Pie from the B&B up the road. That means Tara made it," she explained to his blank look. "Best pie on the planet, trust me."

That was quite the claim but one bite proved it to be true. Ty watched Amy refill his cup, then gestured to the towel she had wrapped around the palm of her left hand. "You okay?"

"Fine."

Bullshit. Her other hand was shaking, and she looked miserable. But hell, if she wanted to pretend she was fine, it was none of his business. Especially since he was the master at being *fine*.

Problem was, there was blood seeping through her towel. "Do you need a doctor?"

"No."

He nodded and ate some more pie. Good. She was fine and didn't need a doctor. And God knew, he sure as hell didn't want to get involved. But when he was done, he cleared his own plate, bringing it to the kitchen himself.

"Hey," Jan yelled at him, not taking her gaze off the TV. "You can't go back there. It's against the rules."

"Your waitress is bleeding. That's against the rules too."

This got Jan's attention. Jan glanced into the back at Amy and frowned before turning back to Ty. "You going to patch her up? She has an hour left on her shift."

He had no idea what the hell he thought he was doing. He hadn't "patched" anyone up in a damn long time. Four years, to be exact. He waited for the sick feeling to settle in his gut, but all he felt was a need to help Amy. "Yeah. I can patch her up."

Amy was standing at the kitchen chopping block, hands flat on the cutting board, head bowed, her face a mask of pain. She jumped when she saw Ty and shook her head. "Guests aren't supposed to clear their own dishes."

"I'm going to ask you again. Do you need a doctor?"

"It was just a silly disagreement with a knife."

Not an answer. He unwrapped her hand himself and looked down at the cut. "That's more than a silly disagreement. You need stitches."

"It's just a cut."

"Uh-huh. And you need the ER."

"No, I don't."

There was something edgy in Amy's voice now, something Ty recognized all too well. For whatever reason, she had a fear or deep-rooted hatred of hospitals. He could sympathize. "You have a first-aid kit?"

"Yeah."

He drew a deep breath, knowing if he didn't help her, she'd go without it. "Get it."

The diner's first-aid box consisted of a few Band-Aids and a pair of tweezers, so Ty went to his car. He always kept a full first-aid kit in there, even though he hadn't ever cracked this one open. He returned to the kitchen and eyed Amy's wound again. He had Steri-strips but the cut was a little deep for that. "Trust me?" he asked her.

"Hell no."

Good girl, he thought. Smart. "Me or the hospital, Amy."

She blew out a breath. "All I need is a damn Band-Aid. And hurry. I have customers."

"They'll wait." She was looking a little greener now. He pushed her onto the lone stool in the kitchen. "Put your head down."

She dropped it to the counter with an audible thunk. He disinfected the wound, then opened a tube.

Head still down, she turned it to the side to eyeball what he was doing. "*Super glue?*" she squeaked.

"*Skin* glue. And hold on tight, it stings like hell." He started, and she sucked in a breath. "You okay?"

She nodded, and he worked in silence, finally covering the wound with a large waterproof bandage.

"Thanks." Amy let out a shuddery sigh. "Men are assholes. Present company excluded, of course."

With a shrug—men *were* assholes, himself included— he gestured to her hand. "How's that feel?"

She opened and closed her fist, testing. "Not bad.

Thanks." She watched him put everything back into his kit. "Does Mallory know that you're as good with your hands as she is?"

"I don't answer trick questions."

She started to laugh, but choked it off at the man who suddenly appeared in the kitchen doorway.

It was Matt, still in uniform, brow furrowed. "Jan said you're all bloody and—" His eyes narrowed on the blood down Amy's white tee. "What the hell happened?"

"Nothing," she said.

"Jesus Christ, Amy." He picked up the bloody towel and jerked his gaze back to her, running it over her body, stepping close.

Amy turned her back on him, on the both of them, and Matt looked at Ty. "What happened to her?"

"She's declined to say."

"A knife," Amy said over her shoulder. "No big deal. Now go away. No big, bad alpha males allowed in the kitchen."

Not even a glimmer of a smile from Matt, which was unusual. Ty hadn't any idea that Matt had something going with the pretty, prickly waitress, which was telling in itself. Usually the affable, easygoing Matt was an open book, not the type to let much get to him. But there was a whole bunch of body language going on, all of it heating up the kitchen.

Then Amy made an annoyed sound and walked to the doorway. For emphasis, she jerked her head, making her wishes perfectly clear. She wanted them out.

Matt waited a beat, just long enough for Amy to give him a little shove. She wasn't tall by any means, though her platform sneakers gave her some extra inches. Still,

Matt was six feet tall and outweighed her by a good eighty pounds. She could push him around only if he allowed it, but to Ty's shock, Matt acquiesced, and with a softly muttered "fuck it," he left.

Ty followed him out, telling himself that he wasn't here to get involved. If he had been, he'd have talked himself into Mallory's bed tonight—and he could have.

Easily.

That wasn't ego, just plain fact. She wanted him. He wanted her right back, more than he could have possibly imagined. Right this minute, he could be wrapped up in her sweet, warm limbs, buried deep. "Shit."

"Yeah," Matt muttered as they strode out to the parking lot side by side. "Shit."

"What was that back there?" Ty asked him.

"I don't want to talk about it."

"Why the fuck does that work for you and not me?"

Matt ignored this to stare in appreciation at the Shelby. "You get the suspension done?"

"Yeah, but there's still a lot left to do. I've been busy on your Jimmy. Almost done, by the way."

"Good. So how's this baby running?"

"Better than any other area of my life."

Matt laughed ruefully and slid into the passenger seat of the Shelby. Apparently Ty was getting company for his late night ride tonight. Silent, brooding company, but that suited him just fine.

Chapter 11

Eat a square meal a day—a box of chocolate.

On Saturday, the doors of the HSC opened to the public. The town hadn't exactly been on board, but enough tentative support had trickled in that Mallory had been able to talk Bill into giving her the one-month trial.

Mallory knew she had Ty to thank for starting that tentative support. After the town meeting, a handful of locals had pledged money for certain programs. Ford Walker and Jax Cullen, co-owners of the local bar, had donated money for a Drink Responsibly program. Lucille was donating supplies from her art gallery for an art program. Lance, Mallory's favorite CF patient, had donated time to help counsel the chronically ill. Every day someone else called. Bill decided it was too much money and goodwill to turn away and had given Mallory approval. But things had to go smoothly or it'd be over.

For now, they'd be open five days a week for services providing crisis counseling, and education and recovery programs. And on Saturdays, the HSC turned into a full-blown medical clinic.

They saw patients nonstop, thanks to their first attending physician, Dr. Scott. As Mallory began to close up at the end of the day, Josh came out from the back.

After a long day, Josh looked more badass ruffian than usual. His doctor's coat was wrinkled and he still had his stethoscope hanging around his neck. His dark hair was ruffled, his darker eyes lined with exhaustion. But there was a readiness to him that said he wasn't too tired to kick ass if needed. He'd worked a double shift to volunteer his time today, but Mallory knew his day wasn't over, not even close. He still had to go home to more responsibility—a young son, not to mention his own handicapped sister, both of whom he was solely responsible for.

"Nice job today," he said to Mallory.

"Thanks to you."

He lifted a shoulder, like it was no big deal. He was a big guy, over six feet and built like a bull in a china shop, which made his talent all the more impressive. He might be serious and just a little scary, but he was the most approachable doctor she'd ever met. He was also her favorite because he treated the nurses with respect. Such behavior should be automatic in doctors, but so often wasn't. This conduct also tended to land him on Lucille's *Most Wanted Single Male* list on Facebook far too often, which drove him nuts.

"I'm glad you got approval for this," he said. "You're doing something really good here."

She glowed over that as she locked up behind him. As the last staff member there, she walked each of the rooms, cleaning up a little as she went. They had two exam rooms, a very small staff kitchen, and the front reception area. There was a back walk-in closet being renovated for their drug lock-up, but for now the drugs and samples were kept in one exam room in a locked cabinet. The reception area was big enough to host groups, which was what they would likely have to do during the week.

Tomorrow night was their first scheduled AA meeting. Monday night would be Narcotics Anonymous—NA. Wednesday nights would host a series of guest speakers, all aimed at teen advocacy programs.

It was all finally happening, and it made Mallory feel useful. Helpful. Maybe she hadn't been able to help Karen, but she could reach others.

By the time she locked the front door and got to her car, yet another storm was rolling in. Night had fallen, and the lot wasn't as well-lit as she'd like. She was on the back side of the hospital, the entrance leading to a narrow side street. She made a note to get the lighting fixed tomorrow and slid into her car just as the sky started dumping rain. She inserted her key in the ignition and turned it.

Nothing, just a click. She tried again anyway and got nowhere. A dead battery, naturally. She peered out her windshield and sighed. Walking home would be a five-mile trek in the pouring rain, which she was far too tired for. Plus her feet hurt from being on them all day. With a grimace, she pulled out her phone and called Joe.

"Yo," her brother said. "Bad time."

"Bad time for me, too. I need you to come jump my car. I have a dead battery."

"You leave your lights on again?"

"No." *Maybe.* "You owe me, Joe." She had to put that one out there right away to start the negotiations. Joe was a deal maker and only dealt at all if the odds were in his favor. "I let you and your idiot friends borrow my car, remember?" she asked. "You needed more seats to get to that stupid trail party out at Peak's Landing. Maybe this is somehow your fault."

"No, the crack in the windshield is our fault. Not the battery."

She stared at the small crack in the windshield on the passenger's side and felt an eye twitch coming on. "Come on, Joe. I could really use your help tonight."

"Christ. Hang on." He covered the phone and murmured something to someone.

A muted female voice laughed, and then Joe was back. "Mal, if all you need is a jump, ask anyone around you." He lowered his voice. "I'm on a date. With *Ashley*."

She had no idea who Ashley was but she was assuming it *wasn't* his blonde. "What happened to whatshername?"

"That was so last week."

Mallory let out a disgusted sigh. "You're a man ho."

"Guilty," he said. And hung up.

Grinding her teeth, Mallory called him back.

He didn't pick up.

"Dammit." She scrolled through her contact list again. Her mother was out of the question. Ella wouldn't have a set of jumper cables, not to mention she'd want to talk about Mallory's social life. Maybe Tammy, she thought, and hit her sister's number. "Can Zach come give me a jump?"

"Honey," Tammy said. "He's a little busy jumping *me* right now."

Oh, for God's sake. Mallory hung up, her usually dormant temper beginning to steam. She would drop everything for any one of her family, and not a single one of them could help her. This depressing thought didn't change the fact that she was still wet, cold, and stranded in a dark parking lot. Again she thumbed her contacts and stopped at one in particular.

Mysterious Cute Guy, aka Ty Garrison.

She had the stuffed animals he'd won at the arcade sitting on her bed, like she was twelve and in middle school, going steady with the town bad boy.

Except would the bad boy really have stood up at a town meeting in front of everyone and defended her? Would he have stopped and helped a stranded woman on the side of the road? Grace had told her what he'd done. And so had Amy, saying that he'd patched her up with calm efficiency.

Yeah, Ty was far more than just some mechanic, though hell if she could figure him out.

She shouldn't call him for help. For one, they'd had inappropriate sex without involvement. To compound that mistake, she'd discovered she liked him. A lot. And to compound *that* mistake, she was dreaming about sleeping with him some more.

All really good reasons not to call him.

But then there was the one really good reason *to* call him.

He would actually come. She hit his number and held her breath. He picked up on the fourth ring, his voice low and calm as always. "Garrison," he said.

"Hi. It's Mallory."

He absorbed that information for a moment, probably

wondering how she'd gotten his number, a conversation she absolutely didn't want to have so she rushed on. "I'm at the HSC," she said, "and my car won't start, and I'm the only one left here, and the stupid parking lot lights aren't working and—"

"Lock your doors. I'll be right there."

"Okay, thanks—" But he was already gone. She slipped her phone into her pocket and put her head down on the steering wheel. So tired... She thought about that and how her feet hurt. She could really use a foot rub. And a body rub. She'd gotten a massage once, last year for her birthday. It'd been a present from Tammy. Her masseuse had been Chloe Traeger, who worked at the Lucky Harbor B&B where there was a lovely day spa. The massage had been fantastic but Mallory wondered what it would be like to have a man rub his hands over her body.

And not just any man, either.

She knew exactly which one she wanted. Ty. She sighed again, picturing lying on her back on a deserted beach at sunset, Ty leaning over her in a pair of low-slung jeans and nothing else, his big hands all over her bikini-clad body.

No, scratch that.

No bikini. And Ty in board shorts. Yeah, board shorts that fell disturbingly low on his hips, his eyes creased in that way he had of showing his feelings without moving his mouth. Mmm, that was a much better image, and she sighed dreamily.

He was aroused. She could feel him when he leaned over her. Big. Hard. She smiled up at him.

Instead of smiling back, he flipped her over, face down

on her towel, leaving her to gasp in shock, waiting breathlessly for him to touch her. When his lips brushed her shoulder, she wriggled for more.

"Lie still." His voice was a thrillingly rough command that she didn't obey, making him groan. He said her name in a warning whisper, running a finger down her spine, then between her legs until she was writhing with a moan of arousal.

He did it again.

And then again, until she was oscillating her hips in small, mindless circles, trying to get more of his fingers. He pushed a thigh between hers to spread her legs, and then pulled her up to her knees and entered her.

She came hard, her cries swallowed when she pressed her face to the forearm he had braced on the towel beneath her. He was right behind her, shuddering in pleasure as he collapsed on top of her—

A rap on her window had her jerking straight up and banging her head on her sun guard.

Mouth quirking, Ty waited patiently while she fumbled to roll down the window.

"Hi," she said breathlessly. "I was just…" God. *Dreaming about you making me come.*

"Sleeping?" he asked.

Or that. Which was far less embarrassing. She nodded and swiped at her sweaty temple with her arm. "Guess I'm tired."

"You look all flushed; you okay?"

She pressed her thighs together. She was more than flushed. "Yeah."

"Try starting it now."

She realized that not only had she slept through him parking next to her, he'd popped both their hoods and had hooked her car up to a set of cables.

Some nap. At least she hadn't screamed out his name. She turned the key, and her car started.

Ty turned and bent over her front end, his head buried beneath her hood. Absolutely *not* noticing how very fine his ass looked from that position, she pushed out of the car and stood next to him.

"You're going to need a new alternator sooner than later," he said.

She stared into the engine compartment, completely clueless about where the alternator might be. "Is that expensive?"

"Not for the part." He was still fiddling around. "The labor's expensive, but it shouldn't be. It's an easy thing to replace."

"So you *are* a mechanic."

He was still messing with... something. He pulled out her dip stick and checked the oil. "Always been pretty good with taking things apart and putting them back together again," he said.

She could vouch for that. A week ago, he'd certainly taken her apart and put her back together again. The ease with which she'd come for him in the storage attic still fueled her fantasies. She'd had sex before, even some pretty good sex, but she'd never gone off like *that*. "I don't think that was much of an answer," she said.

He looked at her. "You don't think so?"

"No."

His mouth curved. "Anyone ever tell you that you're a little—"

"Stubborn? Determined? Annoying?" She nodded. "Yep. Trust me, I've heard it all."

"You need oil. And I work for a government contractor doing the same sort of stuff I did in the military."

"Stuff?" Her inner slut drooled over the sleek back muscles bunching, stretching the material of his shirt taut as he replaced the dip stick. "Like I'd-tell-you-but-I'd-have-to-kill-you stuff?"

He actually turned his head her way and smiled, knocking off a few million of her brain cells. This wasn't good. She needed those brain cells.

"Something like that," he said.

Classified, she thought. Interesting. Disconcerting. But it certainly explained the always-ready air he had and the fact that he looked like a military recruitment poster, only better. She could see him in hot zones all over the world, working on machinery. Tanks. Subs. Missiles. Or maybe his mechanical talents were ship-oriented. He'd said Navy...Her stomach knotted at the thought of how dangerous his life must be. "You patched up Amy at the diner. That was nice of you."

This yielded her a shrug.

She waited for more information, anything, which of course was not forthcoming. "It's a good thing you look good in jeans."

Still beneath the hood, he turned his head and flashed her a quick smile.

"You're a conundrum, you know," she told him. "I mean you've got this whole hands-off thing going about you, and yet you have no problem putting your hands all over me."

"And mouth," he added helpfully. "I like my mouth on you."

Her entire body quivered. "What is it about me that you're attracted to?"

"For starters, the sexy underwear you put on beneath your clothes."

"You've only seen my underwear once."

"Twice," he said. "I looked down your top at the pier."

"You did not."

"Pink-and-white polka-dot bra."

"Oh my God."

"That's what I was thinking." He straightened out from beneath her hood. "And also, while we're on the subject, I like the noises you make when you—"

She covered his mouth with her hand.

He nipped at her fingers, and her knees wobbled. Stupid knees.

"I like your eyes," he said.

"What?"

"Yeah, I like the way they soften when you look at me."

She stared at him, wondering if he was just giving her a line, but he held her gaze evenly. "Keep going," she said slowly.

"I like the way you'd dive into a freak snowstorm to help a perfect stranger. I like how you treat everyone as if they're important, including a homeless drug addict. I like that you give one-hundred percent to every part of your life. You don't hold back, Mallory."

"You...you like all that about me?"

"And also that you like me." He smiled again. "I really like that."

"How about the fact that you're pretty cocky? Do you like that?"

"Mmm-hmm. And I especially like when you use the word *cock* in a sentence."

She pushed him, and he laughed, so she added another push, and of course, he didn't budge, the lout. Instead, he stepped into her, backing her to the car. "What do you like about me?" he asked.

"*Nothing.*"

He grinned. "That's not true. You like it when I—"

"Don't you say it."

"That's okay," he said. "I'm better with showing, not telling, anyway." And he covered her mouth with his. And then his hands got into the fray, and she heard a low, desperate moan.

Hers.

His big palm cupped the back of her head as he changed the kiss from sweet and friendly-like to demanding and firm and...God. *Hungry.* His hand fisted in her hair then, and he kissed her like he was starving for the connection.

Mallory was right there with him. By the time the kiss was over, neither of them were breathing steadily. "Wow," she said and shook her head to clear it. "You ought to be careful with those. A girl might forget herself."

Thoroughly challenged, he reached for her again, but she jumped back. "Oh, no," she said on a laugh. "You're lethal, you know that?"

"Am I still on your list?"

"Well, let's see. It is a list of Mr. Wrongs, and you're just biding your time until you're gone, which pretty much means you *define* Mr. Wrong." She narrowed her eyes and studied him. "But then you show up at the town meeting—after avoiding everyone for months, I might add—and stick up for me." She shook her head. "Who are you, Ty Garrison?"

Apparently he didn't have an answer for that because he was back beneath her hood. "When's the last time you had anyone look at this poor baby?"

"Uh..."

He shook his head and kept fiddling, muttering something about "the lack of respect for the vehicle, even if it *is* a piece of shit."

"Where did you learn respect for *your* vehicles?" she asked, teasing.

"My dad. He was a mechanic in the Navy."

"Ah. So it runs in the family."

"Yeah. And my mom was Air Force."

She smiled at that. "A military brat through and through, huh?"

"All I ever knew," he agreed, tightening some part or another.

"Which is why you're interested in a Vet program at the HSC," she guessed. And personal experience. And he'd made good on his promise too. She'd gotten a nice check, earmarked for what would be a damn good program by the time she was finished with it. Ty had asked her to make sure to get a good counselor involved, one who could help people like Ryan, and she would do just that. "What are they doing now, your parents?"

"My dad died in Desert Storm. My mom a couple of years ago from pneumonia."

Her heart stopped, and her smiled faded as she watched him continue to inspect...whatever he was inspecting. "I'm sorry," she said quietly, knowing better than most how inadequate the words were.

"Everything else looks okay for now." He straightened. "I'll follow you home to make sure."

"There you go again," she said softly, still unbearably touched by his losses. "Wanting to be on my list of Mr. Wrongs but acting like..." *A Mr. Right.*

"Make no mistake," he said quietly. "I'm wrong for you. All wrong."

Of that, she had no doubt.

Chapter 12

*It's not that chocolate is a substitute for love. Love is a
substitute for chocolate. Chocolate is far more reliable
than a man.*

On Sunday, Mallory watched with satisfaction as the
citizens of Lucky Harbor lined up in the hospital's back
parking lot for the car wash. The schedule had been set in
advance, and as heavily advertised, every board member
had agreed to put in two hours.

They were charging twenty-five bucks a pop. Big price
tag but people were paying for the joy of seeing their
well-known town hotshots stripped out of their usual fin-
ery and working like regular joe-schmoes.

Mallory's shift was noon to two, and she was scheduled with Matt, Josh, and Jane. Matt was out of his ranger
uniform. Josh was minus his stethoscope. Both of them
wore board shorts. Matt was listening to the iPod he had
tucked into his shorts pocket, his head banging lightly, an
easy smile on his face as he worked his line.

Without a shirt.

Mallory knew he was a gym rat, and it was time well spent. He was solid sinew wrapped in testosterone.

His line was wrapped around the block.

Josh was wearing a pale blue t-shirt, but he'd gotten wet while washing a large truck, and the thin cotton clung to him like a second skin. He spent up to sixteen hours a day at the hospital, so Mallory had no idea where *his* amazing body came from.

His line was nearly as long as Matt's.

Jane was wearing long Capri-length pants and a man's button-down shirt. The forty-year-old was tall and statuesque, and in the ER, she could wield a cold expression like a weapon, laying waste to all in her path. She was no less ferocious today.

She had no line.

"I don't understand," she said to Mallory. "People hate me. You'd think they'd *want* to line up to see me washing their car, pointing out every spot for me to hand scrub."

"Yeah," Mallory said. "Um…can I make a suggestion?"

Jane slid her a long look. "I don't know. Can you?"

Mallory ignored the Ice Queen tone. "Push up your sleeves. Oh, and tie your shirt tails at your belly button, and undo three of the top buttons."

Jane choked out an offended laugh. "Excuse me? Are you asking me to pimp myself out?"

"Yes. And roll up your pants. You're not even showing knee."

"I have knobby knees."

Mallory stared at her. "Okay, you're my boss, so I'm not going to tell you how much I hate you if *that's* your biggest body issue. But I will tell you that if you undo a few buttons and tie up your shirt, no one's going to be looking at your knees. Oh, and bend over—a lot. Your line will appear in no time."

Jane put a hand on her hip. "I am *forty* years old, Mallory."

"Exactly. You're forty, not eighty. And you have a better body than I do. When was the last time you had a date?"

Jane thought about that and grimaced. "I don't remember."

Mallory reached out and undid Jane's buttons herself. It revealed only the barest hint of cleavage, but it was really great cleavage. Then she gestured for Jane to do the rest.

Jane rolled her eyes, but tied up her shirt.

"I knew it," Mallory said on a sigh. "Great abs. Your pants."

Jane bent over to roll up the hem of her pants, and three cars got in her line.

Mallory was grinning as Jane straightened, looking a whole hell of a lot less like the uptight Director Of Nurses and more like a tousled, sexy, confident woman with attitude.

Jane looked at her line and blinked.

"You see?"

"Hmm . . ." Jane headed for the first car. "They'd better tip well."

Mallory went back to her own decent line. Amy was first up in an old Toyota truck that had seen better days two decades back. "Are you kidding me?" Mallory asked her. "You could have either Matt or Josh slaving over this thing, and you're in *my* line? Maybe *I* should be giving the bad girl lessons."

Amy's eyes locked in on Matt. He was washing Natalia Decker's BMW. Natalia was a CPA who ran her own accounting firm, a cute little blonde who'd dated her way through the men in Lucky Harbor with exuberant glee. She hadn't gotten her nails into Matt yet, though by the way she was hanging out her window watching him, she was working on it.

Oblivious, Matt was bent low over her bumper, scrubbing, the muscles of his back flexing with each movement. He was tan and wet, and looking pretty damn hot.

"Go get in his line," Mallory told Amy. "One of us should get an upfront, close look at him."

Amy slid dark sunglasses over her eyes and muttered something beneath her breath.

"What?" Mallory asked.

"Nothing. I don't want to talk about it. Are you going to wash my car or what?"

"Yeah, but Amy...he looks at you—"

"I *don't* want to talk about it."

"Okay, but this is the *first* order of business at our next Chocoholics meeting. You hear me?"

"You have other things to worry about."

"Yeah? Like what?"

"Like the fact that your Mr. Wrong is behind me."

Mallory turned to look and went still at the sight of the classic muscle car there, complete with the sexy man behind the wheel in dark glasses, dark stubble, and a darker 'tude.

Ty had been awake since before the ass-crack of dawn. He'd gone for a punishing swim and found Matt waiting on the beach. Ty had given him a long look, but Matt didn't appear to care that he wasn't welcome. He'd simply swum alongside Ty—at least until he couldn't keep the pace, and ended up waiting on the shore.

"You're doing good," Matt said when Ty walked out of the water.

It was true; he was doing good. Feeling good. He was making real progress. After the swim, Ty ran, falling only once, and only because a crab had come out of nowhere and startled the shit out of him. Then he hit the gun range, needing to push all his skills. *This* was the week he was going to get cleared. He could feel it.

The range was about thirty miles outside of Lucky Harbor. He'd been coming back into town when he'd seen Mallory amongst the car washers. She was in a T-shirt and shorts, and was wet and soapy. She looked like the Girl-Next-Door meets *Maxim* photo shoot.

Drawn in like a magnet, he'd gotten in her line. When she caught sight of him, she squinted, furtively attempting to see through the bright sun and into his windshield. He felt something loosen deep within him and wasn't sure he could have explained the feeling to save his own life.

She'd piled her hair on top of her head, but it wasn't holding. Loose strands stuck damply to her temples and cheeks, and along the back of her neck.

She was soft there, and he knew that if he put his mouth on her neck, she'd make a little sound that'd go straight through him. Crazy, he told himself. He was crazy in lust with a woman he had no business wanting. Not that *that* seemed to deter him in the slightest.

"Hey, Mysterious Cute Guy!"

Ty nearly jumped out of his skin. He hadn't even heard

Lucille come up to his passenger window. She smiled knowingly. "My neighbor's got a Charger. 1970, I think. Has a front end problem. Told him you might be interested. Are you?"

A Charger was a sweet old thing. Ty wouldn't mind getting his hands on one. "Yeah. I'm interested."

Lucille smiled. "That's right nice of you."

That was him, a right nice guy.

Mallory had finished Amy's car and came up to his driver's window. "Hey," she said. "Thanks for coming."

He let a slow, suggestive smile cross his mouth. Clearly realizing what she'd said, she went bright red. "Roll up your window," she warned. "Or you'll get wet." She paused, then blushed some more. "Dammit, now *everything* I say sounds dirty!"

He was laughing when he rolled up his windows.

She got to work, looking flustered, which he loved. And maybe a little annoyed, too.

Which he also loved.

She was doing a heck of a job washing, her arms surprisingly toned and buffed as she worked the sponge. Her shirt was dark blue, a modest cut knit tee, but she was wet and it was clinging to her. Her denim shorts were snug, and she had a streak of grease on her ass. She was backing away from his car, eyeing it with close scrutiny, clearly wanting to make sure she'd gotten all the soap off, when he rolled down his window. "Watch out," he said. "Or you'll trip over the—"

Soap bucket.

Too late. She tripped and, with a little squeal of surprise, went down.

He leapt out of his car just as she hit, her fingers reflexively gripping the hose nozzle as she landed on her ass in the soapy bucket.

A steady stream of water shot out of the hose and nailed him in the chest.

"Oh God," she said, dropping the hose and trying to get out of the bucket. "I'm sorry!"

Josh and Matt, washing cars on either side of her, rushed over, but Ty got to her first. "Are you all right?" he asked, pulling her out of the bucket.

She immediately took a step back from him, her hands going to her own butt, which was now drenched with soapy water. "No worries. I have lots of padding back there."

"You sure?" Josh asked her, reaching for her arm to brace her upright while she took stock. He was frowning at her ankle. "You didn't reinjure that ankle you broke last year, did you?"

"No." She laughed a little, clearly embarrassed but resigned. "Tell me no one got a picture of that."

"Everyone's too busy staring at Jane," Matt assured her, looking over at Mallory's boss himself. "Who's ... not her usual self today."

They all looked at Jane then, who was indeed looking *very* unlike herself. She was smiling.

Someone from Josh's line honked a horn and yelled, "*Dr. Scoottt...*"

Josh swore beneath his breath, making Mallory laugh and gently pat him on the chest. "Your women are calling, Dr. Scott. Better get back to 'em. And don't forget to give them what they want."

"A clean car?"

"Lots of views of your ass when you bend over."

He grimaced and headed back to his line. Mallory turned to Ty, gasping with shock at how wet he was. "Did I do all that?"

"You going to try telling me that it wasn't on purpose?"

"No," she said on a laugh. "It wasn't on purpose, I swear! If it had been, I'd have skipped the embarrassing bucket part, trust me."

Matt had gone back to washing a car and was busy flirting with the pretty blonde owner of said car. But Ty was extremely aware that Josh was still watching them. Josh was a good man, one of the best that Ty had ever met. But he was also on Mallory's list, and Ty wasn't evolved enough to wish him the best with her. "Mallory."

"Yeah?"

He stepped closer to her. "You can take Josh off your list."

She choked out a laugh as he pulled his now-drenched shirt away from his skin. He was still wearing his gun in a shoulder harness from the range, and he removed the wet Glock, then realized the entire parking lot had gone silent. Everyone was staring at him. Actually, not him. His gun.

Christ. "It got wet," he said. "Guns don't like to get wet."

Matt stepped away from the car he was working on and came to Ty's side, a show of solidarity. Just the supervisory forest ranger and the crazy guy.

"It's okay," Matt said. "Ty's licensed to carry." He said this with his usual easygoing smile, putting a hand on Ty's shoulder, using his other to wave at someone who pulled into the lot.

And just like that, everyone went back to what they'd been doing, giving the two men some privacy.

Matt gave Ty a look. "I keep telling you this is Lucky Harbor, not the Middle East."

Ty returned the look and said nothing.

Matt sighed. "You know that Vet program you're funding at HSC? The one you told Mallory to get a good counselor for? You ought to consider making use of it."

"I'm fine."

"Well, I'm glad to hear it. Maybe you could work on happy. You got any of that? Because you can get away with just about anything if you smile occasionally. Ought to try it sometime."

"Yeah, I'll keep that in mind," Ty said, but he didn't feel like smiling. He had no idea what he was still doing here. His leg was fine. And yet he'd stopped at the small town car wash because Mallory had been looking hot in shorts. He'd just agreed to fix someone's Charger. What the hell was he doing? He was gone, out of here, any day now, moving on as he'd done all his life.

So why the hell was he acting like he was sticking around? Why was he letting people in and making plans? It was not in the cards for him, this small town life. Ties and roots were not his thing. He paid for his car wash. He'd have said good-bye to Mallory but she was busy with another vehicle. He got into his car, but something had him looking back once more at Mallory. From across the lot she was watching him, her gaze long and thoughtful.

No regrets, she'd said.

But he thought that maybe this time, there would be at least one regret. A regret named Mallory Quinn.

* * *

That night, Mallory, Grace, and Amy sat in a corner booth at Eat Me, forks in hand, cake on a plate.

The Chocoholics were in session.

"So," Grace said, licking her fork. "The hardware store is hiring. The owner, Anderson, asked me out."

"Don't do it," both Amy and Mallory said at the same time.

Grace sighed. "He's cute. But I'd rather have the job. I filled out the application. I'm trying hard to find my happy."

"And you think counting nails is going to do it?" Amy asked.

"Is clearing dishes doing it for you?" Grace countered.

Amy shrugged. "It leaves me a lot of free time and brain cells to do what I like."

"Which is?" Mallory asked.

Amy shrugged again. "Drawing."

"You're supposed to be letting people in," Mallory reminded her. "It was your decree, remember? Drawing is a solo sport."

Amy stabbed her fork into the cake for a large bite. "I'm in training." She eyed Mallory. "You want to talk about today?"

"What about today?"

"Gee, I don't know—how about the fact that MCG is carrying?"

"MCG?"

"Mysterious Cute Guy. Ty Garrison. Hot stuff. The guy you smile dopily about every time he's mentioned."

"I do not smile dopily."

Amy looked at Grace. Grace pulled a small mirror from her purse and held it up in front of Mallory.

Mallory looked at her faint glow and—dammit—dopey smile, and did her best to wipe it off her face. "It's the chocolate cake."

Amy coughed and said "bullshit" at the same time.

Mallory sighed and set down her fork.

"Uh oh," Grace said.

"I like him," Mallory said.

"And that's a bad thing?" Grace asked. "You set out to stretch your wings, experience something new. It's happening."

"With a guy that could break her heart," Amy said softly. "Is that it, Mal? You're scared?"

"Like a little bunny rabbit," Mallory said. "Some bad girl I turned out to be."

Ty swam by moonlight, and then hit the beach for another run. He didn't fall this time, not once.

Progress.

When he was done torturing his body and his every muscle was quivering with exertion, he went to bed. Too tired for nightmares, he told himself.

Things started out good. He dreamed about the time his team had been assigned to rescue a diplomat's daughter out of Istanbul. Then the dream shifted to another mission, where they'd "commandeered" certain components from a godforsaken, forlorn corner of Iraq, components that had been waiting for another shipment, which when combined together would have been a huge terrorist threat. Then things transitioned again, to the time they'd managed to get to a bus loaded with

U.S. and British journalists before their scheduled kid-napping...

All successful missions...

But then the dream changed, and everything went straight to hell in a handbasket.

He was thrown from the burning wreckage. When he opened his eyes, his ears were ringing, and although he could see the wild flames all around him, he couldn't hear a damn thing. It was a movie without sound.

His men. He belly-crawled to Kelly, but he was already gone. Ty found Tommy and Brad next and did what he could, then went after Trevor. Trevor was on the other side of the wreckage, gasping for air, his chest crushed, and all Ty could do was hold him as he faded away...

He woke up alone in bed, not on a godforsaken moun-tain. "Christ," he breathed and shoved his fingers through his sweat-dampened hair. *"Christ."*

It was two in the morning but he rolled out of the bed, grabbed his jeans, and shoved his legs into them. His phone, blinking due to missed calls that were no doubt from Frances, was shoved into his pocket. Same with his empty Vicodin bottle.

He got into the Mustang and fired her up. With no idea what possessed him, he did a drive-by of Mallory's house. She wasn't the only one with recon skills, though he fig-ured the only way she could have gotten his cell phone number was through the hospital records.

How very industrious of her.

And illegal.

He found it amusing, and in a world where nothing much amused him anymore, he was also intrigued. A deadly combination.

Distance. He needed a boatload of distance. He was working on that.

Mallory's ranch-style house was in an older neighborhood. Typical Suburbia, USA. The place was freshly painted, the yard clearly cared for, much more than the piece-of-shit car she drove.

Which was why he was here. Or so he told himself.

It took him all of six minutes to replace her alternator with the one he'd driven into Seattle to get for her.

Probably he needed to work harder on keeping his distance.

He really needed to get back to work. He needed to be fucking useful for *something* again. He put his tools back in his car and had started to get behind the wheel when he heard locks tumble. Her front door opened.

In the lit doorway, highlighted by both the porch light and a single light somewhere inside, stood Mallory. Her hair was a wild cloud around her face and shoulders, her bare feet sticking out the bottom of her robe. "Ty?"

So much for stealth.

"What are you doing?" she asked.

Funny thing about that. He had no fucking clue what he was doing. None. Not a single one. He shut his car door and walked up to her, crowding her in the open doorway.

"Ty?"

He didn't answer. If she backed up a step or told him he was crazy, or gave him the slightest sign that he wasn't welcome, he would turn on his heel and walk off.

He was good at that, and they both knew it.

And he definitely expected her to be unnerved. He'd seen her face at the car wash when he'd been holding his gun.

But she surprised him now by stepping into him, meeting him halfway. Reaching for him, her body answered his touch with a slight trembling that made him feel pretty fucking useful, and wasn't that just what he'd wished for? To be useful again?

He kept telling himself that as curious and attracted as he was to her, if Mallory hadn't started things up between them at the auction, he'd have never initiated any sort of intimacy.

He was full of shit. She'd assured him that all she'd wanted was the one night, and he'd tried like hell to believe her, but somehow they kept getting in deeper.

She was like a drug. The most addicting kind, and he had a problem—he was pretty sure that she was developing feelings for him. He no idea what to do with that, or with his own feelings, which were definitely getting in his way. This whole "no emotional attachment" thing had gone straight to shit. Because Mallory Quinn was emotionally attached to every person she ever met, and she had a way of making that contagious. He craved contact with her in a way that he wasn't experienced with.

And he liked to be experienced.

But he couldn't think about that right now because her lips were parted, her cheeks flushed, her eyes telling him that his presence affected her every bit as much as hers did him. Helpless against the pull of her, he caught her up against him and stepped over the threshold, kicking the door closed behind him.

They staggered into the entryway together, mouths fused, bumping into her umbrella stand, knocking it over as she tripped on some shoes and slammed into a coat rack.

They were both laughing as he spun her away from danger, pressing her against a little cherrywood desk and mirror. He trapped her there, and all amusement faded as she gasped, the sound full of desire.

He wanted to hear it again, needed to hear it again. Lowering his head, he kissed the sweet spot beneath her ear, along her jaw, and then the column of her neck. He spent a long moment at the hollow of her throat because, oh yeah, that's where she made the sound again, her shaky hands clutching his shoulders.

"I was dreaming about you," she said softly.

He was glad, even more so since he'd been dreaming of pure hell. He'd had no idea how much he needed this, *her*, until this very minute. "Tell me."

"We were back at the auction." Her fingers wound their way into his hair, giving him a shiver. "Working our way through all the furniture," she murmured.

"Working our way through the furniture?"

"Yeah, you know..." She hesitated. "Doing it on each piece," she whispered.

He drew back far enough to see her eyes. When she blushed gorgeously, he laughed softly. "After what we did that night, you can still be embarrassed to say 'doing it'?"

She pushed at him but he didn't budge. "No," he said, pulling in her tight. "I like it." Hell, she had to be able to feel the proof of that. "What piece of furniture did we do it on first?"

She turned her head away. "I'm not going to say now."

He nibbled her ear. "Tell me," he coaxed, flicking his tongue on her lobe.

She gasped. "A table."

He grinned. "I did you on a table?"

She made a sound that was only *half* embarrassment now, the other half pure arousal.

"Tell me that I spread you out for my viewing pleasure and feasted on all your sweet spots," he said.

Glowing bright red, she stared at his Adam's Apple. "No. You, um, bent me over the table and then, you know, took me from behind."

Yeah, good luck with finding distance now. He was hard as a rock. Maybe distance wasn't the way to go. Maybe they needed this, needed to just go for it, to get each other out of their systems.

Yeah, that was the story he was going with. He turned them both so that she was facing the small foyer desk. "It was just a dream," she murmured into the mirror.

"Doesn't have to be."

She stared at his reflection, watching as his hands ran down her arms to take her hands in his, drawing them up, up around his neck where they'd be out of his way.

The air crackled with electricity. And need. So much need. "What are you wearing beneath the robe?" he asked.

She nibbled on her lower lip.

"Mallory."

"Nothing."

He groaned. Her body was so close to his that a sheet of paper couldn't fit between them. He reached for the tie on her robe. "Do you want this?"

"I—" She closed her mouth.

"Yes or no, Mallory."

"*Yes.*"

One tug of the tie and the robe began to loosen.

"Wait," she gasped. "I—I'm..." She hesitated. "I can't watch."

And yet she didn't take her hands from his neck, or her hungry gaze off the mirror, eyes glued to his fingers as they gripped the edges of her robe.

"Full access this time," he said.

"Oh, God." She nodded. "Okay, but I—" She broke off when he slowly spread the robe open, eyes riveted to her own body.

Which he already knew was the body of his dreams. "Mallory," he breathed. "You're so beautiful." He stroked his hands up her stomach to cup her breasts, his thumbs brushing her velvety nipples, wringing another gasp out of her lips. He did it again, a light teasing touch before he took his hands off her.

She whimpered.

He pulled her hands from around his neck and pushed the robe off her shoulders to puddle at their feet. Taking her hands again, he pinned them out in front of her on the table, which forced her to bend over. He gently squeezed her fingers, signaling he wanted her to stay like that.

"Ty—" she choked out, holding the position with a trusting sweetness that nearly undid him, especially when it was combined with the sexy sway of her breasts and the almost helplessly uncontrolled undulation of her hips into his crotch.

He cupped those gorgeous full breasts, teasing her nipples before skimming one hand south, between her legs.

"H—here? We really shouldn't..."

"No?"

"No," she whispered and then spread her legs, giving him more room.

Dipping into her folds was pure heaven, and he groaned when he found her very wet. His fingers trailed her own moisture over her, exploring every dip and crevice, until she was undulating again, her fingers white-knuckling their grip on the table, her eyes closed, her head back against his chest.

"Watch," he reminded her.

Her eyes opened and locked on the sight of her own body, naked, bent over the table, his tanned hand on her pale breast, the other slowly, languidly moving between her legs. "Oh," she breathed. "We look..."

"Hot." He slid a wet finger deep inside her, and she gave an inarticulate little cry, straining against him.

"Ty—"

"Tell me."

"In me," she gasped, breathless. "Please, in me."

"Come first."

Giving her another slow circle with his thumb, he watched as she shuddered, still holding obediently onto the desk's edges for all she was worth. He could feel her tremble as the tension gripped her and added another finger and some pressure with his thumb, nibbling along the nape of her neck to her shoulder. Strung tight, she breathed in little pants, her spine and ass braced against him, her arms taut, her face a mask of pleasure.

"*Ty.*"

"Right here with you," he assured her, and sent her skittering over the edge. She cried out as she shattered, and would have dropped to her knees if he hadn't caught her.

"*Now*," she demanded breathlessly. "Right now."

Not one to argue with a lady, he stripped, grabbed a condom from his pocket and put it on before pushing inside her.

She cried out again. With one arm supporting her, his

other hand found hers where it gripped the wood, and he linked their fingers. She was still shaking from her orgasm. Bending over her, pressing his torso to her back, brushing his mouth against her neck, he tried to give her a moment. But when she pressed her sweet ass into him, restless, he began to move, stringing them *both* up this time. She took each thrust, arching her back for more, insistent demand in her every movement.

Not so shy now, he thought with a surge of hunger and a rather shocking possessive protectiveness.

He couldn't tear his eyes from her, even as his every single nerve ending screamed at him to let go and come already. The fire she'd started in him was flashing bright, the ache for her tight and hard in his gut. He wasn't going to be able to hold on, but then it didn't matter because she went rigid and skittered over the edge again, her muscles clenching him in erotic, sensual waves.

It was not enough.

It was too much.

It was everything.

Gripping her hard, he growled out a heartfelt "oh fuck" and buried his face in her hair as he followed her over, coming so hard his legs buckled.

He managed to gain enough control to make sure his knees hit the hard wood floor and not hers. He turned her to face him and pulled her tight, nuzzling her neck. After a minute, he pulled back to look at her.

Her smile tugged a helpless one from him as well. "Good?" he asked.

She traced a finger along his lower lip. "That's a pretty weak word for what that was. I bet you could come up with something better."

He nipped gently on her finger. "I'm more of a show-not-tell kind of guy."

"Yeah?"

"Yeah."

"So..." she said, softly. "Show me."

Chapter 13

Forget love—I'd rather fall in chocolate!

Mallory didn't know what had brought Ty to her in the middle of the night, or what he'd planned on doing, but sitting in her entryway naked was a pretty damn good start.

Or finish.

She blushed as he bent in to kiss her, and he laughed softly against her lips as if he could read her mind. To distract them both, she trailed a finger down his chest, over a hip, and found an unnatural ridge. She took a look at the jagged scar that ran the length of his body from groin to knee, and she stilled in horror for what he'd suffered.

She realized that she was all comfy cozy, cuddled up against his chest. The position couldn't possibly be comfortable for him. "Is your leg okay?"

"I can't feel my leg right now."

She laughed breathlessly, relieved at the lessening of the sudden tension in his big, battle-scarred, *perfect* body.

"Good," she said. "I know it gives you pain from the car crash."

"The pain's faded." He paused, then grimaced. "And it wasn't a car crash. It was a plane crash."

She controlled her instinctive gasp of horror. "You survived a plane crash?"

"That wasn't as bad as the several days that went by before rescue."

"Oh, Ty," she breathed, feeling her throat tighten in pain for him, trying to imagine it and not being able to. "How bad was it?"

"Bad enough."

"Your injuries?"

"Cracked ribs, broken wrist, collarbone fracture. Some internal injuries and the leg. That was the worst of it for me. All survivable injuries." He paused again. "Unlike everyone else."

She couldn't even imagine the horrible pain he'd suffered. *For days.* And the others... *He'd been the only one to survive.* Aching for him, she ran her fingers lightly over his chest, feeling the fine tremor of his muscles. Aftershocks of great sex, maybe.

Or memories.

"Your friends," she said softly. "The ones you've mentioned before. That's where you lost them."

"Yeah. My team."

"Were you—"

"Mallory." He shook his head. "I *really* don't want to talk about this."

"I know." She clutched the infinity charm around her neck, knowing the pain. "No one ever wants to talk about Karen either. But she was really important to me. For a long time after she was gone—after I failed to save her—I couldn't bear to remember her, much less talk about her."

He sighed, a long, shuddery exhale of breath and drew her in closer, burying his face in her hair. "How did she die?"

"She took a bottle of pills." She felt him go still. "She was eighteen," Mallory said. "And pregnant. It was ruled an accidental OD but..." She closed her eyes and shook her head. "It wasn't. Accidental, I mean. She did it on purpose."

"Oh, Christ, Mallory." He tightened his grip on her. "Doesn't sound like you could have saved her."

"We were sisters. I knew she had a drug problem. I should have—"

"No," he said firmly, pulling back to look into her eyes. "There's nothing you can do, *nothing*, to help someone who doesn't want to be helped."

It was so regretfully true, she could barely speak. "How do you get past it?"

"You keep moving. You keep doing whatever keeps you going. You keep living." His hands were on the move again, tender and soothing... until her breath caught, and she murmured his name, hungry for him again.

His touch changed then, from tender and soothing to doggedly aggressive and doggedly determined, stealing her breath.

"Keep living," she repeated. "That's a good plan—Oh, God, Ty," she whispered when he sucked a nipple into his mouth, hard. "I thought we were talking."

"You go ahead and talk all you want," he said gently, then proceeded to not-so-gently once again take her right out of her mind, in slow, exquisite detail.

Much, much later, she lay flat on her back on the floor, completely boneless. "Good talk," she whispered hoarsely.

Ty woke up flat on his back, the wood floor stuck to his spine and ass, a warm, sated woman curled into him. He'd taken her on the floor and had the bruises on his knees to prove it. Somehow he staggered to his feet, then scooped up Mallory. He'd have to tell Josh that if his leg could hold out through marathon sex, it could hold out through anything, and see if *that* got him cleared.

"No," she muttered, the word a slur of exhaustion as she stirred in his arms. "Don't wanna get up yet."

He knew she'd been working around the clock, on her feet for twelve hours and more at a time. She worked damn hard. "Shh," he said. "Sleep."

Her muscles went taut as she woke. "Ty?"

Well, who the hell else?

"Where we going?" she asked groggily, slipping her arms around his neck.

"Bed." He was going to tuck her in and get the hell out, before he did something stupid like fall asleep with her. Sex was one thing. Sleeping together afterwards turned it into something else entirely.

You idiot, it's already something else . . .

At her bed, he saw the two big stuffed animals he'd won for her leaning against her pillows. An odd feeling went through him, the kind of feeling that stupid, horny teenage boys got when they had a crush. This was immediately chased by wry amusement at the both of them.

He leaned over the bed to deposit Mallory into it, but

she tugged and he fell in with her. "Cold," she murmured with a shiver and tried to climb up his body.

Pulling her close—just for a minute, he told himself—he reached down and grabbed the comforter, yanking it up over the top of them. He'd share some body heat with her until she stopped shivering. Once she was asleep, he'd head out.

"Mmm," she sighed blissfully, pressing her face into his throat, tucking her cold-ass toes behind his calves. "You feel good."

"I'm not staying," he warned, not knowing which one of them he was actually telling, the woman cuddled in his arms or his own libido. So he said it again.

It didn't matter. Two minutes later, Mallory was breathing slow and deep, the kind of sleep only the very exhausted could pull off. She was out for the count.

And all over him.

Her hair was in his face, her warm breath puffing gently against his jaw, her bare breasts flattened against his side and chest. She had one hand tucked between them, the other low on his stomach. In her sleep, her fingers twitched, and she mumbled something that sounded like "bite me, Jane."

Smiling, he ran his hand down her back. "Shh."

She immediately settled in with a deep sigh, trusting. Warm. Plastered to him like a second skin.

Christ. He didn't want to wake her, but he didn't do the sleepover thing. He never did the sleepover thing.

Ever.

But unequivocally lulled in by her soft, giving warmth, he closed his eyes. Just for a second, and fell asleep wrapped around her.

At some point, he felt the nightmare gathering, pulling him in. Luckily, he managed to wake himself up before he made a complete ass of himself. It was still dark. Too dark. Rolling off the bed, he grabbed up his jeans and was halfway out the door before he felt the hand on his arm. He nearly came out of his skin and whipped around to face Mallory.

Way to be aware of your surroundings, Soldier. Unable to help himself, he twitched free and took a step back, right into the doorknob, which jabbed him hard in the back. "Fuck, Mallory."

"I'm sorry. I didn't mean to startle you." Lit only by the slant of moonlight coming in through her bedroom blinds, she stayed where she was, a few feet away, concern pouring off her in the way that only hours before passion and need had. "You okay?"

And here was where he made his mistake. He should have lied and said yes. He could have done it, easily. If he'd added a small smile and a kiss, she'd have bought it for sure. She'd have bought anything he tried to sell her because she trusted him.

That was who she was.

But it wasn't him. He didn't want to do this, get this close. So he shoved his feet into his running shoes and grabbed up his wallet and keys.

"Ty?"

He headed down the hallway. She came after him; he heard the pad of her bare feet. *She's going to get cold again* was his only inane thought.

She caught him at the front door. It wasn't until he felt her fingers run down his bare back that he realized he'd forgotten his shirt.

"Did you have a bad dream?"

He went still. "No," came the instant denial.

She merely stroked his back again. "That night in the storm," she said quietly. "you had a nightmare. I thought maybe it happened again here."

He dropped his head to the door. "That's not it."

"Then what happened? Things get a little too real?"

He straightened. "I have to go, Mallory."

"Without your shirt?"

He turned to face her, and she smiled.

She was wearing his shirt. "Stay," she said with a terrifying gentleness. "Sleep with me. I won't tell."

He knew she was treading softly around the crazy guy, only wanting to help. But he didn't want her help. He didn't want anyone's help. He was fine. All he needed was to be able to get back to work. And maybe to be buried deep inside her again, because there he didn't hurt. There he felt amazing. But if he took her again, he'd never leave. "Can't."

"But—"

He pulled open the door and stepped into the chilly night sans shirt, leaving before she could finish the rest of her sentence.

Mallory plopped back onto her bed and stared up at the ceiling, haunted by the expression on Ty's face as he'd left. He'd been rude and abrupt, and she should be pissed.

She wasn't.

But she couldn't put a finger on exactly *what* she was.

This, with him, was supposed to have been about fun. Just a little walk on the wild side.

But it had become so much more. Unnerving, but it was the truth. She wanted even more.

And he was so Mr. Wrong it was terrifying.

She wanted him anyway. *How was it that she wanted him anyway?*

She was good at making people feel better, at helping them heal. Or at least she liked to think she was. But this, with him... She couldn't heal what ate at him, any more than she'd been able to heal herself.

The next morning she got up and went to work. A few hours in, she was paged to the nurses' station. "What's up?" she asked Camilla, who was sitting behind the desk when she got there.

Camilla jerked her head toward the hallway. Mallory turned and found a very familiar, tall, broad-shouldered man propping up the wall. His stance was casual, his body relaxed.

But she knew better.

"I'm on break," she said to Camilla and walked toward Ty. "Hey," she said.

"Hey." His eyes never wavered from hers. "Got a minute?"

"Maybe even two."

He didn't smile. Huh. That didn't bode well. All too aware of Camilla's eyes—and ears—on them, she gestured for him to follow her. They took the stairs down to the ground floor cafeteria, and Mallory led him to a corner table.

It was too early for the lunch crowd so they had the place to themselves, except for a janitor working his way across the floor with a mop.

"Smells like a mess hall," Ty said.

"I bet the food was better at mess hall."

"I bet not."

He was sitting close, his warm thigh against hers beneath the table. He wore jeans that were battered to a velvety softness and a midnight blue button-down with the sleeves shoved up to his elbows.

He looked edible.

And she was afraid he was here to tell her his time was up, that he was leaving. "You want anything?" she asked. "Coffee? Tea? Pancakes?" *Me...* "They have great pancakes—"

"Nothing. Mallory—"

"A sandwich," she said desperately. "How about a sandwich? Hell, I could use a sandwich myself." She hopped up, but he grabbed her wrist.

Fine. She could handle this, whatever *this* was, and slowly sat back down, braced for a good-bye. Dammit.

He was looking at her in that way he had, steady, calm. "You okay? You seem jumpy."

"Just say it," she said. "Say good-bye already. I can't imagine it's that hard for you."

His brows went up. "You think I'm here to say good-bye? And that it wouldn't be hard for me to do?"

"Would it?"

He stared at her, his eyes fathomless, giving nothing away. "I'm not here to say good-bye. Not yet anyway."

"Oh." She nodded, knowing she should be relieved, but she wasn't. Tension had gripped her in its hard fist, and she let out a slow, purposeful breath. "I think I need a favor from you, Ty. When it *is* time to go, I want you to just do it. Don't say good-bye. Just go."

"You want me to just leave without a word."

"Yes." Her throat was tight. Her heart was tight too. "That would be best, I think." She stood and started to walk away.

"I wanted to apologize for last night," he said, catching her hand. "I was an ass."

She softened, and with a gentle squeeze of his fingers, sank back into her chair. "Well, maybe *ass* is a bit harsh. I was thinking more along the lines of a scared-y cat."

He let out a rough laugh. "Yeah. That too."

"I understand, you know."

"You shouldn't," he said.

"Why? Because I've never faced anything that haunts me?"

His gaze never left hers. "I'm sorry about Karen," he said. "And you're right. You're stronger than anyone I know. But I meant you shouldn't understand, because you deserve better from me."

Before she could respond to that, the elevator music being piped into the dining area cut off and was replaced by an authoritative male voice. "Code Red."

Mallory jumped up. Code Red meant there was a fire, and personnel were to report in immediately. Today was a scheduled drill but she'd expected it later in the day. "You're either about to be evacuated," she told Ty, "or it's going to be a few minutes before you can leave." She slapped her employee card on the table. "When the drill's over, help yourself to something to eat."

"Code Red," the voice repeated. "All personnel re-spond immediately. Code Red. *Repeat, Code Red.*"

Her life had great timing.

Chapter 14

When the going gets tough, the tough eat chocolate.

With the hospital in temporary lockdown, Ty leaned back and waited. From where he sat, he could see out the cafeteria and across the reception area to the front door of the hospital. In less than four minutes, firefighters and other emergency personnel came pouring in.

A drill, he thought, since no one was being evacuated. Ten minutes later, the hospital employees reappeared, though Mallory didn't.

"You want something to eat?" the cook called out to Ty.

He realized he was starving. He stood and walked over to the cook's station and eyed all the various ingredients. A few more people came in behind him. Two women in scrubs took one look at him and began whispering between themselves.

"Quesadilla?" the cook asked. "Or maybe a grilled turkey and cheese? A burger? I have a hell of a Cobb salad today, but that's not going to fill up a big guy like you."

"Burger," Ty decided. If the plane crash hadn't killed him, or the second-story jump, then a little cholesterol couldn't touch him.

The women behind him were still murmuring. "In the Vets' Hall," one of them whispered, "where *anyone* could have seen them."

"How do you know that?" the other whispered back.

"Sheryl told Cissy who told Gail. It's really unlike her. I mean, you'd expect it of any of the other Quinns but not her..."

The cook slid Ty an apologetic glance as she flipped his burger. "Cheese?"

He nodded.

The whispers continued. "...thought she'd be more careful with her image, what with the HSC at stake and all. She's still short a lot of money and needs everyone's support."

"Do you think they did it in one of the closets *here*?"

Ty had never given a shit about image, and he didn't think Mallory did either, but this was really pissing him off. He turned to face the two nosy old bats.

They both gasped and immediately busied themselves with their trays. He stared at them long and hard, but neither of them spoke.

So he did. "Mind your own business."

They didn't make eye contact and he turned back to the cook, who handed him his plate. She gestured to the card he still held in his hand, the one Mallory had left him. "Just swipe it," she said, indicating the machine alongside the register. "Mallory's card will get you anything you want on her account. Should I add a drink? Chips?"

Mallory had given him her employee pass. She was still trying to take care of him. He wasn't used to that. Shaking his head, he pulled out cash.

"But—"

He gave the cook a look that had her quickly making his change. Extremely aware of the two women behind him boring holes in his back with their beady eyes, he took his burger and headed back to his table.

The two women bought their food and walked past him, giving him several long side glances that told him that all he'd done was make things worse.

And what the hell did he think he was doing anyway, messing around in Mallory's life? He was leaving soon but Lucky Harbor was her home, her world. He ate, feeling confused and uncertain, two entirely foreign emotions for him. He'd actually believed that *he* was the one giving here, that he was the experienced one imparting a little wildness and the dubious honor of his worldly ways. How fucking magnanimous of him.

Especially since the truth was that Mallory had done all the giving, completely schooling him in warmth, compassion, and strength. In the process, with nothing more than her soft voice and a backbone of steel, she'd wrapped him around her pinkie.

Christ, he really was such an asshole. He cleared his plate and headed out, slowing at the front entrance. There was a box there, similar to a mailbox where people could drop donations for the Health Services Clinic. He'd given money for the Vets' program, which wouldn't help if Mallory couldn't get the support for the HSC to remain open. He stared at the box and knew exactly what he was going to do to give back to the woman who'd given him so much.

*   *   *

On Mallory's drive home, she stopped at Eat Me. Grace had sent a text that said there was an emergency.

Mallory went running in and found Grace and Amy waiting for her with a box.

A shoe box.

"Bad girl shoes," Amy said, pushing the box toward her. "Happy birthday."

"My birthday was last month."

"Merry early Christmas."

"Oh no," Mallory said. "These meetings are always about me. It's one of you guys' turns."

"Nope," Grace said. "We can only concentrate on one of us at a time."

"Then let it be Amy," Mallory said.

"Yeah," Jan said from where she was watching TV at the other end of the counter. "She's screwed up. She's got that big, sexy, forest ranger sniffing around her, and all she does is give him dirty looks."

"Hey," Amy said. "That is none of your business."

Jan cackled.

"Not talking about it," Amy said firmly, and nudged the shoe box toward Mallory again.

Because they both looked so excited, Mallory relented and opened the box to find a beautiful pair of black, strappy, four-inch heels that were dainty and flirty and pretty much screamed sex. "Oh," she breathed and kicked off the athletic shoes she'd worked in all day, replacing them with the heels.

Two counter stools over, Mr. Wykowski put a hand to his chest and said "wow."

"Heart pains?" Mallory asked in concern, rushing over there in her scrubs and bad girl heels.

"No," he said. "Not heart pains."

"Where does it hurt?"

He was staring at her heels. "Considerably lower."

Amy snorted. Mallory went back to her stool.

Grace was grinning. "See? Use them wisely. They have the power."

"Power?"

"Bad girl power," Amy said. "Go forth and be bad."

The next day Ty brought Ryan dinner. Ryan was living in a halfway house outside of town, in a place that Mallory had arranged for him to stay in through HSC.

It was infinitely better, and safer, than living on the streets.

After they ate, Ryan asked Ty for a ride, directing him to HSC.

"What's up here tonight?" Ty asked.

"A meeting."

The sign on the front door explained what kind of meeting:

NA—Narcotics Anonymous

Someone had attached a sticky note that said: *EMPHASIS ON THE* A, *PEOPLE!*

Ty didn't know whether to be amused that only in Lucky Harbor would the extra note be necessary, or appalled that the town was trusted with the *anonymous* at all.

But part of the process was trusting.

He'd always sucked at that. He turned to Ryan, who'd

gone still, seeming frozen on the top step. "I'm too old for this shit," Ryan muttered.

"How old are you?" Ty asked.

"Two hundred and fifty."

"Then you're in luck," Ty said. "They don't cut you off until you're three hundred."

A ghost of a smile touched Ryan's mouth. "I'm forty-three."

Only ten years older than Ty. Ryan's body was trembling. Detoxing. Not good. Ty would have paid big bucks to be anywhere else right now but he figured if anyone was interested in him as a crutch, they had to be pretty bad off. "How long has it been since your last hit?"

Ryan swiped a shaking hand over his mouth. "I ran out of Oxycontin four days ago. Doctor says I don't need it anymore. Fucking doctors."

Ty slipped his hand into his pocket and fingered the ever-present empty bottle. Two months, two weeks, and counting. He thought about saying that he'd wait outside, but that felt a little chickenshit, so he went in.

He survived the meeting, and so did Ryan. An hour later they walked out side by side. Quiet. Ty didn't know about Ryan, but he was more than a little shaken by the stories he'd heard, at the utter destruction of lives that those people in there had been trying to reboot and repair. He knew he had to be grateful because he hadn't fucked up his life. At least not completely.

He was halfway back to Ryan's place when Ryan spoke. "So are you and Mallory a thing?"

Ty had been asked this many times in the past few weeks. By the clerk at the grocery store. By the guy who'd taken his money at the gas pump. By everyone who'd crossed his path. By the very same people who—until Mallory—had been content to just stare at him.

Mallory. Mallory was the heart and soul of this town, or at least she represented what its heart and soul would look like in human form. And while maybe he'd treated her like someone he could easily walk away from, he knew different. *She* was different. Still, there was no denying the fact that while *she* was grounded here, in this place, in this life, *he* was chomping at the bit to get back to his. "No," he finally said. "We're not a thing."

Ryan scratched his scruffy jaw. "She know that?"

It'd been Mallory's idea that this be just a one-time affair, though she'd accepted his latest visit as just an addendum to the original deal. And she'd let him off the hook for being an ass.

And then asked him to leave without a good-bye. "Yeah. She knows that."

The question was, did *he*.

"Because she's a real nice lady," Ryan said. "When I was living on a bench at the park, she'd bring me food at night. She ever tell you that?"

Ty shook his head, his chest a little tight at the thought of Mallory, after a long day in the ER, seeking Ryan out to make sure he was fed.

"Yeah, she can't cook worth shit," Ryan told him with a small smile. "But I ate whatever she brought anyway. Didn't want to hurt her feelings."

Ty heard himself choke out a laugh.

Ryan nodded. "If I was…" He lifted a hand to indicate himself and trailed off. "You know, *different*," he finally said. "I'd try for her. She's something special. Way too special for the likes of me, you know?"

Ty's chest tightened even more. Yeah. He knew. He knew *exactly*. "She'd be pissed off to hear you say that."

"She's pretty when she's pissed off," Ryan said wistfully. "One time she came to the park and some kids were trying to bean me with rocks. She chased them, yelling at them at the top of her lungs. I was in a bad way then, and still I think I looked better than she did. Her hair was all over the place, and she was in her scrubs. She looked like a patient from the place I'd stayed at after I got back from my third tour."

A mental facility. Ty pictured Mallory furious and chasing the kids off. He could see it: her scrubs wrinkled after a long day of work, those ridiculous fuzzy boots, her hair looking like it had rioted around her face.

Christ, she was so fucking beautiful.

"You've seen the stuff on Facebook, right?" Ryan asked.

Ty slid him a look. "How are you getting on Facebook?"

"There's a community computer at the house." Ryan shrugged. "Facebook's the homepage. There's a pic up of you two. You two seem pretty cozy for not being a thing."

Yeah. Cozy.

Except what he'd had with Mallory had been just about the opposite of cozy. It'd been hot. Bewildering.

Staggering.

And what the hell pic was up on Facebook?

He dropped Ryan off, then went home and worked on the Jimmy for Matt until late. He showered, then eyed his blinking phone. He glanced at the missed calls, getting a little rush at the thought that maybe Mallory had called him. The last time she'd been stuck. Maybe this time she just wanted to hear his voice. He sure as hell could use the sound of her voice right about now.

But the message wasn't from Mallory. It was from Josh. Ty was expected at the radiology department at seven for scans, and then at a doctor's appointment at eight.

Ty tried to read the tone of Josh's voice to ascertain whether the news was going to be good or bad, but Josh was as good as Ty at not giving anything away.

The next morning, Ty was led to Josh's office and told to wait. He'd perfected the art of hurrying up and waiting in the military, so when Josh strode in carrying a thick file that Ty knew contained his medical history, he didn't react.

Josh was in full doctor mode today. Dark blue scrubs, a white doctor coat, a stethoscope around his neck, and his hospital ID clipped to his hip pocket. Hair rumpled, eyes tired, he dropped Ty's file on his desk, sprawled out into his chair, and put his feet up. "*Christ.*"

"Long day already?"

"Is it still day?" Josh scrubbed his hands over his face. "Heard from Frances today. Or yesterday. Persistent, isn't she?"

"Among other things. What did you tell her?"

"That your prognosis was none of her goddamned business and to stop calling me."

This got a genuine smile out of Ty. "And she thanked you politely and went quietly into the night."

"Yeah," Josh said, heavy on the irony. "Or told me what she was going to do with my balls if she had to come out here to get news on you herself."

"Sounds about right." Ty looked at his closed file. "Verdict?"

"Scans show marked improvement. With another month of continued P.T., you could be back in the same lean, mean fighting shape you were. For now, I'd say you were probably up to where us normal humans are."

Another month off would fucking kill him. "So I'm good to go then."

Josh gave him a look. "Depends on your idea of go. You're not up to leaping out second-story windows."

"Yeah, but that hardly ever happens."

Josh put his feet down and leaned forward, studying Ty for a long, serious moment. "You're really going back."

"I was *always* going back."

"But you want to go back *now.*"

"Hell, yeah," Ty said. "I wanted to go back the day I got here. Especially in the past few weeks, since I've been swimming and running again."

"So why didn't you? Go back?"

"I want to work," Ty said, gesturing to the file. "Need clearance."

"Yes, and that's going to come soon, but my point is that you haven't been exactly handcuffed to Lucky Harbor. You could have left."

A flash of Mallory's face came to Ty. Looking up at him while lying snuggled against him in her bed, wearing only a soft, sated smile and a slant of moonlight across her face.

It was no mystery what had kept him here.

"Mal know that you're just about out of here?" Josh asked quietly.

"This has nothing to do with her," Ty said flatly. "Sign the papers."

"You'd have to be on light duty."

"Fine. I'll push fucking papers around on a desk if I have to. Just clear me."

Josh shook his head, looking baffled. "You'd leave here for a desk job? Man, you're not a desk-job kind of guy and we both know it."

He'd deal. He needed to get close to the action, to get back to his world. He needed the adrenaline. He was wasting away here in Lucky Harbor.

"You know," Josh said with that infuriatingly calm voice, leaning on the desk, his elbows on the release papers. "Maybe we should get back to the real reason you're still here."

"Sign the papers, Josh."

Josh stared at him.

Ty stared back, holding the other man's gaze evenly. Steadily.

With a shake of his head, Josh signed the papers.

Ty spent two days *not* making any plans to get back to his life. First, he told himself he needed to finish up the Jimmy. Then he told himself he had to finish up the Charger for Lucille's neighbor, and the other two cars he'd taken on as well. And people kept calling him with new car issues. He couldn't just ignore them. Plus he needed to finish the Shelby, just for himself, but the truth there was that she was running like a dream.

After that, he ran out of excuses and decided he'd give himself a day off from thinking about it.

Which turned into yet another day...

Then he woke up to a message from Josh to stop by his office at ten. Ty got up and swam. He ran, hard. He played WWE with Matt at the gym for an hour until they fell apart gasping, sweating, and equally worked over. Then Ty dragged himself to the shower and drove to Josh's office.

Josh was in dress clothes today, a white doctor's coat over his clothing, the ever-present stethoscope acting as a tie. He looked up from the mountain of paperwork on his desk and scowled at Ty. "You call The Queen yet about being cleared?"

"No."

Josh gave him a long look, then stood and shut his office door. Back in his chair, he steepled his fingers, studying Ty like a bug on a slide. "Problem?"

"No. I've just got a little pain is all." He straightened his leg and winced.

"No doubt," Josh said dryly. "I was at the gym this morning; you never even noticed me. You were too busy wiping the floor with Matt. Who, by the way, is the best street fighter I've ever met. And you kicked his ass. How much pain can you be in?"

"I pulled something."

Josh's smile faded. "Yeah?"

"Yeah."

Josh was quiet a moment. "Then maybe you should give it another week," he finally said.

Ty nodded his agreement and left. He left the back way, which meant he stood in the bright sunshine in the hospital parking lot staring at Mallory's POS car. He wondered what the hell was wrong with him, but since that was probably way too big a problem to solve in this decade, he went home. He fiddled on the Shelby until he realized it'd gotten dark. He was just getting out of his second shower of the day when he heard the knock at his door.

He'd been off the job for more than six months, and still the instinct to grab his gun before answering was second nature. But this was Lucky Harbor. The only real danger was being killed by kindness.

And nosy-ass gossip.

Shaking his head, he grabbed his Levi's up off the floor and pulled them on, then opened the door to...Mallory.

She gave him a small smile, a sweet smile. Clearly she hadn't yet heard through the cafeteria grapevine that he was single-handedly ruining her life. "Hey," he said. A chronic idiot. That was him.

"Hey yourself." Her gaze ran over his bare torso. Something went hot in her eyes as she took in the fact that all he wore were Levi's, which he hadn't yet buttoned up all the way. He did that now while she watched, and the temperature around them shot up even more.

She stepped over the threshold, and since he hadn't moved she bumped into him. He thought it was an accidental touch but then her hands came up and brushed over his chest and abs. No accident.

Nor was the fact that she was wearing a halter top, low-riding jeans and a pair of really hot heels that brought her up four point five inches and perfectly aligned their bodies. Her pulse was beating like a drum at the little dip in the base of her throat. Lifting a hand, he ran a finger over the beat, watching her pulse leap even more.

Her hand came up to join with his. "In the name of full disclosure," she murmured, "you should know that I talked to Ryan this afternoon."

Ty lifted his gaze.

"He landed in the ER," she said.

"What happened? Is he all right?"

"Someone on the highway caught sight of him wandering around and brought him in. He had a bottle of Jack and some dope he'd scored off some kids."

"*Shit.*"

"Yeah." She kept her hand on his, squeezing his fingers reassuringly. "He's fine. He's currently sleeping it off, but before that...he was talking."

"Was he?"

"You took him to NA."

That was a statement of fact so he let it sit between them.

"You...went into the meeting," she said. "You stayed."

Another statement of fact.

"Was he...unsteady?" she asked. "Did he need the assistance?"

Ah, and now he got it. She was on a fishing expedition. "He wasn't that bad off, no."

She nodded, and he waited for her expression to change but it didn't. There was no leaping to conclusions, no trial and jury, no pity, nothing.

Hell, he didn't know why that surprised him. She never did the expected. She was the warmest, most compassionate, understanding woman he'd ever met.

"Did you need something there?" she asked.

And she was also one of the most curious.

"Why don't you just ask me what you really want to know, Mallory?"

"Okay." She drew a deep breath. "Are you an addict, too?"

Unable to resist, he again stroked his thumb over that spot at the base of her neck before slipping his hand into his pocket to finger the ever-present Vicodin bottle. It was a light weight. Empty. And both those things reassured him. He'd fucked up plenty, but at least not with that. "Damn close," he said.

"Oh," she breathed, and nodded. "I see."

No, she didn't. But that was his fault. "After the plane crash, I wasn't exactly the best of patients. I was on heavy meds. A wreck, basically."

"You'd just lost your team," she said softly.

Something warm unfurled in him at that. She was defending him. To *himself*. "When I went back to work, I gave up the meds." He paused, remembering. "It sucked. Christ, it sucked bad. I liked the oblivion, too damn much."

Her eyes were on his, absorbing his words, taking it all in without judgment. So he gave her the rest. "Six months ago, I got hurt again. In the ER they got me all nice and drugged up before I could refuse the meds."

Something flickered in her eyes, and he knew she was remembering how he'd refused drugs the night of the storm.

"Then I was released," he said. "With a 'take as needed' prescription. I found myself doing exactly that and living for the clock, for the minute I could take more. That's when I stopped refilling."

"You went cold turkey?"

"I never understood that saying, cold turkey," he said with a grim smile. "It's more like *hot hell*, but yeah." He blew out a breath. "And I still crave it."

She was quiet a moment. "I think the craving part is normal. We all have our cravings. I gave up chocolate once. The cravings *sucked*."

He choked out a laugh. Christ, he liked her. A whole

hell of a lot. What was he supposed to do with that? "I don't think it's exactly the same."

"True. I mean, I can't be arrested for hoarding chocolate cake," she said. "But it ruins my life. Costs money. And it makes my scrubs tight. You know how bad that is, when your drawstring pants are too tight? Pretty damn bad, Ty."

He was smiling now. He rocked back on his heels and studied her. "You're looking pretty damn good from where I'm standing."

"Because I only let myself have it once a week. Or whenever Amy calls. She's a very bad influence."

"Still crave, huh?" he asked with genuine sympathy.

"I'd give up my next breath for a piece of cake right now," she said with deep feeling. She sighed, as if with fond memories. "I think it helps to keep busy. Distracted. I know that much."

"I've been distracted plenty," he said, and her cheeks flamed. He loved that she could initiate sex in a storage room above about five hundred of her closest friends and family and *still* blush.

"Were you working on a car?" she asked. "I heard you're the new go-to mechanic guy."

"I was working before I showered."

"Show me?"

"The shower? Sure. I might have used all the hot water though."

She gave him a little laugh and a shove that took him back a step. He could have stood his ground but he liked the way she was letting her hands linger on his chest. He took one of those hands and guided her through to the kitchen and out the back door to the garage.

She looked around, taking in the cars and the slew of tools scattered across the work table. "What were you doing?"

"Brake line work on my Shelby."

"Show me," she said again.

"You want to learn how to put in new stainless steel brake lines," he said, heavy on the disbelief. "Mallory, those shoes aren't meant for working on a car."

"What are they meant for?"

"Messing with a man's head."

She smiled. "Are they working?"

"More than you can possibly imagine. Listen, this car shit, it's messy."

"So?" she asked, sounding amused, and he had to admit she had a point. She saw blood and guts and probably worse every single day. A little dirt wasn't going to bother her. Shaking his head at himself, he popped the hood. He grabbed a forgotten sweatshirt off the bench and handed it to her.

"I'm not cold."

His gaze slid to her breasts. Her nipples were poking at the material of her halter top. If she wasn't cold, then she was turned on. It would seem hard to believe since he hadn't touched her, but every time they got within five feet of each other he got a jolt to the dick, so who was he to say? "It's to keep your clothes from getting dirty." He pulled the sweatshirt over her head, unable to stop himself from touching as much of her as possible as he tugged it down her torso, only slightly mollified to hear her breathing hitch.

Yeah. They were on the same page.

The sweatshirt came to her thighs. She pushed back the hood. "It smells like you."

He felt that odd pain in his chest again, an ache that actually had nothing to do with wanting to get her naked. "And now it's going to smell like *you*," he said.

"Is that okay?"

It was so far beyond okay he didn't have words. Fucking sap. He kicked over the mechanic creeper, then his backup, and gestured her onto it. When they were both flat on their backs, she grinned at him. "Now what?"

"Under the car."

She slid herself beneath the car, and he joined her. Side by side, they looked up at the bottom of the chassis.

"What's first?" she asked.

He looked at her sweet profile. What was first? Reminding himself that he'd been cleared to leave Lucky Harbor. He handed her a roll of brake line. "You bend it to fit the contours of the frame as you go." He pointed out the route, and she began to work the brake line.

"It's peaceful," she said. "Under here."

He slid her a sideways look, and she laughed at him. No one ever laughed at him, he realized. Well, except for Matt, and Matt didn't look cute while doing it either.

"I'm serious," Mallory said, still smiling. "You don't think so?"

It was dirty, grimy, stuffy... and yeah. Peaceful. "I'm just surprised you think so."

"You don't think I can enjoy getting dirty once in awhile?" She bit her lower lip and laughed. "Okay, you know what I mean."

"Yeah. Here—" She wasn't able to put enough muscle into bending the line so he put his hands over hers and guided her. "Unravel another foot or so."

"'kay." She frowned, eyeing the space. "How long is that?"

"Like nine inches. I need twelve." He paused. "Twelve inches would be great."

He felt her gaze, and he did his best to look innocent, but she didn't buy it. "What the hell would you do with twelve inches?" she wanted to know.

He waggled a brow. "Plenty."

She shook her head. "Like you aren't lethal enough with what you have," she said, making him laugh.

They worked the brake line in companionable silence for a few moments, but Mallory didn't do silence all that well. "What do you think about under here?" she asked. "Besides your...inches?"

He smiled, but the truth was, he usually tried like hell not to think at all. "Sometimes I think about my dad."

"He was a Navy mechanic, too, right? He taught you all this stuff?"

Ty's dad had been a mechanic in the Navy, but not Ty. Yet correcting the misconception now, telling her that he'd once been a SEAL medic, wasn't something he wanted to get into. It was far easier to deny that part of himself rather than revisit it. "My dad didn't want me to learn mechanics, actually. He wanted more for me. I think he hoped that if he kept me away from anything mechanical, I'd become a lawyer or something like that."

"And...?"

"And when I was fourteen, he bought a Pontiac GTO." He smiled at the memory. "A '67. God, she was sweet."

"She?" Mallory teased, turning her face to his. She was so close he reached out and stroked a rogue strand of hair from her temple, tucking it behind her ear.

"Yeah, she," he said. "Cars are always a she. And do you want to hear this story or not?"

"Very much." She nudged her shoulder to his. "Every single detail."

"I took apart the engine."

"Oh my God," she said on a shocked laugh. "Was he mad?"

"It was a classic, and it was in mint condition. *Mad* doesn't even begin to cover what he was."

She stared at him, eyes wide. "Why did you do it?"

He shrugged. "I couldn't help myself. I liked to take things apart and then put them back together again. Only I couldn't. I had no idea what I was doing." Ty could still remember the look on his father's face: utter and complete shock at the empty engine compartment, horror that his baby had been breached and violated, and then sheer fury. "I can still feel the sweat trickling down the back of my spine," he said, shaking his head. "I hadn't meant to take it so far. I'd just kept undoing and undoing..."

"What happened?"

"I was pretty sure he'd kick my ass."

She gasped. "He beat you?"

"Nah, he never laid a hand on me." Ty felt a smile curve his mouth. "Didn't have to. He was one scary son of a bitch. He'd talk in this low, authoritative voice that dared you to defy him. No one ever did that I know of."

"Not you?"

"*Hell* no."

She was grinning wide, and he shook his head at her. "What's so funny?"

"You," she said. "You're so big and bad. It's hard to imagine you scared of anything." She touched his jaw, cupping it in her palm and lightly running her thumb over his skin.

He hadn't shaved that morning, and he could hear the rasp of his stubble against the pad of her thumb. As she touched him, he watched the flecks in her eyes heat like gold.

"I like being under a car with you," she said.

Working on cars was his escape. Beneath a hood or a chassis was familiar ground, no matter what part of the world he was in or where he lay his head at night. It was his constant. A buffer from the shit.

And Mallory was a single-woman destruction crew, outmaneuvering him, letting herself right into his safety zone, and then into his damn heart while she was at it. Because no matter what bullshit he fed himself, he liked being here with her, too.

"You ever going to tell me what you *are* scared of?" she asked.

He let out a short laugh. "Plenty," he assured her.

Her eyes softened, and she slid her hand into the hair at the back of his neck, fisting lightly, bringing him a full-body shiver of pure pleasure.

"Such as?" she asked.

You, he nearly said.

And it would be God's truth.

"Tell me."

"I'm afraid of not living," he said. He rolled out from beneath the Shelby, then crouched beside Mallory's creeper, putting his hands on her ankles to yank her out, too.

Sitting up, she pushed her hair back and met his gaze. "Don't worry, Ty. I know."

"You know what?"

"That this isn't your real life, that you're just killing time with me until—"

He put his finger over her lips. "Mal—"

"No, it's okay," she said around his finger, wrapping her hand around his wrist. "You're not the small-town type. I know it."

And yet here he was. Free to go, but still here.

"Are we done working on the car?" she asked.

"Yeah." Her legs seemed endless in those jeans and fuck-me heels. "We're done working on the car."

"So I can teach you something about *my* work now?"

He took in her small but sexy smile and felt himself go hard. "What did you have in mind?"

"Ever play doctor?"

Chapter 15

There is nothing better than a good friend, except maybe a good friend with chocolate.

The next morning, Mallory woke to a disgruntled *meow*. It was Sweet Pea, letting the world know it was past time for breakfast.

When Mallory ignored this, the cat batted her on the forehead with a paw.

"Shh," Mallory said.

"*Meow.*"

Mallory stretched, her body sore. She hadn't been to the gym since her membership had expired a year ago, which left only one thing to attribute the soreness to.

Ty, and his own special brand of workout.

She sighed blissfully and rolled over. She hadn't gotten home until late. Or early, depending on how you looked at it. She'd have liked to stay at Ty's all night but that would have been too much.

Not for her. For *him*.

She'd promised him that this was a simple fling. No use in telling him she'd broken that promise. Besides, she was pretty sure he was more than just physically attracted to her as well, but she wasn't sure if *he* knew it.

She loved being with him. That was the bottom line. The only line. There were no preconceived notions on how she should behave. It was freeing, exhilarating.

Amazing.

And also unsettling. She was in the big girls' sandbox when she played with Ty, and she was going to get hurt. There was nothing she could do about that so she showered. When she went to the closet for her white athletic shoes, she sniffed, then wrinkled her nose. "Oh no, you didn't," she said to Sweet Pea.

Sweet Pea was in the middle of the bed, daintily washing her face. She had no comment.

"You *poo'd in my shoe*?"

Sweet Pea gave her a look that said "see if you come home that late again" and continued with her grooming.

"Two words," Mallory told the cat. "*Glue. Factory.*"

Sweet Pea didn't look worried, and with good reason. It was an empty threat, and they both knew it. Mallory cleaned up the mess, thankful Sweet Pea hadn't used her bad girl shoes. She flashed to Ty tossing her onto his bed in the shoes and nothing else... Yeah. She was going to bronze those suckers.

She grabbed her phone off her nightstand and headed out her front door to get to work.

Joe was in her driveway, head under her opened hood. "Hey," he said. "Who did your alternator?"

"No one. What are you doing? You said you were busy."

"And now I'm not. I picked up a new alternator for you this morning, but someone beat me to it."

"What?" She stepped off the front porch and took a peek at the thing he was pointing out, the one shiny, clean part in the whole car.

"See?" Joe said. "Brand new alternator. Maybe it was Garrison."

"Why would you think that?"

"Because he helped this guy...Ryan, I think...get a job at the welding shop. And Ryan told me you're seeing Garrison."

Ty had gotten Ryan a job. Everything in her softened at the thought of Ty caring that much, and she wondered if it was too soon to go back over there. She'd wear her heels again. And maybe a trench coat and nothing else...

"Hel*lo*," Joe said, irritated.

"What?"

"Are you seeing Garrison or not? Would he have done this for you?"

Mallory flashed back to finding Ty in her driveway in the middle of the night. She'd never questioned what he'd been doing here, figuring it had been about sex. She hadn't minded that; she'd wanted him, too, but she got a little warm fuzzy that it hadn't been about *just* sex.

She had no explanation for last night, which had been all her own doing. She'd have to tell Amy that she was right: bad girl shoes were awesome. Amy loved to be right.

She drove to work with the smile still on her face. She'd parked and was just getting out of the car when her phone vibrated. Odd, because she'd have sworn she'd set it to ring. Pulling it out of her pocket, she didn't even attempt to see the screen in the bright morning sun before she answered with a simple "Hello?"

There was a long beat of silence and then, "Who the hell are you and where the hell is Ty?"

Mallory blinked at the very sexy, snooty female voice sounding damn proprietary, then said, "Who is this?"

"I asked first. Oh, for fuck's sake. Just put him on the phone. *Now*."

Oh hell no, Mallory thought, feeling a proprietariness of her own, even though on some level she'd known that Ty had to have other women in his life. It made perfect sense, but that didn't mean she liked how it felt.

"Fine, have it your way," the woman snapped. "Tell him Frances called. Make sure you tell him that it's important, do you understand?"

"How did you get this number?"

"Cookie, you don't want to go there. Now listen to me. I don't care how good you suck him, I've known him longer, I know him better, and I'm the only one of us who will know him by this time next week. Give him the damn message."

Click.

Mallory stared at the phone, realizing that it wasn't her phone at all. It was an iPhone just like hers, but the background was of only the date and a clock, not the picture of the beach she'd taken last week.

She had Ty's phone.

Mallory tried calling *her* phone but it went directly to voicemail, signaling that Ty had either turned it off or she'd run out of battery. She chewed on the situation for a minute, then punched out Amy's number. "It's me," she said. "I'm using someone else's phone. Life is getting nuts."

"Nuts is all relative on the Bad Girl scale."

"Is that right?" Mallory asked. "So where on that scale would you put getting yelled at by the ex of the guy I'm sleeping with?"

Dead silence. Then, "So the bad girl shoes worked?"

Mallory blew out a breath. "Yes. Now concentrate." She told Amy all about the call. "And really," she said. "I have no one but myself to blame. *I* wanted this one-time thing. I mean I wanted the second time too, *and* the third, but now—"

"Now you're in this, and you're worried that maybe you're in it alone."

Mallory's throat tightened. "Yeah. I mean three times. To me that's..."

"I know." Suddenly Amy wasn't sounding amused. "It's a relationship."

"And I'm pretty sure Ty's allergic to relationships."

Amy paused again. "Mallory, are you sure you haven't bitten off more than you can chew?"

Mallory choked out a laugh. "*Now*? You think to ask me this now? *You* started this. You egged me on with the list of Mr. Wrongs! Hell, yes, I've bitten off more than I can chew!"

"Okay," Amy soothed. "We can fix this. You'll just downgrade to a *less* Mr. Wrong. Someone easier to drag around by his twig and berries, you know?"

Yeah, but she didn't want just anyone's twigs and berries. "Look, I'm at work. We'll have to obsess over this later. Have cake waiting. I'm going to need it."

"Will do, babe."

Mallory clicked off and went into the hospital.

Five minutes into her shift, Jane called her into her

office. "Two things," her boss said cryptically, giving nothing away. "First up." She laid a piece of paper on her desk, facing Mallory. It was a receipt for a sizeable amount.

"Anonymous donation," Jane said. "For HSC."

"My God." Mallory sank to a spare chair. "Am I looking at all those zeroes correctly?"

"Yes," Jane said. "And they're all very pretty."

Mallory's eyes jerked up to Jane's. "Did you just make a joke?"

"Tell anyone, and I'll skin you." Jane let out a rare smile but it was fleeting. "Nicely done."

"How do you know I had anything to do with this?" Mallory asked, still astonished.

Jane gave an impressive eye roll. "Mallory, without you, there would be no HSC. Even *with* you, it's barely there, and it's on tentative footing. Someone you know or talked to donated this money."

Mallory absorbed that a moment. "Someone I know? I don't *know* anyone with a spare 10K."

"Don't you?"

"You're not talking about Ty," Mallory said, but Jane's eyes said that's exactly who she was talking about. "He already donated money for the Vets' program," Mallory protested. "Besides, he doesn't have this kind of money. But truthfully, she had no idea what Ty had or didn't have. *Ten thousand dollars* . . . "Why would he—"

"Don't ask me that," Jane said quietly. "Because honestly, Mallory? I don't want to know why he'd give you so much money for a Health Services Clinic in a town he has no ties to, a place he apparently plans on leaving very soon."

"Not me," Mallory said. "He didn't give the money to me. He gave it to HSC. If it was even him."

"Hmm," was all Jane said to this. She paused. "I really don't like to delve into my employees' private lives, but..."

Oh boy. "But...?"

"But since yours is being discussed over the water cooler, it's unavoidable. You're dating a man who no one knows anything about."

Well, technically, there was little "dating" involved. She was flat out boinking him. "No disrespect, Jane, but I really don't see how this affects my job."

"Whether he was the anonymous donor or not, he's been seen socializing with known drug addicts. And he yelled at two aides in the cafeteria."

Mallory's temper was usually non-existent but it flared to life at Jane's cavalier description of Ryan. "That's not quite how either of those two events went down," she said as evenly as she could. "Ty's involved in the Vets' program. He and Ryan connected because of their military backgrounds, and Ty's been helping him, giving him rides and bringing him food." Which she only knew because Lucille had told her, and thinking about it *still* melted her heart. She also knew about the hospital cafeteria incident, thanks to Lucille. "As for the radiation techs, they were just downright rude, so—"

"My point," Jane said, "is that you're not just an employee now. You're *running* the HSC. You're in a position that requires a certain public persona, and you have no one to blame but yourself for that one. You chose this, Mallory, so you have to understand that certain aspects of your life are now up for scrutiny. You have a moral and financial obligation to live up to that scrutiny."

Mallory was having a hard time swallowing this. "Are you saying I can't have a private life?"

"I'm saying that private life can't conflict with your public life. You can't date a man who might need the services HSC provides, wrong as that sounds. You just can't."

The words rang through Mallory's head for the next few hours as she dealt with her patients. She had a vomiter—oh joy—a teenager who'd let her new tattoo get infected, and an eight-months-pregnant woman who ate a jar of pickles and put herself into labor with gas pains.

Alyssa was little to no help. She was far too busy flirting with that cute new resident doctor, hoping to score a date for her night off. All of Alyssa's patients kept hailing Mallory down, until finally she physically yanked Alyssa away from the new resident and reminded her that she had actual work to do.

Mallory pretty much ran ragged until there was finally a lull. She used the rare quiet time to sit at the nurses' station and catch up on charting.

"Mallory!"

She looked up to find one of her patients, Jodi Larson, standing there beaming from ear to ear. Jodi was ten years old, a leukemia patient, and one of Mallory's all-time favorite people. She'd been in for her six-month check, and given the smile also on Jodi's mom's face behind her, the news had been good.

"Officially in remission," Jodi said proudly.

Jodi's mom's eyes were shining brilliantly as she nodded affirmation of the good news. Thrilled, Mallory hugged them both tight, and Jodi presented her with a plate of cookies. "Chocolate chip and walnut. I baked them just for you."

They hugged again, then Mallory got paged and had to go. It turned out the page was from her own mother.

"Mallory," Ella whispered, dragging her daughter into a far, quiet corner. "People are talking about how you were seen driving home at 3:20 in the morning. Why do I have a daughter coming home that late? Nothing good happens that late, Mallory. Nothing."

Oh, for the love of God. "Actually, it was only 2:30, so your source is dyslexic." And pretty damn annoying, but Mallory didn't bother to say so. Her mother had a point and she was winding up for it.

"You were with *that* man," Ella said.

Uh huh, and there it was. Mallory's left eye began to twitch. "That man has a name."

"Cute Guy."

"A *real* name."

Her mother's lips tightened. "Yes, I believe The Facebook is calling him *Mysterious* Cute Guy."

Mallory put a finger to her twitching eye. "Okay, for the last time, it's not *The* Facebook, it's just *Facebook*."

"Honey, please. It's time you came to your senses. You're going to end up as wild and crazy as Joe and Tammy, and that's not who you are."

"Mom, Joe is only twenty-four. He's not ready to settle down, so a little wild and crazy is okay. And Tammy is settled down in her own wild and crazy way. Maybe it's not what you wanted for her but she's adjusted and happy. What's wrong with being like them?"

Her mom's mouth tightened. "That's not what I mean, and you know it."

"No," Mallory agreed quietly, her chest tight. "That isn't what you mean, and I do know it. You're talking about Karen."

"No, we're not."

"Well, we should."

Her mother closed her eyes and turned away. "I have to go."

"She started dating a guy no one knew."

"I don't want to talk about this, Mallory!"

"He encouraged her to take a walk on the wild side, and—"

"*Don't*," Ella said stiffly. "Don't you—"

"And she changed. She stopped being who you thought she should be. And—"

Her mother whirled back, eyes blazing, finger pointed shakily in Mallory's face. "Don't you *dare* say it."

"Mom," Mallory said through a tight throat, suddenly *very* tired. "It's not the same this time. You know it's not the same for me. Karen was doing drugs."

"Your young man went to NA."

Mallory shook her head in disbelief. "That's *confidential*."

"It's Lucky Harbor," Ella said with a shrug that said Ty's privacy was nothing compared to her need to make sure her daughter was okay. "Remember that stormy night, when he ended up in the ER? He refused narcotics for pain. *Adamantly*."

"So?"

"Don't play dumb, Mallory. You know what I'm saying. He's an outsider, and I realize that sounds rude, but you've got to admit people are getting the wrong idea about you two."

Actually, given what she and Ty had been doing in the deep, dark of the night—and sometimes in the middle of the day—people had the exact *right* idea.

Ella took one look at Mallory's face and got a pinched look of tension. "See? It's happening. It's happening again, just like Karen with Tony."

"No," Mallory said firmly. God, no. "Tony got Karen both hooked and then pregnant, and she spiraled downward. I can't believe we're comparing my life to Karen's now, after all these years. Why not back then, when I *was* in danger of spiraling?"

Her mother looked as if Mallory had slapped her. "You... you weren't. You were our rock."

Mallory let out a breath and shook her head, feeling weary to the bone. And sad. Way too damn sad. "Forget it, Mom."

"I can't. Oh my God." She covered her face. "I thought—you were so sweet during that time. I never thought—Oh, Mallory. I'm so sorry. Are you... spiraling again?"

Mallory drew a shaky breath and stepped forward, putting her hands on her mom's arms. "No," she said gently. "I'm not spiraling again. I'm not going to kill myself, Mom." The big, fat elephant in the room. "I'm not Karen."

Ella nodded, and with tears in her eyes, hugged Mallory in tight. "I know," she whispered. Then, in the Quinn way of bucking up, she sniffed and pulled back to search her pockets, coming up with a tissue that she used to swipe her eyes. "You're really okay?"

"Really," Mallory promised.

"So can I have my sweet daughter back?"

A low laugh escaped Mallory. "I'm still sweet, Mom. I'm just not going to be amenable all the time, or compliant. And I'm not going to live my life exactly as you'd have me do."

"Are you going to keep seeing that man?"

Lucille walked by in her candy-striper uniform. "Well, I hope so," she said. "He's the hottest thing you've dated since...well, ever."

"Don't encourage her," Ella said. "This isn't just a silly thing. It's affecting her job."

"Phooey," Lucille said.

"Jane is concerned about it affecting the HSC as well."

"Phooey," Lucille said again. "And shame on you, Ella, for buying into that. It's about time our girl here stops paying for others' mistakes and regrets, don't you think?"

Ella turned and looked at Mallory for a long beat, seeming stricken by the thought of anyone thinking she wasn't fully supporting her own flesh and blood. "I never wanted you to pay for our mistakes and regrets."

"Well, she has," Lucille said, brutally honest as always, though her voice was very kind. She moved behind the nurses' desk, poured Ella some coffee, pulled a flask from her pocket, and added a dash of something that smelled 100 proof.

"Lucille!" Ella gasped. "I'm on the job!"

"You're clocking out, and it's time."

"Time for what?"

"Time for Mallory to not be the only one to stretch her wings. And speaking of wings," Lucille said to Mallory, "you're going to need wings for your next patient, and she's ready for you."

The new patient turned out to be Mrs. Burland.

"You," Mrs. B said when Mallory entered her room.

"Me," Mallory agreed and reached for the blood pressure cuff. "It says on your chart that you passed out after your bath again. Did you take your meds at the right time?"

"Well, of course I did. I'm not a complete idiot. They didn't work."

"Did you space the pills out with food, as explicitly instructed on the bottles?"

Mrs. Burland glared at her.

"I'll take that as a no," Mallory said. Mrs. B's color was off, and her blood pressure was far too low. "When was your last meal?"

"Hmph."

"Mrs. Burland." Mallory put her fingers on the woman's narrow, frail, paper-thin wrist to check her pulse. "Did you eat lunch today?"

Mrs. Burland straightened to her full four-foot-eight inches, quivering with indignity. "I know what I'm supposed to be doing."

Mallory looked into her rheumy, pissy eyes and felt her heart clench. *Dammit.* She had a feeling she knew the problem—Mrs. B didn't have any food. Probably she wasn't feeling good enough to take care of herself, and since she'd long ago scared off family and friends with her mean, petty, vicious ways, she had no one to help her. Mallory picked up the room phone and called the cafeteria. "Stella, it's Mallory. I need a full dinner tray for room three."

"Sure thing, Sweet Cheeks. Is your hunk-o-burning love going to be making any more visits my way?"

Mallory rubbed her still-twitching eye. "Not today."

When the tray came, Mallory stood over her grumpy patient. "Eat."

Mrs. Burland tried to push the tray away but Mallory was one step ahead of her, holding it still. "Oh no, you don't. You're not going to have a little tantrum and spill it, not this time."

Mrs. Burland's eyes burned bright with temper, which Mallory was happy to see because it meant her patient was already feeling better. Mallory leaned close. "I'm stronger and meaner, and *I've* eaten today."

"Well *that's* obvious." Mrs. Burland sniffed at the juice on the tray. "Hmph."

"It's apple."

"I have eyes in my head, don't I?" Mrs. Burland sipped the juice. In sixty seconds, her color was better. "You didn't used to be so mean."

"It's a newly acquired skill," Mallory said.

"I'm ready to go home now."

"You can't go home until I see you eat."

"You're making that up. This cafeteria food isn't fit for a dog," Mrs. Burland said.

Well, she had her there. Even Mallory, who'd eat just about anything, didn't like the cafeteria food, not that she'd ever say so to the cook. "Fine." Mallory went to the staff kitchen and pulled out her own lunch, which she brought back to Mrs. Burland's room. "Try my sandwich. Turkey and cheese with spinach." Which she'd only added because her mom kept asking if she was eating her vegetables. "There's a little bit of mustard and probably too much mayo but your cholesterol is the least of your problems." Mallory also tossed down a baggie of baby carrots and an apple.

Mrs. Burland took a bite of the sandwich first. *"Awful,"* she said, but took another bite. And then another, until there was nothing left but a few crumbs.

"The carrot sticks and the apple too," Mallory said.

"Are they as horrid as the sandwich?"

"They're as horrid as your bad attitude. And I'll tell you this right now. You're going to eat it all if I have to shove it down your throat myself."

"Mallory," a voice breathed in disbelief from the doorway.

Jane. *Perfect.* Mallory turned to face her boss, but not before she saw triumph and evil glee come into Mrs. Burland's eyes.

"A moment," Jane said, face tight.

"Certainly." Mallory jabbed a finger at the carrots and apple. Mrs. Burland meekly picked up the apple.

In the hallway, Jane led Mallory just out of hearing range of Mrs. Burland. "New tactic?"

"Yes," Mallory said, refusing to defend herself. "She finish it all?"

Jane took a look over Mallory's shoulder at Mrs. B. "Every last bite. How did you do it?"

"By being a bigger bitch than she is."

"Nicely done."

By the time Mallory got in her car and left work, she was starving and exhausted. She solved the first problem by eating a handful of Jodi's cookies. Then she pulled her phone out and took a quick peek to see if she had any texts before remembering she had Ty's phone. She paused and eyed the remaining chocolate chip/walnut cookies. Fifteen minutes later, she pulled into Ty's driveway.

The garage door was open, and the man himself was

flat on his back beneath his car, one long denim-clad leg straight out, the other bent. His black T-shirt had risen up. Or maybe it was his Levi's that had sunk almost indecently low on his hips. In either case, the revealed strip of his washboard abs had her mouth actually watering. She thought maybe she could stand here and just look at him all day long, but he seemed to enjoy looking at her right back and she'd had a hell of a long day and couldn't possibly be worth looking at right now.

Not that it appeared to make any difference. Ty's attraction to her was apparently based on some intangible thing she couldn't fathom. She knew she could think about that for a million years and not get used to it, to the fact that no matter what she did or what she looked like, he seemed to want her.

The feeling was far too mutual.

Chapter 16

Nothing chocolate, nothing gained.

Ty sat up on the mechanic's creeper and took in the sight of Mallory standing there. She was packing a plate of cookies, which he hoped to God were for him. He assumed she'd discovered the phone fiasco by now, but other than that, he wasn't sure what sort of mood to expect from her.

The last time he'd seen her, she'd been face down on his bed, boneless and sated right into a coma of bliss. He'd stroked a strand of damp hair from her face and she'd smiled in her sleep. His heart had constricted at the sight, his sole thought, *oh Christ, I am in trouble.* He'd been torn by the urge to tug her close, but then claustrophobia had reached up and grabbed him by the throat. Just as he'd chosen retreat, she'd awakened and gotten dressed to go.

That must have been when she'd grabbed the wrong phone, although he hadn't realized it then. He'd followed her home to make sure she got there safely, then driven back to his place and expected to crash. Instead he'd missed her.

Clearly he was losing it.

He had no idea what she was thinking, but he hadn't expected to see her smile at the sight of him, a smile that was filled with relief.

Relief, he realized, and surprise that he was still here in town.

Yeah, join my club. He was surprised, too.

She was in pale purple scrubs and white Nikes. She had two pens sticking out of her hip pocket, one red, one black. There were correlating ink marks on her scrubs. She followed his gaze and rubbed at the stains. "I'm a mess. Don't ask."

"Not a mess," he said. "Are those cookies?"

"Yes. And I had to fight the staff to keep them for you."

"Girl-on-girl fight?" he asked hopefully. "Did you get it on video?"

"You are such a guy." She came closer and crouched at his side, holding the plate out for him. He took a big bite of a cookie and moaned in deep appreciation.

"Did you give the HSC ten thousand dollars?"

Ah, there it was, he thought, swallowing. He'd been hoping she wouldn't find out, but he supposed that was unrealistic in a town like Lucky Harbor. Taking his time, he ate cookie number two, then reached for a third.

She held the plate out of his reach. "Did you?" she asked.

He eyed her for a long moment. "Which answer will get me the rest of the cookies?"

"Oh, Ty," she breathed, looking worried as she lowered the plate. Worried for him, he realized.

"Why?" she asked. "You already gave."

"HSC needed it."

"But it's *so* much money."

"If you're asking if I can afford it, I can."

She just stared at him, so he shrugged. "The job pays well." He paused. "Really well."

She let out a breath. She was already hunkered at his side so it took little effort to lean over toward him and press a kiss to his cheek. "Thank you," she whispered, and went to kiss the other cheek, but he turned his head and caught her mouth with his. They were both gratifyingly out of breath by the time he pulled back.

"You're welcome," he said, surprised when she rose and sat on the stool at his work bench.

"Don't let me keep you from what you were doing," she said. "I'll watch."

He arched a brow, feeling amused for the first time all day. "You want me to get back under the car?"

"I just don't want you to lose any time because of me."

"Is that right?"

"Absolutely."

Humoring the both of them, he lay back down onto the mechanic's creeper and lifted his hands above his head to the edge of the car.

She nibbled on her lower lip. Watching him work turned her on. The knowledge shouldn't have surprised him—she turned him on just breathing, but he laughed softly.

She blushed. "How did you know?"

"Your nipples are hard."

She made a sound in the back of her throat and covered her breasts, making him laugh.

"It's your jeans," she said. "They're faded at your, um." She waggled a finger in the direction of his crotch. "Stress spots. And your T-shirt, it's tight on your biceps and shoulders. And when you're flat on your back under the car, you look like you know what you're doing."

"That's because I do."

"It's the whole package," she agreed miserably.

He grinned. "If it helps, my *package* likes your package. A whole hell of a lot."

"Work!" she demanded, closing her eyes.

Obliging, he rolled back beneath the car. He heard her get to her feet and walk close, peering into the opened hood above him. "So how much wrenching do you do at your work?"

She was as see-through as glass. He knew that she'd put him back beneath the car because she'd gotten him to talk beneath a car before. But she was so goddamned cute trying to outthink him that he gave her what she wanted.

Which in hindsight made her a hell of lot more dangerous than he'd thought. "I hotwired a tank once," he said. "With my team. We stole it to disable rebel insurgents."

She squatted at his side. "You've led a very different life than mine." Her hand settled on his bad thigh. It'd been only recently that he'd even gotten feeling back in it, but he was having no trouble feeling anything now. It felt like her fingers had a direct line to his groin, and things stirred to life.

"Our phones got switched," she said.

There was a new quality to her voice now, one that had him setting down his wrench and pulling himself back out from beneath the car.

She was still crouched low, and from his vantage point

flat on his back, he looked up into her face. As usual, she could hide nothing from him, and for once, he wished he couldn't see her every thought. They exchanged phones but her expression didn't change. "Problem?" he asked.

"A woman called. Frances? She wants you to call her."

"She always wants me to call her."

Mallory nodded, looked down at the ground and then back into his eyes. "Are you dating her?"

"I'm not much of a dater."

"You know what I mean."

Yeah, he did. And he didn't want to go there.

"I know," she said quickly. "We agreed that this thing with you and me was...casual."

He didn't like where this was going.

"A fling," she went on. "Right? Not a relationship." She rose and turned away from him. "But I was thinking that maybe that last part isn't true. I mean, we never actually said there *wasn't* a relationship."

"I'll say it," he said. "It's not a relationship."

She went still, turning back to stare at him with those eyes he'd never once been able to resist. "Why is that?" she asked. "Why can't there be an us, if there's a you and a someone else?"

He looked into her expressive face and felt a stab of pain right in the gut. He'd survived SEAL training. He'd lived through a plane crash. He'd kept on breathing when the rest of his team, his friends, his brothers, hadn't been able to do the same. But he didn't know how to do this. "There are some things I can't tell you," he said slowly. "Things that even if I wanted to, I couldn't."

"So the reason we can't be a *we* is classified?" she asked in disbelief. "Really, Ty?"

Well, hell. Yeah, that had been pretty fucking lame. Chalk it up to the panic now residing in his hollow gut. Whatever he did here, whatever he came up with, he needed her to want to keep her distance. Except Mallory Quinn was incapable of distance when her heart was involved. That was both painfully attractive and terrifying. "Don't fall for me, Mallory. That wouldn't be good for either of us. We're too different. You said so yourself."

She sucked in a breath like he'd slapped her. "And what, you and Frances are alike? Compatible?"

"Unfortunately, yes."

Hands on hips, she narrowed her eyes. "If you're sleeping with her, then why wouldn't she just roll over and talk to you? Why is she yelling about you not returning her phone calls?"

"Frances doesn't yell."

"*Strongly* suggested then," she said with mock politeness. She paused. "You're not sleeping with her."

Gig up. "I'm not sleeping with her. And as for the why she's pissed, there are a variety of reasons. I haven't seen her in six months, for one."

She stared at him, then turned away again.

Ty rose to his feet and walked around her to see her face. "Get the rest out," he said. "Let's finish this."

A wry smile twisted her mouth. "You aren't familiar with the Quinn pattern of holding onto a good mad, I see."

"Holding onto your mad only tortures *you*," he pointed out. "If you're mad at me, let me have it."

"Are you always so logical?" With a sigh, she shook her head. "Never mind. Don't answer that." She put a finger to her eye. "Damn twitch," she muttered to herself, then looked at him, chin up. "I snooped in your phone."

"I would expect nothing less from Walking-On-The-Wild-Side Mallory."

"I thought about not telling you. But stealth isn't one of my special talents."

"You have other special talents," he said, and made her laugh.

"Dammit," she said. "I don't want to laugh with you right now."

Lifting a hand, he wrapped it around the nape of her neck and drew her in. "You need some more time to be mad at me?"

"Yes."

"Let me know when you're about done." He knew he had no right to touch her, crave her like air, but he did both. And when he put his mouth on hers, he recognized the taste of her, like she'd been made for just him. Which made him far more screwed than he'd even imagined.

But suddenly she was pulling free, shaking her head. "Ty—I can't."

"You can't kiss and be mad at me at the same time?"

"Oh, I can do that. What I can't do is this. I can't do this and keep it…not real."

"It's real."

"Yes, but real for you means an erection. For me, it means…" She rubbed her chest as if it hurt and closed her eyes. "Never mind." She took a step back and then another. "I'm sorry, this really is my fault. I shouldn't have—"

"Mallory—"

"No, it's okay. Really. But I'm going now."

He watched her get into her car and drive off. Yeah, he thought, definitely time to go back to work. Past time.

Mallory parked behind her brother's truck in her mother's driveway.

Dinner with the Quinns.

It'd been a full day since she'd left Ty standing in his garage, hot and dirty and looking a little baffled, like maybe he'd lost his copy of the rule book for their little game.

But even though she'd started the game in the first place, she no longer wanted to play. Somewhere along the way, her heart had flipped on her. She could pretend to be a bad girl all she wanted. It was only an illusion. The truth was, she needed more than just sex. And that really pissed her off about herself.

And what pissed her off even more was how much she already missed him.

Her mother was in the kitchen pulling a roasted chicken out of the oven. It looked perfect. Mallory wouldn't even know where to begin to make food that looked like that and she sniffed appreciatively.

"Did you bring the dessert?" her mother asked. "That cake you brought to Joe's birthday party was amazing. I had no idea you were so talented. Tell me you made another of those."

Mallory held out the tray of cupcakes she'd gotten from the B&B this morning. Tara had promised they were absolutely to die for. Mallory knew this to be true because she'd already inhaled two of them.

"A woman who can bake like this," her mom said,

"should have kids. I wouldn't mind some grandchildren."

"Mom."

"Just sayin'."

"Well, stop just sayin'."

Joe walked in and rumpled Mallory's hair. "Hey, think you can convince that cute new LN to go out with me?"

"No, Camilla's too good for you. And how do you know her?"

"I work with her brother at the welding shop. She brought him lunch."

"Stay away from Camilla," Mallory said.

Ella was shooing everyone to the table. "Joe, put your phone away. Oh, Mal, I almost forgot. Tammy wanted me to ask if you'd take Alyssa's shift this weekend so she and Tammy can have a girl's night out."

Mallory grabbed two rolls. "Can't."

Ella took one roll back. "You'll hate yourself in the morning. And why can't you take the shift?"

"I'm working at the HSC this weekend."

"Both days?"

"No, but I need a day off."

Ella blinked. "You never say no. You're always so good about helping everyone."

Oh how she hated that adjective applied to her—*good*.

Joe grinned and took two rolls without comment from Ella, the skinny rat-fink bastard. "I don't think Mallory likes being called *good*, Mom."

"Of course she does. Why wouldn't she?"

Right. Why wouldn't she...

She escaped as soon as dinner was over. Her family was...well, her family. She loved them but they had no idea how much their opinion of her wore her down, that she yearned for so much more, that she wanted to be seen. Seen for herself.

Ty saw her for herself.

Too bad he didn't see her as someone he wanted in his life.

She was halfway home when her phone rang. She pulled over and answered Amy's call.

"You see Facebook lately?"

Mallory's heart sank. "What now?"

"Someone caught a picture of you and Ty in what looks like the hospital parking lot. He was...under your hood."

Oh boy. "Tell me you really mean that. And not as some sort of euphemism."

"The picture is hot, Mal. No one can deny that you don't look good together."

"We're *not* together. And what the hell are we doing in the picture?"

"Kissing. And he's got a hand on your ass. They've relabeled him from Mysterious Cute Guy to Good-With-His-Hands Guy."

"Oh, God."

"And Mal?"

"Yeah?"

"I think you're ready to teach your own Bad Girl Lessons now."

Mallory thunked her head on the steering wheel.

"Oh, and chocoholics unite tomorrow. I'm getting a chocolate cake from Tara. It's got yours, Grace's, and my name on it. *You've* got a story to tell."

"So do you. I want to hear more about this thing with Matt—"

"There's no 'thing.'"

"Amy—"

"Sorry, bad connection. Must be going through a tunnel."

"You're at the diner!"

"Oh, well then it must be something I don't want to discuss." And she disconnected.

Mallory shook her head and got back on the road, hitting the gas hard. She wanted to see that Facebook pic. Two blocks from home, red and blue lights flashed in her rearview mirror.

Shit.

She pulled over, rolled down her window, and glared at Sheriff Sawyer Thompson as he ambled up to the side of her car. She and Sawyer had gone to high school together, though he'd been a couple of years ahead of her. She'd done his English papers, and he'd handled her math and science. Later, she'd patched him up several times when his wild, misspent youth had landed him on the injured list.

Then he'd settled down and become a sheriff of all things, now firmly entrenched on the right side of the law. There'd been a time when having the big, bad, sexy sheriff pull her over might have made her day. But that time wasn't now. "What?" she demanded a little crankily. "You don't have a bad guy to catch? You have to pull over people who are just trying to get home?"

"Give me a break, Mal. You were doing fifty-five in a thirty-five zone. I whooped my siren at you twice, and you never even noticed. What the hell's up with you?"

Crap. She sagged in her seat. "Nothing."

He shook his head and leaned against her car, apparently perfectly happy to take a break on her time. She sighed. "Long day?" she asked sympathetically.

"Yeah." He slid her a look. "But clearly not as long as yours."

"I'm fine."

"Is that right?" He pulled out his iPhone and thumbed his way to a page, then turned it to her.

Facebook.

A picture had indeed been posted, just as Amy had said. It was small and grainy but it was her. In Ty's arms.

With his hand on her ass.

She stared at herself. She had a dazed, dreamy smile on her face. Not Ty. His expression was possessive as he stared down at her hungrily, and she felt herself getting aroused all over again in spite of herself. This was quickly followed by a surge of her supposedly rare temper. "Are you *kidding* me?"

Sawyer slipped the phone back into his pocket.

"That's an invasion of privacy!" she said. "Arrest someone!"

"You were in a public place."

"I didn't know someone was taking pictures!"

"Obviously," Sawyer drawled, still leaning back against her car as if he had all day.

"I'm going to kick someone's ass."

His brow shot up at that. "You don't kick ass, Mal. You *save* people's asses."

"I'm over it! Give me my damn speeding ticket and get out of my way before I run your foot over."

Sawyer flashed a genuine grin now. "Are you threatening an officer?"

"My ticket, Sawyer."

"I'm not going to give you a ticket, Mallory."

"You're not?"

"Hell, no. If I gave you a ticket now, I'd get skinned alive by...well, everyone."

This was thankfully true. "That's never bothered you before." If she wasn't so mad, she might have found humor in this. "It's Chloe. Having a girlfriend has softened you up."

He grimaced. "I'm tempted to ticket you just for saying that."

She found a smile after all.

He returned it and leaned in her window, tugging on a strand of her hair. "Want some advice?"

"I want to run your foot over."

"You're not going to run me over, because then you'd have to give me first aid and you're not in the mood." But he stepped back, proving he wasn't just all good looks. "Slow down," he warned her and tugged on her hair again. "*Everywhere.*"

"What does that mean?"

"It means that I don't want to see you hurt."

Well, it was too damn late for that, wasn't it. She already hurt, thank you very much.

She blew out a breath and eased out into traffic. She was careful not to speed again, even with her phone going off every two seconds. She ignored all calls, parked in her driveway, watered Mrs. Tyler's flowers, watered her grandma's flowers, and fed Sweet Pea.

Some habits were hard to break.

She bent down to scratch the cat behind the ears and got bit for her efforts. Yeah, definitely some habits were hard to break. She walked straight through the house and out the back door. In the backyard, she headed to the sole lounge chair. Plopping down, she hit speaker on her phone and finally accessed the messages, squinting as she did, as if that would help not hear them.

"Mallory," Jane said in her Displeased Voice. "Call me."

No thank you. Clearly her boss had seen the picture. Just as clearly, she assumed that Mallory had ignored her warning. Mallory supposed she should call in and let Jane know that the picture had been taken before their "talk." Or that she was no longer seeing Ty. But tired of being the peacemaker, she hit delete.

"Wow, Mal," came the next message. Tammy. "You're one serious badass lately. If you find yourself heading to Vegas, make sure you buy the wedding package *without* the photos. You don't need any pics; this one is perfect."

Delete.

Third message. "Mallory, this is Deena. From the grocery store? Yeah, listen, I play Bunko with a group every Wednesday night, and this week we had a drawing for who could go for Cute Guy and I won. So you're going to need to back off. He's mine."

He's all yours, Deena.

Delete.

Sweet Pea bumped her head into Mallory's shin. This wasn't a show of love but a demand for more food. "You have no idea how good you have it, cat," she said with a sigh. "All you have to do is sleep for, what, eighteen hours a day? No pressure, no expectations. No Mysterious Cute Guys messing with your head, giving you mixed signals."

Except the mixed signals had been all hers. He'd been honest with her from the get-go. Well, if not exactly honest, he'd at least been up front.

Don't fall for me, Mallory. That wouldn't be good for either of us.

Right. She'd just stand firm and not fall.

Except...

Except she already had.

Chapter 17

What is the meaning of life? All evidence to date points to chocolate.

After a sleepless night, Mallory worked a long shift, then took a detour home by Mrs. Burland's house. Last night the HSC had hosted a healthy living seminar given by Cece Martin, the local dietician, and Mrs. Burland had promised to go. Mallory had looked over the sign-in sheet from the event but Mrs. B hadn't shown up.

Mallory pulled into Mrs. B's driveway. The yard was neglected, as was the house. With a bad feeling, Mallory got out of her car, grabbed the bag of groceries she'd picked up, and knocked at the front door.

No one answered.

Mallory knocked again, knowing that Mrs. B probably wouldn't open the door to her, but something definitely felt off. She wriggled the handle, and the door opened. "Mrs. Burland?" she called out. "It's me, Mallory Quinn."

"Go away."

The voice sounded feeble and weak and somehow arrogant at the same time. Ignoring the command, Mallory walked inside the dark house and flipped on a light.

Mrs. Burland lay on the scarred wood floor at the base of a set of stairs.

Mallory dropped everything in her hands and rushed to her, setting two fingers against Mrs. B's carotid artery to search out a pulse.

Strong.

Sagging back on her knees, she let out a breath of relief. "You got dizzy and fell down the stairs?"

"No, I like to nap here," Mrs. B snapped out. "I told you to go away. You have no right to be here."

Okay, so little Miss Merry Sunshine was stringing her words together just fine, with no obvious disorientation. It was her vasovagal syncope then. Mallory ran a hand down the older woman's limbs and found nothing obviously broken. "Can you stand?"

"Sure. I just chose to be the rug today," Mrs. B snapped. "Why the hell are you here? Don't you ever get tired of saving people? *Why do you do it?*"

"Well, in your case, I do it for your charming wit and sweet nature." And anyway, there weren't enough shrinks or enough time to cover why she really did it... "Can you sit up?"

Mrs. Burland slapped Mallory's hands away but didn't move.

Well, that answered that question. Mallory sat on the floor next to her and rifled through the bag of groceries she'd brought. "What's going to float your boat today? I've got soup, a sandwich, or—"

"Just go away! I'm old. I'm alone. I'm going to die any second now. Just *let me*."

"You're not old," Mallory said. "You're just mean. And FYI, *that's* why you're alone. You could have friends if you'd stop snapping at everyone. Lucille'd take you into her posse in an instant if you were even the slightest bit less evil. She *loves* snark."

"I'm *alone*."

"Hello," Mallory said. "I'm sitting right here! You're *not* alone. You have me." She pulled out a snack-sized box of apple juice. "Your favorite."

"Not thirsty."

"Then how about some chicken soup?"

Mrs. Burland showed another sign of life as a slight spark came into her eyes. "Is it from a can?"

"No," Mallory said. "I spent all day cooking it myself. After raising the chickens and growing the carrots and celery in my garden."

Mrs. Burland sniffed. "I don't eat soup out of a can."

"Fine." Mallory pulled out a bag of prunes.

Mrs. Burland snatched the bag and opened it with shaking fingers.

Mallory smiled.

"You're enjoying my misery?"

"I knew I'd get you with the prunes."

After a minute or two, with the sugar in her system, Mrs. B glared at Mallory. "I'd have been fine without you."

"Sure. You'd be even better if you took care of yourself."

"What do you know? You're not taking care of yourself either."

"What does that mean?"

"In a storage attic?" Mrs. Burland asked snidely, then snorted at Mallory's look of shock. "Yes, I heard about your little interlude. Someone caught your Mr. Garrison coming downstairs from the auction, and then you following him a few minutes later looking all telltale mussed up. Either you were practicing for a WWE tryout or you'd been having some hanky-panky. Don't think just because I'm old that I don't know these things. I remember hormones."

Oh good Lord.

"And what kind of a woman dates a man who takes her to a storage attic?" Mrs. B wanted to know.

A red-blooded one. Ty Garrison was *seriously* potent, and Mallory defied even the most stalwart of women to be able to deny herself a Ty-induced orgasm. Just thinking it made her ache, because in spite of herself, she missed him *way* too much. She hoped he missed her too, that he wasn't planning to fill the void with...*Frances.* "Actually," she said, "it's not really an attic, but more of a storage area. And we're not dating."

"So you're giving away the milk for free?"

"First of all, I'm not a cow," Mallory said. "And second of all, we're *not* discussing this."

"You're trying to save him, right? Like you try to save everyone? Surely even you realize that a man like that isn't interested in a small town nurse, not for the long term."

The jab hit a little close to home because it happened to be true. But Mallory wasn't trying to save Ty.

She wouldn't have minded keeping him, though... "Watch it," she said mildly. "Or the prunes come with me."

"Hmph."

They sat there on the floor for a few minutes longer while Mallory checked Mrs. Burland's vitals again, which were stronger now. Then she glanced up and nearly screamed.

Jack Nicholson from *The Shining* stood in the front doorway.

Or Mr. Wykowski. He stepped inside. "Louisa," he said quietly, eyes on Mrs. B. "You all right?"

The oddest thing happened. Right before Mallory's eyes, Mrs. Burland changed. She softened. She... *smiled*. Or at least that's what Mallory thought the baring of her teeth meant.

"Of course," Mrs. B said. "I'm fine."

"Liar," Mr. Wykowski said, squatting beside her. "You get dizzy again?"

"Of course not."

"*Louisa.*"

Mrs. Burland's eyes darted away. "Maybe a little. But only for a minute."

Mr. Wykowski nodded to Mallory. "Good of you to stop by. She doesn't make it easy. She hasn't figured out that we take care of our own here in Lucky Harbor."

Mallory smiled at him, knowing she'd never be afraid of him again. "It's good to know she's not *alone*." She shot Mrs. Burland a long look.

Mrs. Burland rolled her eyes, but shockingly not a single bitchy thing crossed her lips.

There were more footsteps on the front porch and then another neighbor appeared. Lucille. She was in a neon green track suit today, which wasn't exactly flattering on a body that gravity hadn't exactly been kind to. Her wrinkled lips were in pink. Her tennis shoes were black and yellow.

You needed a pair of sunglasses to look at her.

"There you are, Teddy," Lucille said, smiling at Mr. Wykowski. "Ready for that walk around the block?"

Mrs. Burland narrowed her gaze. "He was visiting with *me*."

Lucille put her hands on her hips. "You don't even like visitors."

"Out of my house."

Lucille smiled. "Make me."

Mrs. Burland narrowed her eyes.

Lucille held out her hand. "Need help getting up first?"

Mrs. Burland struggled up by herself, glaring triumphantly at Lucille when she did it. "I could beat you around the block if I wanted."

"Yeah?" Lucille sized her up. "Prove it."

"I'll do that." Mrs. Burland moved toward the door, where Mr. Wykowski carefully drew her arm into the crook of his. Then Lucille flanked Mrs. Burland's other side.

And the three of them walked out the door and around the block.

Mallory went home. She parked, watered Mrs. Tyler's flowers, her grandma's flowers, and then unlocked her front door. She glanced at the little foyer desk—as she had every time since Ty had shown her a whole new use for it—and sighed. There was chocolate cake in her immediate future. If she wasn't going to have wild, high-calorie-burning sex, she was going to have to resort to some exercise.

"Meow."

"I hear you." She fed Sweet Pea and then changed, forcing herself to the pier for a run.

The quarter of a mile down to the end nearly killed her so she walked back, holding the stitch in her side. When she came up on the ice cream stand, she slowed even more. Lance wasn't working today but his older brother Tucker was.

"Hey Cutie," Tucker called out. "I've got a chocolate double with your name on it. Literally. We just created a new list of specials. Number one is The Good Girl Gone Bad."

She gave him a long, dark look and he laughed. "Come on," he said. "It's funny."

Maybe to someone whose name wasn't Mallory Quinn.

"Want one?"

More than her next breath. "No."

He leaned out the window, all lean, easy grace as he took in her sweaty appearance. "Wow, turning down ice cream. And you're running." His smile spread. "You're on a diet, aren't you?"

She blew out a breath. "Just trying to get some exercise and be healthy."

"You look good to me," he said.

Aw. That was nice. She was thinking maybe he'd be a nice addition to the Mr. Wrong list, but then he said, "And whatshisface should tell you that in every attic he gets you into."

"Okay, first of all, it's a *storage area!*" And dammit. She was going to have to move. She went back to running. Without her ice cream.

It was the hardest thing she'd ever done.

She went home and glared at her foyer desk. "Somehow," she told it, "this is your fault."

The table had nothing to say in its defense.

"Fine. It's not your fault. It's Ty's." Her body ached for him, but it was more than that. Her mind ached for him, too.

Shaking her head at herself, she showered, got caught up in a *Charmed* season six marathon, and then headed over to Eat Me at the appointed time for a meeting of the Chocoholics.

As she entered Eat Me, the comforting sounds of people talking and laughing washed over her, as did scents of foods that made her stomach growl.

She'd skipped dinner. Tonight was very different from their first impromptu meeting. For one, there was no storm. It was fifty degrees outside, clear, and the air was scented with late spring.

For another, it wasn't midnight so the place wasn't deserted. She slipped onto the stool next to Grace and eyed the empty spot in front of her. "You refraining tonight?"

"Waiting on you."

Amy appeared, holding a cake and three forks.

Mallory grabbed one and dug in, guilt free since she'd run.

"No less than five customers have already tried to buy this cake," Amy said. "So you are welcome." She had to come and go at first as the diner emptied out. Then she stood on her side of the counter inhaling her third of the small cake. "God," she said on a moan. "Heaven on earth."

"Amazing," Grace admitted.

Mallory couldn't speak. She was too busy stuffing her face.

Amy swallowed and licked chocolate off her lips. "I'm calling this meeting to order. Mallory, you're first up."

"Nope. Not my turn."

"We've told you, you're first until we fix you." Grace smiled. "So spill. Tell us all."

Mallory sighed. "I'd rather talk about Amy and Sexy Forest Ranger Matt."

Grace went brows up at this and looked at Amy. "You putting out forest fires with that hot ranger who keeps coming in here for pie?"

"We have good pie," Amy said.

"There's all kinds of pie," Grace said.

Mallory nearly snorted cake out her nose, and Amy gave her a dirty look.

"This is *not* about me," she said haughtily and pointed her fork at Mallory.

Mallory stuffed in some cake.

"Uh oh," Grace said. "I'm sensing some slow down in Mission: Bad Girl."

"I wore the shoes," Mallory said. "And it was fun."

"Um, honey, from all accounts, you had more than some fun," Grace said, licking her fork.

"Accounts?"

"FB." Grace turned to Amy. "And thanks for the Facebook tip, by the way. It's a little addictive."

"You can't believe everything you read on there." Mallory sank onto her stool a little bit. "It's only a small percentage of the truth."

"Is that right?" Grace asked. "So what percentage of that picture with you and Ty looking cozy would you say is the truth?"

Mallory blew out a sigh and stabbed into the cake for another big bite. "We weren't...cozy. Then."

Grace grinned. "He's got that look. That big, sexy, I-know-how-to-please-a-woman-in-bed look."

Mallory propped up her head with her hand. With her other, she shoveled in more cake. "I don't want to talk about it."

"Yeah, but see, we *do*," Amy said.

"I broke it off," Mallory said and sighed when they gasped. "I told you, I'm not hard-wired for this bad girl stuff. Every time we were together I would find my-self..." She closed her eyes. "Falling."

Grace reached for her hand and squeezed it.

Amy pushed the cake closer to Mallory.

"Thanks." Mallory shook her head. "I couldn't keep things light. He's just..." She sighed. "Too yummy."

"He was swimming the other day," Grace said. "In the ocean. I was sitting on the beach pouting after spending gas money to get to Seattle for interviews that went nowhere. Anyway, he swam for like two hours straight. Didn't know anyone but a Navy SEAL could do that. Did you know a Navy SEAL can find or hunt down anyone or anything?"

"So?" Amy said.

"So, I bet a guy like that could locate a clit without any problems."

Both Amy and Grace looked at Mallory expectantly. Mallory choked on her cake, and was still choking when someone came up behind her and patted her on the back.

She knew that touch. Intimately. Whipping around, she came face to face with Ty. Her heart clutched at the sight of him. Traitorous heart. And she couldn't help but wonder, had he been a SEAL? It made perfect sense. He'd sure had absolutely no problem finding her clit...

His gaze met hers for an unfathomably long beat, and as always, just at the sight of him, she got a little thrill. And also as always, he looked bigger than life, and a whole lot more than she could handle. But there was something different about him tonight. Tonight he seemed weary and a little rough around the edges, and her heart clenched again.

God, she'd missed him.

She didn't understand it, but he'd never looked more appealing. Or real. She wanted to take his hand in hers and kiss away his problems. Hold him.

She wanted to hold a caged lion.

It made no sense but it was the truth. She knew he was leaving, and he'd be taking a big piece of her heart along with him when he did, but that was a done deal. She also knew something else—that she wanted whatever he had to give her in the meantime. Because with him, she wasn't a caretaker. She wasn't a sister. She wasn't thinking, planning, overseeing.

She was just Mallory. And she felt...alive. So damn alive.

His eyes smiled. He touched the corner of her upper lip, then sucked on his finger. "Mmm," he said. "Chocolate."

Amy's jaw dropped open. Grace fanned herself. Ty looked at them, and they suddenly got very busy. Though Amy did give Mallory a "see, meeting interrupted *again*" look before she went off to serve a customer, and Grace remembered something she had to go do.

Which didn't stop everyone else in the diner from staring at them. "Oh good Lord," Mallory said. "Come on." She took the caged lion's hand and led him outside.

The stars were out in force tonight, like scattered diamonds on the night sky. The waves crashed up against the shore. They walked along the pier, past the dark arcade and the closed ice cream shop. Past everything until there was nothing but empty pier ahead and the black ocean. There Mallory stopped and leaned over the railing. "I'm sorry about the other day," she said quietly, facing the water. "I mean, I started this thing between us. I laid out the rules. So I had no right to change them on you without saying so, and then hold it against you."

He didn't say anything, and she turned to him, searching his impassive face, hoping to see understanding. Forgiveness. Or at the very least, a sign that he understood.

She got none of that, and her heart sank.

After a minute, he mirrored her pose, leaning on the railing to stare out at the water. "I grew up with military parents," he said. "I went into the military. And when I got out, I went to work for a private contractor to the government, doing... more military-like work. It's my job, it's my life. It's who I am."

She nodded. "I know."

"It requires things of me," he said. "Being alone, being the protector, keeping myself protected." He lifted a shoulder. "I don't know how to be anyone else."

"I don't want you to be anyone else, Ty. Ever. I like who you are."

He was quiet, absorbing that. "Frances is my boss. She's... proprietary."

To say the least. But he wasn't giving her all of it. "You've been with her. Sexually."

"Yes," he said, bluntly honest as always. "Before I worked for her, a very long time ago. It's over."

"For you," she said. "It's over for you."

He acknowledged that with a shrug. Not his problem. So it wouldn't be Mallory's either, she decided.

Turning to her, Ty ran a finger over the dainty gold chain at her neck, then beneath the infinity charm, looking at it for a moment. "After I lost my team in the plane crash, I spent the first six months recovering alone, by choice." He let out a breath and dropped his hand from her. "I couldn't... I didn't want anyone close. I still don't want anyone close."

He'd lost his parents, his friends. Everyone. She couldn't imagine how alone he must have felt.

Or maybe she could. Hadn't she, even surrounded by all the people in her life, *still* felt alone? Mallory scooped her necklace in her palm and tightened her fist on it. "Karen gave this to me right before she—" She closed her eyes for a minute, and pictured Karen's own laughing eyes. "It's the infinity sign," she told him. "Forever connected. She wore it all the time, and I always bugged her to let me borrow it. I wanted to be just like her. It used to drive her nuts. Then one day, she took the necklace off and just put it around my neck. She kissed my cheek and told me to be good, that being good would keep me out of the trouble that she'd always found herself in. She made me promise. Then she said she'd be watching me, guiding my way, making sure I was okay. I thought—I thought how sweet, but then..." Her throat tightened almost beyond bearing. "It was the last time I saw her," she said softly. "The next day she..." She let out a shuddery breath and shook her head, unable to speak.

With a low sound of empathy, Ty slid his hand to the

nape of her neck, drawing her in against him. It was her undoing, and she fisted her hands in his shirt as a few tears escaped.

"I know your losses hurt," she managed. "But you're not alone, Ty." She said this fiercely, choking out the words. "You're not. I mean the pain doesn't go away, it *never* goes away, but it gets easier to remember them. And then one day, you'll remember them with a smile. I can promise you that."

He tightened his grip on her and nodded. They stood like that, locked together, a light breeze blowing her hair around. A strand of it clung to the stubble on his jaw and he left it there, bound to her, liking it...

"I thought maybe you'd left," she said.

"Not yet."

But soon... Those words, unspoken, hovered between them. When he got medically cleared, he'd be gone.

"Maybe you can't walk away from me," she said, meaning to tease, to lighten the moment.

"I can always walk away," he said. "Discipline runs deep."

Okay, so he wasn't feeling playful. Shaken, she took a step back and came up against the railing, but he put his hands on her and reeled her back in. "I need to get back to what I do," he said.

"You aren't your work."

"I am." Maintaining eye contact, he tightened his grip on her. "But I'm not ready to go yet."

"It's the sex," she said.

"It's more than sex."

"Not if it's still something that can be walked away from," she said.

He held her gaze, his own steady. Calm. So sure. "It's the way it has to be, Mallory."

She already knew that, oh how she knew it. The question was the same as always—could she live with it?

Yes.

No.

For now…Because the alternative was losing him right now, right this very minute, and she'd tried that. It didn't work for her. She wasn't ready to let him go.

He pressed his forehead to hers. "Your call," he said quietly. "Tell me to fuck off. Walk away from me right now and avoid any more heartbreak, I'm not worth it. Or—"

"Or," she said with soft steel. "I choose the *or*."

"Mallory." His voice was gruff. "You deserve better."

She pulled him farther down the pier, past the yacht club entrance and around the side of the building where no one who happened by could see them. There she pushed him up against the wall and kissed him. She took full advantage of his surprise, opening her mouth over his, causing a rush of heat and the melting of all the bones in her legs.

He was a soldier and knew how to turn any situation to his own advantage, and this was no exception. In less than a single heartbeat, he'd taken complete control of the kiss, stealing her breath and her heart with one sweep of his finger.

"If the decision is mine to make," she said breathing hard, her voice utterly serious, "then I'm keeping you, for as long as I can have you."

Chapter 18

Falling in love is like eating a whole box of chocolates—
it seems like a good idea at first...

The next day, Ty woke up in his bed with a gloriously naked woman sprawled out over the top of him. Not that he was opposed to such a phenomenon, but this gloriously naked woman was all up in his space, and he'd always valued his own space. He was a big guy and he didn't like to feel crowded. Mallory was half his size, and as it turned out, she was a bed hog. She was also a blanket hog and a pillow hog.

It's okay, he told himself. It was okay that they'd slept together because they both knew what this was and what it wasn't. They'd fallen asleep together, that's all. It didn't mean anything. Now if it happened again...well, *then* he'd panic. "Mallory."

She let out a soft snore, and he felt his heart squeeze. Fucking heart. "Mallory. Are you working today?" He already had one hand on her ass. Easy enough to add the other. When he squeezed, then went exploring, a low appreciative moan escaped her lips, and she obligingly spread her legs, giving him more room to work, murmuring something that sounded like "don't stop."

Then she froze and jerked upright. "*Whattimeisit?*"

"Seven," he said, nuzzling his face in her crazy hair.

"Seven? *Seven?* I have to be gone!" She leapt out of the bed, frantically searching for her various pieces of clothing.

Enjoying the Naked Mallory Show, he leaned back, hands behind his head.

"Where are my panties?" she demanded.

"Under the chair."

She dove under the chair, giving him a heart-stopping view that made him groan.

"They're not here!" she yelled, voice muffled from her head-down-ass-up position.

"No? Check under my jeans then," he said.

She straightened, and hair in her face—hell, hair everywhere—gave him a narrowed gaze.

He smiled.

She crawled to his jeans, another hot view, and snatched her panties. With her clothes in her arms, she vanished into his bathroom. Two minutes later she reappeared, dressed and looking thoroughly fucked. "Come here," he said, smiling.

"Oh hell no. If I come over there, you're going to kiss me."

"Yeah," he said. "I am."

"And then you'll... *you know.*'

He laughed, feeling light-hearted and... happy. "I do know. I know exactly what I want to do to you. I want to put my mouth on your—"

"Oh, God." She shook her head and grabbed her keys. *"I have to go!"*

"Five minutes," he said, and thought he had her when she hesitated, biting her lower lip, looking tempted. "It'll be the best five minutes of your day," he promised.

"I usually need more like fifteen minutes."

"Not last night you didn't. Last night you only needed four before you—"

"Bye," she said, laughing, and shut his door.

Ty lay there smiling like an idiot for a few minutes. Then his phone beeped. Rolling out of bed, he accessed his messages. Once upon a not-so-long-ago time, there were only messages from Frances. That was no longer the case. The first message was from Ryan.

"Hey, man," the vet said. That was it, the full extent of the message. Pretty typical of Ryan, and it could mean anything from "let's have dinner" to "I'm jonesing and need someone to talk to."

Matt had called as well, looking for a sparring partner. Josh had called inquiring about his health—and Ty knew Josh meant his mental health, not his leg.

Ty stared at his phone in surprise. At some point, when he'd been busy resenting like hell this slow-paced, sleepy little town and everyone in it, something had happened.

He'd made ties, strings on the heart he wasn't even sure he had. His smile faded as he listened to his last message, which contained no words, just a seething silence.

Frances.

He should call her and check in. After all, he was cleared to go back. But he didn't call. Instead he checked up on Ryan, then he finished the last of the cars lined up for him—Matt's Jimmy.

Now he could go back.

Almost.

He showered and drove to the Health Services Clinic just as it was closing up for the day. It was Thursday, and he knew there were no activities or meetings scheduled there that night.

He'd checked.

The front room was empty, but he could hear voices so he followed them and found Mallory in one of the small rooms, door open. She was facing a woman in her sixties. The woman was sitting in a chair, her face pinched like she'd eaten a sour apple.

Mallory was wearing purple scrubs today, and it was a good color for her. Her hair had been tied back, probably hours ago, and as usual, strands had escaped.

She wasn't good at hiding her feelings, and right now she was on edge, tired, and frustrated.

A long day, no doubt, made longer since they'd spent most of the night tearing up his sheets. He knew exactly what he'd do to relax her, but he had to remind himself that she wasn't his to take care of.

His own choice.

He was leaving, and someday, maybe someday soon, she'd stay up all night with someone else. Someone who would take care of her, help her unwind at the end of the day. Maybe someone from her list.

But if it was Anderson, Ty was going to kick his ass, just on principle. And if it was Josh, Ty'd...Jesus. It'd be whoever Mallory chose, and Ty had nothing to say about it, not even if her new Mr. Wrong used the guise of showing her how to hold a tool to kiss her. Not even if that Mr. Wrong bent her over a piece of furniture, taking her in front of a mirror, forcing her to see how gorgeous and amazing she really was. It was none of his business.

But it sucked.

"Just trust me," Mallory said to her patient, moving to a cabinet. She pulled a set of keys from her pocket and eyed the medicine samples lined up there before grabbing a box. "Take these. One a day."

"What are you poisoning me with now?" the woman asked.

"Vitamins," Mallory said.

The woman set the samples down. "Vitamins are a sham. It's the drug companies' way of making money off all us unsuspecting idiots."

Mallory put the vitamins back into the woman's hands. "Your blood work shows you're anemic. These will help. Or you can keep passing out in the bathroom and waiting until EMS finds you on the floor with your pants at your ankles again. Your choice, Mrs. Burland."

There was a long silence during which the woman glared at Mallory. "You used to be afraid of me. You used to quail and tremble like a little girl."

"Things change," Mallory said in a mild voice. No judgment, no recriminations. "Take the vitamins. Don't make me come over every night and pinch your nose and shove them down your throat."

"Well fine, if you're going to out-mean me."

"I am," Mallory said firmly.

"See, you *have* changed. You've gotten a tough skin. You've learned to hold back and keep your emotions off your sleeve for the world to see. You are very welcome."

"Oh, it wasn't *all* you," Mallory said, and Ty felt an

odd tightening in his chest, because he knew who'd changed her.

Him.

He was such an asshole.

Turning from the woman, Mallory caught sight of him standing there. Her surprised smile only added to the ache in Ty's chest but he nodded to her and stepped back, leaning against the wall in the hall to wait.

Mallory looked at her patient. "I have something else for you; hold on." She came out into the hall, shutting the door behind her. She flashed Ty another smile and vanished into the next room. When she returned, she handed her patient some flyers before guiding her from the exam room and out front.

A few minutes later Mallory was back. "Hey."

"Hey. You need a lock on the front door when you're here alone," he said.

"I wasn't alone until now, and this is Lucky Harbor. I'm as safe as it gets."

"You're not safe here with the drugs."

"The meds are locked."

"Flimsy lock," he said. "Especially for someone who's desperate."

"It's only temporary. We're getting a much better setup next week." She smiled, still not taking her safety seriously enough for him. "So what's up? What brings you here?"

"You owe me a favor," he said. "And I'm collecting."

She sputtered, then laughed. "I owe *you* a favor? Since when?"

"Since the night I pretended to be your date at the auction."

"Pretended? You were supposed to be my date all along," she reminded him.

"But I was concussed and didn't remember making the date. Which means that you owe me for that, too, taking advantage of an injured guy." He *tsk*ed. "Shame on you, Mallory Quinn. Imagine what people would say if they knew you'd done such a thing."

She narrowed her eyes, clearly amused by his playfulness, but not fully trusting him.

Smart girl. He shouldn't be trusted. Not by a long shot.

"So what exactly is this favor?" she asked. "And don't tell me it involves any storage rooms." She paused. "Okay, so we both know I'd hop into another closet with you so fast it'd make your head spin."

With a laugh, he pushed off the wall and came toward her. "It's not that," he said. "I need the same thing you needed that night."

"An orgasm?" she asked cheekily.

"Only if you ask *very* nicely. But I meant a date."

Her expression went dubious. "A date? Now?"

"Yes."

She went from dubious to blank-faced. "A *last* date?"

Well, hell. What could he say to that? It was the truth. "Actually," he said. "I don't believe we ever had a first date." He took her hand and brought it to his mouth, brushing his lips against her palm as he watched her over their joined fingers. "Say yes, Mallory."

Staring at him, she turned her hand, cupping his face, her fingers gliding across his jaw. "Always."

He felt his heart roll, exposing its underbelly. Nothing he could do about that. He was equipped to eliminate threats, protect and serve.

Not to love.
Never to love.

Mallory didn't know what to expect. Ty wouldn't tell her
where they were going, but they were on the highway,
heading toward Seattle. Once there, he drove to a very
swank block lined with designer shops and parked.

"Um," she said.

He pulled her out of the car and into a dress shop.
"Something for the orchestra," he said to the pretty sales
woman who came forward. He turned to Mallory. "Whatever you want."

She was confused. "What?"

"The auction. The night on the town package."

Again, she just gaped at him. "Was that supposed to be
a full explanation?"

"It's tonight," he said. "Tonight's the last night of the
orchestra."

"So you what, kidnapped me to take me to it?"

"Thought you could use a night off. And you said
you never got to date much." He looked endearingly
baffled. "And don't women like this surprise romantic
shit?"

Aw. Dammit. "What, you mean romantic '*shit*'?"

He winced, for the first time since she'd known him,
looking uncomfortable in his own skin. "You're right," he
said. "This was a stupid idea. It's not too late to call this
whole thing off and go get a pizza and beer. Whatever you
want."

The guy had grown up on military bases and then
given his adult years over to the same lifestyle. Mallory
knew he was far more at ease in the role of big, bad tough

guy than romance guy. Certainly he'd rather have a pizza and beer over the orchestra.

And yet he'd thought of her. He wanted to give her a night off. He'd wanted to share that night off with her, and he'd brought her to a place filled with gorgeous, designer clothes to do it so that she wouldn't stress about the lack thereof in her own closet. It was a send off, a finale, a good-bye, and she knew it. But damn. Damn, she wanted this. With him. Stepping into him, she went up on tip-toe and kissed his smooth jaw. He'd shaved for her. "Thank you," she whispered.

He turned his head and claimed her mouth in one quick, hot kiss. "Take your time. I'll be waiting."

If only that was really true.

A limo pulled up front, and that's when she remembered: the package came with a limo. "Oh my God."

He leaned in close. "I'm hoping by the end of the night you'll be saying 'Oh, Ty' ..." And with that, he walked out the front door toward the limo.

She stared after him. "That man is crazy."

"He's crazy *fine*," the sales clerk murmured. "And he did say whatever you wanted..." She gestured around her. "So what would you like?"

Thirty minutes later, Mallory was decked out in a silky, strappy siren-red dress that made her feel like a sex kitten. She kept trying to see the price tag but the clerk had been discreet, and firm. "He said you weren't allowed to look at the prices."

Good Lord.

By the time Mallory exited the shop, she felt like Cinderella. And her prince stepped out of the limo to greet her in a well-fitted, expensive suit that nearly made her trip over her new strappy high-heeled sandals. She'd seen him in a suit before. She'd seen him in jeans, in cargoes, and in nothing at all. He always looked mouth-wateringly gorgeous. But tonight, something felt different... "Wow."

Ignoring that, he took her hand and pulled her in. "You take my breath away," he said simply.

And that's when she realized. It was his eyes. He was looking at her differently. Heart-stoppingly differently.

Dinner was at a French restaurant and was so amazing she was starting to regret not going one size up on the dress. But the wine quickly reduced any lingering anxiety. The problem with that was, combined with a long day and almost no sleep the night before, by the time they got to the orchestra, her eyes were drooping. Still, she accepted another glass of white wine, and they found their seats. The curtain went up.

And that's the last thing Mallory remembered about the orchestra.

When she woke up, the theater was nearly empty, and Ty was leaning over her, an amused smile on his face.

"What?" she said, blinking, confused. "Where?"

His smile spread to a grin. "You snore."

"I do not!" She straightened, stared at the closed curtain on the stage and took in the fact that the few people left around them were leaving. "It's over? I missed the whole thing?"

He pulled her to her feet. "That's okay. You didn't miss the best part."

"What's the best part?"

"Wait for it." He led her back to the limo. He closed the partition between them and the driver, then pulled her onto his lap.

"Is this the best part?" she asked breathlessly when he slid his hands beneath her dress and palmed her butt cheeks, bared by her lacy thong.

"Wait for it," he whispered against her mouth, and spent the drive back to the Shelby creating a slow burn with nothing more than his mouth on hers and his hands caressing her curves.

"More," she demanded.

"*Wait for it.*"

"I'm growing very tired of those three words," she said.

He drove her home, then walked her in, slowly stripping her out of her beautiful new dress and bra and panties, groaning at the sight of her in just her heels.

"So help me, if you tell me to wait for it one more time," she warned, hands on her bare hips.

"Christ, you are the most beautiful woman I've ever seen," he said. He gave her a little push, and she fell to her bed. "I know how tired you are, so feel free to just lay there and relax."

"I'm not tired," she said. "I took a very nice nap at the orchestra."

With a soft laugh, he crawled up her body, taking little nips out of her as he went. "I'm offering to do all the work here."

"I'm more of an equal opportunity type of woman."

He smiled against her mouth. "Is that right? Well, however you want to be is fine with me. But you should know, I'm ready for the best part now."

"Me too. What is it?" she asked eagerly.

He gently bit her lower lip and tugged, then let it go, soothing the ache with his tongue, making every single nerve ending on her body stand up and beg for the same treatment. "You. You're the best part."

Her heart caught. "Me?"

"Definitely you," he breathed, and then set about proving it.

Chapter 19

*I want it all. And I want it smothered in
whipped cream and chocolate!*

The next afternoon, Mallory was in the ER doing her
damnedest not to dwell on the fact that Ty was probably
leaving town at any moment. She kept busy and was
checking in a patient that Sheriff Thompson had dragged
in after breaking up a fight when she took a call from
Camilla.

"I'm at the HSC, just closing after the teen advocacy
meeting," the young LVN said. "And we have a problem."

Mallory raced over there, and Camilla showed her the
medicine lock-up. "I think there's four boxes of Oxycontin missing."

Mallory's heart sank. "What?"

"A month's supply."

Mallory stared at the cabinet in complete and utter
shock. *"What?"*

"Yeah. I called Jane," Camilla said. "I didn't want it to

come out later and have anyone think it happened on my watch. I never got into the lock-up today at all."

Mallory nodded. That meant it had happened yesterday, when *she'd* been in charge. She'd gone into the cabinet several times that she could remember off the top of her head. There'd been the birth control samples she'd given out to Deena and the smoker's patches she'd given Ryan. The vitamins for Mrs. Burland. Mallory recalled that one because Ty had been there. And she flashed back to him admitting he'd gotten too attached to his pain meds.

Cold turkey, he'd said with a harsh laugh. *More like hot hell.*

A tight feeling spread through her chest. Whoever had taken those samples had known what they were taking. There were only two reasons to take Oxycontin. To sell, or to use.

To use, she decided, remembering Ty's words. It was an act of desperation to steal them, and addicts were desperate.

Karen had been desperate, and Mallory had failed her. Badly.

Who else was she failing?

She went back to the ER heartsick. She was in the middle of teaching some brand new firefighter paramedics how to start IVs when she was summoned to Bill's office. She headed that way, expecting to get her hair blown back.

She didn't expect to face several board members, including Jane and her mother.

"Tell us how this could have happened," Bill said, tone stern.

Mallory drew a deep breath. "We received samples early yesterday for the weekend health clinic. I stocked the cabinet myself and locked it."

"Exactly how much is missing?"

He already knew this. He knew everything. He just wanted to hear her say it. "Four boxes," she told him. "Each was a week's supply."

"So a month. You've lost a month's supply of Oxycontin."

Mallory nodded. She was pissed, afraid, frustrated. She'd gone over the inventory a hundred times in her head, hoping she'd just miscalculated.

But she hadn't.

The meds were missing. Someone had stolen them from beneath her own nose. An anguished, distraught, frantic act, by someone she most likely knew by name.

"We'd like the list of everyone who came through the HSC yesterday," Bill said.

This was what she'd been dreading. She didn't know what she wished for the most, that Ty hadn't shown up at all, or that someone else she knew and cared about had. "Bill, we're supposed to be anonymous."

"And you were supposed to make sure something like this never happened. The list, Mallory. I want it by tomorrow morning."

"I can fix this," she said. "Let me—"

"The only way you can fix this is by trusting me to do my job," Bill told her. "And that job is the bottom line. I'm in charge of the bottom line. Do you understand?"

"Of course. But—"

"No buts, Mallory. Don't make this come down to your job being on the line as well as the HSC."

Mallory's heart lurched, and she ground her back teeth so hard she was surprised they didn't dissolve.

"And I'm sure this goes without saying," Bill said, "but until we solve this, the HSC stays closed."

A stab to the gut. "Understood." Somehow she managed to get out of there and through the rest of her shift. All she wanted was to be alone, but her mother caught up with her in the parking lot. "What aren't you telling us, Mallory?"

Mallory was good at hiding her devastation. She'd had lots of practice. "What do you mean?"

"Honey, it's me. The woman who spent thirty-six hours in labor with you. I *know* when you're hiding something."

"Mom, I have to go."

Ella looked deep into her eyes and shook her head. "Oh, no. Oh, Mallory." She cupped Mallory's jaw. "Who are you trying to save this time?"

"Mom, please. Just go back to work."

"In a minute." Ella cupped Mallory's face and kissed each cheek and then her forehead. "You can't save them all. You know that, right?"

"Yes." Mallory closed her eyes. "I don't know what happened yesterday, but whoever it was, it was my fault. Someone I know is in trouble. And it's like Karen all over again." The sob reached up and choked her, shutting off her words, and she slapped a hand over her mouth to keep it in.

Her mother's eyes filled. "Oh, honey. Honey, no. What happened to Karen wasn't your fault."

Mallory closed her eyes. "She came to me that night."

Ella gasped. "What?"

"Karen. She came into my bedroom. She said she needed me." Mallory swallowed hard. "But I'd been...I'd been needing her and she hadn't been there for me. Not once. So I lashed out at her. I said terrible things to her. And you know what she did? She gave me her necklace. She told me she loved me. She pretty much said good-bye, Mom, and I missed it."

"Mallory, you listen to me," her mother said fiercely, giving her a little shake. "You were sixteen."

"She felt like she was alone, like she had no other options. But she *wasn't* alone. There were lots of options." Mallory let out a breath. "I failed her. I have to live with that. And now I'm just trying to make sure I don't fail anyone else. I need to make sure no one else falls through the cracks."

"But at what cost?" her mother asked softly. "You're the one who said it, Mallory. There are just some things that people have to do for themselves. They have to find their own will, their own happy. Their own path."

"Yes, and this is mine."

Ella sighed and hugged her. "Oh, honey. Are you sure? Because this one's going to cost you big. It's going to cost you your job and your reputation."

"It already has. And yes, I'm sure. I have to do this, Mom. I have to figure this out and fix it."

Ella nodded her reluctant understanding, and Mallory got into her car and drove straight to Ty's house. His house, not his home. Because this was just a stop on his life's path, a destination, not the finish line.

She'd admired that about him.

Now it scared her.

Lots of things scared her. Not too long ago, she'd

asked him what he was frightened of, and he'd said he was afraid of not living.

They weren't so different after all, and God, she needed verification of that fact right now.

He didn't answer her knock. The place was quiet. Empty. She put a hand to her chest, knowing damn well that last night had been a good-bye. For all she knew, he was already gone. For a minute, she panicked. After all, she had asked him not to tell her when he left. A very stupid, rash decision on her part. But when she peeked into the garage window and saw the Shelby, she sagged in relief.

Her relief was short-lived, though, because she had no idea where he might go on a night like this. None. And that didn't sit so well.

She was falling in love with a guy that she was afraid she didn't know at all.

Talk about taking a walk on the dark side…

Frustrated and annoyed, she went home. She didn't bother with her usual routine. Screw the flowers. Screw everything, even the cat. She simply strode through her place, intending to get into bed and pull the covers over her head and pretend the day hadn't happened.

Denial. She was thy Queen.

She'd dropped her purse in the living room. Kicked off her shoes in the hallway. She walked into her bedroom struggling with the buttons on her sweater. Giving up, she yanked the thing over her head and got her hair tangled in the buttons. "Dammit!" She was standing there arms up, face covered by the sweater, when two strong arms enveloped her.

She let out a startled scream and was immediately

gathered against a warm, hard form that her body knew better than her own. "Ty," she gasped.

He pressed her back against the bedroom door. "You expecting anyone else?"

"I wasn't expecting anyone at all. Help me, I'm caught."

Instead he slid a thigh between hers.

"*Ty.*" She struggled with the sweater some more and succeeded in catching her hair on a sweater button. "*Ouch*! I can't get loose."

"Hmm." His hands molded her body, everywhere. "I like you a little helpless."

She fought anew. "That's sexist."

"Sexy," he corrected, untangling her, tossing the offending sweater over his head while still holding her captive against the door. "What were you trying to do?"

"Strip." Crash. Forget. "I went looking for you."

"You found me." He tugged, and then her scrub pants were gone.

She gasped. "What are you doing?"

"Helping you strip." He slid a hand into her panties, his eyes dark and heavy lidded with desire. "Tell me why you went looking for me."

There was something in his voice, something edgy, dark. "I wanted to see you." It was God's utter truth. She knew in her heart that he wouldn't have taken those meds. He wouldn't do anything to hurt her, ever. She knew that, just as she knew that her time with him was limited. Too limited.

She was going to be brave about that, later. "I want you," she whispered.

In the dark hallway, his eyes gleamed with heat and intent, and then his mouth was on hers, hard. She sucked his tongue into her mouth, swallowing his rough groan, savoring the taste of him. "My bed," she said. "I need you in my bed."

They staggered farther into the room and fell onto the mattress. "Hurry, Ty."

"Take everything off then," he demanded in that quiet voice that made her leap to obey. She pulled off her top and unhooked her bra. She was wriggling out of her panties when she got distracted by watching him strip. He tugged his shirt over his head, and then his hands went to his button fly, his movements quick and economical as he bared his gorgeous body. In two seconds he was naked, one hundred percent of his attention completely fixed on her. And apparently she was moving too slowly because he took over, wrapping his fingers around each of her ankles, giving a hard tug so that she fell flat on her back.

He was on her in a heartbeat. "I was working on a car, but all I could see was you, running your fingers over the brake line, holding onto the wrench. It made me hard."

She slid her hands down his sinewy, cut torso, planning on licking that same path as soon as she got a chance. "Me touching your tools makes you hard?"

"Yeah," he said silkily. "Your hands on my tool makes me *very* hard."

She laughed, and he nipped at her shoulder. "Your scent was there, too," he said almost accusingly. "In the garage, lingering like you were right there, pestering me with all your questions."

"Well—" She frowned. "*Hey.*"

His lips claimed hers in a hungry, demanding kiss. "I kept hearing your voice," he said between strokes of his tongue. "Pretending to be all sweet and warm, when really you had me pinned to the wall and were drilling me."

"Return the favor," she said breathlessly. "Pin me down and drill me, Ty."

He looked torn between laughter and determination to do just that. "You've had me in a fucking state all day, Mallory Quinn."

"How bad is this state?"

"*Bad*," he said, grinding his hips to hers to prove it. "So bad I couldn't function."

"Mmm," she moaned at the feel of him so hard for her. "So what did you do?"

"Jacked off."

She choked out a laugh. "You did not."

"Did."

The air crackled with electricity, and he kissed her again. His hands were just as demanding as his mouth, finding her breasts, teasing her nipples, sliding a hand between her legs. Finding her already hot and wet, he groaned.

"Please, Ty. I need you. I need you so much."

"Show me," he said.

"Show you?"

"*Show me*."

Knowing what he meant, she bit her lower lip. He'd just admitted to touching himself while thinking about her; surely she could return the favor. In the end, he helped her, entwining their fingers and dragging their joined hands up her body, positioning them on her breasts, urging her to caress her own nipples. When she did, he pulled his fingers free and watched with a low groan. Then, apparently convinced she would continue on, he slid down her body, kissing his way between her thighs. Slowly, purposefully, he sucked her into his mouth, making her writhe so much that he had to hold her down. Her toes curled, her eyes closed, her fingers abandoned her breasts and slid into his hair to hold him to that spot because God, just one more stroke of that tongue—

But he stopped. Just pulled his mouth away until she looked at him.

"Keep your eyes open," he said, and when he lowered his mouth again, she did as he'd told her, watching as he took her right to the edge again. It was the hardest thing she'd done so far with him. But nothing about Ty was in her comfort zone, not his life's experiences, not the way he made her feel, and certainly not how he got her to behave in the bedroom. It felt so absolutely wicked to keep looking at him, to be a voyeur in her own bed, but try as she might to hold on, her vision faded when he pushed her over the edge with shocking ease.

When she could open her eyes again, he easily held himself just above her, making room for himself between her thighs as he cupped her face, his own now struggling with control.

She knew he'd never intended for things to go this far. She hadn't either. But as she tugged him close and kissed him, she felt their co-mingled best intentions go right out the window.

Taking control, he slid his big hands to her bottom and pushed inside her with one hard thrust. "Oh, fuck," he said. "You feel amazing."

It was just the passion of the moment, she tried to tell herself, but she felt him to the depths of her soul. And in her heart of hearts, she knew he felt far more for her than he let on. It was in his actions, and she wrapped her arms around his broad shoulders and melted into the hard planes of his body. Emotion welled up within her, and she had to clamp her mouth closed to hold in the words that wanted to escape.

"Mallory."

Opening her eyes, she stared up into his, her heart clenching hard. His hands slid up to her hips, positioning her exactly as he wanted, and when he thrust again, she gasped as pleasure swamped her. Wrapping her legs around his waist, she whispered his name, needing him to move.

Instead, he lowered his head and traced her nipple with his tongue, causing her to arch her back and shamelessly roll her hips into his. "*Ty.*"

His fingers skimmed roughly up her spine, leaving a trail of heat that she felt all the way to her toes, until his hands gripped hers on either side of her head. "I'm right here," he promised, taking her exactly where she needed to go without words. And that was it, the beginning of the point of no return for her. He was exactly what she'd wanted, what she'd never had the nerve to reach out and grasp for herself before. Ironic, really. He didn't want her to depend on him, and yet he was the one who'd given her the security to be who she was. If only he'd keep looking at her the way he was right now.

For always.

It wasn't going to happen, she knew that. She had to settle for this, for the right now. Telling herself she was stronger than she knew, that she could do it, she cupped his face and let herself go, moving with him in the age-old dance of lovers. And her release, when it came, shattered her apart and yet somehow made her whole at the same time.

At some point in the night, Ty woke up wrapped in warm woman. And it wasn't her clinging to him. Nope, that was all him. He had one hand entangled in her crazy hair, the other on her bare ass, holding her possessively and protectively to him.

Jesus.

The night of the orchestra had been a mistake, and everyone was allowed one mistake. But if he slept with her tonight, it would be mistake number two.

He didn't make mistakes, much less the same one twice. It took some doing, but he managed to get out of the bed without waking her. He gathered his things and walked out of her bedroom, quietly shutting the door behind him. Dumping everything at his feet to sort, he hesitated. In his real life, hesitating was a good way to get dead. And yet he did just that, turning back to her bedroom door, his hands up on the frame above his head. He wanted to go back in there.

Bad.

Don't do it, man. He looked down at his shit. No shirt. One sock. From his pants pocket, his phone was blinking. Frances, he knew. Because she and Josh had finally connected. The gig was up; she knew he was cleared. His last message from her had been something along the lines of *get your sorry ass back to work*. This had been accompanied by a text with a confirmation number for a one-way, first-class airplane ticket back to D.C.

He stubbed his toe on his own shoes. Swearing softly,

he kicked one down the hallway, then went still when the bedroom door opened and the light came on.

Mallory stood there blinking sleepily, tousled and rumpled and wearing nothing but his shirt. "Hey," she murmured. "You okay?"

"Yeah. Sorry. Didn't mean to wake you."

"Are you leaving?"

"Yeah, I... Yeah, I'm leaving." He needed to. Now. Because he was starting to wonder how he was going to leave Lucky Harbor at all.

Mallory made a soft noise in the back of her throat. She was looking at his jeans still on the floor, and the two things that had spilled out of his pockets. His keys.

And the empty Vicodin bottle.

She bent and picked up the bottle, staring at it for a long time. He saw her taking in the two-month-old date of the prescription, the fact that there were refills available to him which he clearly hadn't used. Finally she handed the bottle back to him with a gentle smile. "Stay, Ty. Stay with me for tonight. Just tonight."

He couldn't. Staying would be a mistake. "Mallory—"

She covered his mouth with her fingers, then took his hand in hers, drawing him back into her bedroom and into her bed, and into her warm, soft heart.

Chapter 20

*Exercise is a dirty word. Every time I hear it
I wash my mouth out with chocolate.*

The next day Ty and Matt spent time in the gym, then
Matt went home with Ty to pick up the Jimmy. Matt took
one look around the cleaned-up garage. "You're leaving."

"Always was." Ty held out the Jimmy's keys but Matt
didn't take them.

"The lease on this place is paid up until summer," Ty
said. "Use it if you want. And I want you to take the
tools."

"I'll keep them for you. You'll be back."

Ty looked at him, and Matt shook his head. "Christ,"
he said on a disgusted sigh. "Tell me you're not just going
to vanish on her and not come back at all. You're not that
big a dick, right?"

"You want to test drive this thing or what?"

"So you *are* that big a dick."

"Look, she made me promise not to say good-bye."

"And you believed her?" Matt asked. "Shit, and I thought *I* was stupid with women."

"You are." Ty tossed him the keys at him, leaving Matt no choice but to catch them.

They took the Jimmy out on a test drive. Matt drove like a guy who knew the roads intimately, down-shifting into the hairpin turns, accelerating out of them. He took them along a two-lane, narrow, curvy highway that led almost straight up. On either side were steep, unforgiving, isolated peaks, so lush—thanks to a wet spring—that they resembled a South American rainforest.

When the road ended, Matt cranked the Jimmy into four-wheel drive and kept going, making his own trail.

"You know where you're headed, City Boy?" Ty asked.

Matt sent him a long look. "What, you think you can find your way around these mountains?"

"I could find my way around on Mars," Ty assured him. "Though if you get us dead out here, I'll follow you to the depths of hell and kill you again."

"Told you, not everyone's going to die on you. I'm sure as hell not."

"See that you don't."

Matt drove on, until eventually they came to a plateau. The three-hundred-and-sixty degree vista was staggering. The jagged mountain peaks were still tipped in white. The lower ranges were covered in a thick blanket of green. And to their immediate west, the Pacific shimmered brilliantly.

"Beaut Point," Matt said.

The plateau was about the size of a football field, giving a very decent view of the ocean smashing into a valley of rocks hundreds of feet below. "Good spot," Ty said.

"I chase a lot of stupid teenagers off this ledge. They come four-wheeling up here in daddy's truck to get laid. Then the geniuses get lost, and I end up having to save their miserable asses."

"Tough job."

"Beats scooping gangbangers off the streets of Chicago any day of the week," Matt agreed. "And I imagine it's also a hell of a lot more fun than Afghanistan or Iraq this time of year."

Ty looked over at him. "Don't forget South America. My favorite."

Matt smiled. "Nothing compares to Chicago in high summer in full tactical gear."

"Pussy."

"Sure. If being a pussy means staying in Paradise over leaving for a stupid adrenaline rush in some godforsaken Third World country."

Ty shook his head and stared out at "Paradise."

"Ever climb?" Matt asked.

"Only when I have to."

Matt gestured with his chin out to a sharp outcropping at least three miles across the way. "Widow's Peak. Climbed it last weekend. It's a get-your-head-on-straight kind of spot."

"Was your head crooked?" Ty asked.

"Yeah, actually. But today I figured that was you."

"My head's on perfectly straight, thanks."

"Yeah?"

"Yeah."

"Huh," Matt said.

Ty looked at him. "Okay, let's save some time here.

Why don't you just tell me whatever it is that you're fishing for?"

"All right," Matt said. "Someone stole some samples out of the Health Services Clinic from right beneath Mallory's nose."

Ty's gut tightened. "Today? Was she hurt?"

Matt was watching him carefully. "Yesterday. And no."

"What was taken?"

"Pain meds. She doesn't know when it happened, actually. She says it could have been at a couple of different points during the day."

Ty went still, remembering last night, remembering the look on Mallory's face when she'd seen the empty bottle fall out of his jeans pocket.

She'd known then, and she hadn't said a word. Had she thought he'd taken the pills? He tried to think of a reason that she wouldn't have mentioned the missing meds that didn't involve her thinking it was him. But with a grim, sinking feeling in his gut, he realized he couldn't. "Is she taking shit for it?"

"You could say that, yeah. As of right this minute, HSC is shut down, and if it gets out why, it's going to stay that way."

"She doesn't deserve the blame."

"She accepted the blame."

"How do you know all of this?"

"I'm on the hospital board. Look," he said at Ty's dark expression, "at this point only we board members know. They want her to turn in a list of who was at HSC during the hours that the meds went missing. She's objecting because it's supposed to be anonymous. That put her job in the ER at risk as well as at HSC."

Ty let out a breath and closed his eyes. "Oh, Christ."

"What?"

"I was in there yesterday afternoon." He opened his eyes and looked at Matt. "I was at HSC."

"Did you do it?" Matt asked mildly. "Did you lift the drugs?"

"Hell, no."

"Didn't figure you for being stupid," Matt said, watching as Ty pulled out his phone and hit a number. "And we don't get reception out here. No one does. Listen, this gets a little worse. Jane, her boss, rode her hard about this, and..."

"*And*?"

"Mallory walked off her job. She quit."

Ty held his hands out. "Keys."

"Excuse me?"

"I'm driving back." He needed to see Mallory. Now. *Yesterday.*

"Why are *you* driving back?" Matt wanted to know.

"Because we're in a hurry, and you drive like a girl."

Halfway back to town, Ty finally got phone reception and hit Mallory's number. While it rang in his ear, Matt *tsk*ed. "You need a blue tooth," he said. "Or you're going to get a ticket."

Ty ignored him, thinking *pick up, pick up*... but Mallory didn't. "She's probably at home, phone dead."

And he didn't have her house number.

Matt shook his head. "Nope, she's not at home."

Ty looked at him.

"Oh, did you want to know where she is?" When Ty just narrowed his eyes, Matt smiled. "Yeah, you want to know.

She's at the diner. I was there earlier, heard Amy take a call from her. Something about a chocoholic meeting."

There was something in Matt's voice when he said Amy's name, and needing a distraction, Ty slid him a glance. "So what's with you and the pretty waitress?"

"Nothing."

"There's a whole lot of tension between you two for nothing."

Matt pleaded the Fifth.

"You screw something up?"

Matt's sunglasses were mirrored, giving nothing away. He was not answering, which was the same thing as saying yeah, he'd screwed something up. "What did you do?" Ty asked.

"Jack shit."

Yeah, right. They came into town and bypassed the road to Matt's house.

"Hey," Matt said.

"Hang on, coming in hot." Ty pulled up to the diner with a screech of tires.

Matt let go of the dash and looked at him.

Ty shrugged. "Maybe misery loves company."

"You mean maybe misery loves to watch other people fuck up."

"I'm not going to fuck anything up."

"Uh huh."

Ty shook his head and went into the diner, which had been decorated for spring. There were brightly colored papier-maché flowers and animals hanging from the ceiling tiles, and streamers around the windows. It didn't much match the 50s décor but it was definitely eye-popping.

The place was full with the dinner crowd, the noise level high. Ty recognized just about everyone there, which meant he'd been here far too long. He could see Jan hustling a large tray to a table. And there was Ryan in a far corner with two guys from NA. Blue-haired Lucille was there too, with a group of other blue-haired, nosy old bats. Ty shifted past the small group of people waiting to be seated because he could see Mallory at the counter. Grace was on one side of her, with Amy on the other side of the counter.

Ty came up behind Mallory, who was staring down at a cake that said "Happy Birthday Anderson" as Amy lit the candles.

All around them were the general, noisy sounds of a diner. Dishes clanking, voices raised in conversation, laughter—each table or group involved in their own world. This particular little world, of the three women, was exclusive, and not a one of them was paying their surroundings any attention.

Mallory, the woman who'd claimed to have given up chocolate, licked her lips. "We should skip the candles," she said to Amy. "You have a full house right now. You're too busy for this."

"Oh no," Amy said. "We agreed. When bad shit happens, we meet. We eat." She lit the last candle and handed each of them a fork. "I've already called Tara and told her that Anderson's cake met a tragic demise."

"She believe you?" Grace asked.

"She's smarter than that." Amy looked at Mallory. "But she understood the emergency and is making another cake. The important thing is that we get Mallory through this situation."

Mallory sighed and thunked her forehead to the table.

Amy quickly slid the cake over a little bit, probably so Mallory's hair wouldn't catch fire. "So did you really tell Jane to stuff herself?"

"Yes." Mallory's voice was muffled, and Grace *tsk*ed sympathetically and stroked Mallory's hair.

"But that's not why I'm out of a job," Mallory said. "It's because I yelled it, and everyone heard. Bill said sometimes he wished Jane would stuff it, too, but we have to learn to not compound our errors. He was working up to firing me. He had no choice, really. And that's when I sort of lost it. I told him to stuff it, too, and left."

"Wow," Grace said. "When you decide to go bad, you go all the way."

Mallory let out a combination laugh/sob.

"What are your plans now?" Amy asked her. "Beg for your job back?"

"I'm thinking I'll end up working for some quiet little doctor's office somewhere and try to go back to behaving like myself." Mallory scooped up some cake and stuffed it into her mouth. "I don't want to talk about it."

"Tough," Ty said.

She jerked upright and whirled on her stool to face him. She had chocolate on her lips but she pointed her fork at him like she was a queen on her throne. "You need to stop doing that."

"You'd wither up and die of boredom in a quiet little doctor's office," he said.

She stared up at him, her eyes shining brilliantly. Everyone was looking at them, of course. Well, except Amy, who was looking at Matt. Matt had taken a seat at the counter to watch the circus.

Ty narrowed his eyes at everyone.

No one took the hint to give him and Mallory some privacy. Of course not. It used to be one gaze from him could terrorize people. But it hadn't worked for him in Lucky Harbor, not once. Giving up, he gestured to the candles as the little flames seemed to gather in strength. "You should blow those out," he said.

Amy blew out the candles. Grace feigned interest in a menu. Their ears were cocked.

Resigned at having an audience, Ty looked at Mallory. "Why didn't you tell me?"

"Which?" she asked.

Jesus. There was more than one thing? The candles flickered back to life on the cake, which he ignored. "Let's start with the missing drugs."

"Because I know that you didn't take them." Mallory eyed the cake. "You used trick candles?" she asked Amy.

"Yeah," she said. "They were from Lance's birthday party. His brother's idea. Tucker has a warped sense of humor. They're all I had."

"Excuse me," Lucille said, hopping off her stool and scooting close. "But I couldn't help but overhear. Missing drugs?"

"This isn't an open-to-the-public conversation, Lucille," Mallory said.

"But who would take drugs from the HSC?" the older woman asked. "A teenager? A drug dealer? One of your crazy siblings?"

Mallory pinched the bridge of her nose. "You're just as crazy as Tammy and Joe, and you know it."

Lucille blinked. "Are you sassing me?"

"Yes," Mallory said. "Apparently it's my new thing.

Push me, and I'll even yell at you. Also a new thing. Now stay out of my business; I'm trying to have a private conversation here." She grimaced. "*Please*," she added politely.

Lucille blinked, then smiled. "Well, there it is. Been waiting a long time to see that."

"I *always* say please."

"Not that. Your backbone. You have one, and it looks great on you, my dear."

Mallory just stared at her, then at Ty. But he was still a little stunned at what she'd said before.

I know you didn't take them.

Somehow, in spite of his best efforts to hold back, Mallory knew him, she knew who he was, inside and out, and accepted him. As is.

And she'd believed in him, no questions asked.

This didn't help her now, he knew. Because someone *had* taken the meds under her watch. It could have been anyone. Only Mallory knew the truth, and Ty knew by just looking at her that she *did* know. She knew who it was, and she didn't want to say.

Even now she was trying to save someone.

It slayed him. *She* slayed him. "If you know I wasn't the one who took the pills," he said, "then why didn't you turn over the list of people who'd been inside the building?"

For some reason, this pissed her off. He watched as temper ignited in her eyes. Standing up, she stabbed him in the chest with her finger hard enough to make him wince. "Do you think you're the only one I care about?" she demanded.

"Uh…"

"No," she assured him. "You are not."

She was as mad as he'd ever seen her, in sky blue scrubs with a long-sleeved T-shirt beneath—*his* shirt, if he wasn't mistaken. There was a mysterious lump of things in her pockets and someone had drawn a red heart on one of her white tennis shoes. She still had chocolate on one corner of her mouth, her hair was completely out of control, and she was ready to take down anyone who got in her path.

She'd never looked more beautiful. "Mallory." He knew how much her job meant to her. How much the HSC meant. How much Lucky Harbor meant.

He was leaving, but she wasn't. Her life was here, and in that moment, he made his decision, knowing he could live with it. "I took advantage of you," he said, making sure to speak loud enough for all the eavesdroppers to hear. "Complete advantage."

Two stools over, Matt groaned. "Man, don't. Don't do it."

Mallory hadn't taken her eyes off Ty, and she was still pissed. "*What are you doing?*"

"Attempting to tell what happened," he said carefully.

"Now you all just hold it right there." Mrs. Burland was suddenly right there, pointing at Ty with her cane, almost sticking it up his nose. "Yeah, you little punk-ass," she said. "I'm talking to you."

Little punk ass? He was a foot and a half taller than her and outweighed her by at least a hundred pounds. He stared down at her in shock.

Everyone in the place sucked in a breath and did the same.

Except Matt. He grinned wide. "Little punk ass," he repeated slowly, rolling the words off his tongue in delight. "I like it."

Ty gave him a look that didn't appear to bother Matt at all. It'd been a hell of a long time since anyone had gotten in Ty's face, even longer since he'd been called a little punk ass, and by the looks of her, Mrs. Burland wasn't done with him yet.

"What the hell do you think you're doing?" she demanded.

"I'm trying to have a conversation," he said. "A *private* one."

Lucille leaned in. "There's no such thing in Lucky Harbor," she said helpfully.

Clearly tired of the interruptions, Mrs. Burland slammed her cane onto the floor three times in a row, until all eyes were back on her. She glared at Ty. "You have no right to confess to a crime you didn't commit."

Apparently, as well as being curmudgeonly and grumpy and mean as a snake, Mrs. Burland was also sharp as a tack. "Stay out of it," he said.

"You're trying to be the big hero," Mrs. Burland told him. "You think she's protecting someone, and you don't want her hurt."

Mallory turned to him. "Is that what you're doing?"

Ty opened his mouth but Mrs. Burland rose up to her full four feet eight inches and said, "It was me. *I* took the meds." She eyeballed the entire crowd. "Not a teenager. Not a drug dealer. Not any of the crazy Quinns. And not this—" She gestured toward Ty, and her mouth tightened disfavorably. "*Man*. He might be guilty of plenty, not the least of which is messing with *your* reputation, Mallory

Quinn—not that you seem to mind—but he didn't take the pills. That was me."

"No." A young woman stood up from a table across the room. Ty recognized her as Deena, the clerk at the grocery store. "I was at the HSC yesterday," she said. "For birth control pills. *I* took the Oxycontin."

"That's a lie." This was from Ryan, at the far end of the counter. "We all know I have a problem. *I* took the pills."

Mallory's mouth fell open.

Nothing surprised Ty, but even he could admit to being shocked. The entire town was rallying around Mallory in the only way they knew how. He'd never seen anything like it.

Amy banged a wooden spoon on the counter to get everyone's attention. "Hey, I was there, too. I took the pills." Her eyes locked on Matt's, whose jaw bunched and ticked.

Mallory gaped at Amy. "You were not there—"

"Oh no you all don't!" Mrs. Burland yelled. "Listen you...you egocentric, self-absorbed, narcissistic group of *insane* people. Don't make me smack all of you!" And with that, she pulled a small box from her pocket.

A sample of Oxycontin.

"See?" she said triumphantly. "I have them. I have them all. I took them because I thought they were Probiotics for my constipation. They're the same color box. My insurance is crap, and even if it wasn't, I hate to wait in line at the pharmacy. I've spent the past decade waiting in stupid lines. A line to see the doctor. A line to wait for meds. Hell, I even had to wait in line to go to the bathroom a minute ago. I'm over it, and I'm over all of you."

"You don't need Probiotics," Lucille said. "All you need are prunes and a blender."

"*You* got Mallory fired?" Amy asked Mrs. Burland.

"No, Mallory's big mouth got her fired," Mrs. Burland said.

"I didn't get fired," Mallory said. "I quit."

Lucille tried to lean in again. "Excuse me, dear," she said to Mallory. "But—"

"*Not now*, Lucille. *Please.*"

"Yes, but it's important."

"*What's more important than this?*"

"The candles."

They'd come back to life again, blazing good this time. The cake had been scooted back against the pile of menus, and several had fallen too close. The menus went up in flames just as Ty leaped toward them, grabbing Mallory's glass of water to dump it on the small fire.

The flames flickered and went out.

Except for the middle one, the largest candle. Which turned out to be not just a trick candle but some sort of bottle rocket, because it suddenly shot straight up and into the ceiling like...well, like a bottle rocket.

The fire alarm sounded, and then there was the *whoosh* of a huge pressure hose letting loose, and the sprinklers overhead came on.

And rained down on the entire diner and everyone in it.

Chapter 21

♥

Strength is the ability to break up a solid piece of chocolate—and then eat just one of the pieces.

Mallory was shocked at how fast total chaos reigned. Instantaneously, really. As the overhead sprinklers showered down icy water, people began yelling and screaming. Everyone pushed and shoved at each other to get out.

Adding to the insanity, the decorations hanging from the ceiling soaked up the water and began to fall, pulling down ceiling tiles with them. A papier-maché elephant hit Mallory on the head, along with the attached ceiling tile. For a second she saw stars, then panicked. Someone was going to get seriously hurt. She tried to blink through the downpour to check the crowd for anyone who needed help. She could hardly see two feet in front of her but it appeared that *everyone* needed help. People were either running or down for the count. It was utter mayhem.

Mallory gulped some air and shoved her hair out of her

face. Her hand came away bloody. Her cheek was bleeding, but before she could dwell on that someone grabbed her, tugged her up against his side, and began to steamroll her toward the door.

Ty.

"Let me go," she said, banging on his chest, which was completely ineffective.

"No. I want you safe outside, *now*."

"Forget me, get Mrs. Burland and Lucille!"

"You first, goddammit." Then, still holding her tightly against him, Ty scooped up Mrs. Burland, too. Lucille was nowhere to be seen. Through the sprinklers, Mallory saw Matt grabbing Amy and Grace, shoving them out the door, and going back in for others. Ty dumped Mallory near them and went back inside.

Mallory went to leap in after him. Ty blocked her.

"I'm going in," she said. "People are hurt, Ty. I can help."

His jaw ticked but he stepped aside. The fire alarm was blaring, water from the sprinklers still pouring down. Mallory got several more people outside before she ran into Ty again. He had two of Lucille's posse by their hands but he dropped one and stopped to stroke the wet hair that wouldn't stay out of Mallory's face, ducking a little to look over her bloody cheek, then into her eyes. He was checking on her, making sure she was okay.

But he must know by now. She was always okay. Not that *that* stopped the warmth from washing through her from knowing he cared. It was in every touch, every look.

And he was going to leave.

He had a job; she got that. She'd never want to hold him back from what fueled him, whatever that might be.

But she'd sort of, maybe, just a little bit, wished that *she* could be what fueled him.

By the time the fire department came, they'd gotten everyone out. Several people were injured enough to require several ambulances, which arrived right behind the fire department. Mallory was helping those lined up on the sidewalk. Near her, Matt was assisting the paramedics. Ty, too, looked just as comfortable in a position of medical authority. He had Ryan, who'd somehow gotten a nasty-looking laceration down one arm, seated at the curb. Ty was crouched at the vet's side, applying pressure to the wound, looking quite capable.

Josh pulled up to the scene and hopped out of his car. Ryan was closest to him, so he stopped beside him first.

"He's in shock," Ty said quietly.

It was true. Ryan was shaking, glassy-eyed, disoriented. Definitely in shock. Josh went back to his car and returned with an emergency kit. Ty and Josh wrapped Ryan in an emergency blanket to get him warm, then made sure he was breathing evenly and that his pulse wasn't too fast. Mallory took over then, sitting at Ryan's side, holding his hand as she watched Josh and Ty work together in perfect sync on other victims.

When the paramedics were free, they took over Ryan's care and Mallory moved toward Ty and Josh.

"The least you can do," Josh was saying to Ty, "now that you're cleared and still sitting on your ass, is hire on. You know there's that flight paramedic opening out of Seattle General. That unit runs its ass off, no shortage of adrenaline there. And hell, look at how exciting Lucky Harbor can be."

Ty ignored him and crouched at Lucille's feet. "You okay?"

"Oh, sure, honey." She patted his arm. "You're a good boy."

Ty smiled, and Mallory didn't know if that was at the idea of him being a boy, or good. Then he straightened and turned to Mallory.

She wasn't surprised that he'd known she was standing behind him. He always seemed to know where she was. "Wow," she said with what she thought was remarkable calm. "Look at you."

His eyes locked in on her cheek, and he touched the wound. With a wince, she batted his hand away.

He pulled her away from all the prying eyes and ears. "You need that taken care of," he said. "Let me help—"

"No." She needed more help than he could possibly imagine. "It can wait." She didn't know where to start, but she gave it the old college try and started at the beginning. "How is it that a mechanic knows how to treat trauma victims?"

His gaze never left hers. "I was a medic in the SEALS."

"A medic. In the SEALs." She absorbed that and shook her head. "That's funny, because I could have sworn you told me you were a mechanic. A navy mechanic, who was doing similar work now."

"No," he said. "Well, yes. I work on cars. Sometimes. But that's for me, for fun."

"For fun." She paused, but it didn't compute. "I pictured you working on ships, maybe on helicopters and tanks. Not bodies. Why didn't you tell me?"

He responded with a question of his own. "Why does it matter what I was?"

"Because it's not what you were, Ty, it's who you *are*." How could he not see that? Or hear her heart as it quietly cracked down the center? "You're going back," she said. "You're only here waiting to be cleared..." She stared at him as Josh's words sank in. "Except you already *are* cleared." Oh, God. He could leave now. Any second. "How long have you known? And why would you hide so much from me?" But she already knew the answer to that. It was because they were just fooling around.

Nothing more.

And she had no one to blame but herself. Horrified at how close she was to breaking down, she took a step backward and bumped directly into Sheriff Sawyer Thompson. He'd strode up to the soggy group and now stood there, hands on hips. "What the hell happened here?"

Everyone was still there. No one wanted to miss anything. Every able body in the pathetic, ragtag-looking group immediately gathered ranks around Mrs. Burland, the mean old biddy who'd never done anything nice for a single one of them. In fact, she'd made their life a living hell in a hundred different ways. But they all started talking at once, each giving their story of the drug theft, and how they'd ended up being dumped on by the diner's sprinkler system.

Once again protecting one of their own.

Mrs. Burland still wasn't having any of it. She stood up, wobbled with her cane toward the sheriff and held out her wrists. "Arrest me, Copper. But don't even think about a strip search. I have rights, you know."

Sawyer assured her that he had no interest in arresting her, because then he'd have to arrest everyone else who'd confessed as well. Looking disgusted and frustrated, he started over, talking to one person at a time.

The crowd began to disperse.

Mallory sank to the curb and dropped her head to her knees, exhausted to the bone and far too close to losing it. Ty, holding so much back from her...How was that even possible? She'd given him everything she'd had.

He wasn't going to change now, and God help her, she was going to be okay with that if it killed her.

And it just might.

Two battered boots appeared in front of her, and she felt him crouch at her side.

Ty, of course. Her heart only leapt for Ty. He ran a big, warm hand down her back, made a sound of annoyance at finding her still drenched and shivering, and then she felt one of the emergency blankets from the firefighters come around her.

"I'm fine," she said.

"Yeah." He sat at her side and pulled her in against his warmth. "Extremely fine. But that's not what's in question here."

"What *is* in question?"

"You tell me."

"Fine," she said, and lifted her head. "I don't get the big secret about being a paramedic."

"It wasn't a secret."

"It feels like a secret," she said. "That day you came to the hospital to get your stitches out, you could have done that yourself."

"I wanted to see you."

Aw.

Dammit, *no* aw. "Okay, then what about what happened next?" she asked. "When that patient coded out? You got pale and shaky, almost shocky, as if you'd never seen anything like that before."

Ty was still balanced on the balls of his feet. He lowered his head and studied his shoes for a moment, then looked her right in the eyes. "Do you want to know the last thing I did as a SEAL trauma medic?" he asked, voice dangerously low. She wasn't the only one pissed off and frustrated.

"I dragged my teammates out of the burning plane," he told her. "Tommy was already dead, but the others, Brad, Kelly, and Trevor..." He closed his eyes. "I did everything I could, and they died anyway. Afterward, I couldn't do it. I tried, but I couldn't go back to being a first line trauma responder."

Her gut wrenched for him. "Oh, Ty."

"I was honorably discharged, and when I got work, it wasn't as a medic. I turned down anything like that for four years. Four years, Mallory, where I didn't so much as give out a Band-Aid."

Until he'd come to Lucky Harbor. "Amy's knife wound," she whispered.

He nodded grimly. "The first time I'd opened a first-aid kit in all that time."

And then today. Again, a situation that fell right on him, and he'd stepped into the responsibility as if into a pair of comfortable old shoes. She wondered if he realized that.

"My turn," he said. "Your job? You lost your job?"

"Not lost. *Quit.*" She took a moment to study her own shoes now, until he wrapped his fingers around her ponytail and tugged.

She lifted her head and met his gaze. "Mallory," he said softly. Pained. "Why?"

Why? A million reasons, none of which she wanted to say because suddenly, it was all too much. The job, the HSC, the diner, knowing how she felt about Ty and realizing he was going to leave anyway. Her head hurt, her cheek hurt. And her heart hurt, too. When her eyes filled, he made a low sound. Hard to tell if it was male horror or empathy. But then he wrapped his arms around her, and she planted her face in the crook of his neck.

She should have known he wouldn't be uncomfortable with tears. He didn't seem to be uncomfortable with much, when it came right down to it.

Except maybe his own emotions.

How had things gotten so out of control? All she'd wanted was to stretch her wings. Live for herself instead of for others. Try new things. She'd done that, and she'd loved it.

She loved him.

And therein lay her mistake. "The whole HSC drug fiasco is *my* fault," she said into his chest. "No one else's. I screwed up there." She sucked in a breath as once again her eyes filled. "As for everything else, I always wanted to go a little crazy, but as it turns out, I'm not all that good at it," she whispered.

He made a show of looking at the utter chaos of the diner. "I don't know," he said. "I think you're better at it than you give yourself credit for."

She choked out a laugh, realizing that no matter what she did, he had her back. He'd been there for her, one hundred percent. It was in his every look, touch, kiss. "I just wanted something for myself," she said softly.

"And you deserve that," he said with absolute conviction, warming her from the inside out. From the beginning, he'd treated her like someone special, from before they'd even known each other's names. He'd shared his courage, his sense of adventure, his inner strength.

Once, she'd been a woman terribly out of balance with herself and her hopes and dreams. That had changed.

Because of him.

She was in balance now but even that wasn't enough. Loving him wasn't enough. It wasn't going to get her what she wanted. Nothing was going to get her what she wanted—which was Ty. She really needed to cut her losses now before it got worse, but God. How could she? "Ty."

He pulled back to look into her eyes, his own going very serious at the look in hers.

She cupped his face. "I've screwed up. I'm falling for you." She gently kissed his gorgeous mouth so that he couldn't say anything. "Don't worry, I know you won't let yourself do the same." She kissed him again when he went to speak, because it was in his eyes. Sorrow. "I can't do this anymore," she whispered past a throat that felt like she'd swallowed cut glass. "I'm sorry."

"Are you dumping me, Mallory?"

Was she? The truth was that *he* was the one going, and yet he hadn't. She'd have to think about that later, but for now, for right now, what she had with him wasn't enough for her. "You were never mine to dump," she said.

Something crossed his normally stoic face, but he nodded and lifted a hand to her jaw, stroking his thumb over her lips in a gentle gesture that made her ache. She started to say something, she had no idea what, but someone tapped her on the shoulder. "*Mallory Michelle Quinn.*"

Only one person ever middle-named her. Her mom; just what she needed. She swiped at her eyes and turned, considering herself lucky to be so wet that no one could possibly tell if she was crying or not. "Mom, why are you here?"

"I heard about the diner. You're hurt?"

"Now's not a good time—" Mallory brushed her mom's hand away. "*Mom.*"

"Don't you 'mom' me! You have a cut on your cheek. And you let Jane *fire* you?"

"Okay, someone give me a microphone!" Mallory said as loud as she could. "Because I wasn't fired, I *quit*. There's a difference."

Her mother stared at her for a long beat, during which Mallory did her best not to look as utterly heartbroken as she felt. Finally Ella nodded. "Well, I hope to hell you took Jane down a peg or two while you were at it."

Shock had Mallory gaping. "You're not upset?"

"She's overworked you and taken advantage of your skills. The board's already banding together to try to get you back. I suggest turning down their first offer. According to what I overheard, their second offer will be a much better deal."

Mallory choked out a shocked breath. "Overheard?"

"Fine. I put a glass to the door of Bill's office and listened in. But I'm not proud of it." Ella hesitated. "What I am proud of is you. And Sawyer sent me over here to get you. He needs one last quick word from you for his report."

Sawyer was already headed for her.

He gave her a look of frustration. "You okay?"

No. "Yes."

"Good, because so far I've heard twenty different versions of what's going on. Tell me that you're going to come up with the *right* one."

She told him the entire story the best that she could, then turned to look for Ty and found her mom talking to him. Ella was animated, her hands moving, her mouth flapping, and Mallory's stomach sank. From the looks of things, she could be reading him the riot act, or...hell. She couldn't imagine. "I've got to go," she said to Sawyer.

Her mother saw her coming and met her halfway. "He has a way of looking at you, honey. Like you mean something to him."

Mallory shook her head. "What did you two talk about?"

"Are you asking if I accused him of destroying your reputation?" Ella looked over Mallory's shoulder and found Ty watching them. She sent him a little finger wave.

He didn't wave back but he did almost smile.

"You made it clear what you thought of my way of thinking," Ella said to Mallory. "And you were right. I've been holding the reins too tight, depending on you to be the calm in the storm of this crazy family. That was unfair, maybe even cruel, and I was wrong. I never should have done it. Just as I never should have allowed you to blame yourself for Karen. Or my divorce. Or the general insanity of our family."

"Mom—"

"Hush, honey. I told him I'd make him dinner," Ella

said casually, almost as a throwaway remark, and stroked Mallory's wet hair back from her face.

"You *what*?"

"He's been good to you. I want to thank him. It's simple etiquette."

"You mean it's simple curiosity," Mallory said.

"Okay, that too."

"Mom, we're just..." God. Her heart hurt. "Friends."

"Oh, please," Ella said with a laugh. "I didn't fall for that with Tammy when she brought Zach home, and I'm not going to fall for it with you. He said yes."

"No, really," Mallory said. "We're not what you think we are. He said *yes*?"

"Sweetheart, you're drenched and still shivering. You're going to catch your death out here. Go home and take a hot shower, and put something on that cut on your cheek." Ella hugged her tight, then pushed her toward her car.

Mallory took a last look at the scene. Ty was back to helping. He was hauling things out of the wrecked diner with Matt. Two extremely fine examples of what a good use of gorgeous male muscle could do.

"Mallory." Josh gestured to Mrs. Burland, huddled on the sidewalk. "She's refusing to go to the hospital but mostly, she's just shaken up. If you're leaving, maybe you could drive her home."

Mallory ended up driving the entire senior posse home since Lucille was the only one of them still in possession of her license, and she was going into the hospital for X-rays. It took nearly an hour because each of them took forever to say their good-byes and get out of the car. When she'd finally gotten rid of them all, Mallory told herself to go home, but herself didn't listen. She drove to Ty's.

The garage was open, and he was beneath his precious Shelby.

She bet he'd never walked away from a car in his life.

Still working on adrenaline, frustration, and a pain so real it felt like maybe her heart had been split in two, she stormed up to the mechanic's creeper and nudged at his exposed calf.

Okay, maybe it was more of a kick. "You told my mother she could cook you dinner?"

He rolled out from beneath the car, and arms still braced on the chassis above him, looked up at her. He wisely didn't comment on what was surely a spectacularly bad hair day on her part. She'd been hit with the sprinklers, and then dust from the ceiling tiles, and the whole mess had dried naturally without any of her defrizzing products that never really worked anyway.

"Problem?" he finally asked.

"Oh my God!" She tossed up her hands. "You did. You said yes. *Why?*"

"She said she'd make meatloaf. I don't think I've ever had home-cooked meatloaf. I thought it was a suburban myth."

She'd never wanted to both hug and strangle someone before. "*I'll* make you meatloaf!"

"You dumped me," he said reasonably. "And besides, you don't cook."

Dammit. Dammit, he was killing her. She pressed the heels of her hands to her eyes but she couldn't rub away the ache. Spinning on her heel, she walked out of the garage.

He caught her at her car, pulling her back against him. She felt the shaking of his chest and realized he was laughing at her.

At least until he caught sight of her face.

His smile faded then.

With a frustrated growl, she shoved him away and got into her car, but before she could shut the door, he squatted at her side, the muscles in his thighs flexing against the faded denim he wore. He blocked her escape with one hand on the door, the other on the back of her seat, his expression unreadable now. "This isn't about meatloaf," he said. "This isn't even about me. Tell me what the real problem is."

I'm in love with you…

"My problem," Mallory said, "is that you're blocking me from shutting the door."

"And you're shutting me out."

"That's pretty funny," she managed, throat inexplicably tight. "Coming from you. The King Of Shutting *Me* Out."

"I didn't shut you out intentionally."

"Ditto," she said, with no small amount of attitude.

He studied her for a long moment. "Tell me about the night Karen died."

She felt like he'd reached into her chest and closed his fist around her lungs. She couldn't breathe. "She's not a part of this."

"I think maybe she is. She took a walk on the dark side, and it didn't work out so well for her. She made you promise to be good, and you kept your word. Until me."

"Someone has a big mouth."

"*Many* someones," he agreed. "But then again, you

love it here. You love all those someones. And they all love you."

Mallory dropped her head to the steering wheel. "Look, I'm mad at you, okay? This isn't about me. I know my painful memories are relative. My life is good. I'm lucky. This isn't about how poor little Mallory has had it so hard. I'm not falling apart or anything."

He stroked a hand down her back. "Of course you're not. You're just holding the steering wheel up with your head for a minute, that's all."

Choking out a laugh, she closed her eyes. "I'm okay."

"Yeah, you are. You're so much more okay than I've ever been. You're the strongest woman I've ever met, Mallory. Do you know that?"

"But that's just it. I'm not strong at all. I always thought I could save everyone. If I was good, I'd excel. If I was good, my family would stay together. If I was good, nothing bad could happen."

Ty's hand on her was calming. So was his voice, low and even, without judgment. And the dash of affection didn't hurt. "How did that work out for you?" he asked. "All that being good?"

Another laugh tore out of her, completely mirthless. "It didn't. All that work, all that time spent trying to please everyone, and it fell apart anyway. I failed."

"You know better than that."

"Do I?" She tightened her grip on the steering wheel. It was her only anchor in a spinning world. Nothing was working out for her. Not her job. Not the way she wanted people to see her. And not her non-relationship with Ty. "I don't want to talk about the past anymore. My sister made her choice. My family each made their own choices after that. My parents handled everything the best they could, including their divorce."

"Maybe," he said. "But it still chewed you up and spit you out."

"I'm okay."

"You don't always have to be okay."

"Well, I know that."

"Then say it. Free that sixteen-year old, Mallory. Say it wasn't her fault; not your parents' divorce, not Karen, none of it."

"Ty."

"Say it."

She gulped in some air and let it out. "It wasn't my fault."

He wrapped his hand around her hair and gently tugged until she'd lifted her head and was looking at him. "That's right," he said with terrifying gentleness. "It wasn't your fault. You did the best you could with what you had. You made the decision to progress beyond that little girl who lived to please. You stepped outside your comfort zone and went after what you wanted."

She felt the heat hit her cheeks. They both knew what she'd gone after.

Him.

Naked.

And she'd gotten him.

"Stop carrying all the responsibility for everyone," he said quietly. "Let it go, let it all go and be whoever the hell you want to be."

She gave him a little smile. "Are you going to take your own advice?"

"I'm working on it."

"You're pretty amazing, you know that?"

"Yeah." He flashed his own small smile. "Too bad you dumped my sorry ass."

She looked at him for a long beat. "I might have been too hasty on that," she whispered. "Twice now."

"Is that right?"

"Yeah. Because your ass is anything but sorry."

He gave her a smile. "Come here," he said, and then without waiting for her to move, rose to his feet and pulled her from the car.

She curled into him, wrapping her arms around his neck. "Where are we going?"

"To show you how much more amazing I can be when we're horizontal."

Chapter 22

A life without chocolate is no life at all.

Ty set Mallory down in his bathroom, and she looked around in confusion. "I'm not horizontal."

Leaning past her, he flipped on his shower and cranked the water to hot. Then he stripped. And oh good Lord, he looked so damn good without his clothes that it almost made her forget her problems, including the fact that *he* was her biggest problem. "What—"

"You're wet and frozen solid. Kick off your shoes."

While she was obeying that command, he peeled the wet clothes from her and let them hit the floor. And while she was distracted by his mouth-watering body, he checked the temperature of the shower, then pushed her in.

She sucked in a breath as the hot water hit her, and then another when he reached for the soap. He washed her with quick efficiency while she stared down at the erection brushing her stomach.

"Ignore it," he said.

She stared at it some more, and it got bigger.

He shook his head at her and washed her hair, his fingers heaven on her scalp, making her moan. Then he set her aside, soaped himself up with equally quick efficiency, which absolutely shouldn't have turned her on, but totally did.

It must have showed because his eyes went dark and hot. Turning off the water, he wrapped her up in a towel and sat her on the counter. With just a towel low on his hips, he crouched down, rooted in a drawer, and came up with a first-aid kit and a box of condoms. Both unopened. Saying nothing, he set the condoms on the counter at her hip.

She went hot looking at them.

Grabbing the first-aid kit, he straightened to his full height and pushed her wet hair from her face. He dipped his knees a little and eyed the cut over her cheek. "A few butterfly bandages will do you, I think." He disinfected the cut, and when she hissed out a pained breath, he leaned in and kissed her temple.

"Nice bedside manner," she murmured. "You patch up a lot of wet, naked women?"

"Almost never." He carefully peeled back the plastic packaging on the sterilized butterfly bandages and began to cover her wound.

"So what exactly happened that you're okay with handling this sort of thing again?" she asked.

"You happened."

"Come on."

He slid her a look. "You think you're the only one making changes in your life?" he asked. "You work your ass off, no matter how much shit you see, and you see plenty. You just want to help people, heal them. I used to be like that. I didn't realize I missed it, but I do."

"The job you're going back to," she said. "It's obviously very dangerous work."

"Not as dangerous as being a SEAL. That was about as bad as it can get."

"Like the plane crash," she said softly.

"Yeah. Like the plane crash."

"Do you have PTSD, Ty?"

"Maybe." He shrugged. "Probably, a little. Not debilitating though. Not anymore anyway."

He was still damp from the shower, his hair pushed back from his face. He concentrated on his task, leaving her free to stare at him. His mouth was somehow both stern and generous at the same time, his jaw square and rough with a day's worth of scruff that she knew would feel deliciously sensual against her skin. He had a scar along one side of his jaw and another on his temple. His chest was broad, his abs ridged with muscle.

He was beautiful.

"You really miss it," she said softly. "The action."

"Once an adrenaline junkie, always one, I guess." He finished with the cut on her face and lifted her hand, turning it over to gently probe her swollen and already bruised wrist. She had no idea how he'd noticed it.

'It's not broken," she said.

He nodded in agreement, then lifted it to his mouth and brushed a kiss to her skin.

While she melted, he expertly wrapped it in an Ace bandage, then looked at her shin.

Bleeding.

She hadn't even realized.

He dropped to his knees and attended to that with the same concentration and professionalism he'd given everything else. His head was level with the counter she was sitting on, and his hands were on her bare leg. And all she could think was if he shifted her leg an inch more to the left, her towel would gape, and he'd be eye level with her bare crotch.

It was a suggestive, erotic thought that led to others, and she squirmed, wondering how she could get her towel to drop without being obvious about it.

"You okay?" he asked.

"Why didn't you leave when you were cleared?"

He looked up into her face. "I think you know why."

"Me."

"You," he agreed.

There were some advantages to changing her life around, to living for herself instead of for others' expectations, she decided. For one thing, it had given her new confidence. So she accessed some of that and unwrapped the towel, letting it fall to the counter at her hips.

Ty went still, and a sensual thrill rushed through her.

He let out a breath and slid his hands up her legs, applying gentle pressure until she opened them for him. He groaned at his new-found view and pressed a kiss to first one inner thigh, and then the other.

And then in between.

His hands were on her, rough and strong but tender at the same time, and her body quivered, rejoicing in the rightness of his touch. He murmured something against her skin and though she couldn't hear him, she urged him on, clutching at his shoulders until her toes curled, until she cried out his name, until there were no more thoughts.

She opened her eyes and found him rising to his feet, eyes hot, mouth wet, as he helped her off the counter. Then she was staring at him as he turned and walked out of the bathroom. "What are you—"

Since he was gone, she followed him into his bedroom, watching as he quickly dropped his towel, but instead of finishing the horizontal lessons, he pulled on black knit boxers that barely fit over his massive erection. "What are you doing?"

"Someone's at the door." He slid his long legs into jeans and grimaced when he tried to button them up.

Still in her orgasmic glow, she was thinking that she'd like to trace the cords of every one of his muscles, starting with his chest and working her way down. It'd take a while but she thought it would be time well spent. Then what he'd said sank in. "Someone's at your door? I didn't hear anything."

A small smile escaped him. "That's because you were making more noise than the doorbell."

"I was not—" God. She covered her hot cheeks. "Who is it?"

"Your mother."

She squeaked. "*What*?"

"I caught sight of her walking up to the door from the bathroom window." He glanced down at his hard-on. "You're going to have to get it." He eyed her body from head to toe and groaned. "And probably you should get dressed."

"*Why is my mother here?*"

"Meatloaf."

She'd forgotten about the meatloaf. Panicked, she

turned in a circle. "My scrubs are wet and in a pile on your bathroom floor!"

"Hydrogen, helium, lithium—"

She stared at him. "What are you doing now?"

"Listing the chemical elements so I can answer the door without a boner."

"And knowing my mother is on your porch isn't taking care of that?"

"Good point." He threw her a pair of sweats that had been lying on a chair and left the room.

In the end, she tossed dignity and wore his sweats instead of her wet scrubs, but by the time she got to the living room, it was empty.

She found Ty in the big kitchen setting down a large bag. "She didn't stay," he said. "She said she figured I had my hands full making sure you were okay. She said she'd water your flowers and feed the cat for you, that you were to just sit your tired patoot down and relax, and I was to make sure you did just that."

"My mother, the Master Manipulator."

"Is your patoot tired?" he asked, sounding amused though his eyes were very serious.

"No. Are you hungry?"

His eyes roamed hungrily over her features. "Yes, but not for food. You?"

"I'll have whatever you're having."

Ty had been wanting to get his hands on Mallory since he'd heard from Matt about the missing drugs. Hell, he'd been wanting to put his hands on her since... always. He *always* wanted to put his hands on her. His hands, his mouth. *Everything*.

He stood her by the bed, making short work of the sweats she'd pulled on. When he dropped to his knees before her, he found her still warm and wet, already making those noises he loved, and when he slid a finger inside her, she gasped and opened her legs even wider for him.

A woman who knew what she wanted.

He loved that about her.

Her fingers were in his hair, holding him to her as if she was afraid he'd stop too soon.

Not a chance.

He wanted to hear her cry out his name again, wanted to feel her fly apart for him, so he worked her slow and easy, driving her right to the edge before backing off. She'd tightened her hands in his hair, doing her best to make him bald. He smiled against her and finally took her to the end. She was still shuddering when he surged to his feet and tossed her to the bed. She lay back, arms stretched out at her sides and gave him a little smile.

Sweet.

Hot.

"Why are you still dressed?" she wanted to know.

It was a good question. He stripped, grabbed a condom and rolled it on. When he had, he pushed inside her, just one long, slick slide that had them both sucking in a harsh breath of sheer, unadulterated pleasure.

Nothing had ever felt so good as being buried deep inside her.

Nothing.

"Ty?"

He drowned in her eyes. "Yeah?"

"This is far more than I thought it would be."

He knew that. He knew it to the depths of his soul.

With one hand in her hair, holding her for a hard, deep kiss, the other cupping her sweet ass, he began to move, thrusting into her slow and steady, and for the first time all day—hell, all damn *week*—his world started to make sense.

He'd been a military brat who'd never landed in one place for long, then a soldier himself. There'd been next to no softness in his life. He'd taken the time for the occasional relationship, although none of them were serious; none stuck long enough to affect him deeply. Certainly no previous relationship had managed to fit what his idea of love was.

Mallory was different.

In his heart of hearts, he knew that much. Hell, from that first stormy night, his tie to her had been undeniable. It'd happened in an instant and only strengthened with time, and he wanted to be with her. Talking, touching, kissing, fucking—whatever he could get, because she beat back the darkness inside him. But being with her was a double-edged sword, because every minute he spent with her absolutely changed his definitions of... *everything*.

She made him yearn for things he'd never yearned for before: home, family, love. And Christ if that didn't stump him. What did he know about any of those things?

All he did know was that this—her mouth open on his, her body warm and soft and welcoming, her hands sliding up his chest and around his neck—felt right. *Real*. "Careful," he murmured, kissing her swollen cheek, then her wrapped wrist. "Don't let me hurt you."

"You healed me," she murmured. "Now let me heal

you." Her hands slid down his back and then up again, and that felt so good he nearly purred. She melted into him and he warned himself that she'd had a rough time of it, that he needed to go slowly, but then she wrapped her legs around his waist and he sank in even further. With a moan, she arched beneath him, head back, eyes closed, hunger and desire etched on her face. "Oh, Ty…"

He nuzzled her exposed throat, then sucked a patch of skin into his mouth, making her gasp and tighten her grip on him.

Everywhere.

It set him on fire.

She did it again, and he let it roll over him: the feel of her heat gripping him like a vise, her scent, the scent of them together, the sound of her ragged breathing combined with wordless entreaties. Yeah. This. *This* was what he'd needed, her body hot and trembling against his, everything connecting. She was rocking into each thrust, her cries echoing in his mouth as he drove deeper, then deeper still. She was saying his name over and over now, straining against him, and then she was coming, shuddering in his arms as she went straight over the edge, taking him right along with her.

It was so good. That was his only thought as he let himself go. So good, so damn good…

Her hair was in his face, but he didn't breathe because he didn't want to disturb her. Her body, still overheated and damp, was plastered to his. She had one leg thrown over him, her cheek stuck to his pec, her hand on his favorite body part as if she owned it.

She did own it. She owned his heart and soul as well.

Jesus. It had started out so innocuously. Innocent, even.

Okay, not innocent. They'd had sex that first night in an attic. Some pretty fan-fucking-tastic sex.

He'd not been in a good place then. He hadn't felt good enough for his own life, much less anyone else's.

Certainly not good enough for a woman like Mallory, who'd give a perfect stranger the very shirt off her back.

But watching her, being with her, made him feel good. Worthy.

It was unbelievable to him that one little woman could do that, but she had.

And where did that leave him? He'd never intended to be anything to Mallory other than a good time, but best laid plans...

Maybe he should have run hard and fast that very first night, but there'd been something about her, something that had drawn him in.

Even when he'd cost her, with her job, with her relationships with her family, she'd never hesitated. She'd given him everything she had. And in return, she'd only asked one thing of him. Just one.

Don't say good-bye. Just go.

His arms involuntarily tightened on her, and although she gave a soft sigh and cuddled deeper into him, she didn't waken. Nor did she stir when he finally forced himself to let go of her and slip out of the bed.

Mallory came awake slowly, thinking about all that had happened the day before. The HSC being shut down, her quitting, the diner's destruction... Ty making it all okay. It was subtle, he was subtle, but last night he'd given her just what she'd needed. Responsive but not smothering, encouraging her to talk when she'd needed to, and letting her be quiet when it'd counted.

She stretched, feeling her muscles ache in a very delicious way. He'd worshipped her body until nearly dawn.

Not just sex.

In truth, it hadn't been just sex for her since their first time, but she hadn't been sure how Ty felt.

Until last night.

Last night, the way he'd touched her, how he'd looked while deep in the throes, shuddering against her, claiming her body and giving her his... that had been lovemaking at its finest. Smiling at the memory, she rolled over and reached for him, but he wasn't in the bed. His pillow was cold.

And something inside her went cold as well.

She grabbed her buzzing phone off the nightstand. She put it there before falling asleep, as was her habit. She thought it might be Ty, but it was a text from Jane:

Bill refused your resignation. Also, due to a new donation earmarked specifically for HSC, the place has been granted a stay of execution for the next six months. On top of that, you are no longer pro bono for your hours there. Your next shift is tomorrow at eight. Be there, Mallory.

A new donation... *What had Ty done now?* Wrapping herself in his sheet, she walked through his house, her glow quickly subsiding. There'd never been much of him anywhere in the place to begin with, but the few traces of his existence were gone. His clothes, his duffle bag on the chair, his iPhone.

Gone.

Running now, she got to the garage and flipped on the light. The Shelby was still there, pretty and shiny.

Finished.

Confused, she went back through the house and into the bedroom. There she found the note that must have been on his pillow but had slipped to the floor, weighted down by a single key. A car key. The note read:

Mallory,

It was far more than I thought it would be, too.

I left you the Shelby. Sell it, it's worth enough that you can take your time deciding on the job thing. Matt'll get what it's worth for you. If you keep it, don't park it on the street.

No regrets.

Love, Ty

She stared at the note for a good ten minutes. He'd left her his baby? Given her permission to sell it so she wouldn't have to worry about money?

And then signed the note *Love, Ty*?

She let out a laugh, then clapped her hand over her mouth when it was followed by a soft sob.

He loved her.

The fool.

Or maybe that was her. *She* was the fool, because she loved him, too. Oh, how she loved him. "No regrets," she whispered, and wrapped her fingers around the key.

Chapter 23

Life is like a box of chocolates—full of nuts.

Mallory sat in Bill's office staring at him in disbelief. "Wait," she said, shaking her head. "Tell me that last part again. Ty tried to give you another donation, and you turned him down?"

"Yes," Bill said. "He's done enough for HSC, and I mean that in the best possible way."

Mallory swallowed hard. It was true. He'd done a lot for her, too. And even as he'd gone back to his life, he'd tried to make sure she'd be taken care of. She wished he was still here so she could smack him.

And then hug him.

"You turned down money?" she asked. "You never turn down money."

"It's not always about the bottom line." He smiled briefly but warmly. "See, even an old dog can learn new tricks."

"But Jane told me there was a donation."

"Yes. Another donation did come in. Mrs. Burland donated one hundred thousand dollars and—"

Mallory gasped and Bill held up a hand. "And she wanted it to be clear that everyone know she was the donor. She said, and I quote, *'I want it yelled from the rooftops that I was the one to save HSC.'*"

Mallory just stared. "Mrs. Burland," she repeated. "The woman who hates all of us, especially me?"

"Yes," Bill said. "Although I don't think she hates you as much as the rest of us. I believe Jane told you, there's a special condition on her donation."

"Me."

"Yeah. Consider your new salary for HSC a raise since I don't have it in the budget to offer you one for your RN position in the ER."

"But I quit."

"So un-quit. Take the knowledge that HSC is now secure, and so is your job, and get out of my office and back to work."

She thought about that for all of two seconds. "Yes, sir." She got up and moved to the door.

"Oh, and Mallory?"

She turned back.

"Don't ever quit again. My voice mail and e-mail box is overloaded with just about everyone in town demanding I'd best not lose you. Your mother has been hounding my ass since you walked out. Hell, *my* mother is hounding me. Understand?"

For the first time since she'd woken alone that morning, Mallory managed a smile. "I understand."

* * *

One week later, Mallory's life looked good—on paper. She had her job back, the future of HSC was secured, and the town was behind her.

What she didn't have was Ty.

Get used to it, she told herself, but on Saturday she rolled out of bed with a decided lack of enthusiasm. She'd done as she'd wanted. She'd stepped out of her comfort zone. She'd been selfish and lived her life the way she wanted, and it'd been more exciting than she could have imagined.

But how did she go back to being herself?

You don't, she decided. She'd put her heart on the line for the first time in her life but she'd made the choice to do it.

No regrets.

That was the day she got the delivery—a plain padded envelope, the return address too blurry and smeared to make out. She opened it up and a carefully wrapped package fell out. Opening the tissue paper, she stared down at the beautiful charm bracelet she'd coveted from the charity auction all those weeks ago.

There was no note, but none was necessary. She knew who'd sent it, and she pressed her hand to her aching heart at what it meant.

Ty, of course. He'd understood her as no other man ever had. He got that she was vested in this town, maybe in the same way he'd yearned to be, that the bracelet meant something to her. He'd added a charm, a '68 Shelby. She had no idea where he could have gotten it from, or what it'd cost him.

What did it mean?

It meant he cared about her, she told herself. Deeply.

It meant she was on his mind, maybe even that he missed her.

She missed him, too, so very much.

Throat tight, she put the bracelet on, swallowed her tears, and shored up her determination to continue stretching her wings.

Two weeks later, Ty was on a flight back to the U.S. after an assignment that had involved escorting diplomats to a Somalian peace treaty.

The team he'd been with were all well-trained, seasoned men with the exception of one, who was fresh out of the military. Their first night, there'd been a kidnapping attempt, but they'd shut it down with no problem.

There'd been no injuries on Ty's team unless he counted the newbie, who'd gotten so nervous when it was over that he'd thrown up and needed an IV fluid replacement. Ty had done the honors.

"Sorry," the kid muttered to Ty that night, embarrassed as he watched Ty pull the IV. "I lost it."

Ty shook his head. "Happens."

"But not to you, right?"

On Ty's first mission, and on every assignment up to the plane crash, he'd thrived on what he'd been doing. He'd believed in it with every fiber of his soul, understood that he'd belonged out there doing what he could to save lives.

After the crash, he hadn't just lost four friends. He'd also lost something of himself. His ability to connect. To get attached.

Until Lucky Harbor. Until the nosy, pestering people

of Lucky Harbor, who cared about everyone and every-thing in their path. Including him.

And Mallory. God, Mallory. She'd been the last piece of his shattered soul fitting back into place. "Hell yeah, it happens to me."

The kid looked surprised to hear Ty admit such a thing but he nodded in appreciation. "I can do this," he told Ty. "I'm ready for whatever comes our way."

But nothing did.

They spent two entire weeks doing nothing more than cooling their heels in the African bush, where the most exciting thing to happen was watching through the long-range scope of a rifle as an elephant gave birth in the distance.

Ty had come back to this because he thought he'd needed the rush of the job to be happy.

So where in the holy hell was his happy?

He knew the answer to that. It was thousands and thou-sands of miles away, with a woman who'd decimated the carefully constructed wall around his heart. And that's when it hit him between the eyes: It wasn't the job that fueled him, that kept him sane.

It was Mallory.

She was his team. She and Lucky Harbor. When he was there with her, she filled him up. Made him whole.

Made him everything.

Christ, he was slow. Too slow. It was probably far too late for such realizations. He'd been a fool and walked away from the best thing to ever happen to him, and Mal-lory didn't suffer fools well.

He looked out the airplane window as they finally cir-cled D.C. Normally, at this point he'd be thinking about his priorities: sleeping for two days, fueling up on good food, and maybe finding a warm, willing woman.

He could get behind the sleep and the food, but there was only one woman he could think of, only one woman he wanted.

He'd left Lucky Harbor certain this had been his future, the nomadic, dangerous work he'd given his life to. He'd told himself it was the right thing to do, that he had to do this to make his team's deaths mean something. Plus, he could never give Mallory the kind of life she wanted. It just wasn't for him.

He'd been wrong on all counts. He knew it now. Brad, Tommy, Kelly, and Trevor's deaths would *always* mean something. And *his* life meant something, too. Probably he'd always known that, but he hadn't had his head screwed on right for a long time. He had it on tight now.

Debriefing took far too long. Frances was waiting for him. A tall, stacked blonde, she had mile-long legs that looked so good in a power suit she was her boss' sole weapon for recruiting.

Once upon a time, she'd recruited the hell out of Ty.

Now there was nothing between them but an odd mix of hostility and affection. She looked him over from head to toe and then back again. "You look like shit."

"Aw. Thanks."

She didn't offer him a smile, just another long gaze, giving nothing away. "You're not staying," she guessed.

"I'm not staying." He tossed her his security pass and walked.

"Do you really think a place like Lucky Harbor has anything to offer you?" she called after him.

He knew it did. He had connections there, real ones.

"Dammit, Ty," she said to his back when he kept walking. "At some point, you have to stop running."

"That's exactly what I'm doing."

Ty caught a red-eye flight into Seattle, and as he landed he brought up Lucky Harbor's Facebook. He'd resisted until now, but as the page loaded, he felt a smile curve his mouth at the latest note posted on the wall:

By now, you've all heard about Mrs. Burland's $100,000 donation to HSC, and how she single-handedly saved the clinic, brought back Mallory Quinn, AND created peace on earth.

Okay, maybe not quite peace on earth, but we do worship the ground she walks on. (Did I get that right, Louisa?)

ANYWAY, last week's raffle raised an additional $5K for the hospital. Thanks to our own Mallory Quinn for her tireless efforts. The grand prize— a date with Hospital Administrator Bill Lawson— was won by Jane Miller, Director of Nurses. Rumor has it that there was a good-night kiss. Wonder if Bill put out? Sources say yes. Look for a summer wedding . . .

Dawn hit the eastern sky as Ty drove a rental car into Lucky Harbor. He wondered if Mallory was still asleep in her bed, warm and soft.

Alone.

Christ, he hoped so. It'd only been two weeks but he'd

left abruptly. Cruelly. He had no right to be back, no right at all to ask her to forgive him.

But that's exactly what he was going to do.

The ocean was still an inky purple as he drove past the pier, then hit the brakes.

The Shelby was in the lot at the diner.

Heart pounding, he parked and entered. The place smelled like fresh paint. The floors looked new and yet seemed to be made of the same timeless linoleum as they'd been before the sprinkler situation. He found Amy, Grace, and Mallory seated at the counter eating chocolate chip pancakes.

Or they had been eating, until he entered.

Three forks went still in the air.

Grace's and Amy's gazes slid to Mallory, but she was paying them no attention whatsoever. She was staring at Ty, her fork halfway to her mouth.

He'd walked through fire fights with less nerves, but he took hope from the sight of the charm bracelet glinting on her wrist.

"This is a private meeting," Grace told him. "Locals only."

"Grace," Mallory said quietly, her eyes never leaving Ty, but for once not giving anything of herself away, either. Ty had absolutely no idea what she was thinking; her face was carefully blank.

A lesson she'd probably learned from him.

Chapter 24

♥

In the cookies of life, friends and lovers
are the chocolate chips.

Mallory stared at Ty and got light-headed, which turned out to be because she wasn't breathing.

"I thought you chocoholics met over cake," Ty said.

Two weeks. It'd been two weeks since she'd seen him, and he wanted to discuss cake. She hungrily drank in the sight of him. He wore battered Levi's and a white button-down, looking as good as ever. But he'd lost some weight, and his eyes were guarded.

"We've been banned from cake," Grace said. "On account of the candles."

Amy pointed at Ty with her fork. "You planning on walking in and out of her life again?"

"Just in," he said, his gaze never leaving Mallory's. "We need to talk."

"So talk," Grace said.

Amy nodded.

Heart pounding, Mallory stood up and gave both of her friends a shake of her head. "You know what he's asking. Give us a minute."

"Okay, but this is his third time interrupting us," Amy pointed out. "And—"

"*Please*," Mallory said to her friends.

Amy looked at Ty, using her first two fingers to point at him, going back and forth between his eyes and hers, silently giving him notice that she was watching him and not to even *think* about misbehaving.

Grace dragged her away.

Mallory waited until they were out of earshot to look at Ty. Her entire being went warm as she drank him in. She had no idea why he was back but she hoped like hell she was part of the reason.

"You still trying to save me, Mallory?" Ty asked quietly.

Her heart was hammering so loud she couldn't hear herself talk. "I can't seem to help myself."

"I don't need saving."

No. No, he sure didn't. He was strong and capable, and more than able to take care of himself. "What *do* you need?"

"You," he said simply. "Only you."

"Oh," Grace breathed softly from behind them. "Oh, that's good."

Both Mallory and Ty turned to find that Amy and Grace had scooted close enough to eavesdrop. Grace winced and held up an apologetic hand. "Sorry. Continue."

Mallory turned back to Ty, who took her hand in his big, warm one to entwine their fingers, bringing them up to his chest. His heartbeat was a reassuring steady thump. "I know you've looked for Mr. Right," he said. "And then Mr. Wrong. I was thinking maybe you'd be interested in a Mr. . . . Regular."

Her throat went tight. "That'd be great," she managed. "But I don't see any regular guys standing in front of me."

The corner of his mouth tipped up and melted her but she wasn't going to be distracted by his hotness right now. "Your job," she said.

"Yeah, I thought that's what drove me, gave me what I needed. I was wrong, Mallory. It's you. *You* fulfill me, like no job or no person ever has. You make me whole."

There was a sniffle behind them. Two sniffles. Mallory ignored them, even as she felt like sniffling herself. "Won't you go crazy here?"

"There's an opening in Seattle for a trauma flight paramedic. Also, I was thinking I want to work with veterans at HSC. I think I could help. And if I get bored and need some real action, there's always the arcade."

Mallory was absorbing this with what felt like a huge bucket of hope sitting on her chest. "And me," she whispered. "I could show you some action. You know, once in awhile."

"Mallory," he said, sounding raw and staggered and touched beyond words. "God, I was so stupid. So slow. I didn't know what to do with you. I tried to keep my distance but my world doesn't work without you in it."

She melted. Given the twin sighs behind her, she wasn't the only one. "But is a trauma paramedic job enough for you?"

"There's more important things to me than an adrenaline rush. There's more important things than *any* job. But there's nothing more important than you," he said. "Mallory, I lo—"

"*Wait!*" This was from Amy, and she looked at Mallory. "I'm sorry, but don't you think you should tell him about the car before he finishes that sentence?"

"*No*," Mallory said, giving Amy the evil eye. She wanted the rest of Ty's sentence, dammit!

Ty frowned. "What's wrong with the Shelby?"

"*Nothing*," Mallory said quickly.

"Nothing," Amy agreed. "Except for the dinged door where she parked too close to the mailbox."

"Oh my God," Mallory said to her. "What are you, the car police?"

"The *classic* car police," Amy said smugly.

"You parked the Shelby on the street?" Ty asked Mallory incredulously.

She went brows-up.

"Okay," he said, lifting his hands. "It's okay. Never mind about the car."

"I've got this one," Grace said, wrapping an arm around Amy, covering the waitress's mouth while she was at it. "Go on."

Mallory turned back to Ty, who pulled her off her stool and touched the small scar on her cheek before leaning in to kiss her. "I love you, Mallory," he said very quietly, very seriously. "So damn much."

Warmth and affection and need and so much more rushed her. "I know."

"You know?"

"Yes."

"Well, hell," he said with a small smile and a shake of

his head. "You might have told me and saved me a lot of time."

"How about I tell you something else?" she said. "I love you, too."

The rest of the wariness he'd arrived with drained from him. "Tell me what you need from me for there to be an us," he said.

Hope blossomed, full and bright. "You want an us?"

"I want an us. Tell me, Mallory."

"I like what we had," she said. "Being together after a long day, maybe dinner out sometimes. That was nice. We could skip the orchestra, though."

"Mallory," he said on a short laugh. "Tell me you want more from me than that."

She bit her lower lip, but the naughty grin escaped anyway. "Well, maybe a little bit more."

He laughed softly, his eyes going dark. He pulled her in and kissed her hard, threading his hands in her hair. "How do you feel about sealing the deal with a ring?" he murmured against her lips.

All three women gasped.

"What?" Mallory squeaked. "You mean an engagement ring? To be *married*?"

"Yes," he said. "You're it for me, Mallory. You're everything."

He was serious. And suddenly, so was she. "I'd like that," she said softly.

"Good," he said. "Anything else we need to work out?"

Only a hundred things. Where was he going to live? *With her*, she thought possessively. She wanted him with her. Wait—Did that mean that she'd have to learn to cook? Because that might be a stretch. And she didn't have any room in her closet to share. And the cat. What if Sweet Pea pooped in his boots?

Ty cupped her face and made her look at him, deep into his eyes, and it was there she found the truth. All these worries were inconsequential. They didn't matter. Nothing mattered but this.

Him.

Besides, she had time to make room for him in her closet. The cat had time to get used to him. They had all the time they needed, because he'd told her he was hers, and he was a man of his word. "I've got all I need," she told him.

He leaned down and kissed her again, then stroked a finger over her temple, tucking a loose strand of hair behind her ear. "I want you to know," he said. "That you're the best choice I ever made."

"No regrets?"

"No regrets."

Heart full to bursting, she tugged him down and kissed the man she was going to spend the rest of her life with.

The Chocoholics' Wickedly Awesome Chocolate Cake

Cake

1 8-ounce bag of dark chocolate chips
½ cup and 3 extra tablespoons butter
1 ¼ cups cake flour
½ cup cocoa
1 box of instant chocolate pudding mix
½ teaspoon salt
½ teaspoon baking powder
¼ teaspoon baking soda
4 large eggs
¼ cup vegetable oil
½ cup white sugar
⅓ cup dark brown sugar

1 ½ teaspoon vanilla extract

⅔ cup milk

Melt the chocolate chips in a microwave-safe bowl by combining the chocolate chips and 3 tablespoons of butter and microwaving on power level 3 for 2 minutes. Take the bowl out of the oven, stir, and put back in the microwave for 2 more minutes. Take it out, stir, and put back in the microwave for 2 final minutes. Stir until the melted chocolate is fully incorporated with the butter.

Mix the dry ingredients together in a medium bowl: cake flour, cocoa, pudding mix, salt, baking powder, and baking soda.

In a large bowl, using an electric mixer, beat the eggs, oil, and sugars together until it thickens, approximately five minutes. Reduce mixer to low speed then add in vanilla and milk. Gradually add in the dry ingredients and beat together.

After it's fully mixed, pour batter into a greased 8-inch square cake pan. Bake at 350 degrees until you can put a toothpick in the middle and it comes out clean, approximately 35 to 45 minutes.

Frosting

½ cup powdered sugar
¾ cup cocoa
2 tablespoons butter (softened)
1 8-ounce package of cream cheese (softened)
1 teaspoon vanilla
¼ cup milk

Mix the powdered sugar and cocoa together.

In a separate bowl, using an electric mixer, beat the butter and cream cheese together. Add vanilla and mix it in. Slowly start incorporating some of the sugar-cocoa mixture. When it starts to firm up, slowly mix in some of the milk. Alternate sugar-cocoa mix and milk until you have the right frosting consistency.

Frost the cooled cake and then…yum!

Amy Michaels is looking forward
to her first weekend hike
through the mountains.

But when a wrong turn takes her off
the trail, she finds herself up close
and personal with forest ranger
Matt Bowers...

At Last

Please turn this page for a preview.

Chapter 1

Everything's better with chocolate.

I'm not lost," Amy Michaels said to the squirrel watching her from his perch on a tree branch. "Really, I'm not."

But she so was. And actually, it was a way of life. Not that Mr. Squirrel seemed to care. "I don't suppose you know which way?" she asked him. "I happen to be looking for hope."

His nose twitched, then he turned tail and vanished into the thick woods.

Well, that's what she got for asking a guy for directions. Or asking a guy for anything for that matter... She stood there another moment, with the high-altitude sun beating down on her head, a map in one hand and Grandma Rose's journal in the other. The forest around her was a profusion of every hue of green and thick with tree moss and climbing plants. Even the ground was alive with growth and running creeks that she constantly had to leap over while birds and squirrels chattered at her. A city girl at heart, Amy was used to concrete, lights, and people flipping other people off. This noisy silence and lack of civilization was like being on another planet, but she kept going.

The old Amy wouldn't have. She'd have gone home by now. But the old Amy had made a life-long habit out of running instead of taking a stand. She was done with that. It was the reason she was here in the wilds instead of on her couch. There was another reason too, one she had a hard time putting into words. Nearly five decades ago now, her grandma had spent a summer in Lucky Harbor, the small Washington coastal town Amy could catch glimpses of from some of the switchbacks on the trail. Rose's summer adventure had been Amy's bedtime stories growing up, the only bright spot in an otherwise shitty childhood.

Now Amy was grown up—relatively speaking—and looking for what her grandma had claimed to find all those years ago—hope, peace, heart. It seemed silly and elusive but the truth was sitting in her gut—Amy wanted those things, needed them so desperately it hurt.

It was harder than she expected. She'd been up since before dawn, had put in a ten-hour shift on her feet at the diner and was now on a mountain trail. Still on her feet.

Unsure she was even going in the right direction, she flipped open her grandma's journal, which was really more of a spiral notepad, small enough that it fit in the palm of her hand. Amy had it practically memorized, but it was always a comfort to see the messy scrawl.

It's been a rough week. The roughest of the summer so far. A woman in town gave us directions for a day hike, promising it'd be fun. We started at the North District Ranger Station, turned right at Eagle Rock,

*left at Squaw Flats. And with the constant roar of
the ocean as our northward guide, headed straight
to the most gorgeous meadow I've ever seen, lined
on the east side by thirty-foot-high prehistoric rocks
pointing to the sky. The farthest one was the tallest,
proudly planted into the ground, probably sitting
there since the Ice Age.*

*We sat, our backs to the rock, taking it all in. I
spent some time drawing the meadow, and when I
was done, the late afternoon sun hit the rock perfectly, lighting it up like a diamond from heaven,
both blinding and inspiring.*

*We carved our initials into the bottom of our dia-
mond and stayed the night beneath a black velvety
sky...*

*And by morning, I realized I had something I'd
been sorely missing—hope for the future.*

Amy could hear the words in her grandma's soft, trembling voice, though of course she would have been much
younger when she'd actually written the journal. Grandpa
Scott had died when Amy was five so she couldn't remember much about him other than a stern face and that
he'd waggled his finger a lot. It was hard to picture the
stoic man of her memories taking a whimsical journey to
a diamond rock and finding hope, but what did she know.

She hiked for what felt like forever on the steep mountain trail that sure had looked a whole lot flatter and
straighter on the map. Neither the map nor Rose's journal
had given any indication that Amy would be going
straight up until her nose bled. Or that the single-track
trail was pitted with obstacles like rocks, fast-running

creeks, low-dropping growth, and in two cases, downed trees that were bigger than her entire apartment. But Amy had determination on her side. Hell, she'd been born determined. Sure, she'd taken a few detours through Down-On-Her-Luck and then past Bad-Decisions-Ville, but she was on the right path now.

She just needed that hope. And peace would be good, too. She didn't give much of a shit about heart. Heart had never really worked out for her. Heart could suck it, but she wanted that hope. So she kept moving, amongst skyscraper-high rock formations and trees that she couldn't even see the tops of, feeling small and insignificant.

And awed.

She'd roughed it before, but in the past, this had meant something entirely different, such as giving up meals on her extra lean weeks, not trudging through the damp, overgrown forest laden with bugs, spiders, and possibly killer birds. At least they sounded like killers to Amy, what with all the manic hooting and carrying on.

When she needed a break, she opened her backpack and went directly for the emergency brownie she'd pilfered from work earlier. She sat on a large rock and sighed in pleasure at getting off her feet. At the first bite of chocolaty goodness, she moaned again, instantly relaxing.

See, she told herself, looking around at the overabundant nature, this wasn't so bad. She could totally do this. Hell, maybe she'd even sleep out here, like her grandparents had, beneath the velvet sky—

Then a bee dive-bombed her with the precision of a kamikaze pilot, and Amy screeched, flinging herself off the rock. "Dammit." Dusting herself off, she stood and eyed the fallen brownie, lying forlorn in the dirt. She gave herself a moment to mourn the loss before taking in her surroundings with wariness.

There were no more bees, but now she had a bigger problem. It suddenly occurred to her that it'd been awhile since she'd caught sight of the rugged coastline, with its stone arches and rocky sea stacks. Nor could she hear the roar of the crashing waves from below as her northward guide.

That couldn't be good.

She consulted her map and her penciled route. Not that *that* helped. There'd been quite a few forks on the trail, not all of them clearly marked. She turned to her grandma's journal again. As directed, she'd started at the North District Ranger Station, gone right at Eagle Rock, left at Squaw Flats...but no ocean sounds. No meadow. No diamond rock.

And no hope.

Amy looked at her watch—six thirty. Was it getting darker already? Hard to tell. She figured she had another hour and a half before nightfall, but deep down, she knew that wasn't enough time. The meadow wasn't going to magically appear, at least not today. Turning in a slow circle to get her bearings, she heard an odd rustling. A human sort of rustling. Amy went utterly still except for the hair on the back of her neck, which stood straight up. "Hello?"

The rustling had stopped, but *there*, she caught a quick flash of something in the bush.

A face? She'd have sworn so. "Hello?" she called out. "Who's there?"

No one answered. Amy slid her backpack around to

her front and reached in for her pocket knife. Once a city rat, always a city rat.

Another slight rustle and a glimpse of something blue—a sweatshirt maybe. "Hey!" she yelled, louder than she meant to but she *hated* being startled.

Again, no one answered her and the sudden stillness told her that she was once again alone.

She was good at alone. Alone worked. Heart still racing, she turned back around. And then around again. Because she had a problem—everything looked the same, so much so that she wasn't sure which way she'd come.

Or which way she was going. She walked along the trail for a minute but it didn't seem familiar so she did a one-eighty and tried again.

Still not familiar.

Great. Feeling like she'd gone down the rabbit hole, she whipped out her cell phone and stared down at the screen.

One bar...

Okay, don't panic. Amy never panicked until her back was up against the wall. Eyeing the closest rock outcropping, she headed towards it. Her guide book had said that the Olympics' rock formations were made up of shales, sandstone, soft basalts, and pillow lava. *She* would have said they were sharp and craggy, a fact attested to by the cuts on her hands and legs. But they were also a good place to get reception.

Hopefully.

Climbing out onto the rocks was fine. Looking down, not so much. She was oh-holy-shit high up.

Gulp.

But she had *two* bars now for her efforts. She took a

moment to debate between her two closest friends, Grace or Mallory. Either of the Chocoholics were good in a tough situation but Mallory was local, so Amy called her first.

"How's it going?" Mallory asked.

"Taking a brownie break," Amy said casually, like she wasn't sitting on a rock outcropping a million feet above earth. "Thought you could join me."

"For chocolate?" Mallory asked. "Oh, yeah. Where are you?"

Well, wasn't that the question of the day. "I'm on the Sierra Meadows trail...somewhere."

There was a beat of accusatory silence. "You lied about meeting you for a brownie?" Mallory asked, tone full of rebuke.

"Yeah, that's not exactly the part of my story I expected you to fixate on," Amy said. The rock was damp beneath her. Rain-soaked mosses adorned every tree trunk in sight, and she could hear a waterfall cascading into a natural pool somewhere nearby. Another bush rustled. Wind?

Or...?

"I can't believe you lied about chocolate," Mallory said. "Lying about chocolate is...*sacrilege*. Do you remember all those Bad Girl lessons you gave me?"

Amy rubbed the spot between her eyes, where a headache was starting. "You mean the lessons that landed you the sexy hunk you're currently sleeping with?"

"Well, yes. But my point is that maybe you need *Good* Girl lessons. And Good Girl Lesson Number One is *never* tease when it comes to chocolate."

"Forget the chocolate." Amy drew a deep breath.

"Okay, so you know I'm not all that big on needing help when I screw up, but..." She grimaced. "*Help.*"

"You're really lost?"

Amy sighed. "Yeah, I'm really lost. Alert the media. Text Lucille." Actually, in Lucky Harbor, Lucille *was* the media. Though she was seventy-something, her mind was sharp as a tack, and she used it to run Lucky Harbor's Facebook like New York's *Page Six.*

Mallory had turned all business, using her bossy ER voice. "What trail did you start on and how long have you been moving?"

Amy did her best to recount her trek up to the point where she'd turned left at Squaw Flats. "I should have hit the meadow by now, right?"

"If you stayed on the right trail," Mallory agreed. "Okay, listen to me very carefully. I want you to stay right where you are. Don't move."

Amy looked around her, wondering what sort of animals were nearby and how much of a meal she might look like to them. "Maybe I should—"

"No," Mallory said firmly. "I mean it, Amy. I want you to stay. People get lost up there and are never heard from again. *Don't move from that spot.* I've got a plan."

Amy nodded, but Mallory was already gone. Amy slipped her phone into her pocket, and though she wasn't much for following directions, she did as Mallory had commanded and didn't move from her spot. But she did resettle the comforting weight of her knife in her palm.

And wished for another brownie.

The forest noises started up again. Birds. Insects. Something with a howl that brought goose bumps to her entire body. She got whiplash from checking out each and every noise. But as she'd learned long ago, maintaining a high level of tension for an extended period of time was just exhausting. A good scream queen she would not make, so she pulled out her sketch pad and did her best to lose herself in drawing.

Thirty minutes later, she heard someone coming from the opposite direction she *thought* she'd come from. They weren't making much noise, but Amy was a master at hearing someone approach. She could do it in her sleep—and had. Her heart kicked hard, but these were easy, steady footsteps on the trail. Not heavy, drunken footsteps heading down the hall to her bedroom...

In either case, it certainly wasn't Mallory. No, this was a man, light on his feet but not making any attempt to hide his approach. Amy squeezed her fingers around the comforting weight of her knife.

From around the corner, the man appeared. He was tall, built, and armed and dangerous, though not to her physical well-being. Nope, nothing about the tough, sinewy, gorgeous forest ranger was a threat to her body.

But Matt Bowers was *lethal* to her peace of mind.

She knew who he was from all the nights he'd come into the diner after a long shift, seeking food. Lucky Harbor residents fawned over him, especially the women. Amy attributed this to an electrifying mix of testosterone and the uniform. He was sipping a Big Gulp which she'd bet her last dollar had Dr. Pepper in it. The man was a serious soda addict.

She understood his appeal, even felt the tug of it herself, but that was her body's response to him. Her brain was smarter than the rest of her and resisted.

He wore dark, wraparound Oakley sunglasses, but she

happened to know that his eyes were light brown, sharp, and missed nothing. Those eyes were in complete contrast with his smile, which was all laid-back and easygoing, and said he was a pussy cat.

That smile lied.

Nothing about Matt Bowers was sweet and tame. Not one little hair on his sun-kissed head, not a single spectacular muscle, nothing. He was trouble with a capital T, and Amy had given up trouble a long time ago.

She was still sitting on the rock outcropping, nearly out of sight of the trail, but Matt's attention tracked straight to her with no effort at all. She sensed his wry amusement as he stopped and eyed her. "Someone send out an SOS?"

She barely bit back her sigh. *Dammit, Mallory. Out of all the men in all the land, you had to send this one...*

When she didn't answer, he smiled. He knew damn well she'd called Mallory, and he wanted to hear her admit that she was lost.

But she didn't feel like it—childish and immature, she knew. The truth was, her reaction to him was just about the furthest thing from childish, and that scared her. She wasn't ready for the likes of him, for the likes of any man. The very last thing she needed was an entanglement, even if Matt did make her mouth water, even if he did look like he knew exactly how to get her off this mountain.

Or off in general...

And if *that* wasn't the most disconcerting thought she'd had in weeks...

Months.

"Mallory called the cavalry," he said. "Figured I was the best shot you had of getting found before dark."

Amy squared her shoulders, hoping she looked more capable than she felt. "Mallory shouldn't have bothered you."

He smiled. "So you *did* send out the SOS."

Damn him and his smug smile. "Forget about it," she said. "I'm fine. Go back to your job doing..." She waved her hand. "Whatever it is that forest rangers do, getting Yogi out of the trash, keeping the squirrels in line, etc."

"Yogi and the squirrels do take up a lot of my time," he agreed mildly. "But no worries. I can still fit you in."

His voice always seemed to do something funny to her stomach. And lower. "Lucky me."

"Yeah." He took another leisurely sip of his soda. "You might not know this but on top of keeping Yogi in line and all the squirrel wrangling I do, rescuing fair maidens is also part of my job description."

"I'm no fair maiden—" She broke off when something screeched directly above her. Reacting instinctively, she flattened herself to the rock, completely ruining her tough-girl image.

"Just the cry of a loon," her very own forest ranger said. "Echoing across Four Lakes."

She straightened up just as another animal howled, and she barely managed not to flinch. "That," she said shakily, "was more than a loon."

"A coyote," he agreed. "And the bugling of an elk. It's dusk. Everyone's on the prowl for dinner. The sound carries over the lakes, making everyone seem like they're closer than they are."

"There's elk around here?"

"Roosevelt elk," he said. "And deer, bobcats, and cougars, too."

Amy shoved her sketch book into her backpack, ready to get the hell off the mountain.

"Whatcha got there?" he asked.

"Nothing." She didn't know him well enough to share her drawings, and then there was the fact that he was everything she didn't trust: easy smile, easy nature, easy ways—no matter how sexy the packaging.

ER doc Josh Scott has his future
all mapped out.

But Grace has a different plan...

Forever and a Day

Please turn this page for a preview.

Chapter 1

Chocolate makes the world go around.

Tired, edgy, and scared that she was never going to get her life on the happy track, Grace Brooks dropped into the back booth of the diner and sagged against the red vinyl seat. "I could really use a drink."

Mallory, in wrinkled scrubs, just coming off an all-night shift at the ER, snorted as she crawled into the booth as well. "It's eight in the morning."

"Hey, it's happy hour somewhere." This from their third Musketeer, Amy, who was wearing a black tee, a black denim skirt with lots of zippers, and kickass boots. The tough girl ensemble was softened by the bright pink Eat Me apron she was forced to wear while waitressing. "Pick your poison."

"Actually," Grace said, fighting a yawn. She'd slept poorly, worrying about money. And paying bills. And keeping a roof over her head... "I was thinking hot chocolate."

"That works too," Amy said. "Be right back."

· Good as her word, she reappeared with a tray of steaming hot chocolate and big, fluffy chocolate pancakes. "Chocoholics unite."

Four months ago, Grace had come west from New York for a Seattle banking job, until she'd discovered that putting out for the boss was part of the deal. Leaving the offer on the table, she'd gotten into her car and driven as far as the tank of gas could take her, ending up in the little Washington state beach town of Lucky Harbor. That same night she'd gotten stuck in this very diner during a freak snow storm with two strangers.

Mallory and Amy.

With no electricity and a downed tree blocking their escape, the three of them had spent a few scary hours soothing their nerves by eating their way through a very large chocolate cake. Since then, meeting over chocolate cake had become habit—until they'd accidentally destroyed the inside of the diner in a certain candle incident that wasn't to be discussed. Jan, the owner of Eat Me, had refused to let them meet over cake anymore, so the Chocoholics had switched to pancakes. Grace was thinking of making a motion for chocolate cupcakes next. It was important to have the right food for those meetings, as dissecting their lives—specifically their lack of love lives—was hard work. Except these days Amy and Mallory actually *had* love lives.

Grace did not.

Amy disappeared and came back with butter and syrup. She untied and tossed aside her apron and sat, pushing the syrup to Grace.

"I love you," Grace said with great feeling as she took her first bite of delicious goodness.

Not one to waste her break, Amy toasted her with a pancake-loaded fork dripping with syrup and dug in.

Mallory was still carefully spreading butter on her pancakes. "You going to tell us what's wrong, Grace?"

Grace stilled for a beat, surprised that Mallory had been able to read her. "I didn't say anything was wrong."

"You're main-lining a stack of six pancakes like your life depends on it."

"Because they're amazing." And nothing was wrong exactly. Except...everything.

All her life she'd worked her ass off, running on the hamster wheel, heading toward her elusive future. Being adopted at birth by a rocket scientist and a well-respected research biologist had set the standards, and she knew her role. Achieve, and achieve high. "I've applied at every bank, investment company, and accounting firm between Seattle and San Francisco. There's not much out there."

"No nibbles?" Mallory asked sympathetically, reaching for the syrup, her engagement ring catching the light.

Amy shielded her eyes. "Jeez, Mallory, stop waving that thing around, you're going to blind us. Couldn't Ty have found one smaller than a third world country? Or less sparkly?"

Mallory beamed at the rock on her finger but otherwise ignored Amy's comment, unwilling to be deterred. "Back to the nibbles," she said to Grace.

"Nothing to write home about. Just a couple of possible interviews for next week, one in Seattle, one in Portland." Neither job was exactly what Grace wanted, but available jobs at her level in banking had become nearly extinct. So here she was, two thousand miles from "home," drowning beneath the debt load of her education and CPR because her parents had always been of the "build character and pave your own road" variety. She was still mad at herself for following that job offer to Seattle at all. But she'd wanted a good, solid position in the firm—just not one that she could find in the Kama Sutra.

Now late spring had turned to late summer, and she was *still* in Lucky Harbor, living off temp jobs. She was down to her last couple of hundred bucks, and her parents thought she'd taken that job, that she was in Seattle counting other people's money for a living. They believed in hard work and achieving greatness. Since they were both esteemed in their respective fields, it was safe to say that they'd accomplished their goals there.

Grace had strived to do the same, strived to live up to the standards of being a Brooks, but there was no doubt she fell short. In her heart she belonged, but her brain— the part of her that understood she was only a Brooks on *paper*—knew she'd never really pulled it off.

"I don't want you to leave Lucky Harbor," Mallory said. "But one of these interviews will work out for you, I know it."

Grace didn't necessarily want to leave Lucky Harbor either. She'd found the small, quirky town to be more welcoming than anywhere else she'd ever been, but staying wasn't really an option. She was never going to build her big career here. "I hope so." She stabbed a few more pancakes from the tray and dropped them on her plate. "I hate fibbing to my parents so they won't worry. And I'm whittling away at my meager savings. Plus being in limbo sucks."

"Yeah, none of those things are your real problem," Amy said.

"No?" Grace asked. "What's my real problem?"

"You're not getting any."

Grace sagged at the pathetic truthfulness of this statement, a situation made all the worse by the fact that both Amy and Mallory *were* getting some.

Lots.

"Remember the storm?" Mallory asked. "When we almost died in this very place?"

"Right," Amy said dryly. "From overdosing on chocolate cake, maybe."

Mallory ignored this and pointed her fork at Grace. "We made a pinky promise. I said I'd learn to be a little bad for a change. And Amy here was going to live her life instead of letting it live her. And you, Miss Grace, you were going to find more than a new job, remember? You were going to stop chasing your own tail and go after some happy and some fun. It's time, babe."

"I *am* having fun here." At least, more than she'd ever let herself have before. "And what it's time for right now is work." With a longing look at the last stack of pancakes, Grace stood up and brushed the crumbs off her sundress.

"What's today's job?" Amy asked.

When Grace had first realized she needed to get a temporary job or stop eating, she'd purposely gone for something new. Something that didn't require stuffy pencil skirts or closed-toe heel, or sitting in front of a computer for fifteen hours a day. Because if she had to be off-track and a little lost, then she *was* going to have fun while she was at it, dammit. "I'm delivering birthday flowers to Mrs. Burland for her eightieth birthday. Then modeling at Lucille's art gallery for a drawing class."

"Modeling for an art class?" Mallory asked. "Like...nude?"

"Today they're drawing hands." Nude was *tomorrow's* class, and Grace was really hoping something happened before then, like maybe she'd win the lottery. Or get beamed to another planet.

"If I had your body," Amy said. "I'd totally model nude. And charge for it."

"That's called something different than modeling," Mallory said dryly.

Grace rolled her eyes at the both of them, dropped the last of her pocket money onto the table and left to make the floral deliveries. When she'd worked at the bank, she'd gotten up before the crack of dawn, rode a train for two hours, put in twelve more at her desk, then got home in time to crawl into bed.

Things were majorly different here.

For one thing, she saw daylight.

So maybe she could no longer afford Starbucks, but at least she wasn't still having the recurring nightmare where she suffocated under a sea of pennies that she'd been trying to count one by one.

Two hours later, Grace was just finishing the last of the deliveries when her cell phone buzzed. She didn't recognize the incoming number, so she played mental roulette and answered. "Grace Brooks," she said in her most professional tone, as if she was still sitting on top of her world. Sure, she'd given up designer wear, but she hadn't lost her pride. Not yet anyway.

"I'm calling about your flyer," a man said. "I need a dog walker. Someone who's on time, responsible, and not a flake."

Her flyer? "A dog walker?" she repeated.

"Yes, and I'd need you to start today."

"Today...as in *today*?" she asked.

"Yes."

The man, whoever he was, had a hell of a voice, low and a little raspy, with a hint of impatience. Clearly he'd misdialed. And just as clearly, there was someone else in Lucky Harbor trying to drum up work for themselves.

Grace considered herself a good person. She sponsored a child in Africa and she dropped her spare change into the charity jars at the supermarket. Someone in town had put up flyers looking to get work, and that someone deserved this phone call. But dog walking... Grace could totally do dog walking. Offering a silent apology for stealing the job, she said, "I could start today."

"Your flyer lists your qualifications, but not how long you've been doing this."

That was too bad because she'd sure like to know that herself. She'd never actually had a dog. Turns out, rocket scientists and renowned biologists don't have a lot of time in their lives for incidentals such as dogs.

Or kids...

In fact, come to think of it, Grace had never had so much as a goldfish, but really, how hard could it be? Put the thing on a leash and walk, right? "I'm a little new at the dog walking thing," she admitted.

"A little new?" he asked. "Or a lot new?"

"A lot."

There was a pause, as if he was considering hanging up. Grace rushed to fill the silence. "But I'm very diligent!" she said quickly. "I never leave a job unfinished."

Unless she was asked how she felt about giving blow jobs during lunch breaks... "And I'm completely reliable."

"The dog is actually a puppy," he said. "And new to our household. Not yet fully trained."

"No problem," she said, and crossed her fingers, hoping that was true. She loved puppies. Or at least she loved the *idea* of puppies.

"I left for work early this morning and won't be home until late tonight. I'd need you to walk the dog by lunch time."

Yeah, he really had a hell of a voice. Low and authoritative, it made her want to snap to attention and salute him, but it was also...sexy. Wondering if the rest of him matched his voice, she made arrangements to go to his house in a couple of hours, where there'd be someone waiting to let her inside. Her payment of forty bucks cash would be left on the dining room table.

Forty bucks cash for walking a puppy...

Score.

Grace didn't ask why the person opening the door for her couldn't walk the puppy. She didn't want to talk her new employer out of hiring her because hello, *forty bucks*. She could eat all week off that, if she was careful.

At the appropriate time, she pulled up to the address she'd been given and sucked in a big breath. She hadn't caught the man's name, but he lived in a very expensive area, on the northern-most part of the town where the rocky beach stretched for endless miles like a gorgeous postcard for the Pacific Northwest. The dark green bluffs and rock formations were piled like gifts from heaven for as far as the eye could see. Well, as far as *her* eye could see, which wasn't all that far since she needed glasses.

She was waiting on a great job with benefits to come along first.

The house sat across the street from the beach. Built in sprawling stone and glass, it was beautiful though she found it odd that it was all one level, when the surrounding homes were two and three stories high. Even more curious, next to the front steps was a ramp. A wheel chair ramp. Grace knocked on the door, then caught sight of the Post-it note stuck on the glass panel.

Dear Dog Sitter,

I've left door unlocked for you. Please let yourself in. Oh, and if you could throw away this note and not let my brother know I left his house unlocked, that'd be great, thanks. Also, don't steal anything.

Anna

Grace stood there chewing her bottom lip in rare indecision. She hadn't given this enough thought. Hell, let's be honest. She'd given it *no* thought at all past "easy job." She reminded herself that she was smart in a crisis and could get through anything.

But walking into a perfect stranger's home seemed problematic, if not downright dangerous. What if a curious neighbor saw her and called the cops? She looked herself over. Enjoying her current freedom from business wear, she was in a sundress with her cute Payless-special ankle boots and lace socks. Not looking much like a banking specialist, and hopefully not looking like a B&E expert either...

Regardless, what if this was a set up? What if a bad guy lived here, one who lured hungry, slightly desperate, act-now-think-later women inside to do heinous things to them?

Okay, so maybe she'd been watching too many late-night marathons of *Criminal Minds*, but it could totally happen.

Then, from inside the depths of the house came a happy, high-pitched bark. And then another, which seemed to say: *"Hurry up, lady. I have to pee!"*

Ah, hell. In for a penny... Grace opened the front door and peered inside.

The living room was as stunning as the outside of the house. Wide open spaces, done in dark masculine wood and neutral colors. The furniture was oversized and sparse on the beautiful, scarred, hardwood floors. An entire wall of windows faced the Indian Summer sky and Pacific Ocean.

As Grace stepped inside, the barking increased in volume, intermingled now with hopeful whining. She followed the sounds to a huge, state-of-the-art kitchen that made her wish she knew how to cook beyond the basic soup and grilled cheese sandwiches. Just past the kitchen was a laundry room, the doorway blocked by a toddler gate.

On the other side of the gate was a baby pig.

A baby pig who barked.

Okay, not a pig at all, but one of those dogs whose faces looked smashed in. The tiny body was mostly tan, the face black with crazy bugged-out eyes and a tongue that lolled out the side of its mouth. It looked like an animated cartoon as it twirled in excited circles, dancing for her, trying to impress her and charm its way out of lock up.

"Hi," she said to him. *Her*? Hard to tell since its parts were so low as to scrape the ground along with its belly.

The thing snorted and huffed in joyous delirium, rolling over and over like a hotdog, then jumping up and down like a Mexican jumping bean.

"Oh, there's no need for all that," Grace said, and opened the gate.

Mistake number one.

The dog/pig/alien streaked past her with astounding speed and promptly raced out of the kitchen and out of sight.

"Hey," she called. "Slow down."

But it didn't, and wow, those stumpy legs could really move. It snorted with sheer delight as it made its mad getaway and Grace was forced to rethink the pig theory. Also, the sex mystery was solved.

From behind, she'd caught a glimpse of dangly bits.

It—*he*—ran circles around the couch, barking with merry enthusiasm. She gave chase, wondering how it was that she had multiple advance degrees, and yet she hadn't thought to ask the name of the damn dog. "Hey," she said. "Hey you. We're going outside to walk."

The puppy dashed past her like lightning.

Dammit. Breathless, she changed direction and followed him back into the kitchen where he was chasing some imaginary threat around the gorgeous dark wood kitchen table that indeed had two twenty dollar bills lying on the smooth surface.

She was beginning to see why the job paid so much.

She retraced her steps to the laundry room and found a

leash and collar hanging on the doorknob above the gate. Perfect. The collar was a manly blue and the tag said: *Tank*.

Grace laughed out loud, then searched for Tank. Turned out, Tank had worn off his excess energy and was up against the front door, panting.

"Good boy," Grace cooed, and came at him with his collar. "What a good boy."

He smiled at her.

Aw. *See?* she told herself. *Compared to account analysis and posing nude, this job was going to be a piece of cake.* She was still mentally patting herself on the back for accepting this job when right there on the foyer floor Tank squatted, hunched, and—

"No!" she cried. "Oh, no, not inside!" She fumbled with the front door, which scared Tank into stopping mid-poo. He ran a few feet away from the front door and hunched again. He was quicker this time. Grace was still standing there, mouth open in shock and horror as little Tank took a dainty step away from his *second* masterpiece, pawed his short back legs on the wood like a matador, and then, with his oversized head held up high, trotted right out the front door like royalty.

Grace staggered after him, eyes watering from the unholy smell. "Tank! Tank, wait!"

Tank didn't wait. Apparently feeling ten pounds lighter, he raced across the front yard and street. He hit the beach, his little legs pumping with the speed of a gazelle as he practically flew across the sand, heading straight for the water.

"Oh, God," she cried. "No, Tank, *no!*"

But Tank dove into the first wave and vanished.

Grace dropped the purse off her shoulder to the sand. *"Tank!"*

A wave hit her at hip level, knocking her back a step as she frantically searched for a bobbing head.

Nothing. The little guy had completely vanished, having committed suicide right before her eyes.

The next wave hit her at chest height. Again she staggered back, gasping at the shock of the water as she searched frantically for a little black head.

Wave number three washed right over the top of her. She came up sputtering, shook her head to clear it, then dove beneath the surface, desperate to find the puppy.

Nothing.

Finally, she was forced to crawl out of the water and admit defeat. She pulled her phone from her purse and swore because it'd turned itself off again. Probably because she kept dropping it.

Or tossing it to the rocky beach to look for drowning puppies.

She powered the phone on, gnawed on her lower lip, then called the man who'd trusted her to "be on time, responsible, and not a flake." Heart pounding, throat tight, she waited until he picked up.

"Dr. Scott," came the low, deep male voice.

Dr. Scott. *Dr. Scott?*

"Hello?" he said. "Anyone there?"

Oh, God. This was bad. Very bad. Because she knew him.

Well, okay, not really. She'd seen him around because he was good friends with Mallory's and Amy's boyfriends. Dr. Joshua Scott was thirty-four—which she knew because Mallory had given him thirty-four chocolate cupcakes on his birthday last month, a joke because he was a health nut. He was a big guy, built for football more than the ER, but he'd chosen the latter. Even in his wrinkled scrubs after a long day at work, his dark hair tousled and his darker eyes lined with exhaustion, he was drop-dead sexy. The few times that their gazes had locked, the air had snapped, crackled, and popped with a tension she hadn't felt with a man in far too long.

And she'd just killed his puppy.

"Um, hi," she said. "This is Grace Brooks. Your... dog walker." She choked down a horrified sob and forced herself to continue, to give him the rest. "I might have just lost your puppy."

There was a single beat of stunned silence.

"I'm so sorry," she whispered.

More silence.

She dropped to her wobbly knees in the sand and shoved her wet hair out of her face with shaking fingers. "Dr. Scott? Did you hear me?"

"Yes."

She waited for the rest of his response, desperately gripping the phone.

"You *might* have lost Tank," he repeated.

"Yes," she said softly, hating herself.

"You're sure."

Grace looked around the beach. The empty beach. "Yes."

"Well then, I owe you a big, fat kiss."

Grace pulled her phone from her ear and stared at it, then brought it back. "No," she said, shaking her head as if he could see her. "I don't think you understand, I *lost* Tank. In the water."

He muttered something that she'd have sworn sounded like "I should be so lucky."

"What?" she asked.

"Nothing. I'm two minutes away. I got a break in the ER and was coming home to make sure you showed."

"Well, of course I showed—"

But he'd disconnected.

"Why wouldn't I show?" she asked no one. She dropped her phone back in her purse and got up. Two minutes. She had two minutes to find Tank.

When Jill's neighbor decided to have an extension built, she was suddenly gifted with inspiration: a bunch of cute, young, sweaty guys hanging off the roof and the walls. Just the type of men who'd appeal to three estranged sisters forced together when they inherit a dilapidated beach resort . . .

Meet Maddie, Tara and Chloe in

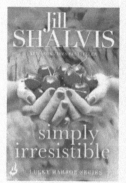 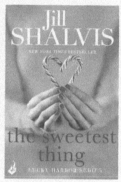 

'Count on Jill Shalvis for a witty, steamy, unputdownable love story'
Robyn Carr

headline
ETERNAL

*W*hen the lights go out and you're 'stuck' in a café with potential Chocoholic-partners-in-crime and nothing else to do but eat cake and discuss the mysteries of life, it's surprising just what conclusions women will come to. But when they decide to kick things into gear, they'd better be prepared for what happens once they have the ball rolling . . .

Here come Mallory, Amy and Grace in

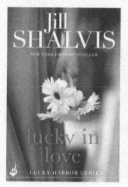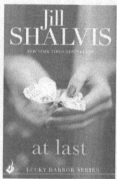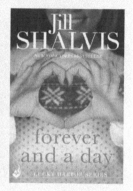

'An abundance of chemistry, smoldering romance, and hilarious antics'

Publishers Weekly

headline
ETERNAL

The women of Lucky Harbor have been charming readers with their incredible love stories – now it's time for some very sexy men to take center stage. They're in for some *big* surprises – and from corners they'd least expect it.

Really get to know Luke, Jack and Ben in

 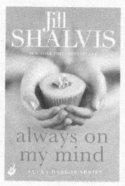 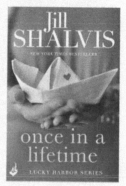

'Hot sex, some delightful humor and plenty of heartwarming emotion'

Romantic Times

headline
ETERNAL

$\mathcal{L}$ucky Harbor is the perfect place to escape to, whether that means a homecoming, getting away from the city or running from something a whole lot darker. Whatever the cause, Lucky Harbor has three more residents who are about to discover just how much this sleepy little town really has to offer.

Escape with Becca, Olivia and Callie in

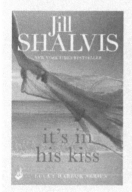 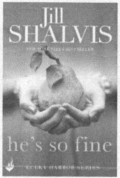 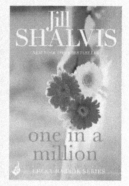

'Clever, steamy, and fun. Jill Shalvis will make you laugh and fall in love'
Rachel Gibson

headline
ETERNAL